The Cruelest Month

The Cruelest Month

Ernest Buckler

Introduction by Alan Young
General Editor: Malcolm Ross

New Canadian Library No. 139

McClelland and Stewart Limited

Copyright © 1963 by McClelland and Stewart Limited
Introduction © 1977 McClelland and Stewart Limited

This book was originally published by
McClelland and Stewart Limited in 1963

0-7710-9247-4

The Canadian Publishers
McClelland and Stewart Limited
25 Hollinger Road, Toronto
M4B 3G2

Printed and bound in Canada

Acknowledgements

Faber and Faber Ltd. for extract from "The Waste
Land" from *Collected Poems 1909-1962* by T. S. Eliot.

McGraw-Hill Ryerson Ltd. and Gregory M. Cook for
extracts from *Ernest Buckler*, ed. Gregory M. Cook.

T. Fisher Rare Book Library at the University of Toronto and Ernest Buckler for permission to quote
from the Ernest Buckler Manuscript Collection.

CONTENTS

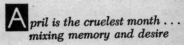

April is the cruelest month . . .
mixing memory and desire

T. S. ELIOT

Introduction

In January 1952, a few days after *The Mountain and the Valley* had been accepted for publication, Ernest Buckler wrote to his literary agent about his ideas for a second novel: "Maybe a more sophisticated novel, with a background of Greenwich's Belle Haven district, where I spent a good deal of time working, in the 20s" (Letter to Harold Ober, 21 Jan. 1952, Univ. of Toronto Buckler Collection). This idea seems eventually to have developed into *The Cruelest Month* (1963). In the letter Buckler is alluding to the six summers that he spent between 1920 and 1925 working at Kent House, an exclusive and expensive summer hotel in Greenwich, Connecticut. Undoubtedly this early teen-age contact with the wealthy urbanites who patronized Kent House was what provided him with his model for the clientele and general concept of Endlaw, the imaginary Nova Scotian rural retreat (its name a partly ironic anagram of "Walden") which is the principal setting of *The Cruelest Month* and the meeting place for its cast of sophisticates, three of whom significantly come from Connecticut.

Nine years after telling his agent about the proposed novel, Buckler finally completed the manuscript of *The Cruelest Month*. After rejections by Henry Holt and Doubleday, it was accepted by McClelland and Stewart in 1962. Like *The Mountain and the Valley* it is set in the Annapolis Valley, the rural area of Nova Scotia where Buckler grew up and now lives. As in the earlier work, a central theme concerns the opposition between natural, non-intellectual rural values and the complexity, sophistication and potential speciousness of the world outside the valley. Both novels also depict potential artists (David Canaan and Paul Creed), each of whom opts for the pastoral experience and, perhaps ironically, never writes the novel he has planned. Such similarities, however, are relatively superficial. In *The Mountain and the Valley*, the focus of interest is principally upon a single, semi-autobiographical character, David Canaan, and his psychological and artistic development during his thirty years from childhood to death. Our attention is taken up with Buckler's portrait of a pre-World War Two rural way of life that has now largely disappeared, with the disintegration of a rural family, and above all with the inner dilemma that David faces when he discovers that he "belongs" neither in the rural community where he has grown up nor in the world a mere train or automobile ride away. However, in *The Cruelest Month* Buckler is no longer concerned with focusing upon a single individual but instead involves himself with the members of a group of sophisticated and highly articulate urbanites aged between thirty and fifty-five. Where David belongs to the Valley, these are largely outsiders, and Buckler's chief preoccupation is not so much with the kind of dilemma that David faces, though there is something of this in Paul's situation, but with the interrelationships that develop among them during a brief encounter at Endlaw during the April of 1951. Buckler himself appears to have seen the novel as being in part an exploration of the nature of love relationships. His title when he submitted the manuscript to McClelland and Stewart was "The Cells of Love," which was "supposed to cover (in a kind of double, somewhat ironic, application) both the cellular variegation of love and love's sometimes prisoning aspects" (Letter to Jack Rackliffe, 14 Oct. 1961, Buckler Collection). In his second novel Buckler is thus consciously exploring new possibilities of theme, character and form, and, as may be expected, the end product is very different from his first novel.

The form of *The Cruelest Month* is analogous to the process alluded to in the opening lines of T. S. Eliot's *The Waste Land*, as Buckler's epigraph and eventual title (his original first choice for the novel) appear to acknowledge:

April is the cruelest month, breeding
Lilacs out of the dead land, mixing
Memory and desire, stirring
Dull roots with spring rain.

Eliot's lines also explain the choice of April (not normally the season for a forest fire in Nova Scotia) for Endlaw sequence, and they provide a hint of the rationale for the four-part division of the novel. In Parts One and Two Buckler reveals the spiritual "dead land" inhabited by the various characters who visited Endlaw in 1946 and the manner of their lives during the subsequent five-year interval that occurs prior to their return in 1951. These first two sections are concerned with memory, as Buckler seems to hint in the epigraph, and they deal with the background of the characters (Part One) and the motivations or "desires" (Part Two) which then draw them back to Endlaw. As the characters gather together at the end of Part Two, we discover that each is in some way an "amputee," an image used several times by Buckler in the novel. Originally part of one suggested title ("Nest of Amputees"), the image suggests the manner in which some vital part of each character is now dead or lost, and this proves to be so. The talents of Morse, a succesful writer, appear to have dried up; the wealthy Rex and Sheila Giorno face the loss of their love for each other, and Rex is further confronted by his loss of self-respect; Kate Fennison has yet to adjust to the recent death of her widowed father, a university professor, to whom she has devoted herself at the cost of her youth; Bruce Mansfield has yet to accept the deaths of his wife and son for which he feels responsible and which have consequently ended his ambition for a career in medicine.

The figure around whom the guests with their burdens of bitter memories and blighted desires all gather is Paul Creed, the owner of Endlaw. As Kate realizes, those who congregate around this man are "People orphaned from something that had once been the big nerve and jugular of their whole lives." Paul possesses "some rare credential which gave people the urge to make it you-and-I with him almost at first sight," but, as he himself discovers before Part Two ends, he too is one of the "amputees": "He saw what his life had been, a refusal to visit inside the house of anyone's spirit because if the visit were returned he must always speak to them from the doorway of his own." He also learns that he has a heart condition that could claim his life, and, like that of David in *The Mountain and the Valley*, Paul's physical problem is presented as symbolic of an inner limitation that prevents true personal fulfillment. Even Letty Spence, Paul's widowed housekeeper and born and bred locally, though representing the very antithesis of those who come to Endlaw, nonetheless is initially unfulfilled and suffers chiefly from her inability to communicate with Paul whom she secretly loves:

> He lived in the country of those people who seemed to know exactly what the world was *saying*, anyway, and she could only stare at the world like a child at the fair. She could only catch its short simple sentences. That was the wall between them. A dreadful wall for love to have recognize the height and thickness of.

If parts One and Two of the novel concern "memory" and "desire," Part Three, which takes up more than half the work, is concerned with the shedding of the past and the movement of the characters towards renewal and fulfillment. Significantly Buckler once described the novel in a letter to Vance K. Henry as being "very broadly speaking, an investigation of the way in which various people of various temperaments meet personal loss and the challenge of nihilism which, at times, seems to be the only logical creed" (Buckler Collection). The process of shedding the past and facing the challenge of the future is inevitably a painful one, and again Eliot's poem provides an apt parallel with its focus upon "the cruelest month" and the suffering involved in the transition from winter to spring, from death to life, and from past to future. Part Four of the novel concludes the process begun in Part Three by depicting the departure of Paul's guests and the accompanying forest fire that symbolizes the inner purgatory that all have experienced. Again one is reminded of Eliot's poem, and even more so when the fire is followed by rain, something that takes us back to the opening promise of *The Waste Land* with its allusion to the stirring of dull roots with spring rain and the consequent promise of new life. Part Four is above all a composite portrait of those who have been made whole again, their faith in themselves and life restored after their brief sojourn at what Morse earlier refers to as a "Home for Incroyables." Morse has recommenced writing; Rex and Sheila are reunited; Kate and Morse are to be married; Bruce has decided to return to medical school; and Paul and Letty found each other.

Such an interpretation of the form of *The Cruelest Month* fails to do justice, however, to the ironic manner in which Buckler undercuts the positive vision inherent in the "Waste Land" pattern. Such irony seems to have been intentional on Buckler's part and is not merely the result of inconsistency within the novel. He once stated, for example, that he had used Eliot's lines for epigraph and title "to indicate the ironies of existence which the novel portrays," and that he had introduced the lilacs mentioned in the opening lines of *The Waste Land* as an intentional ironic symbol, since "their annual growth and rebirth mocks the inability of the characters to imitate the natural cycle" (Bernita Harris, M.A. Thesis, Univ. of New Brunswick, 1969, pp. 1-2). Elsewhere Buckler has commented upon the fundamental self-deception that marks his characters at the end of the novel:

(When you see someone maybe made over the way you'd

thought you wanted them to be, do they seem suddenly worse? Kate's reaction to Morse's almost "soft" idealism at the end, her notice of her almost silliness with love; the irony that Paul thinks he's found an answer in Letty—when, anyone should see, particularly with Letty changing herself ("proper" speech, etc.), that this is maybe an ignis fatuus too). The way people continue to fool themselves.)

(*Ernest Buckler*, ed. G. M. Cook, 1972, pp. 80-81)

In addition to the recurring irony of the lilacs in *The Cruelest Month*, the exposure at the end of Chapter 32 of Kate's "silliness" and Morse's "soft idealism," which, as Kate realizes, is as false as his former cynicism, and, at the very end of the novel, Paul's self-deception over Letty and her false attempt to join the world of words, further ironies and attendant incongruities suggest themselves to the reader. One senses, for example, that Paul is mistaken when he doesn't permit the love between himself and Kate to develop, an error symbolized by his handing her the lilac root. He is entirely mistaken also in his judgement that Endlaw is the one place "that nothing could ever turn inside out." What too is one to make of Paul's suggestion to Letty at the end of the novel that they install a telephone at Endlaw, the telephone being symbolic of the world of words which he renounces when he destroys the plans for his novel and against which Letty has always revolted? What too could be more alien to the spirit of a place which Paul advertizes at the opening of the novel as a "quiet cave" in which to recreate oneself, free from Cadillacs, entertainment and telephones?

The underlying pattern of irony suggested here is further enforced by the manner in which Rex's thoughtlessness is the initial cause of the forest fire that almost engulfs Endlaw. Though he may have changed superficially, the qualities of character that caused the automobile accident as he approached Endlaw have remained unaltered so that one cannot fully share his wife's faith in their future relationship. The reader is also aware that their reconciliation is based upon Rex's deceit, since he has trapped Sheila into returning to him by allowing her to believe that his shooting accident was really an attempt at suicide. In addition even the final symbolic reappearance of the deer at the end of the novel is marked by irony. The deer is "a wild, secret, beautiful thing that not even the grown men of the place had ever set eye on." It represents a new domain of experience and awareness that significantly no one possesses when the novel opens, since the animal remains unnoticed as the guests make their way to Endlaw. When they depart, however, all see it, but Morse fails to share in its wonder. Symbolically his continued inner blindness is demonstrated when his response to the deer is to follow "every leap it made, keeping the cross of an imaginary gun's telescopic sight focused exactly over its heart." The destructive cynicism that characterizes his writing presumably remains a part of his nature. No spell in any Nova Scotian Walden can transform this side of his nature.

Buckler's characters thus for the most part retain their human imperfections and leave the green world of Endlaw to fare as best they may in the harsher world from which they have temporarily taken shelter. One senses there is some hope in varying degrees for all of them, but, due to Buckler's continual ironies, one retains the uncomfortable awareness that there is indeed a sad discrepancy between the regenerative processes of the natural cycle and the inability of the human being to imitate it fully.

When it appeared, *The Cruelest Month* received some measure of adverse criticism, the chief complaints being concerned with the bookish, pseudo-intellectual talk of its characters, and the mechanical manipulation of their interrelationships and encounters. It may not be possible to defend the novel completely from these attacks, but it should be pointed out that those who have made the first charge have largely ignored the fact that the use of language is an important sub-theme of the novel. Buckler wishes to demonstrate that, though words may be the chief form of human communication, as the presence of one writer and one would-be writer reminds us, they may also be the means of distorting truth and distracting their users from what really matters in life. Kate perceives the point: "Books and ideas, I'm right in there when that's the game. But how tongue-tied and defaulting with ignorance would they find me in a matter of flesh and blood?" Letty, who represents, according to Buckler, "the soundness of the 'natural' country person" (*Buckler*, ed. Cook, p. 81), possesses throughout the novel an antipathy to words that is summed up in her belief "that all the readin' and writin' that was ever done [...] wouldn't amount to a fart on the plains of Arabia." When Paul destroys the plans for his novel, rejects the book Letty profers him, and accepts Letty herself, the defeat of the Word in favour of more fundamental aspects of experience is virtually complete, though, as pointed out above, there is a disturbing moment at the conclusion of the novel when Letty attempts to speak "as proper as 'they' did." It is important therefore to Buckler's purpose that the words of his characters should frequently appear hollow and glib (perhaps like those of the characters in *The Waste Land*), smacking too much of the head and too little of the flesh.

However, it would be more difficult to argue that Buckler's somewhat artificial handling of character relationships and encounters is also an intrinsic expression of the emptiness of the characters' lives and of their refusal to come to terms with reality. Some readers may here feel that Buckler is not totally convincing, and it is perhaps significant that in succeeding books he has never returned either to the kinds of characters dealt with in *The Cruelest Month* or to the exploration of the intricacies of character interrelationships that provide the central focus of the novel.

Such possible flaws in this ambitious, carefully-wrought and complex work have to be acknowledged, but the strength of the novel must be too. These latter include the skilfully maintained irony which climaxes in the novel's ambivalent conclusion and which counterpoints the working out in theme and form of the "Waste Land" pattern described above. To this must be added the pervasive demonstration in *The Cruelest Month* of one of Buckler's greatest strengths as a writer — his subtle delineation of minutiae and of the variegated shades of emotional response to situation and place. Nor does one quickly forget the symbolic power of the novel's concluding section, as strong in its own way as that of his first novel, or the narrative brilliance of a passage like the Bruce/Peter story in Chapter Three (originally published separately as "The Rebellion of Young David"). This is a novel that has undoubtedly yet to be awarded its true worth.

Alan R. Young
Acadia University

PART

At first glance, Paul's place was no more than a small, white, friend-faced house standing beside a lake still as theorems. Someone else's snapshot. And then you saw what was perfect about it. Simple though it was, and chanced together though it had been by builders who as architects were total innocents, it had the inevitability of a master painting.

That first season they were together there – Morse, Kate, Paul, and Letty – they were all still young enough not yet to have glimpsed the inevitable set of their own bone. Their personal patterns still felt as pliable to them as flesh.

Letty was Paul's housekeeper. She glanced at the forwarding addresses he had just given her to drop off at the post office in town. This was the last week of the season, these the last of the summer's guests :

Morse Halliday, Simsbury, Connecticut.

Dr Clarke Fennison, 11 University St., Halifax, NS.

Kate Fennison, ditto.

Morse was a writer. Dr Fennison was a widowed professor of archaeology; Kate his only child and companion.

Letty's forehead puckered. She wasn't quite sure which group of letters stood for which person. She had come to know the months on the calendar (it said September, 1946) and the days of the week. And her own name : Letty Spence. And Paul's : Paul Creed. And the short words you lived by. But the long unfamiliar words gave her a lost feeling.

She heard Paul talking and laughing with Morse and Kate in the next room. Her eyes flickered as if a small coal had touched her. She thought the sun rose and set in him. But they were his kind. She was not.

Paul called his place Endlaw, an anagram of Walden. Himself, the poor man's Thoreau. "Heavens !" Kate had exclaimed at Endlaw. "*C'est merveilleux! Incroyable!*" Morse had promptly dubbed it the "Home for Incroyables." That's the way they talked then.

Endlaw was nothing like an ordinary hotel. Only once had Paul advertised for guests.

"Limited accommodation," the ad ran, "April through September, for such as seek a quiet cave wherein to mind their own business.

8

Good shelter, board, view. No telephone. No entertainment. Come sort yourself out, if you dare. Bring no Cadillacs, cats, or bitches."

It was by sheerest chance that Morse had seen Paul's ad in the *Saturday Review*. Someone had discarded that particular issue on a bench beside him in Grand Central Station, open at that particular page. In sheer boredom he'd picked it up and examined it. And sheer impulse had sent him to the ticket window to book immediate passage to Nova Scotia. Maybe at Endlaw the novel that had him sitting and staring in New York would fall into place.

It did. Like one of those chain puzzles at just the right twist. The novel was *Each in His Narrow Cell*. The book that was to make his name.

He had just now finished it. They were drinking on that. With the last comma in place, he had a sense of enormous release, as if he'd been liberated from some stunning illness. Everything's particular charge was so tinglingly heightened that it was like a glorious violence.

"Do you know how this place first struck me?" he said. This was Kate's last day with them. They were all in a retrospective, recapitulatory mood. "I felt as if whatever ragged hound had been at my heels had suddenly lost the scent."

As usual, he steered the conversation, but it was Paul who commanded its atmosphere.

Morse had a massive leonine head. The unfeaturelike black hair that grew on it and on the backs of his hands and in a dickey to the hollow of his throat was like some rank crop of animality seeded beneath the skin. And yet he had a peculiarly antiseptic quality, as if every body orifice was always immaculate of smear or sediment. His eyes had the jungle glitter of an Arab's. And his teeth made you suddenly aware that teeth were really for biting. They were an unsettling constituent of his smile. Yet there was nothing fearsome about him. He had no gentleness himself. But there was no one that gentleness, true gentleness like Paul's, could safer go right up to and touch. He "swore in his common talk," as Letty put it, but this was not really blasphemous of anything.

"With me," Kate picked it up, "it was the time thing." She and her father had happened on Endlaw through a wrong turning at the crossroads in Granfort during the course of a motor trip itself unplanned from day to day. "You know time. Anywhere else, you hear its meter ticking whether you're using it or not. Here, that meter's stopped. You only get charged for what you use."

"Since we've come over all lit'ry," Paul said with his characteristic grin, "do you want to know what impression I got when *I* first laid eyes on it? It seemed like the one pocket in the universe that

9

nothing could ever turn inside out. That was seven years ago this very day and I've never changed my mind."

It is always surprising to find that the spirit is not of the same colouring as its integument. Paul had a blond Scandinavian spirit in a dark Mediterranean face. It was one of those thin-skinned faces that the eyes perpetually instruct. Without resemblance in any physical detail, it made you think of the Duke of Windsor's. As if some unlived part of his life stayed macabrely youthful in its flesh alongside time's normal ravage. He looked like one of those extraordinary people who have outlived the active memory in others' minds of the original circumstances which made them memorable.

But this was not a plaintive look. If you examined his face closely enough you saw, beyond the flesh look and the thought look, a third expression that was in absolute command of both these two.

"You actually came here through Letty, didn't you?" Kate said.

"Yes," Paul said, "God bless her."

They all smiled. They always smiled whenever Letty's name was mentioned. Morse had loved her from the day he'd heard her sniff that all the readin' and writin' that was ever done ("mollyhawkin' things over," she called it) wouldn't amount to a fart on the plains of Arabia.

Letty had been the cook at the hotel Paul stayed at when he first came to Granfort. One morning he'd heard her discussing this place with her sister-in-law beneath his window. A farmer called Mansfield had owned it then. The Brewster Lumber Mills had made a clean sweep buying up the other farms along the road, but he'd held out for a stiffer price. Then the company had gone bankrupt. Letty's sister-in-law said he was offering the place at a real bargain now – if anyone could stand to live way out there alone.

"And what were you doing in Granfort?" Kate said. "You were born in Vancouver, weren't you? I thought once a Vancouverite, the rest of the world had no charm."

"I know," Paul said. "But I'm a bit of an expatriate."

"A bit!" Morse said. "You know by now what he's like, don't you? The old conjurer's pea. He's never under the walnut shell you pick up. But I did manage to wheedle this much out of him. A bit of an expatriate! He's worked at a weather station in Alaska. He's been a timekeeper in the Labrador mine fields. An oil rigger in the Caribbean. He taught solid geometry for two years in Nigeria, for God's sake."

"Come now," Paul said. "You make me sound like the enigmatic chap in a Maugham concoction. I'm nothing of the kind."

10

He wasn't. He was elusive, but without any hint whatever of the secretive. You might know nothing about him, but such was his immediacy that somehow you knew *him* before you'd exchanged ten words.

"Well, anyway," he said to Kate. "You know the mind has like a thirsty eye that floats around all the time. It's always looking for some place that will have exactly the same – lighting, I guess you'd call it – as the mind itself has right then. One day I happened to see this picture of Granfort in a government travel folder. It clicked. Another day, another digestion, it might have been Portugal." He could talk that way without sounding that way in the least.

Endlaw was twenty miles from Granfort. Trees older than men lined the dirt road that led to it. Centuried spruces, lonelied by their own height. It was the last house on the road. All the others the lumber company had promptly demolished as fire hazards.

Morse had put down some impressions of his journey there. His romantic streak was still in the ascendant then.

"You drive from Yarmouth to Granfort through disembodied villages, with the man walking from the porch to the well looking like a man in a primitive painting walking from the porch to the well. I've never seen a place quite like Granfort. It washes you clean of whatever your chronic mood. This is the very soil where settlers from the Old World first set foot on the New. You really feel it. An ancient rampart mounds graveyard-green from the horseshoe harbour. Shell-coloured buildings pocketed in the living green above it still catch the light from another time. You look out over this historied water, eternally cryptic with the sheen of the sun, to the narrow gap where it joins the sea and you know exactly how it felt to stand here and watch for a friendly or an enemy sail.

"You ask someone the way on from here. His sudden liveliness astounds you. All Nova Scotians are like that, the moment they can do you a favour. He almost pleads that you understand the maps he draws on the palm of his hand.

"Roads partake of their destination. Trees along a road that ends in disappointment dissociate themselves from it. These trees, for once taking the melancholy *out* of the fields they've trespassed on, hint you constantly forward. Through them and past the old fields and down the sharp hollow before the brook and up the opposite rise, and over the brook and past the meadow and through the trees again – until you round the blindest bend of all and there you are so suddenly it's like a shock.

"You feel as if you are stepping into the very domicile of peace.

11

And yet – an odd acceleration. As if the natural drift of all things interpersonal develops here with the short-cut pace of shipboard or dream . . ."

In an ordinary hotel, this room where they now sat would have been the lobby. Here, it was simply a room asteep with the quality of a house in which books live and breathe. There was no accounting for the house's spell. It was baffling in the way that certain celebrated places confound the stranger expecting to locate their cachet in something picturesque. Finding nothing of the kind, he looks for it in their very plainness. But even that is not a studied one.

This room looked out on the lake. The lake, so smooth the clouds could read themselves on it where it was deep, lapped ceaselessly against the rocks and the bone-clean barkless trees along its shore. A small groved island rested like a weight on its geometric centre. The eyes and ears of the house were gentled out of all wariness by the sight of nothing but trees and the sound of nothing but water.

"And to find a character like this in charge here!" Morse said. He was leaning against the mantelpiece, his just-short-of-brawling face alight with that affectionate needling which constitutes the final compliment. "Tell us, Paul . . . and I'm serious, they don't come any more serious than I am when I'm on the sauce this early in the day . . . tell us, how does it feel to be a character? Oh yes you are. In a Hemingway book, you'd rate one of his special nicknames. That's the kind of character you are. How does it feel?"

"You know," Paul took off on one of his outlandish tangents, "I wish Hemingway had just once teamed up with Ivy Compton-Burnett. Then we'd really have got an economical novel, wouldn't we? Not a scrap of that inconsequential nonsense about which is wearing what and who is sitting where and why's the price of eggs. That excelsior's all right for cups and saucers, but not for verbs."

"Amen!" Morse bit on it. "Amen!"

"I've always liked Hemingway," Kate said. "Loved him. That saving streak of good old-fashioned sentiment. Just like me. And it's always been such pleasure to watch him with the literary matadors. Just when they've thought they had him down and their little capes fluttering all over the place, the old bull's made one surge to his feet and driven a horn right through their guts. Shish kebab!"

Thinking: Books and ideas, I'm right in there when that's the game. But how tongue-tied and defaulting with ignorance would they find me in a matter of flesh and blood?

Kate Fennison was not quite yet a professor's daughter. Spirit

12

flashed like colour in her face. Her eyes, at times so drowningly dark they looked almost blind, made her big white teeth as brilliant as a Negro's. Not yet did wind-straggle in her hair point up her age. Her hair was the colour of spaded earth, and sleeping never matted it against her head in the way that turns the skull-shape of some women no longer young into an obscenity.

Morse turned to Kate, nodding his head toward Paul. "You know what this old bastard's doing, don't you? He's just using my Hemingway remark to draw the scent away from himself. Look at him. The old partridge trick – faking a broken wing to draw you away from her nest."

"I see him," Kate said, in the fondly rueful tone you use with that remark to children.

She was perched on the arm of a Morris chair, her legs crossed at the knee, one hand holding her glass flat on the palm of the other as drinker-talkers do. From one corner of her consciousness she could see the black leaves of crows floating over the wooded knolls. For this minute she was protected from the stitch of melancholy that flying birds had always given her before. In all the other corners of her consciousness that shimmering lift of the first drink was awash in her, when all the little nettles that have never ceased to press against you, beyond distraction to abstraction, loose their hooks from your flesh. She felt a kind of emancipating impudence.

Thinking: This place really is exempt from the arithmetic of time. This hour is pure bonus.

And, most mercifully of all, the blurring of the drink obscured in her the knowledge that her father's absence was what made this special taste of freedom possible, and so absolved her from penance for that knowledge.

"Paul doesn't like to be invaded," she said.

"That's right," Paul said. "We all have our moats. I defend that one like my young."

"You see?" Morse said. "All of a sudden, Ivy Compton-Burnett in person. *Look* like her, Paul. He can look like any damn person he ever saw or heard tell of. Go on, look like her, for Kate."

Paul shook his head. "Shhh!" he said. "I didn't want Kate to know I could mimic. I don't know why such a harmless gift should give people the idea you're malicious, whether you use it that way or not, but it does. I suppose it has something to do with that same invasion syndrome."

"You couldn't be malicious if you tried," Morse said. "*Do* it, I said."

Paul's lightning reproduction of a face so totally unlike his own was yet so stunningly exact that Kate was almost too amazed to laugh.

"*Paul!*" she exclaimed. "You do sort of scare me. But you'd never take *me* off, would you?"

"No," he said. "Never."

And the moment he knew he meant that, he knew how close he'd come to loving her. No, he could never take her off. It frightened him. He felt his independence man its entrances like a threatened life. He was thankful she was leaving.

"Now *there's* someone," Kate said, "who knows how to get at character. Old Aunt Ivy. She knows that what identifies people is simply the thing that troubles them. She strips them right down to that and nothing else."

"Uh uh," Morse said. "That doesn't work with this character here. He lines up with *my* theory. I hold that what identifies people is the kind of thing that happens to them. Not what they instigate themselves, mind you, but what *happens* to them. The kind of thing they attract. Paul, tell Kate about the bees. My God, yes, tell her about the bees!"

"You think that's a story for mixed company?" Paul said.

"What do you mean, mixed company?" Morse said. "Who the hell's mixed company here? I don't like women much, but that's only because I've been married to a couple of them. When a woman's in love with you, she's all adrool with it like a rotten squash – and when she isn't, I'd as soon sleep with a piranha. But never mind. I'm damn sure you're not mixed company either. And I've seen nothing to suggest that Kate here isn't . . . you're heterosexual, aren't you, Miss Fennison?"

"As a rabbit," she said. "I give you my oath."

The drink had her almost giggling. None of her long sentences sounded pontifical to her and all her short ones wonderfully witty.

"No," Paul said, shaking his head. "It's a pointless juvenile's story. One of those gratuitous Tennessee Williams bits."

"Ah, but you're wrong, my friend," Morse said. "It's nothing of the kind. 'Character' is the text for today and nothing could set forth your character better."

"No," Paul said again.

"All right," Morse said. "I'll tell her myself. And you needn't worry about Kate's sensibilities. I'll euphemize that never-never land between kneecap and belly button so Jane Austen wouldn't turn a hair. What happened . . ."

He turned to Kate and parodied a kind of Beerbohm naughtiness. This was the first time she'd really wondered if she loved him, to see him quite unconscious that he wasn't altogether bringing something off.

"What happened . . ." he said. "One day whilst gleaning in the

14

fields and thinking God knows what grave and sub-tile thoughts – as is his wont, I assure you – our hero felt an urgent call of nature. He quickly hied himself to the depths of a neighbouring ravine, undid his nether garments, and with the most enormous relief . . ." he paused meaningfully ". . . right *fair* into a bee's nest!"

The picture itself struck Kate so funny that she let out a yelp of laughter. Morse held up a cautionary forefinger, absolutely sober.

"Whereupon the bees – and who wouldn't be justly *enough* outraged by such brazen desecration of his hearth? – swarmed up and attacked him smartly on either flank. See him now. Scrambling up the embankment, wrestling with the drawers that hung around his ankles like a hobble, and the bees in hot pursuit. Somehow he made it. Scaled the summit, outdistanced his assailants, righted his clothing. And then. It was then he heard this ominous buzzing in the general region of what we'll call his . . . oh hell, his crotch. And the next second this bee he'd unwittingly gathered up inside his drawers stung him beautifully, truly, right on the end of the *sine qua non.*"

Kate was struck with such laughter it splayed her.

"Wait!" Morse said, the index finger up again. "And *just* as he was baring his southern exposure once more and flapping the bee off his ichabod like crazy he looks up and there is Letty – straightening up out of the bracken with her basket of ras'bris and regarding him with one shudders to imagine *what* enormities of misconstruction. Now isn't that Paul for you?"

"It is!" Kate cried. "Oh it is, it is!" All at once her merriment snubbed itself. "You know, it's so *darn* typical I'm not sure I don't find it more *affecting* than funny. Does that make sense? I mean, it's one of those cases when people are so much like themselves it makes you love them. Paul," she said, as if it were that compelling, "will you marry me?"

Paul immediately ducked into the docility of a simple. "I guess," he mumbled. He gave a hick's meaching chuckle. "Sure."

"I'd guess not," Morse said, abruptly serious again. "Don't you see? To hark back before the bees a bit – definitive though they are in a different way – that's just the point. That's the whole puzzle. Paul doesn't marry *any*thing. He's just about the singlest damn character that ever lived."

He was. He was nothing like selfish, in no way egotistical or proud. Least of all was he anything like withdrawn. His doors were never locked. Others went in and out of him, and he the same with them, as if they were home. He had some rare credential which gave people the urge to make it you-and-I with him almost at first

15

sight. As if he were that section of themselves they made the privileged communications to. And yet they were forever baffled that despite this openness there was some final fusion with them, some final self-forgetfulness, that he would never quite hand over.

It had always been like that. He'd always had to feel that he belonged entirely to himself. The moment real involvement threatened he would have an instant picture of his own boundaries, map-stained with their own inviolable ink. It was nothing narcissistic, but he felt a loyalty to them as if they were some homely, family kingdom. As if real trespass on them, any yielding of autonomy that fusion brings, would cloud that inner eye which he could focus with such clarity. And this astringent clarity was his Samson's hair against whatever lance of fortune. He had kept himself, quite literally, as free as air. It was the only way that he could seem to breathe.

"He just *rents* people," Morse said. "Why do you suppose he set up this establishment here? Just so he could rent people a few months at a time . . . and then he's only too glad to set his consciousness on 'simmer' and cocoon along for the rest of the year absolutely alone."

Morse was refilling the glasses without consulting anyone's decision for or against a drink, talking around what he was doing like actors punctuating a long speech with the comma and dash of body movement.

"And get this. He doesn't give a damn that no more than a handful of people know that he *knows* everything. He does. He knows everything. He could reproduce the whole bloody *Encyclopaedia Britannica* if he had to. He knows that silly old George IV killed himself straining at stool. He can swap dichotomies with Huxley. He's letter-perfect in the nesting habits of the heath hen. He can integrate 'sine x cosine x,' for God's sake . . ."

Kate accepted her second drink like a remark, feeling as if she were watching herself in one of those improbably pleasant dreams wherein, miraculously, no one questions your right to belong.

"More than that," she said, "he knows the other kind of thing . . . why that new hat of Letty's isn't a comic but a heartbreaking touch, for instance. Doesn't he?"

Piecing Paul together had come to be a kind of beaming intercourse between each other. Right from the beginning it had been one of those peculiarly close threesomes wherein two members, in varying combinations, are always playing straight man or mock-inquisitor to the third.

"Exactly," Morse rattled on, taking none of his usual pains to pre-edit the clinkers from his speech. "It's like that phrase in the

16

Book of Common Prayer. He's insight-wise – not told-to wise, but insight-wise – to 'all manners and conditions of men.' You couldn't surprise him with anything. Just the nod in him – 'Yeah, I know.' And this is what I'm getting at. Say some meathead drives along this road one winter dusk. He sees this anonymous-looking character here traipsing out of the woods with his axe. The cold has bleached his face out so it looks like someone's after a funeral. And his clothing has that darned-look it always has – "

"Well, of all the mitigated gall!" Paul said.

"And the meathead thinks: What do people like that ever *think* about? And here's this character that could – " Morse made a gesture of frustration. "Just to think of a character like that with his label turned toward the wall, don't you want to protest?" He made another gesture, of exasperation. "And this crazy clown doesn't have one damned ounce of protest in him! Look at him now. Just sitting there grinning. Old Papa Lisa. That bloody decoy grin. That bloody matador's cape of his!"

It was Paul's typical grin. A wobbly amateur affair, not shored up at all, looking as if with heckling it might deteriorate into a smirk. So farcically unsymptomatic of the pith behind it which you tried to lock with that it was, indeed, the perfect decoy.

Kate saw precisely what Morse meant by the slouchiness of work clothes making Paul look negligible. He had a face that needed clothing to be absolutely right. A hat one shade too small or one too large would persecute it. It would jar with any kind of cap. Above all, his was such a speaking face – so helplessly externalized a feature – that you couldn't imagine even death's making it a closed one.

And yet if you were to turn the two men inside out and render them down you would find a matching residue of iron in the one and of whipcord in the other to explain this friendship so apparently implausible.

"You ask what makes me grin," Paul said. "Well, I'll show you."

The impersonal eyes of a newspaper lying on the floor had been continually staring at them, as they had from time to time while they talked returned its stare. He reached for it.

"I didn't ask what made you grin," Morse said. "I asked what made you, period. But all right. Let's hear what makes you grin."

Paul opened the paper. "Come here," he said.

Morse and Kate stood behind him, looking over his shoulder. Their hands rested on the back of his chair, almost touching. Hers, Kate thinking, so plainly memoried with the touch of teacups only and his with the true contactual knowledge of all things flesh and blood had to offer.

17

She recognized her thought for what it was, a sozzled one. For a second she came up like her own periscope through the lapping waters of her euphoria. For a fleeting second she saw herself as the classic spectacle of fatuity: an old maid in her cups, pathetically deluded that she had membership with anyone.

"Now here," Paul brought her back, "we have an album of the *earnest* types."

He pointed to the picture of a Cabinet Minister ringed by a platform aggregation. All had cast themselves for the photographer's benefit in that attitude of whimsical submission to the chairman's flattery.

"We will bend to this project," Paul trumpeted, "every last resource of mind, strength and determination at our command..."

He pointed to another cut. TEMPERANCE DELEGATES ASSEMBLE FOR ANNUAL MEET.

"Three whole days," he said, "haggling how to phrase a resolution about as world-shaking as a sneeze."

He pointed to a group of local players who were putting on *The Cherry Orchard* ... to an athlete who had jumped two inches higher than anyone had ever jumped before ... to an author cuddling his cheek in one hand as if it were a breast ... to a moustached colonel strutting like a little boy with Daddy's hat on down the line of soldiers drawn up for review...

He flipped the page and pointed to a redoubtable type who'd just become president of a ball-bearings outfit. He jerked back, as if startled—striking a precise duplicate of the fingers clasping the pen just so and the bristling purpose in the eye.

"Mind you," he said, "these are no candid camera shots. These characters have picked that pose, they're *holding* it."

"I suppose our ball-bearings boy must once have been a child," Morse said. "A child of some sort."

"You wonder, don't you," Paul said.

He flipped another page.

"And bless the ladies." He pointed at random. At Mrs Roger Tompkins who had just been made the corresponding secretary of a Garden Club. (Plant a Fuchsia Week had been her last crusade.) At Mrs J. L. W. Ruffin, with her arm outstretched to grasp the Scroll and Jewel some fraternal body was awarding her. At the group of hatted vestry wives clotted round the coffee urn, with a seated arch-matron holding out the immemorial cup...

"She's someone's mother," Kate murmured.

"I know," he said, "I know. Don't get me wrong. They don't incense me in the least. I bear them no ill will. But look at them. Smiling in most cases, yes. But not a grin in the whole lot. How *can* they play it so straight? Don't they know that someone, some-where in the world, is surreptitiously breaking wind?"

"If it could only be our Lady of the Urn!" Morse said. Kate giggled. She felt wonderful again.

"No," Paul said, "I'm serious. Not sermonizing, though. Please note, I didn't point a finger at that gang of cutthroats in the dock at Nuremberg. I didn't say one word about the killboys and the killjoys – all earnest types. I didn't drag in a thing about the whole menagerie of human didoes being no more than a nit on the galaxies of time and space. Not a word about the nonsense spec-tacle of serious thought. Well, only a few. Look up and the macro-cosms slap you down. Look down and the microcosms stagger you. And Plato gets not one scintilla closer to the riddle than Dale Evans. But that's not my point. All my point is, that . . ."

He read. " 'A group of citizens concerned in how the city's street names had their origin met at the home of Mr and Mrs Angus Burns to discuss . . .' 'The gift table was artfully arranged in the semblance of a parasol . . .' 'Mayoralty contestant willing to swear that . . .' 'Nickel magnate attributes success to . . .' "

He dropped the paper. "Do you see what I mean? How can they be so deadly intent? How can they *not* grin at their own intent-ness? Me, I'm so constituted that I can't help grinning, that's all. My God," he said, "I *am* running off at the mouth."

Again he took on subtle distance, like a child who shrugs off the encroaching garment that your propinquity has suddenly turned into.

"You are, you know," Morse said, "for you! Be damned if you're not! But while for once we've got that valve pried open, what's the serious word on Kate's proposal? The girl's waiting for an answer."

Paul made no reply. He merely kept himself the old familiar grin away from it all. But the earth around its roots was strangely shaken.

"Because if you're not going to take her up on it – " Morse was gathering the glasses for another refill – "I think it might not be a bad idea if I married her myself."

"You're *joking*, Mr Halliday!" Kate cried, in the spirit of it. "Now you're just joking!" But underneath the joke she too felt the mere letter of his words take on a startling grip.

They hadn't heard her father's car drive in. Its shadow passed a cutter-bar across the window, felling the moment's antennae in one quick swath.

Everything subsided. Morse seemed to fold the glasses away, put a bookmark in the conversation.

It was a cruelty – to Dr Fennison. He was as young in heart as they were. And looked it. He had no stamp of the professor. His still fine, mountain climber's head, with the face that never bothered to prepare itself for the occasion, was still ingenuous even at the neckline. Not with the ghost of youthfulness, like Paul's, but as if somewhere along the years he had become his own son. No parent could be less parentally afflictive. But once his wife had died and he was left alone with Kate, there was no escaping that father-daughter brand the circumstance had put on them.

Kate knew exactly how he'd act when he came in. Hearing her have fun, he'd promptly make his presence scarce, not to inhibit anything. She felt the cramp of sensing his cramp – yet mixed in with it a kind of militance in his behalf, defiantly against the others.

"We're in here," she called, the moment he set foot inside the hall.

Translating her, Morse made a mental note: She has this haemo-philic sympathy; she can never see that it bleeds both subject and object white. Some day he must write about her. There were sup-posed to be no convincing women in American fiction. Perhaps he could correct that – if he could manage to detail their soft centres without gagging.

Thinking: Women! They believe they're so subtle and they're transparent as glass. They spend their whole lives making mud pies out of their emotions. Or stringing them up on a frigging harp and twanging them for every possible chord, until their fingers are raw. But just the same, I damn near love her.

Thinking: I wish we had a fresh new word for "love." One that didn't pastry-scent every sentence it shows in . . .

"Oh well – " he said, winding it up glibly, "how does it go? Kate proposes, God disposes?"

Glibness was the thing with them that first summer. They still were confident that they could get on top of anything, with words. Each one of them still confident that he himself, in fact, could still dispose. They had yet to meet Bruce Mansfield. Or Rex and Sheila Giorno.

They had seen a picture of the Giornos. Last Sunday's edition of the *New York Times,* to which Paul subscribed, had run the Giornos' wedding picture in a leading spot; but no prophetic hint from these strange faces had snagged their scrutiny for longer than a skimming glance.

Letty was wearing the preposterous hat in town. Its flummery suggested that some prankster had sneaked it onto her head without her knowledge. She was one of those country women whose vital face goes so blunt, like a talent, when there is no longer anyone to love it alive. No one had noticed that she wasn't pretty until her husband died. She had extraordinarily delicate, voiceful hands.

Everyone in town knew Letty. Everyone had a smile for her, a word about her after she'd gone by. Recalling some daisy amongst the growing legend of her scandalous remarks. For as her face had gone blunt her tongue had taken on an edge.

Three times a week she drove Paul's decrepit old Ford into town for the mail and the groceries. Drove it fair down the middle of Main Street, yielding not an inch to the long tourist cars that tried to honk her out of their way.

"I was just noticin' her hands," one customer said to another when Letty left the grocer's. "I remember the day after her husband was killed – it was a derrick struck him, wasn't it, loadin' pulpwood off the wharf? I was just a kid then and Mother sent me over with some hot biscuits for her. I remember it shocked me, kind of – I thought she'd be settin' there cryin', and she was workin'. Her hands looked kind of scared. They looked as if they was scared to stop movin'. You just watch her hands sometimes. They still keep movin' like that."

From the grocer's Letty went to the cemetery. She had a bunch of the flowers she called "Chinese lanterns" to put on Harry's grave. Their dried parchment globes, exactly the colour of lamplight, would last all winter.

Twenty years ago today Harry had been brought here. She remembered the day like yesterday, but Harry's presence no longer came back for these anniversary visits. The dead lose their senses one by one. First they go deaf. Then they turn their faces away and go blind. And then motionless. Last of all, they go dumb. Harry had, at last, given in to his own stillness. It was as if he had not crumbled, but evaporated. When Letty plucked the moss from his name's lettering on the marker her hands touched only stone. She sighed, but she didn't implore. When the unbelievable fact that Harry's face was not the only face in the world had become believable, she had given in to it. When the past no longer asserted its own jealousy of the present distraction she never tried to maintain one on its behalf.

From the cemetery she went to her sister-in-law's. Huldah was her only female relative. This was the Granfort of the dingy side streets. Huldah cleared a place on the mussy kitchen table for the teacups and the inevitable plate of gingersnaps with the thimble stampings at their centre.

In between visits she'd forget how Huldah always ruffled her. She'd come there brimming with small confidences, having no other woman to air them with. But Huldah had a habit of snapping up the very first bait so eagerly it was somehow oppressive. She crowded you so close with her avid receptiveness that your next impulse was, perversely, to pull in your lines altogether.

"Do you remember what happened twenty years ago today, Huldah?" Letty said.

"Today!" Huldah echoed, gently-preying, her voice walking on eggshells. "Twenty years ago today!"

It embarrassed her to be caught with food in her mouth. Would it be quite fitting to swallow it without a commemorative pause?

Letty reached for another cookie. The perverse impulse was working already.

"You had your oven too hot for these, didn't you?" she said.

Huldah swallowed. Then sighed.

"I guess that's a day you'll never forget, Letty, isn't it?" she said. "There's bin some changes since then. Little did you know back then that you'd be buried out there on the old Mansfield place now. No mail service. No phone even. I guess it's a good thing we can't see ahead."

"What ever become of the Mansfields?" Letty switched the topic again.

Huldah looked thwarted. "Well," she said, "the last I heard . . ."

She cleared her throat and Letty thought, she'll give me their whole pedigree. I never saw the beat of that woman. What she don't know about people ain't worth knowin'.

The last Huldah had heard, the Mansfields were still up Truro way. The parents, that is. They'd moved up there, to another farm, after Paul bought them out. And the boy. Bruce. Did Letty remember him? The smart one. Took all the prizes in school, did Letty remember? Well, she understood he went to college later. And then enlisted and went overseas. And now they said he was back in college again.

"He married the Westhaver girl, you know. Molly Westhaver.

22

They went together right back from kids. They've got one child, I know. And I don't doubt but two now. The last I heard she was expecting again."

Where does she *get* all her information? Letty marvelled. I'll bet there ain't another soul in town could tell you anything about the Mansfields after all these years.

"Letty," Huldah interrupted herself suddenly, "I wish you'd give up that job out there. It's too hard a work for a woman your age. Forty-three isn't twenty-three, you know. Why don't you come in town here . . . with Jim and me? Where it's like living."

Letty glanced at the window with its listless curtains pierced by a faded Remembrance Day poppy, two Coronation buttons, and needles trailing thread. A row of soup cans housing some sickly aster transplants lined the sill.

She glanced through the window to the backyard, with the whitewashed rubber tire enclosing a bed of rotted nasturtiums. And across the yard to the gutter of the pavement where the chewing-gum wrappers were dammed up, like sodden leaves by a branch across a brook. In the street an empty beer carton gave yet another death twitch each time a car passed over it.

She glanced across the street to the old wooden theatre painted the green of a caterpillar's insides . . . to the tattered poster in front of it where all day long a bangled slave girl lifted her supplicating arms to the remnants of a Roman centurion.

"You needn't feel beholden to us," Huldah was saying. "You could apply for the Widows' Pension. I don't see how they could keep you out of it."

"I'd see myself!" The offishness that Huldah always sparked in her became outright anger. "Them pension navigators with their little satchels, pokin' and pryin' into your affairs! I guess I ain't in the poorhouse jist yet, Huldah. When I get so I can't work no longer – well, I may have to come to it. But as long as these hands . . ."

She looked at her hands as if she were beseeching them never to make a separate peace with age.

"And how would Paul get along without me?" she said.

"Now, Letty," Huldah said. "Be reasonable. In this world there's always someone to take your place – anyone's place – don't you know that? Do you think Paul couldn't get another housekeeper? That's your trouble, Letty – you're too easy. You've got to look out for yourself in this world or no one else will. Do you think he'd think twice about looking after you if it was the other way around?"

That was another trait of Huldah's. She was forever trying to weld others to herself by pointing out to them how shamelessly

23

their friends exploited them; just how much more they gave their friends than they could ever hope to get in turn, were the tables reversed.

But the welding never quite worked out. The truer her words and the stauncher her alignment with their rights the more they seemed to sidle off. Just when she'd counted on her championship to melt them totally toward her they switched the conversation. They looked as if they wished they were somewhere else.

She made a quick excuse to the back porch now, for a hod of coal. Maybe if she gave her words a chance to sink in . . .

They were sinking in, all right. For the life of her, Letty couldn't have expressed her thoughts. The only way she could really talk to Paul was with the language of her hands. (It was terrible that hands could be so congested with fluency and yet so powerless to lend one smidgen of it to your speech.)

Yes. Maybe Huldah was right. Housekeepers were invisible somehow, as human beings. When Paul was alone with her, he didn't shutter up that personal switchboard the others reached him through, exactly; but she could see he kept no operator there to take the calls. He only brought that operator back when they came back, the talking people, and spoke to him in his own tongue.

He lived in the country of those people who seemed to know exactly what the world was *saying*, anyway, and she could only stare at the world like a child at the fair. She could only catch its short simple sentences. That was the wall between them. A dreadful wall for love to have to recognize the height and thickness of.

She knew he was content enough to be alone with her throughout the winter months. Idling along in the kitchen of his mind, knowing that its living rooms would be reopened when the talking people come back in the spring. But what would it be like if he hadn't that to look ahead to? – if he knew there was to be just the two of them, always? It would be a dreadful thing to hear him listening to the hum of vacancy in those best rooms inside him – and yet be powerless to cross their thresholds, open though they were, and give him company . . .

Huldah wiped the coal dust from her hands, glancing at Letty's face. She couldn't understand it. The more anyone tried to make common cause with Letty, the more alone she looked. She looked as if she'd been dealt a blow.

"Well," Letty said, packing herself up, "I shouldn't be settin' here." Whenever the talk with Huldah struck a split rail like this the clock's demands seemed way overdue. "It's time I got home and got some dinner goin'."

"Now, that's exactly what I was saying," Huldah harked back.

"You shouldn't be at the beck and call of a job like that. At your time of life. You should be able to set down and talk all day if you wanted to."

Letty exploded.

"No, thank you!" she said. "I've *seen* people that got nothin' to do but set down and talk all day! We get plenty specimens like that out there. They don't know what an honest day's work feels like. Nothin' but talk, talk, talk. Talkin' ain't *livin'*. Workin's livin'. Makin' things and doin' things for people. They never made anything you could lay your hands on. Not as much as an axe handle or a loaf o' bread. If they'd ever bin right down to hardpan . . . if they'd ever had to scratch for a livin', maybe they'd have something to take their minds offa their*selves*. But, talk, talk, talk. All they've ever done is wag the air around with their tongues. It's like they're jist feedin' off the *smell* o' things. Their heads need a good dose o' salts." She caught her breath. "And when they get tired o' talkin', they're kinda like cannibals . . . then they start pawin' around in each other's feelin's . . . and eatin' offa *them*. *Them's* yer people that got nothin' to do but set around and talk all day. No, thank you. Kids could handle theirselves better."

Her tirade broke off suddenly. It wasn't Huldah she was talking to, anyway, but herself.

"Who's that?" she said, glancing at the street. "That ain't old Mayor Gill's wife, is it . . . with that pisspot stuck on her head?"

Huldah's teeth clutched her lower lip in the nervous shocked-impish giggle that tries to dispose of outrage by pretending it was a slip.

"Them hats's all the style this year," she said. She had a sudden inspiration. "Now *there*, Letty. I happen to know Nora Gill's looking for a cook right now. That'd be a wonderful spot for you. You'd be in town. And you could get around . . . to meetings and things."

"You kin have yer meetin's and things," Letty said.

The minute she'd set eyes on Nora Gill the anger she'd taken out on Paul's friends left her. Huldah was always doin' that somehow; gettin' you to say things you didn't mean. Reallegiance to Paul's friends swept over her in a quite dizzying lift.

They wasn't like Nora Gill. They really *was* something. Not jist here, but in the world's eye. Nora jist thought she was something. She was jist perched up on like a little bunch of rickety crates. A little bit of money. A little pinch of this. A little pinch of that. Knock them out and she'd go ass over kittle. You could never topple them that way. They was too wide and solid on the ground.

And yet no matter how much paraphernalia they had in their

minds, in some ways they was opener than anyone else. She knew that in a way they took her right in with them – when they wouldn't give the likes of Nora Gill the time of day. It had something to do with anyone's bein' themself, she couldn't come any closer to it than that. She knew that she could meet them anywheres in the world, it wouldn't matter who they was with, and it'd be "Hi Letty!" with them right away. They wouldn't even think of havin' to make apologies for her. She loved them.

She gave Nora Gill's retreating figure another scathing glance. "I'd knock the feathers outa that old crow," she said, "before I was there a fort'nit."

Huldah changed her tack.

"Well then, Letty," she said, as if it might surprise Letty to find out how broad-minded she could be, "why don't you get married again? I don't see how anyone could say a word. You've respected Harry's memory all these years. You've kept yourself decent." She went coy. "Why don't you set your cap for Paul?"

"Huldah," Letty said, "sometimes I think you ain't got the sense you was born with."

Huldah chose to take this in a burst of good part. She laughed outright, shaking her head from side to side.

"Letty," she said, "you're a caution!"

But why didn't Letty laugh with her? Again she looked as if she'd been struck.

Yes, Letty was thinking. I'm a caution. But if Harry had lived I wouldn't have been a caution. With Harry . . . with children . . . I'd have been just like anyone else.

Paul would be a caution too, she thought, if he couldn't talk like that. They all would. But they can talk like that. I can't. I'm just a caution.

Letty was halfway home before the self-confrontments that Huldah had stirred up in her ceased to dismay.

Halfway there, as she drove through a long cleansing stripe of tree-shadow on the road, they vanished all at once, as if light or music had scattered them. In a moment home would be nearer than town. The road itself began to welcome her and reinstate her. The dreadful spectre of life with Jim and Huldah, with Nora Gill, dropped behind her. She felt that great gust of freedom which comes with knowing that whatever little you're content to settle for in the place you love, and in the company that makes all other company seem blank and eyeless, is worth far more than anything you might exact in any other circumstance.

What did it matter who gave and who took? All she asked was

that her strength be spared. So that she could go on looking after Paul (as which of his talking friends would?) in all the ways he was so careless about, himself. That's the only thing that was like livin'.

She felt young and lively with the very thought. She felt the years and years of strength before her. There was no one to see her smile as she touched a hand to her face; but all at once she was a pretty woman. The hat almost became her.

She still believed that everything turned on her keeping her strength. She had never heard of Rex and Sheila Giorno, either. She scarcely knew where Connecticut was.

CHAPTER 3

Nor did Bruce Mansfield know anything of the Giornos. He was at his father's farm in Truro and they were in Greenwich – hundreds of miles and the climate of money away.

His father's Truro place had never seemed like home to him. You can't transfer your feeling for the home farm to another. If the one you were raised on has crudities, they're no more noticed than the rawness of a family face. But such crudities as the new place may have – the curling grey shingles on its long dark porch, the clutter of stock pails with cakes of middlings on their sides – strike you, even more than they do the city-born, as alien and dismal.

But it didn't matter much to Bruce where he was then. He was only twenty-seven years old. He had Molly. And Peter. He was back from the war. And with another year's earnings and his service grants he could go back to the University, to the studies that were like another heart and spine to him.

They were staying at his father's until Molly's second child was born. Yesterday he'd taken her to the hospital in Halifax. A week ahead of time, just to make sure. She'd had a little trouble carrying this one. Today his parents had gone in to see her. He and Peter were all alone.

Once when Bruce was a child at the place that was now Paul's, the roof had leaked next to the flue. It was only a small leak but a stubborn one, and sometimes rain water would trickle down the side of the flue and stain the wallpaper in his bedroom. His mother stopped that with meal bags spread out on the attic floor. But even if he couldn't see the leak he could never enjoy the rain, knowing that the house wasn't tight. His father patched the shingles next to the flue, and the first storm after that Bruce took the lantern up into the attic, tremblingly to test if everything was now snug. But the water was still trickling through. He went back downstairs, but he couldn't feel indoors. Someone said, maybe the rain was seeping through the bricks; and they mounted a cover over the flue's mouth. The next rain, he thought: surely this time . . . but when he put his hand against the flue it came away wet, and he felt half-sick. Someone said maybe the flashing was gone, and his father tore some bricks out and put in new flashing . . . but when it next rained his hand still came away wet.

And then, as a last resource, his father ran a thick wide collar of cement all around the flue where it entered the roof. The work was hardly done before the driving rain of a hurricane came down. Bruce went into the attic that night, not daring to hope, and he touched the flue and it was dry as kindling. He examined it from top to bottom and there wasn't a single stain of moisture. And he hugged it and the driving rain was pounding on the roof but the wind couldn't force one drop of it inside and he was indoors at last and it was truly wonderful.

Being married to Molly was like that.

When she was out of sight her face had a way of springing up behind his eyes clearer than the objects before them. The dark-eyed face that sparks of fun saved from being too gentle to be comfortable with. The certainties of maturity setting on it, some-how touchingly, like punishment she was unconscious of. The hair in which a girlish vulnerability lingered like some disarmingly naïve defence.

Not that sophistication was a mystery to her. She was the kind of country girl who, if she can take a polish at all, takes it so grace-fully: the soft glow that makes no mention of itself, like good wood glowing under lamplight. But whenever she practised urbanity it was with the relief, when she could stop practising it, of a house-wife slipping into her everyday garments again when the company leaves.

Next to the flesh-eyed physical tie which they both found welding, unshackling, enlarging, engulfing, sense-grunting, homing (and, savingly, a little comic) in exactly the same way, this was the greatest bond between them.

He too had often practised urbanity, but never with the tempta-tion to make it part of him. They shared the matchless island of one's content being so satiatingly the other's as never to give it a fret that they themselves were unremarkable. It was enough merely to watch and report to each other on the remarkable, the sophisticated – "they" – with exactly the same knowing but un-vaccinated eye.

Molly wasn't beautiful. Her face was in no way distinctive, except as such faces are at certain moments loved so fiercely for their particular ordinariness. But she had that unlocatable delicacy in her flesh that so binds you to the woman you know is all your own.

Peter wasn't his own in quite the same way.

He'd been scarcely more defined than a baby when Bruce went overseas. When Bruce came back, he'd found an uncommonly individual child of six, who seemed in most behaviour to be twice that age. They were still feeling their way around with each other. And almost as often as they were close as touch they'd be a total bafflement apart.

There were times when Bruce could only look at him and say his name over and over in his mind.

He would say, "Peter, Peter . . . ," nights when he'd look at him asleep – the involuntary way you pass your hand across your eyes when your head aches, though there is no way for your hand to get inside. Any six-year-old has a look of accusing innocence when he's asleep, an assaulting grudgelessness. But it seemed to Bruce as if Peter had it especially. It seemed incredible that when he'd told him to undress he'd said, "You make me!" – his eyes dark and stormy. It seemed incredible that those same legs and hands, absolutely pliant now, would ever be party to such isolating violence again. His visible flesh would be still; yet he was always moving in a dream. Maybe he'd cry, "Wait . . . Wait up, Bruce." Where am I going in the dream, Bruce would think, what am I doing, that even as I hold him in my arms he is falling behind?

Peter called his father "Bruce," not "Dad." The idea was, they were pals or something.

Bruce had never laid a hand on him. A curious suggestion of vulnerability about his wire-thin body, his perceptive face, so con-trasted with its actual belligerence that the thought of laying a hand on him – well, Bruce just couldn't do it. They were supposed to *reason* things out.

Sometimes that worked. Sometimes it didn't.

Peter *could* reason, all right. His body would seem to vibrate with obedience. His friendship would be absolutely unwithholding.

"You stepped on my hand," he'd say, laughing, though his face was pinched with the pain of it, "but that doesn't matter, does it, Bruce? Sometimes you can't see people's hands when they stick them in the way." Or if they were fishing, he'd say, "You tell me when to pull on the line, won't you Bruce . . . just right *when?*"

Then, without warning whatsoever, he'd become possessed by this automatic inaccessible mutiny.

That's when Bruce would feel the staggering helplessness. That whatever he'd done wrong had not only failed, but that Peter would never know he'd been *trying* to do it right for him. Worse still, that his child-mind was rocked by some blind contradiction that he himself would never be able to fathom at all.

Maybe Bruce would be helping him with a reading lesson. (Peter could read at four.) He'd try to make a game of it, totalling the words Peter named right against the words he named wrong. Peter would look at him, squinting up his face into a twist of deliberate ingratiation. He'd say, "Seventeen right and only one wrong . . . wouldn't that make you *laugh*, Bruce?"

Then maybe the very next word Bruce asked him, he'd slump against the table in a pose of indolence; or flop the book shut while the smile was still on his father's face.

Or maybe they'd be playing with his new baseball bat and mitt.

His hands were too small to grasp the bat properly and his fingers were lost in the mitt. But he couldn't have seemed more obliviously happy when he did connect with the ball. "Boy, that was a solid hit, wasn't it Bruce? You throw them *just* right, Bruce, just *right*." He'd improvise rules of his own for the game. His face would contort with the delight of communicating them to his father.

Then, suddenly, when he'd throw the ball himself, he'd throw it so hard that the physical smart of it on Bruce's fingers would sting him to exasperation.

"All right," Bruce would say coolly, "if you don't want to play, I'll go hoe the garden."

He'd go over to the garden, watching Peter out of the corner of his eye. Peter would wander, forlorn, about the yard. Then Bruce would see him coming slowly toward the garden – where his tracks still showed in the carrot rows he'd raced through yesterday.

He'd come up behind his father and say, "I have to walk right between the rows, don't I? Gardens are hard *work*, aren't they, Bruce? . . you don't want anyone stepping on the rows."

Peter, Peter . . .

The strange part, it wasn't that correction lacked effect because it left no impression.

One evening he'd said out of a blue sky, "*You're* so smart, Bruce . . . I haven't got a brain in my head, not one. You've got so many *brains*, Bruce, *brains* . . ."

Bruce was completely puzzled. Then he remembered: Peter had called him "dumb" that morning and he had snubbed him with total silence. He'd forgotten the incident entirely. But Peter hadn't.

Though he'd been less rather than more tractable since then, he'd been carrying the snub around with him all day. Now he was trying to override it.

Or the afternoon there was only one nickel in his small black purse. Bruce saw him take it out and put it back again, several times, before he came and asked for another. He never asked for money unless he wanted it terribly. Bruce gave him another nickel. He went to the store and came back with two Cokes. For some reason he had to treat his father. Bruce's face must have shown his gratification.

"You look happier with me than you did this morning," Peter said with his devastating candour, "don't you, Bruce?"

That time, Bruce could recall no morning offence at all. Peter must have sensed a displeasure which he himself had been quite unconscious of.

Peter, Peter . . .

Oddly enough, it was only when they were absolutely alone, when no one else was anywhere near, that it seemed as if they'd never been apart.

They were alone this morning. They were going fencing. It was one of those mornings when even the trees seem to breathe out a clean water-smell. Peter was very excited. He and his mother had lived here all the years Bruce was away, but he'd never been to the back pasture before.

Bruce carried the axe and mall. Peter carried the staple-box and the two hammers. Sometimes Peter walked beside him, sometimes ahead.

There was something about the child that always affected Bruce when he watched him walking back-to. He'd made him wear his rubber boots because there was a swamp to cross. Now the sun was getting warm, he wished he'd let him wear his sneakers and carried him across the swamp. There was something about the heavy boots *not* slowing up his eager movement . . . and the thought that they must be tiring him without his being conscious of it. He asked him if his legs weren't tired.

"Noooo," Peter scoffed. As if that were the kind of nonsense question people kid each other with to clinch the absolute perfection of the moment. Then he added, "If your legs do get a little tired going some place, that doesn't hurt, does it, Bruce?"

You may love your child's company, but it is seldom good company in the adult sense. Peter was good company in that sense too. The unusual twists of comment that continually popped up in his speech were more engaging than most adults'. No one would ever

31

believe it, but just last week he'd said, "How come your conscience can tell your mind to tell your tongue *not* to say 'Goddamit'?"

Yet there was no shadow of unnatural precocity about him. His face had a kind of feature-smalling brightness, like Molly's, that gave him a peaked look when he was tired or disappointed, and when his face was washed and the water on his hair, for town, a kind of shining. But when his face was without its smashing look, it was as child-like and unwithholding as the clasp of his hand.

Father and son were not unlike, but Bruce's face never gave him away like that.

Except for the slightly clamped expression of one who is too stringent a self-judge, he was typically the medical student in appearance as in fact. No hint whatever of the pure scholar he might as easily have been. He had the hockey player's build whose averageness in street clothes somehow surprises you; and the kind of squarish, blondish face, dull-complexioned with the very soundness of health, which suggests a sculpture in which the final finish is withheld deliberately for some realistic touch. Its flesh looked as if it weighed as solid as bone.

This was one of the days when Peter was intensely, jubilantly communicative. One of his "How come?" days. As if by his questions and Bruce's answers they, and they alone, could find out about everything.

If his father said anything remotely funny he worked himself up into quite a glee. Bruce knew his laughter was a little louder than natural. His face would twitch a little, renewing it, each time Bruce glanced at him. But that didn't mean his amusement was false. Bruce knew that his intense willingness to think anything funny that was said was as funny as anything could possibly be, tickled him more than the joke itself.

They came to the place where the horse had been buried. Dogs had dug the earth away from it. The brackets of its ribs and the chalky grimace of its jaws stared whitely in the bright sun.

Peter was suddenly quiet beyond mere attentiveness. As if something invisible were threatening to come too close. He had never seen a skeleton before.

"Those bones can't move, *can* they, Bruce?" he said.

"No," Bruce said.

"How can bones move?"

"Oh, they have to have flesh on them, and muscles, and . . ."

"Well, could he move when he was just dead? I mean right then, when he was right just dead?"

"No."

"How come?"

Bruce was searching for an answer when Peter moved very close to him.

"Could you carry the hammers, Bruce, please?" he said.

Bruce put the hammers in the back pocket of his overalls.

"Could *you* carry an axe and a mall both in one hand?" Peter said.

Bruce took the axe in his left hand, with the mall, so that now each had a hand free. Peter took his hand and tugged him along the road. He was quiet for a few minutes.

Then he said: "Bruce? You study about that, don't you? What goes out of your muscles when you're dead?"

He was a good boy all morning. Really a help. Bruce couldn't have carried all the gear through the bush at once. He'd have had to replace a row of rotted posts with the axe and mall, then go back to where he'd left the staple-box and hammers and go over the same ground, tightening the wire. As it was, Peter carried the staple-box and hammers and they could wind things up as they went.

He held the wire taut while Bruce drove the staples. He'd get his voice down very low. "The way you do it, Bruce, see, you get the claw of the hammer right behind a *barb* . . . so it won't slip Bruce, see?" As if he'd hit on some trick that would now be a conspiratorial secret between the two of them alone. The hum of manual labour stitched their presences together.

They started at the far end of the pasture and worked toward home. It was five minutes past eleven when they came within sight of the skeleton again. The spot where the Mansfield section of the line fence ended.

That was fine. They could finish the job before noon and not have to walk all the way back again after dinner.

Bruce cursed when he struck three rotten posts in a row. But they could still finish, if they hurried.

He thought Peter looked tired and pale.

"You take off those heavy boots and rest," he said, "while I go down to the intervale and cut some posts." There were no trees growing near the fence.

"All right, Bruce," Peter said. "But don't be long."

He was very quiet. There was that look of suspension in his flesh that he'd get sometimes when his mind was working on something it couldn't quite manoeuvre.

It took Bruce less than half an hour to cut the posts. But when he carried them back to the fence, Peter was nowhere in sight.

"Bring the staples, chum," he shouted.

Peter didn't pop from behind any bush.

"Peter! Peter!" he called, louder.

33

There was only that hollow stillness of the winds rustling the leaves when you call to someone in the woods and there's no answer. Peter had completely disappeared.

Bruce felt a sudden irritation. Of all the damn times to beat it home without a word!

He started to stretch the wire by himself. But disquiet began to insinuate itself. Anyone could follow that wide road home. But what if . . . he didn't know just what . . . but what if something . . . ?

Oh, goddam it, he'd have to go find him. The obbligato of concern for Molly, which had maintained its own unconscious strain against his nerves, now made itself insistent too.

He kept calling all the way along the road. There was no answer. How could Peter get out of the woods so quickly, unless he ran? He must have run all the way.

Bruce began to run, himself.

His first reaction when he saw Peter standing by the house, looking toward the pasture, was intense relief. Then all at once his irritation was compounded.

Peter seemed to sense his irritation even from a distance. He began to wave, as if to disarm. He had a funny way of waving, holding his arm out stiff and moving his hand up and down very slowly. Bruce didn't wave back. When he came close enough that Peter could see his face, Peter stopped waving.

"I thought you'd come home without me, Bruce," he said. "Some other way."

"Why should you think that?" Bruce said, in the sarcastic calm you use with an adult.

Peter wasn't defiant, as Bruce had thought he'd be. The way he so often was. He looked as if he was relieved to see his father; but as if, seeing him come from that direction, he knew he'd done something wrong. Now he was trying to pass the whole misunderstanding off as an amusing twist in the way things had turned out – but not too sure this would go over. His tentative over-smiling brushed at Bruce's irritation, but didn't dislodge it.

"I called to you, Bruce," he said.

Bruce just looked at him. As much as to say: Do you think I'm deaf?

"Yes. I called. I thought you'd come home some other way."

"Now I've got to traipse all the way back there this afternoon to finish one bloody rod of fence," Bruce said.

"I thought you'd gone and left me!" Peter said.

Bruce ignored him and walked past him into the house.

Peter didn't eat much dinner. But he wasn't defiant about that either, as he usually was when he refused to eat. And after dinner he went out and sat down on the banking, by himself. He didn't know that his hair was sticking up through the heart-shaped holes in his skull-cap with all the buttons pinned on it.

When it came time to go back to the woods again, he hung around Bruce with his new bat and ball. Tossing the ball up himself and trying to hit out flies.

"Boy, you picked out the very best bat there was, didn't you, Bruce?" he said.

Bruce could read his mind: his father would toss him a few. He didn't pay any attention to what Peter was doing.

When he started across the yard for the woods, Peter said, "Do you want me to carry the axe for you this afternoon? That makes it *easier* for you, doesn't it, Bruce?"

"I'll be back in an hour or so," Bruce said in a level voice, the way you'd snub an adult. "You stay here and play with Max." Max was a neighbour's boy.

Peter followed as far as the gate. Then he stopped. Bruce didn't turn around.

It wasn't until he bent over to crawl through the barbed wire fence that he stole a glance at Peter. He was tossing the ball up and trying to hit it. But it always fell to the ground, because the bat was so big for him and because he had one eye on his father.

Bruce noticed he was still wearing his hot rubber boots. He had meant to have him change into sneakers, and then forgotten. Peter was the kind of child who seems to invest his clothes with his own mood. The thought of his clothes, when he was forlorn, struck Bruce as hard as the thought of his face.

In the pasture Bruce picked up the tools and began to work. But he couldn't seem to work quickly.

The hammer would go slack in his hands and he'd catch himself thinking about crazy things like Peter's covert pride in his new corduroys the Saturday he'd taken him to the matinee . . . so singling him out from the other kids, totally thoughtless of their slip-shod dress, that he'd felt an unreasonable rush of protectiveness toward him. Of his laughing dutifully at the violence in the comedy, but crouching toward his father a little, while the other kids, who weren't half as violent as he, shrieked together in a seizure of delight . . .

Bruce thought of his scribblers, with the fixity of the letters there which his small hand had formed so earnestly but so crooked. Of the times when the freak would come upon him to recount all his transgressions of the day, insisting on his guilt with the very phrases Bruce himself had used, phrases that had seemed to make no impression whatsoever on him at the moment . . .

35

He thought of him playing ball with the other children.

At first they'd go along with the outlandish variations Peter would suggest in the game – he had so damn much imagination! They'd go along with it because the equipment was his. Then somehow *they'd* be playing with his bat and glove and he'd be out of it, watching.

Bruce thought now of him standing there, saying, "Boy, I hope my friends come to play with me early tomorrow, Bruce, *early*" – when he himself knew that if they came at all, their first question would be, "Can we use your bat and glove?"

He thought of him asleep. He thought: If anything should ever happen to him, that's the way he would look. He laughed, trying to kid himself for being such a sentimental fool.

But a sudden feeling came over him that something *was* happening to Peter. Right now. It was as clear as the sound of a voice.

When Bruce came in sight of the barn he could see the cluster of children by the horse stable.

He couldn't see Peter among them. But he saw the ladder against the roof. He saw Max running toward the stable, with a neighbour running behind him.

The children looked at Bruce with that uneasy awe that was always in their faces whenever Peter had been reckless beyond anything they'd dare themselves. He knew what had happened.

"He fell off the roof," Max said.

Bruce knew that somehow he'd driven him to this.

He held him and he said, "Peter . . . Peter . . ."

Peter stirred. "Wait," he said drowsily. "Wait up, Bruce . . ."

Bruce had the oddest feeling then. He had an absolute conviction that if he hadn't been right there, right then, to call Peter's name, Peter would never have come back. It was foolish. The child was only stunned and bruised. But he felt it just the same.

Peter didn't whimper when Bruce examined him. He was always as quiet and brave as an adult whenever he was hurt.

Bruce read to him for a while. He'd sit quiet all day, with the erasure on his face as smooth as the erasure of sleep, if you read to him.

After supper, Bruce decided to wind up the fencing job.

"Do you want to help me finish the fence?" he said. He thought Peter would be delighted.

"No," Peter said. "You go on. I'll wait right here. Right here, Bruce."

"Who's going to help me stretch the wire?" Bruce said.

Peter hesitated. "All right," he said.

He scarcely spoke until they got almost to the spot where the

36

skeleton was. Then he stopped and said, "We better go back, Bruce. It's going to be dark."

"G'way with ya," Bruce said. "It won't be dark for hours."

It wouldn't be, although the light *was* an eerie after-supper light.

"I'm going home," Peter said. His voice and his face were suddenly defiant.

"You're not going home," Bruce said. He almost shouted at him. "Now come on. Hurry up."

He was carrying an extra pound of staples. Peter snatched the package from his hand. Before Bruce could stop him he broke the string and strewed them far and wide.

Bruce was so keyed up from the whole day's several strains that he did then what he'd never done before. He took him and held him and he put it onto him, hard and thoroughly.

Peter didn't try to escape. For the first few seconds he didn't make a sound. He didn't pull back his defiance. There was only a kind of crouching in his eyes when he first realized that his father was actually going to strike him.

Then he began to cry. He cried and cried.

"You're *going* home," Bruce said, "and you're going straight to *bed*."

He could see the marks of his fingers on Peter's bare legs when he undressed him.

Peter went to sleep almost immediately. It was so quiet downstairs that Bruce decided to study. But he couldn't study. The words on the page might have been any others.

He'd forgotten to make Peter go to the toilet before he sent him to bed. Peter awoke, to go to the toilet.

Bruce went upstairs and Peter was sitting on the side of the bed. He had on his bright, communicative face again. His father sat down beside him.

"Bones make you feel funny, don't they, Bruce?" was the first thing Peter said.

Bruce remembered then.

He remembered that the skeleton was opposite the place where Peter had sat down to rest while he cut the posts. He remembered how Peter had shrunk back from it on the way in. He remembered then that the wind had been blowing *away* from him when he was in the intervale. That's why he hadn't heard Peter call.

He thought of Peter calling, and then running along the road alone in the hot, heavy rubber boots . . .

Bruce put an arm around his shoulder. Peter was warm from the bed and from his night-childishness. Somehow Bruce had never so felt Peter's being his own son, felt it to the very end of every nerve.

But he didn't know what to say. He could still see the red marks of his hands on Peter's legs.

Peter sensed his feeling. He was so like an adult sometimes. And like the perceptive adult, he knew exactly when the way to preserve the peak of a splendid moment was to break away from it to something else.

"Do you think Mum's got the baby yet?" he said quickly. It was the first time he'd ever mentioned the baby coming.

"I don't think so," Bruce said. "They'd have phoned. It's not due for a little while yet."

"What will we call him, Bruce?" Peter said. He thought a moment. "I wish you would have called *me* Bruce," he said, "and then we could have called *him Peter,* couldn't we?"

"But maybe it won't be a boy," Bruce said.

"No. But if it is." Peter was suddenly all child again. "You won't call *him* Bruce, *will* you?" he said.

"No," Bruce said.

Peter pulled his father's arm down around his own waist and wormed his hand in under his father's palm.

"I'd like to seen when you were little, Bruce," he said. "Will you take me there sometime – where you were little? Just the two of us?"

"Yes," Bruce said. "I'll take you there sometime. I promise."

Yes, yes. He would take him back there. He would take him to so many, many places. He would show him so many, many things. And whenever Peter got that other look, he would remember this day. He would see to it that enough understanding took that smashing, unreachable look from his face forever.

He had never felt so happy in his whole life.

CHAPTER **4**

"How's your headache now?" Kate said to her father.

"It'll be all right," he said. His health had always been so extroverted that any physical distress perplexed him, made him look younger than ever. "It's nothing much. Driving into the sun, I suppose." It had been one of those fall days of glaring sun all the way from Endlaw.

They were back home now, making those first disjointed movements toward this object or that; waiting for the house, drugged with such a stretch of its own silence, to recognize them.

Their house looked out on the University campus and the Northwest Arm of Halifax harbour. In the Arm the convoy-memoried water of the harbour changes into sailboat water. Over it, tinted cloud-maps of Italy and Greenland and Asia Minor geographied the deep ocean colour of the dusking sky.

"We'll get something to eat," Kate said, "and then you'd better take some aspirin and go to bed."

"I think I will," he said. "But won't it be sort of dreary for you here all alone? Why don't you go out somewhere? It worries me, Kate, you don't get out more."

"No," she said. "I've got lots of things to do."

It *would* be drearier for her than for him. Immediately he returned from a trip now, the pleasantness of being home superseded all memory of the trip's pleasantness. She was younger. She was still half at Paul's.

She knew he was helpless not to recognize that. It trapped her with empathy.

They had supper and he went to bed. Fire had roused the house to their presences again. When the household chores were done, she poured herself a drink and went into the study, to read.

Her father had never seemed like a professor. But this was a professor's brownstone house. This was a professor's room – the bookcase its centre of gravity. The dark roll-top desk stood weather-grained with the climate of abstract thought that had so often clouded above it. The walls were hung with pictures of her father's undergraduate companions, severely young in the clothing and cut of hair that had now grown so old on them: those team pictures posed in innocence of posterity's realignment, in which the two front figures sprawl against each other on the ground and the present celebrity is not appropriately centred but an anonymous third from the right.

On the desk top, the photograph of her mother's delicate, imperilled face smiled (so tirelessly for one whom any concentration tired so quickly) her "album smile." Kate looked like both her father and mother, though they had never resembled each other in the least.

The room was outwardly tidy. But it had that atmosphere of clutter which pervades all houses wherein it has always seemed so much more important to *know* than to *do* (or to *have*) that the things of convenience are never sorted into any order of precedence.

Its capricious pieces of furniture had not been chosen to match, nor yet for contrast. They were stared down by the archaeological fragments which her father had brought back from other civilizations and other centuries. They had an air not quite shabby or dispirited, but of having had to resign themselves once and for all to their absolutely incidental status.

Kate read a while: the book reviews in the *Times* that Paul had given her to bring along.

And then she stopped reading. An inner dialogue had begun too steadily to interrupt her conversation with the page. It was nothing like the drinking dialogue at Paul's. Home was claiming her again as quickly as the first twinges of a recurrent illness put their sufferer back into the faithful country of his malaise.

She put the paper down and began to discuss her situation with herself, as if for the millionth time she were trying to revise some recalcitrant text. Strangely enough, her lonesomeness vanished.

I know what it looks like to the others, she thought. That father-daughter thing. The joke. The father devouring the daughter more and more and the daughter starving primmer and primmer. Vicarish little jollities the only leaven in their life together.

But it's not a bit like that, she defended herself almost angrily. And, really angrily, him. He was so much more helplessly than she the victim of this circumstantial evidence.

She felt a sudden imperative cry that there must be someone to whom she could make that clear. She sighed. She knew there was no one *that* concerned. She began, once again, to explain it to herself.

This was the way it was.

It was simply that he and she saw *behind* things with such identical vision (even behind the way others would misjudge their situation) that it made them the freest, if the closest, kind of friends. Exactly how someone's clothing or action or turn of speech was ludicrous or moving or sham, they spotted at exactly the same instant. Each was the only one the other could have gone to, without feeling traitorous, to discuss some disturbing flaw in a second person he might love. And yet they didn't feed congestingly on each other's presence. They were as family-free, as family-flexible, as if they belonged to a large family whose other members just happened to be somewhere else at the moment.

She got up and poured herself another drink. The drink became her audience. Almost at once it made her more glintingly objective and at the same time more leniently subjective.

All right, she thought objectively. Grant them that she fooled herself about all this. Granted that – what (she gave rein to the subjective) could she have done?

She couldn't have left him that first year after her mother's death. Not while he was still using those big clumsy boy-hands, even to carry food to his mouth, as if they were insupportably heavy. No one could be that cruel. It would be like executing meanness on a brave child.

And after that . . . it was easy enough to prescribe. But how could you not postpone from day to day the *exact* moment to take the knife in your hand? The moment when you must deny the ultimate loyalty, loyalty to the familiar. How in that touchstone moment, of all moments the only one shorn to its bone, could you draw on your gloves and go out and close the door – to look back through the window and see him turn like his own ghost to adjust some little dishevelment of the house that the most orderly packing always leaves behind it?

Two people living together have an island to stand on. Accreted like coral from the little skeletons of their daily intercourse. He alone would have nothing under his feet at all.

How then could you . . . ?

You needn't be such a soft exploring fool, she thought objectively. That's one way. You don't have to keep turning everything around and around until you *find* the facet of it that catches the minor light.

But what if, once you alone had seen that light, you were simply helpless not to give because the other never exacted?

And yes, yes – the drinks were gaining steadily on her now – their days together had been happy days, let the others poke wise looks at them however they liked. He was such good company, that was it. They had somehow matched, and so kept alive in each other, some original insight of youth. Something spontaneous. Outrageous. (He said the Registrar's wife danced like Trigger.) Irreverent. Unseducible by the prudence of age.

She knew that he could detect the old's stigmata with as clear an outsider's eye as her own. Their little slynesses and cautions. The little tick of some interior silence that seemed to fascinate them when they thought they were unobserved. That curious enzyme in the craw of their minds that worked reflectively on what the young digested in a flash.

She had seen old men twist a matchstick inside their ear and then regard the end of it with almost steeping fascination when they withdrew it. Or screw a finger up inside a nostril with that curling sensual expression. She had seen them harkeningly absorbed in some small body function or in the content of their handkerchiefs. He would never be *anything* like that.

But . . . she caught her breath. The years *were* piling up on him. And there was the cruelty.

41

If the end of your days and the end of your awareness approached their intersection, as with most old people, at an angle so obtuse their courses seemed to have been in almost perfect parallel . . . But to be guiltless of age nor any way anaesthetized by it, yet to know that the death sentence would be carried out on you within a space of time scarcely less certain than the murderer's "between midnight and dawn." While, breath by innocent breath, time's relentless subtraction went on . . .

Oh God, she thought, what must it be like for the old? Was being old anything they could help? Was it their fault if people were made half-angry at them by whatever it is in people which makes them half-angry at anything they might, if they let themselves consider it, pity?

When the others heard tragic news of the young their thinking was struck still. All at once the young seemed like blood relatives. What must it be like to be old and to know that you had passed that point when any blow whatever on you could put you in a tragic light? That you were only in others' minds like someone read about? Like a blind spot on the wall where a mirror had hung?

What must it be like one day to have heard some grey croupier pronounce the words *Les jeux sont faits, rien ne va plus*? And to see all the things you would never do, now, like a child finally forced to recognize that he "can't go"?

Her stinging pity became almost lyric, filling in the picture down to its last punishing detail.

You were old . . . you were old . . . and the sensations of your own body were the only real voices of intimacy you ever heard. The others still came to see you but they came as a duty, just before some second engagement they could pretend to remember all of a sudden. They never believed that your heart or senses felt things like anyone else: when they were with you their faces slipped automatically into a kind of neutral gear.

You didn't dare let the cast of any dread, any nostalgia, show on your face. They quickened to it in the young. In *you* they snubbed it as an imposition. And if at any time your joy or anger or concern claimed equivalence with theirs, their faces seemed to change the subject, as if sidling off from a touch that was slightly obscene. Even your thoughts and your feelings had somehow to stay in their room.

Yes, and waking each morning to know that the shadow of time's dark goalpost had not been the cast of a dream that the light would wash away. And when daylight went again, to be locked up (no matter who was there) with the speechless part of evening.

You were old . . . you were old . . . and now your life was like the end of a visit. If a child's visit were ending, someone would make certain that its final days were filled with special entertainment. But who, in the company of the old, didn't sit content to let these minutes of his own go by, dull and uneventful, because there were boundless more to come? – while the old (and with what awful unprotestability?) saw these same minutes slip away empty though numbered among their last?

He hasn't denied me anything, she thought. They think he's denied me marriage. But he hasn't. There was never a man – except for Morse Halliday, she had suddenly to admit – there was never a man I liked physically who didn't bore me otherwise. With the reverse ten times as true.

He hasn't denied me husband and children. Nothing would have made him happier than to see me married and happy. If there has ever been a question of denial, it is I – my ranklings, my doubts – who have denied them to him. I denied *him* the family stir which should be there to shield anyone old from the bare still face of things as they are . . .

And then her thought of Morse became not parenthetical but dominant.

She picked up the *Times* again. But the book reviews had no taste. She glanced through the society pages.

And this time the picture of Sheila and Rex really engaged her attention. She thought she had never seen such an extraordinarily happy-looking couple. Certainly she had never seen such an arrestingly handsome man. Or such a look of love as they gave each other. As if they were listening to some euphoric inner statement, like drunks. As if, when they spoke to each other, their tongues would be thick with it. As if each found the other the complete eyeful, to brimming.

Her own eyes felt the faculty of vision in them suddenly excessive. Had Morse ever looked like that at either of the women he'd married? If anyone . . . if Morse . . . were ever to look at her like that . . .

Her father was moving about upstairs. She thought she heard him stumble and curse. She smiled. He had that youthful clumsiness about his body movements too.

"You still got your headache?" she called. "Is there anything I can bring you? The aspirin's down here."

"No," he called back. "It's not bad. Just enough that I can't sleep."

"Do you want me to call the doctor?" she said, more than anything to hear him denounce the sheer absurdity of such a move.

"The doctor? No. But you can call the carpenter to rip out that

43

confounded threshold in the bathroom, if you like."

She laughed. He would never be an old man.

She was as unprepared for her shock the next morning as he had been for his. She was in the pantry when he came downstairs. He sat beside the kitchen table.

"Will you settle for some apple juice this morning?" she said, coming out of the pantry. "We don't seem to have an orange."

He looked back at her in the unseeing way that animals with horizontal pupils seem to look at you. He repeated the word after her.

"Orange . . ." he said, as if the word were some pleasantly mystic little novelty.

She stared at him. It wasn't his face at all. The face that always looked as if alert for the point of a story or a joke wasn't there at all.

No! she cried silently; she couldn't speak. Oh, Father, don't! Please don't! Come back.

He repeated the word. "Orange . . ." The word, she thought crazily, that nothing rhymes with. And then he chuckled. And then repeated the chuckle. As if he were testing it from every angle, turning it over and over in some absolutely inaccessible cranny of his mind.

"Father!" she said, her eyes grabbing to save him. "What's the trouble?"

"Orange," he said, chuckling again.

The doctor was brisk and cheerful.

"It's a stroke," he said. "But keep him perfectly quiet for a week or so and I'm certain he'll come out of this one all right. Just make sure he takes it as a warning, that's all."

Yes, yes, she would make sure. She would take it as a warning too. If he'd only come back . . . that's all she asked. She'd see to it, she *promised* it, as fervently as if in some unnatural fit of brutishness she herself had struck him with a murderous weapon, that that frightful look would never come into his face again.

CHAPTER **5**

It was that wedding picture in the *Times* which gave Rex Giorno away.

Adelaide Kirby was no spy. Her part in the thing was quite

44

innocent. She'd merely phoned Bloomingdale's to send her one of the bridge lamps featured in their *Tribune* ad. Ordinarily, the *Tribune* was the only New York paper she saw. But amongst the insulation the lamp came packed in was this particular section of the *Times*. She'd spotted Rex's face at once. It was only natural that she send along the clipping to her old friend, Julia Merritt, next time she wrote.

And now Sheila Giorno and Julia Merritt were face-to-face at the Plaza this very afternoon.

It wasn't really strange that Sheila was so ignorant of all but the scantiest details of her husband's past. Rex himself seemed to care so little about the past, to find something fretful about remembrances. They just brought on a lot of "yakking." He couldn't be bothered digging around in that deadwood. And he was so unsecretive, so just the opposite of "dark" in any way, that to pry beyond what facts he volunteered seemed niggling.

She had a general picture of his home in Philadelphia, of course. She also knew that he'd run away from home at seventeen. He'd told her so. But their conversation on that subject was typical of all their talks about his background.

"Why did you run away?" she'd said.

"Now why the hell does anyone run away from home?" he'd answered.

"And you never went back?"

"No. Who the hell'd want to go back to a place like Philadelphia?"

"You've never written either?"

"No. What the hell's the use of stirring up that business all over again?"

And then he'd launched at once into some farcical trivia about the random jobs he'd bounced around in before enlistment in the army.

He did nothing to court it, but the impression she was always left with was that of an uncommonly spirited youngster fleeing the clutches of a harshly staid, oppressive family. She hated them for having tried to smother him. She was glad he'd broken clear.

How could she foresee the disenchantment that Julia Merritt was to spring unwittingly on her today?

Sheila could make nothing of the short note she'd had from Julia Merritt. Here was this perfect stranger saying she'd be at the Plaza all day Thursday and could Sheila possibly have lunch with her there? There was no explanation of her request. The whole tone of the letter assumed that Sheila would need none. Nor was there any explanation of the added plea that the meeting be arranged without Rex's knowledge. As if Sheila would know at once the reason for that, too.

If Sheila could come, just have her paged. If she couldn't – well, *please* not to mention a word of all this to Rex, regardless. Could she trust her not to?

There was no originating address on the letter. Nothing but the postmark. Boston. But Sheila had known intuitively that it was no crank letter.

She went. And now, for the first time in her life, she knew anger against Rex.

For different reasons, Rex's face and Sheila's were of the kind that seemed raised above their context, like the heads on coins.

Sheila's had always been the lead face among the rich linen girls driving up to the Westchester Country Club in a Sunday covey for luncheon and golf. She reflected her father's house in Belle Haven – the Rossiter place, with as unimpeachable a certainty in its own grace as the interior of a Tiffany ring box. Greenwich was on her like a watermark. Her eyes seemed always to have known their way around.

But her face owed its real effect to quite other things. Her blondeness had such emphasis it insisted on itself as the total statement of her. But it wasn't. It was altogether different from the blondeness of the other girls, which never ceased its chatter even when their lips were still. Or the blondeness which ease and money so quickly ravage and raddle. It was a kind of Helen Hayes blondeness, so fluid and cognizant that the dies of passing time always stamped it with the grain.

More than that, she had this special talent.

She herself was in no way a noted person. But the thing was (and it was the definition of her least far-fetched), she could deliver you from the sense of belittlement by the noted : the feeling that nothing happening outside their mystic circle has any intrinsic value . . . that all the amateurish subplots of ordinary intercourse, all the self-buildup you enact with others no less anonymous than yourself, are all blind farce for not having that circle's attention.

When Sheila came into the room, bringing with her a curious ventilation, she could erase that feeling as immediately as an experience of the flesh can eviscerate a preoccupation of the mind. It was her special gift that she could turn that feeling upside down. She made you see that an offhand insight into any performance on the world's stage, so long as it was canny enough and empathetic, put you on a level with the actors. She made you see that chance, not godhead, sets some people on one side of the footlights and some on the other. She made you feel, in fact, one up on your superiors. By a margin precisely that of the distance which any superiority, even that of the comic, inflicts on its holder. She was contagious to a degree – and oddly curative.

It was for these gifts – to him – that Rex had first loved her.

They made a striking couple, her vivid blondeness against his tawny counterpart. But if Sheila's looks were incidental, Rex's were not. He was startlingly handsome, and that was his whole point.

His face was of the kind photographers delight in, accenting the chin line or the nostril with shadow to catch in them something like the flare of breeding in a horse. A Latinish health-pallor set off the coal-black hair and the type of blue eyes so arresting when they have the depth of brown; giving his features an overall cast like the bloodshot sensuality of an adolescent after swimming. His features had that once-in-a-million congruity which makes the ordinary face look like a patchwork of stray pieces.

Rex's was, in fact, the kind of handsomeness so qualitatively beyond its runners-up that it seems to have been something that "struck," like genius. The kind that can make you or ruin you.

Naïve good nature saved him then. It forestalled any resentment. He had traded on his looks quite shamelessly. He had accepted everything they brought him, without care or conscience. Good times. Popularity. A self-confidence fed by the envy of the others, the envy itself disarmed by his ingenuousness. But he had never been anything like vain. He took his good looks as if they were something as fortuitous as plainness.

"Of course I loved you the first time I saw you," Sheila had kidded him. "Haven't you ever read any fairy tales? It doesn't take the little old princess two seconds to know it's the little old prince, no matter where she first sets eyes on him or what disguise he's in. If you'd been the little old frog that day, I'd have known you were the prince."

He was on leave that first day she'd seen him.

When the war came, he was a kind of king. Handsome in uniform, the very things that would have been faults in a quieter season – thoughtlessness, taking whatever offered itself to him not indebtedly but as his due, asking for nothing but the vividness of the moment – all these gave him the facile lordliness of one whose looks and disposition make him perfect for the part the times have cast him in.

He was hitch-hiking from Rye to Cos Cob that day. He knew "this guy" in Rye and "this other guy" in Cos Cob. (He never seemed to have any real friends. Just "guys.") She saw his face when the car ahead of hers didn't stop to pick him up. He couldn't believe it had ignored him. She stopped. It was more with this ingenuousness than with his looks that he had first captured her.

The next week she had his first letter. From camp. With the hard words all spelled right because he'd looked them up, but the easy ones he'd been so sure of full of the wildest mistakes.

And the next week he came to visit her.

She met him in Grand Central. She stood and watched him a minute before she waved: that wonderful free-hand handsomeness laid out even for strangers to help themselves to. And yet, she thought (she was to recall this thought today), if you only knew it, you'd be as lonely as a child.

She drove him around the city and he looked at all the sights the way a child does. As if they were his inheritance. And when they came to the Algonquin she said, just to see, "That's the Algonquin. You know. The Round Table and all that," and he said – he didn't know at all – "Maybe if we told them we were Indians they'd give us a reservation." He was quite proud of his dreadful little joke.

That captured her too. But what would her father and mother make of him?

She needn't have worried. His uncalculating behaviour completely disarmed them. He acted as if they were perfectly welcome to this good thing he was letting them in on, in the three of them getting to know each other. No one else could have brought it off without being brash or offensive. And yet right in the midst of his naïveté there'd be a sudden sprinkling of grace notes (she was to see today where he'd picked them up) to redeem it instantly from monotone or definitiveness.

Her mother couldn't resist a little gentle prying. But her father cut that short with a single sentence of solemn parody: "I came of poor but honest parents . . ." And with this acceptance of him so totally without side glance, she had never been so happy.

Yet the few times she did have to be defensive of him, the bond seemed stronger still.

The next night he'd gone with her to Ginny Cutter's engagement party. Sometime during the evening he'd suddenly clasped his arm around Ginny's bare shoulders. It wasn't to paw her. It was just the great, shaggy, hiya-kiddo way he had then. "Thanks," Ginny said, with a gleamingly innocent smile right into his face, "but I don't find it at all cold here, really." She lightly disengaged his arm, then turned her own face instantly-questioningly toward what someone else was saying.

Sheila longed to slap Ginny's face. It wasn't natural to her to harbour pettiness for an hour; but when it came time to select

Ginny's wedding gift, she picked out the most tastelessly deriva-
tive set of mantel china she could find.

One day she took him to Sardi's.

The waiter said, *"Vous voulez, m'sieur?"* and he said, "Come
again?" and the waiter said, "That means, 'What do you wish?',"
not repeating the "sir." She could gladly have choked the waiter
because Rex didn't even know he'd been slapped down.

And just to think of those old country club bitches—who'd been
born with the luncheon hat on and never had an orgasm in their
lives, she was sure, except the clinical one with Grand Slam bid,
doubled, made, and vulnerable – an immediate anger flamed in
her. Their gaze, with its insulting blind-spot, seemed to hover just
a centimetre above Rex's little gaucheries. She'd have liked to see
them lose continence of their urine, and throw up all over a Miro
at the Guggenheim.

She was completely captured when he came back (wounded in
the foot) from France and married her. When for as long as all
young men's injuries were taken to be battle scars he walked as if
his limp were a badge; but after that like a child who tries to keep
facing front, so that no one can see the patch on the back of his
jacket . . .

And Kate was quite right about that look of Rex's in the wedding
picture. He so loved Sheila that each time he came near her he
couldn't tell in which sense he felt that last little falling-short of
total absorptiveness the more piercingly, sight or touch.

Sheila didn't have to page Mrs Merritt. The moment she set eyes
on her in the lobby she'd been clairvoyantly certain that this gentle
but blow-schooled and somehow gallant face was the one that
matched the letter.

"You're Rex's mother," she said, *"aren't you.* I might have known.
It was the new name that confused me." She supposed that Mrs
Giorno had remarried.

Mrs Merritt wasn't quick enough to hide the stroke of dismay
on her face.

"You didn't tell Rex, did you?" she said.

"No," Sheila said, "but –"

Mrs Merritt interrupted her quickly. "– Shall we go in to lunch
then? We can talk after we've ordered."

She had to gain time. It had simply never occurred to her that
Sheila wouldn't recognize her name, that she wouldn't know the
whole story. If there was one thing about Rex as a child, it was his
almost pathological frankness. But he must have kept this secret.
She had wanted merely to meet Rex's wife and to hear firsthand

news of him. It would be like news of the dead. And now she had betrayed him.

She had to tell Sheila that she was not Rex's mother. That she and her husband had been foster parents only. There was no escaping that. But as they ate she tried desperately to limit all discussion of Rex to the present. How was he? How was he getting on? She'd heard what a lovely place Greenwich was to live in. Tell her about Greenwich. She'd never been there . . .

It didn't work. Each time Sheila glanced at this woman's demandless face, she became angrier. She could see that the notion of Rex's having been driven into vagabondage by these people was completely false.

"No, Mrs Merritt," she said. "I'm sorry. I can't keep this visit quiet any longer. I know he ran away from home. He told me so. But for him to neglect you like that! Never to write even. It's shameful. Heartless! And he's got to be faced with it. If you don't do it, I must. He's got to make amends. You live in Boston now. There's no reason in the world why we all shouldn't see each other as often as you like."

And so, to re-exact the promise of secrecy from her, Mrs Merritt had to tell her everything. Maybe then she would understand – as she herself could now – why Rex disliked having his childhood even mentioned.

Rex, the truth went, was born on one of those morningless streets where you step over the drunks and the children shoot dice on the sidewalks. His mother had left his father when Rex was three years old. His father had a tiny shoe-mending shop on the ground floor of a grubby tenement. He and Rex lived in a single room above it.

His father was not a drunkard. But when he did drink he locked Rex in their room and was gone for twenty-four hours at a stretch. The Welfare people had found Rex there one day when he was five. Locked in and crying with hunger. They had put him in a Home. The Merritts had taken him from the Home when he was ten.

"We always wanted to adopt him," she said, "but somehow he clung to his own name." Maybe Sheila knew those rare obstinacies of his that, airy as they appeared, were so earless and tongueless. Argument could no more pit them than water iron. "We didn't press it," she said. "He'd had cages enough. We didn't want to add the suggestion of another. My husband always said that if there was one thing we must make sure we gave him it was a sense of complete freedom."

"But why did he run away?" Sheila said.

"We don't know to this day," Mrs Merritt said. "He seemed so happy with us. And then one morning his bed was empty and his suitcase gone. No note. Nothing." They'd had little trouble locating his first stop. "Scranton, of all places." She had to smile. "I expect it was simply because that's where the first car that picked him up was going. He was like that." He was working in the coal mines there. They'd located his boarding house. "We decided not to go see him right away," she said. "I wrote to him instead. I told him that any time he ever changed his feeling about us he'd find that nothing had ever changed our feeling about him. Least of all this. I didn't plead – we so wanted him to feel no *obligation* toward us, we so wanted him to feel free – but I asked him to come home and give us another try. I registered the letter, return receipt. We got the return receipt but nothing else. Ever."

And so they hadn't pursued it. It was plain that he wanted to shuck off everything connected with Philadelphia. They must concur.

"But now," Sheila said. "Surely now . . ." Her anger was gone.

Mrs Merritt shook her head.

"No," she said. "I can see now just how *much* he must want to avoid anything . . . or anyone . . . that reminds him of his childhood. What a sore spot it must be with him. Why he fled. *Any* thing that Rex could keep secret." She sighed. "And I had to be the one to give him away. How wrong and foolish it was of me to come here. My husband would have discouraged me. I didn't tell him. That's why I gave no address in my letter. I didn't want an answer I couldn't explain. But it never entered my head that you wouldn't know . . ."

"I'm glad you came," Sheila said quietly. "Do you think it makes one particle of difference to me whether Rex was born on a good street or a bad one? I mean, I hate to think of . . . that helpless child . . . but surely you don't believe it makes any difference to me in any other way?"

"I don't," Mrs Merritt said. "And . . . yes . . . perhaps I'm glad I came, too. To know that. But will you promise never to tell him?"

Sheila hesitated. "It's hard to refuse," she said. "But if . . . somehow . . . I could bring you together again. I don't know. I've got to think it over."

She thought it over on the way home.

Yes, she would tell him. There was no scar that enough sincerity and understanding couldn't erase. Nothing that, between them, they couldn't put straight.

And then, driving past the Boys' Farm at Stamford in the evocative fall dusk, Mrs Merritt's words about the first time they had ever seen Rex came back to her.

"I think it was mostly the season and the time of day that accounted for the whole thing. Fred and I were on our way home from the country. It was that odd October light just before dark when . . . if you're the age we were then and have no children you realize . . . well, that you have no children. The boys at the Home were all in a field across the street. I remember they were playing one of those noonday games. The kind that always look so lonesome when *any* children play them in that kind of light, do you know what I mean?

"Anyway, we heard the bell ring for the children to come in. Rex was the last in line. They were almost across the street when he stopped short. Right in front of the car. Defying us. Or no, not really defying – just daring us, for the benefit of the others. Fred had to ditch the car almost, not to strike him.

"But somehow we weren't angry. He was such a handsome child. And – I don't know, he was always the least thoughtful or lonesome-*natured* child I ever saw, no matter what – but just the same he looked so indescribably lonely. I can't explain it. So . . . separate."

No, Sheila thought. Mrs Merritt was right. She'd write and tell her so. The scars were all healed now. It would be cruel to open them again, before everyone's eyes. They might not heal so thoroughly a second time . . .

And all at once she had this rash and fierce wish that she could take him off some place where nothing or no one could ever close in on him again. Some island. Some simple, innocent spot. Just the two of them. Some wide, free, country place. Like Nova Scotia . . .

PART

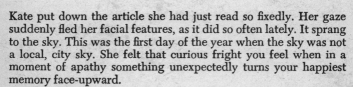

CHAPTER 6

Kate put down the article she had just read so fixedly. Her gaze suddenly fled her facial features, as it did so often lately. It sprang to the sky. This was the first day of the year when the sky was not a local, city sky. She felt that curious fright you feel when in a moment of apathy something unexpectedly turns your happiest memory face-upward.

Her gaze fastened on the sky for a moment. Then it descended rung by rung, touching foot on the indrawn stone of the University towers and, beneath them, onto the movements of the two students playing the year's first tennis. She couldn't see the ball and, far off, the game had the peculiar sadness of all games played out of season. Descending still, it touched the first venturesome moth of sail on the Arm; and then came back into the room.

For five years her father's face had kept coming back and going away again. Until gradually he'd turned into the vacant husk she looked at now. His face still had a young man's freshness, but now the eyes never came back at all.

She turned to him.

"What do you think I've just been reading?" she said. "There's a piece here in the *Clarion* about Morse Halliday!"

He didn't reply.

"You remember Morse, don't you?" she said. "Paul's place? Endlaw? That summer just after the war?"

There was no sign that he remembered anything. Sometimes he remembered things. Sometimes he didn't.

"Do you want to hear what it says?" she asked him.

Her father nodded. His gentle gaze, if on anything more than on nothing, was centred on the delta of veins on the backs of his hands.

She began to read aloud.

"Morse Halliday, well-known journalist, war correspondent and novelist, who lives in virtual isolation at Simsbury, Connecticut, was interviewed recently in New York en route to Nova Scotia. He expects to spend the summer there, near Granfort. Asked why he had had no new book lately, he replied: 'It was a nasty habit. Haven't you boys ever heard that it can drive you crazy, or blind?'

"About the present literary scene he had this to say: 'There's a notion abroad that the first thing writers must do is make an exact count of the flyspecks on the light bulb. Convince the reader that you've seen inside the man's room—or the Men's Room—and he'll believe you've seen inside the man. It's the biggest hoax since Piltdown. Then we have the psychology boys with their tissue slides. They use fifty times as many words as Christ took for the Sermon on the Mount to show why our hero still picks his nose at forty-three. You know, when I was a kid in Minnesota, there was a thing I used to watch the farmers do with a pig's bowels after the slaughter. There's a film of fat over the bowel exactly like Valenciennes lace. The farmers had a wonderful knack of stripping this off, hand over hand. They called it "riddling the guts." Almost any modern novel I can think of should have its guts riddled like that.' "

Kate looked up automatically to exchange a smile with her father.

Her father didn't return her smile. He was smiling at some secret on the backs of his hands.

She resumed her reading with a blunted sigh :

" 'Not that the primer stylists get it right either. Only a simpleton believes you can say anything complex simply.'

"Asked to comment on a recent remark of his third wife (Natalie Condor, the tobacco heiress) that 'Morse and I would probably still be married if I'd been shaped like a Chianti bottle,' he said, 'Natalie must have read that somewhere. Natalie got so she could read quite good.'

"He refused the photographer a picture. 'Nobody wants to look at web-skinned old parties like me any more,' he said. 'Give them what they want. The T-shirt boys. Or the Babyface half-Nelsons. Or the lady novelists that look as if they'd just combed that dreadful hair of theirs with one of their own gap-toothed adjectives.'

"Mr Halliday is fifty-five years old today."

It sounded like the man Kate remembered and it didn't. No reporter could fake Morse's unfakeable way of speaking. But this was self-caricature, almost.

Each in His Narrow Cell hadn't sounded that way. That first novel had been savage enough, but it was the savagery of compassion. She'd detected a change in his second, *The Cock Crew Thrice.* It was like derisive grinding on a festered tooth, an animal biting its own wound. Now she detected that change sharper still. What had happened to him?

Had she really been in love with him that summer at Paul's? She tried to remember. She didn't know. She only knew that when she'd been with him a sense of freedom had amplified her the way nothing had before or since.

Her eyelids fell for a moment, like an animal's trying to squint pain away. Then, abruptly smiling, she brought her glance back to her father's face.

"You remember Morse Halliday, Father," she said again. "Don't you?"

"Morse . . ." he echoed her softly, ". . . Halliday . . ."

Oh God! she thought, looking at him. Now there's nothing to show for anything. She felt the curious anger that pity is never far from when the object of it is loved.

All the days of her five-year captivity came up in her throat at once.

The mornings, when seconds after waking, the bright petulant words she would rehearse, but never utter, sprang up.

And then the afternoons, when these aborted words would melt into one formless lump and it seemed as if each breath her lungs drew they had to dip down for with a weighted bucket.

And then the evenings, when the terrible exhaustion of the circumscribed would fell her. (There are no bars at the prison window but the guard saunters suddenly at every exit you approach.) She would have a taste of herself almost physically in her throat, as of snow melted down to drink or of tea cold and tasting of its container. She couldn't read, not even in her own room. Even with the door closed, the unprotesting abusedness of his silence seemed to creep like smoke through the crack above the sill. It encompassed her like a bell jar.

"Day after day after day . . ." People used that expression so glibly to describe their trivial monotonies. She knew what it really meant.

Sometimes she'd have the brainsick impulse to clutch, physically, at anyone who came to the door. The grocery boy. The meter reader. Or, once, a strange young girl, to use the telephone. Not sensually, but as if she could capture freedom like an object of prey by pouncing on the flesh it was incarnate in.

In his green years, her father had traced the countless centuries of civilization along the Nile. Now he traced the tiny canals in the palm of his left hand with the trembling forefinger of his right. Over and over and over . . .

Kate watched him. She braced her cheeks with the grip of her teeth against each other. Her body went so rigid that she could hear each part of it defining itself. Mouth said mouth. Arm said arm. Foot said foot.

The doctor's last report stamped itself like a ribbon of text onto everything she looked at: "He could go out like the snuff of a candle. Or he could last for years."

"Years." For an instant the word was like a spectre.

She righted herself with a frantic blush. She silently pleaded her father's forgiveness for the thought. For all the times of her forgetfulness that the old had feelings too. She intensely promised him all the things she'd never done for him or bothered to tell him. She promised him they'd take that trip, this very week, she'd always known he longed to take. If he'd only come back . . .

"Father . . ." she said quickly. "Father, you remember that lovely summer holiday we had at Paul's place . . . Endlaw . . . *don't* you? Paul Creed? And Morse? And Letty? You remember how funny Letty was? Don't you?"

"Lovely . . . summer . . ." he repeated after her.

And then he screamed. "Holiday!" he screamed.

She had never seen his eyes like that before. They started from his face like fang-bared animals.

CHAPTER 7

Letty was sitting on the porch steps when Paul came home from town. This was the first of the April noons when the sun came close enough to bleach the wood's texture with warmth, to polish the lake's glass with touch rather than glance. She was transplanting a slip from what she called her "male and female" fern.

I never noticed her hands before, Paul thought; how beautiful they are. In her face he saw the shadow of all that was in abeyance there. Two hours ago his life had been turned full circle and left facing directly against its own grain. Since that moment he had noticed everything with a stinging clarity.

"Was it any mail for me?" Letty said. She never got any letters, but she always asked.

"No," Paul said. "But I had a letter from Morse Halliday. He's coming again this spring. You remember Morse, don't you? He was here five years ago."

"I think likely," Letty said. "Anyone with a gift o' gab like that!" Despite her bristling tone she touched the fronds of the plant with a little access of indulgence. "I'll have to make him some o' that blueberry fungy he was always braggin' up so. I got a few jars o' berries left in the cellar."

Paul grinned.

"When's he comin'?" Letty said.

"In a week or so," he said. "He's in New York now. Or he could turn up any minute – you know him. You know, Letty," he said, "I think we'll just take it a bit lazy this summer. Morse. And Bruce. And two or three others maybe. Anyone else that comes can go."

Letty's hands paused, reminiscing. "I was just thinkin' about Kate Fennison," she said. "Do you mind the nice girl was here the same summer as Morse? With her father? I mind how off-handed she was. She always knew ya no matter where she saw ya. No lugs about her at all."

She stopped, flushing. Had she overstepped herself talking to Paul that way about his own kind?

"Yes," Paul said, "I remember her."

He'd remembered her two hours ago. For the first time he'd known he'd really loved her. That he'd loved her to the point of its being a kind of information about all things.

"Where *is* Bruce?" he said quickly.

"Choppin'," Letty said. "As soon as you went to town."

"I thought that must be him I heard," Paul said.

"You know," Letty said, "it's strange him turnin' up here agin. Huldah's all exercised over it. She give me his whole pedigree agin yesterday." She shook her head. "That woman's as good as a witch. She *swears* he had a wife and child. If not two children. Did he tell you where they are now?"

"No," Paul said. "He told me he used to live here, that's all. And asked if I could use someone to chop the wood and help with the outside chores. It's a little hard to thaw him out."

"I know," Letty said.

She'd seen that kind here before. Lookin' as if their brakes was draggin' agin their face. They just wanted to be let alone.

"Huldah m'ntains he was studyin' for a doctor," she said.

"A doctor!"

Sooner or later with everyone there comes to be one word that springs at him like an animal. Paul had one now. Letty had just spoken it.

"That's what she said." Letty patted the earth tight around the roots of the slip and stood up. "Did you see anyone in town?"

"No," Paul said.

"I don't suppose you went to the doctor!" she chided.

"No," he lied.

He didn't want to talk about the doctor or the people in the courtroom.

Paul had always shied clear of doctors. They invaded you to the core. He hated to have anyone come that close. He had no explicit theory about this, but he acted on one. And it had rooted and grown into an unconquerable obsession.

His body, no less than his mind, was a citadel of his freedom. He must have autonomy there too.

It had nothing to do with the bearing of pain. Bright natural pains held no threat. They were glancing things, speaking in your own voice, like sex. Casual, therapeutic sex. That kind of sex (and it was abundant hereabouts) had never threatened control of his own boundaries in the least. It was the pains with the dark voices that threatened. The strangers. Not strange for their viciousness, but for their alien tongue. They threatened like love.

And it was these that seemed to gather speech only when they had their special linguist, the doctor, to talk to. It was like the old superstition about cancer: once you opened it to the air it raced like wildfire.

He had no fear whatever of death. But he was acutely, obsessively uneasy with doctors for their congress with these blind, unassimilable strangers inside your very skin.

The first chest pain he'd ignored. He had tried to disbelieve it out of existence. But being ignored, it had only raised its voice the louder. And then he had recognized in it one of the dark voices. He'd been *forced* to bring it to Dr Anders.

Dr Anders was a springy, youthful, blunt-spoken man, with professional gravity only in his hands. Half the women in town, Letty said, were "lallygaggin' over him, they run to him if they had a fart crossways." His own looks were quite unremarkable, but his wife was such a beauty that she gave him a sort of mystique. The town men's first thought whenever they met him on the street was of her. What must it be like to be getting stuff like that all the time?

Paul scarcely knew him. He was counting on a clinical atmosphere. That way he could preserve something of his distance. He met just the opposite.

Dr Anders had talked to Paul only twice before. Once in his office when he'd dressed a cut on Paul's hand. Once at the blood donor clinic when some remark of Paul's had kept him chuckling the length of the ward, with a look almost of discovery on his face. But, for the doctor, twice was enough to provoke that curious rapport. He shed his professional category altogether, putting the whole thing on a first-name basis right from the start.

He never smoked with patients. He smoked with Paul. The waiting room was full, but he made Paul's call into a visit. He showed him an ingenious new instrument for examining the retina and had Paul look through it at the back of *his* eye. And then, as was never his habit with anyone else, he made an off-the-record comment about the next patient coming up.

Paul's mood was restlessness; but it was compulsive in him to match whatever attitude the doctor struck.

"Well, Paul," the doctor got down to business at last, "what is it? Anything special? Or just a general check-up? A good thorough check-up doesn't hurt once in a while, you know."

"I know," Paul said. "But no, I feel fine generally. It's just this little . . ."

He stopped, grinning. "That reminds me of Letty one day. Her brother-in-law had her out for a spin in his new car – this was back when cars were quite a novelty here – and the first gas pump he came to he said, 'I wonder if I hadn't better stop here and get some gas.' And Letty said, 'The car's workin' all right, ain't it? What the thunder do you want tamperin' with it fer!' Maybe that's the case with me."

The doctor's man-laugh broke wide of his doctorly laugh.

"Well now, you know Letty might have something there, at that," he said. "We'll see."

He opened his card file, still chuckling while he riffled through the C's.

"Hmmm," he said. "I don't seem to *have* a card for you, Paul. Unless the nurse mislaid it somewhere. Oh well."

He picked out a blank card and wrote Paul's name on it. Paul felt invaded.

"Age?"

"Forty-eight."

The doctor inked in the figure without attention. The other entries he wrote in quickly, pronouncing the answers to himself, without interrogation at all.

"Single . . . Farmer. The innkeeping's just on the side, isn't it? . . . Five – eleven?"

"Six even."

"Hundred and – seventy?"

"Two."

"Ever had any sickness?"

"No." Paul wished he hadn't come.

All at once the doctor laid his pen down across the card and smiled predictively.

"Age," he repeated. "You know, I had a funny one the other day. This old character came in. Seventy-nine. I said, 'What's your trouble, George?' And what do you think he said? 'Doc,' he said, 'I caught the old woman puttin' saltpetre in my porridge this mornin'. She thinks I'm ruinin' my health. I wish you'd tell her a little night work don't do e'er a one of us any harm.' Seventy-nine!" He shook his head, with a retroactive chuckle. "I just hope I can still take a piece when I'm seventy-nine."

A photograph of the doctor's delicious wife, with their child, sat catty-cornered on his desk. Her eyes seemed to Paul to be staring at him. He felt his boundaries at another's mercy. Only a doctor could make you feel like that. He wanted to escape. He couldn't.

"I'll be lucky when *I'm* seventy-nine," he said, "if I have enough of the old mucilage left to stick a postage stamp."

The doctor's man-laugh exploded again. It kept re-detonating itself. He seemed to have to sober himself, unwillingly, with briskness.

"Okay, Paul," he said, when he'd finished the case history. "What's your trouble?"

"Well, nothing much, really," Paul said. "It's just this cramp I get sometimes in my chest."

"Where exactly?"

Paul motioned where. Under the breast bone, with occasional tentacles in his arm.

"And how would you describe this cramp?"

Paul said it felt a bit like something grabbing. Teeth maybe. Or maybe a tourniquet.

"You have it right now . . . at all?"

"Just a twinge," Paul said. Suddenly he did have the pain. And more than a twinge of it.

"All right," the doctor said. "Let's just take off your shirt and have a listen."

Paul took off his shirt. He felt more and more invaded. His heart was pounding.

His arms and chest were muscled coarse and suddenly primitive alongside his face. Gross hair triangled down from his throat to meet the apex of the hair hinting upward from his belly. It made the doctor's face-flesh hands seem in propinquity almost dainty. But those hands could seek out the dark stranger, that voice could speak the word that ended the autonomy of these very muscles. It could disclose a traitor in your own house. It could make you a slave.

The doctor took his pulse and blood pressure. And then he explored his chest with the stethoscope. Listening, considering; palpating, considering; questioning, considering. Questioning, questioning, questioning . . . about this, that, and the other . . .

Paul began to get a trapped feeling. He wished the doctor would hurry.

"You say the pain isn't severe . . . never *was* severe?"

"No." Paul began to lie. "Maybe I was a little fanciful there at first. It's hardly a pain at all, really. More like the way a strained muscle catches you sometimes."

"Hmmm." The doctor considered. "You say you don't get it often?"

"No," Paul lied. He wanted to escape. "You know, I just thought. That's probably what it is. A strained muscle. I've been making a stone wall below the garden and lifting quite a bit. And of course I smoke too bloody much. Maybe it's that."

The doctor nodded. But absently.

When the actual examination of the chest and elsewhere was over, he still sat there in front of Paul, still considering. Paul felt more and more cornered. He wished the doctor would move away.

"You say the pain was *never* severe," the doctor said again.

"No," Paul lied. "Never."

He reached quickly for his shirt. He wanted so desperately to get back to belonging to himself that he almost believed he was speaking the truth. He disowned the pain. He scrapped the hope he'd brought with him that the doctor could relieve it. He was willing to take that loss the way you take the loss on furniture the water ruins when your house itself is threatened with fire.

The doctor stood up.

"The pain was never at any *time* severe," he harped yet again, puzzling declaratively to himself.

"No," Paul lied.

Now that he was back into his clothing again he felt less vulnerable; his autonomy returned its grip.

The doctor shook his head.

"Well, Paul," he said, "I might as well be honest, I can't say for certain what this is." He mentioned several things it could be. Then, soberer : "Of course, it lines up with the angina picture too – and where there's angina there are often other coronary faults that . . . but you say there's never been any real pain!"

Angina.

The window was open. A wave-edge of one of those first April breezes that seem to stray with a one-day innocence to the brazenness of towns and cities came through. It was astir with life breaking open. It touched Paul at that focus of evocation in the hollow of the throat.

The simple coincidence of word with breeze did it, as the simplest synchronisms sometimes will.

This might be serious. He might die. The bright piano wire of mortal threat piercing out of the word "angina" put a heightened eye in every sense. The breeze showed him everything as it might have been. Showed him in a flash what half a lifetime of self-scrutiny had never shown him.

Had he ever had any sickness? Yes, he'd been sick all his life. All those years he'd been fencing against the wrong threat altogether. His autonomy did lie sieved by the doctor's one word. But that was not the thing. He saw exactly what his freedom had been. Nothing. He saw the doctor's wife and child. He saw Kate's face. He saw that if he'd let her love take charge of him, it could have been as if life were a baffle of equations in x and y and suddenly you were good in algebra.

And now it was too late. It was hopeless.

He saw what he was really like to the others. So jealous of his own image, he'd kept their eyes off it by reflecting back their own, like a mirror. And who thought of a mirror as anything but blank glass when he wasn't regarding his own face in it? He saw what price he'd paid for the luxury of being master within his own boundaries. Everything. He saw what his life had been, a refusal to visit inside the house of anyone's spirit because if the visit were returned he must always speak to them from the doorway of his own. Books the flesh of it. Talk the touch . . . Nothing.

The breeze died, and as suddenly as it had come, the pain; but the heightened eyes in every sense multiplied themselves in every nerve.

And with the death of the breeze Paul had the most punishing insight of all. He saw that he'd had his freedom far too long not now to be forever bound by it. Mere act or not, he would keep on defending it. There'd be no satisfaction left to him like that of gripping consistency to the very end.

"So what I'd like you to do," the doctor was saying, "I'd like you to go to the hospital in Halifax and have a thorough investigation. I can't do it properly here. I simply haven't got the apparatus. Stethoscopic information has all kinds of gaps in it, you know. I mean, you ought to have a cardiogram and . . . Then you'll know."

"Well, we'll see," Paul said. "If it gives me any more trouble. I couldn't leave right now . . . but we'll see."

"Or, wait a minute!" The doctor's eyes clicked. "The best damn chest man in Canada is in Halifax right this minute. Dr Claude Lennick from the Renfrew Memorial Hospital in Montreal. A good friend of mine. At a medical convention. I'm driving in tomorrow for the wind-up sessions and you could go along with me. Lennick's only here to lecture, of course, but I know damn well I could set it up for him to examine you. What do you say?"

"Well, I say thanks one hell of a lot," Paul said. "But I honestly couldn't leave tomorrow. We've got some guests coming soon and . . . later though, maybe. We'll see."

The doctor looked at him. "You'll see!" He gave his head the shake of resignation that is somehow a gesture of fondness. "You know, Paul, I don't believe you have the faintest damn notion of taking my advice. I suppose I'm just wasting my breath to tell you to go easy even."

Paul grinned.

"I was thinking about Letty again," he said. "She wouldn't want me to hold everything up for maybe just a little gas."

The doctor grinned too. "I know, I know," he said. "But gas or no gas, I feel this thing warrants further investigation. You should have a cardiogram and . . ."

"Well," Paul hedged again, "we can always set that up later, can't we . . . if, as I say, I have any more trouble."

With a final grimace of tolerant exasperation, the doctor let it go at that. He went back to general talk.

"I wonder how the trial came out," he said, halting Paul with one last remark at the door.

"I don't know," Paul said. He felt like running. "I don't think it's over yet."

"Did you ever *see* Corbett's wife?" the doctor said. "I don't know why any fool'd put his neck into the halter for the likes of that."

Paul stepped out into the street. The shriving clarity when you've first come face-to-face with mortal threat still heightened him. Everything he looked at he saw with a penetration that was absolutely new. Every face, every brick, every blade of grass, teemed at him with its own infinite bibliography.

The day's mood was intently benign, breaking with sap. The breeze touched his throat again. It gave a grubby anachronism to whatever pieces of winter clothing he still had on. Every cast of wear in them was suddenly emphasized.

In spots the pavements were almost hot. Pavements could never accept the sun's warmth without turning up its volume somewhere into a threat of punishment. Paul's heart took a great leap toward the pure peace of Endlaw.

His car was parked in the courthouse square. He was in that tinglingly unanchored state of mind when all remarks sound exactly equal, so that the last one addressed to you has ascendancy simply by virtue of place. The doctor's parting remark still clung. He went into the courthouse.

It was like stepping underneath the skin of the day, underneath its breath.

Paul saw everything in the room as if his own vision had shed a skin. He knew the accused. The accused was not a vicious man, but a gentle one. He had simply loved his faithless wife too much. In a blind gust of jealousy he had shot her, then tried to shoot himself. Scarcely a man in the courtroom but had known impulses nearly as violent. But the accused had made his explicit. And so – Paul sensed the spectator reaction – he'd become an enormity.

The spectators were no longer the fellow-men they had been before. They shrank back. Thank God the eye of Justice was not turned on them! Paul saw it in the way they sat. Disowning their own bodies, as it were, lest the Law's glance should shift their way. Their glances focused on the accused like rays through a burning glass. They devoured his face as if it were an obscene picture – avariciously, yet somehow stopping just short of touching it. And when his back bent forward with supporting the insupportable, the same not-quite-touching stares fed on his back. Fed like flies on the spot between his shoulders where they said the bullet had so narrowly missed his heart.

Paul looked at the accused's fellow-farmers. Their necks had been fudge-scored by the same wind and sun as the accused had felt. Now they were statued with righteous dissociation. And, most terrible of all, he saw the women watching. He had never seen a woman stripped of her womanliness before.

A sense of shame mounted in him. He felt soiled clear through for being there in this company of Brahmins. Of *voyeurs*. He had seen the courtroom face that each man carries behind his neighbour face. He had seen how that face came front when you made something fallible about yourself explicit. When you signed your name to it.

He got up and went out into the day.

It was then, quite suddenly, that the old lifetime obsession reclamped itself on him more fervently than ever; like a surging backwash. The idea which struck him was statureless, he knew that. He felt a self-contempt to have a selfish plan engendered in him by another's tragedy. But he knew he would enact it.

No one must ever look at him that Brahmin way. Not even the way they looked at someone sick. Not even the way they looked in pity. Pity was the prime invader of them all. Knowing that you were marked for death, they looked at you as if their look had put on gloves. He wouldn't suffer that look from anyone. Not even from a doctor.

And this was how he could prevent it. He was unknown in Montreal. He had the specialist's address. He would arrange to go and see him there, have the critical examination there. But he needn't sign his name to it. He could use a false one. And under that false name he could will a kind of self-annulment. So complete that it would be as if the fatal verdict (if that's what it turned out to be) and the *look* were falling on a total stranger.

Passing the woodlot on the way home, Paul heard Bruce chopping.

Yesterday, he thought, I was free to chop. A great gust of the glory it had been to be free to chop almost stifled him.

He caught himself close to the wispily elegiac plaintiveness that unconsciously poeticizes itself, frighteningly close to rehearsing his deprivation with that toxic "lingering" regard of the self-commiserative. It was the thing that more than anything in God's world he loathed.

He grinned.

CHAPTER 8

Kate's father did not go out like the snuff of a candle. Gentleness took leave of him first; all dignity second. "Gradually," by whatever its capricious acceleration, became "suddenly." His hardened arteries suddenly cut his mind loose and set it ablaze. They gave his muscles the strength of frenzy.

The first day in hospital there was nothing to do but to bind him to the bed.

Kate watched him struggling until the hypodermics won over. Not even touch could reach him. She felt like an animal, without hands to help its young.

When he became quiet she sat there and looked at the years gone by. She tried to configure in them, as others must be able to do in theirs, an unexpungeable army at her back, thick with time and deed.

But hers seemed to have no density whatever. Their colour was the colour of patches of frozen flesh over a cheekbone.

She searched among them for certain days that would stand up as proof and testimony that she had really existed in them. But the only days with surviving shape seemed to be those which owed it to the distinctiveness of having been peculiarly hurting.

There were enough of those. She sighed, trying to swallow them back into shapelessness. It didn't work. They came at her one after another.

The day struck her in the mouth when she'd said, "Oh, I can't be *bothered* going to the doctor. Who wouldn't sooner be dead than alive here anyway?" and he'd merely said, "Now, Kate . . ." and it hadn't been his face, somehow, but his hands that had looked defenceless and shattered. She remembered glimpsing through his bedroom door that night the body which sleep so cruelly bore unconscious past half the landscape of the little journey left to him.

All the young teachers at the University had loved him like sons – or brothers. She remembered the day the youngest archaeology instructor, off on a two-year sabbatical, had come to say good-bye to him. When watching him, she'd thought: He must know that this half-hour is a death watch. He must know that any half-hour he spends with anything two years away in the coming again, in fact or in thought, is a death watch.

And the day at table when she'd seen the subtle pulse of transience beating in his temple veins. Even while he smiled. Even while a *young* man's enjoyment of the food was giving him its cruel lie . . .

The second day he was himself – just long enough to be humiliated to tears that he couldn't hold his faeces until the pan came.

And then the morphia, this time in a caprice of benevolence, gave him visions. It was a noon of drifting rain, of hospital grey. Through the window he saw the most beguiling sunsets. He described them to her, smiling.

She listened to him and thought of other days.

When it had become too late for new clothing to be a possible gift for him. He would never wear out what he had . . .

Those days at the change of any season, whose mute and incommunicable sadness doubled the piercing cast of any other severance. He must have known, with each of them, that this might be the last of any changing season he would ever see . . .

She listened to his details of the phantom sunsets and she saw his face again the day he'd told her how the sun came up in Alexandria. He'd been quite lost to the present, back once more in the absolute "now" of something rediscovered for the first time in years and years. And she had seemed to see, as if they were physical, the slipping-past minutes of the present put their thieving hands in his pocket while he wasn't looking . . .

What day, she wondered, had *he* first heard those words, *Les jeux sont faits*? Had it been as far back as the day he'd dressed for her mother's funeral? . . . putting the same arms with the same motions into the same shirt . . . but with the arms and every other member of his body standing *around* him now, intimately strange . . .

Or was it some day when he'd heard the whistle but not the clatter of a distant train and for some reason gone to the window to know its direction, only to catch a glimpse of its hindmost car disappearing along the crooked track out of sight?

Or had it been just some ordinary day, without provocation at all? Some day when he'd escaped into one of those treacherous daytime naps . . . to awaken and see the message of "gone" and "forever" waiting for him, written in the afternoon's particular cast as clearly as if it were written on a paper in his hand? . . .

On the third day, his last convulsive movement was to strike Kate in the face when she leaned over to change the ice pack on his forehead.

"Get out of this *room*!" he screamed. "You've tormented me long enough!"

She left the room, to placate him.

Her face was still smarting from the blow when the nurse (glancing covertly at her wristwatch: could she perhaps catch the early bus home now?) came to tell her that he was dead.

Kate drew her first companionless breath.

She heard the thunderclap of "never." She felt a great silence disjoin itself from the ordinary silence. A great tide of something went out. It left her standing on the shore.

And then a kind of harsh, impervious freedom took possession of her.

Not freedom from him, but . . . Decency, nor anything else, could claim she owed it one second's observance now. Not after this. Even the ending couldn't be allowed to come decently. It had to be monstrously, squalidly wrong.

She felt the glittering right – the mandate even – to be defiant.

Or better than defiant: sacrilegious toward everything, everywhere. Now there was no one she must consider lest her attitudes wound him. She was bayed into that terrible freedom of owing no act and of fearing none's consequence. She felt nothing but a blind scraping anger.

A cleric was standing under the ceiling light, ticking off ward calls in his notebook. He approached her and introduced himself. He began to talk about a Higher Power's knowing best.

Kate cut him short, blazingly calm and fluent.

"I have never liked bullies," she said. "If God asks people to be kind to each other, He should set a better example Himself. I'm

afraid I must ask you to reserve your comfort, if you don't mind . . .
until He stops torturing old men to death and burning children in
their beds."

The head floor nurse came over. Not even now quite able to
throttle her chronic briskness; her smile so long an automatic tic
that it could not even now be varied.

"His wedding ring . . ." she said to Kate. "Would you like us to
take it off before . . .?" Kate knew what she meant. The stiffness.
"Or do you want it left on?"

Kate slashed out at her almost joyously. "Would you want ghouls
at your wedding ring," she said, "if, God forbid, you'd ever had
one?"

But her salt, harsh freedom was short-lived. It lasted no longer
than it takes the salt of tears which unconsciously expected com-
miseration to dry on the face after a snub. It dried on her face
the first moment the taxi from the hospital brought her within sight
again of their house. What insanity had let her say those dreadful
things?

CHAPTER **9**

Kate sat at her father's desk now. She was acknowledging the
sympathy cards she'd had.

A soft spring dusk lay on the drowsing street outside. Promised
green, like a faint oil slick, was starting to redeem the campus trees
from their skeletal anonymity of the winter. The moments had a
curious tick of suspension, as when you follow the second hand
of a watch, taking a temperature. The empty rooms drew at her
presence constantly. At once leaden and importunate.

Her work went slowly. She hesitated over each card. Shouldn't
she add some personal line to the formal acknowledgement? There
had been none on most of the cards she'd received. But wouldn't it
please her father to make this extra little gesture of appreciation?
Wouldn't not doing it be like all those other little things she hadn't
done when he was alive? For the not doing of which the silence
of his never having asked them of her, even in thought, was the
keenest rebuke.

She wrote a few extra lines on almost all the cards.

She glanced through the window at the dwindling light. She had
the feeling of so many windows, always; the more bleaching that

it did not state itself. She had always looked *out* at others passing by. They had never looked *in* at her.

She saw a bareheaded boy on a bicycle. He was no more aware of the dusk than of the breeze in his hair. He had one palm on the handlebars, his wheels describing a series of inconsequent ellipses on the street. In the other hand he held a mouth organ. He was playing a shrill ragged tune.

All at once the empty rooms drew at her presence so assertively that she nearly cried out.

But what good would it do to cry out? No one would come. There was no one now to whom she was the one person who meant more than any other. For no one did she cast a shadow. Her cry wouldn't even shatter the stillness of the house. The house would merely close over the sound like a pool over a stone. The rooms would once again suck at her presence, attenuating it, drawing it out over them like foil. She felt white and diffuse. She poured herself a drink.

Sick people look into mirrors to see how they are. People ascatter with loneliness go to them to see who they are.

Kate sought the long mirror over the fireplace. It would scarcely have surprised her to see her image condense on the mirror in the edgeless pattern of fog condensing on a pane.

But no. There was her physical shape, no less precisely bounded than if she were happy. It stabilized her, like another presence; stopped up all the leaks in her vagrant antennae and poured her back into her own definition. Her thought, endlessly cobwebbed with adjectival orchestration, snapped back to noun and verb.

You *are* what you look like, she thought. If I were poured into different flesh that flesh would soon show the same disfigurements as this. The marks of things not there. Other faces were daily disarrayed and reassembled. Hers was a face that time stamped belatedly, and with all sorts of omissions, once every ten or fifteen years. It lacks, she thought, whatever it is that the cleverest illustration lacks and the crudest photograph has : a living resemblance to someone else.

It was in a no-man's-land between old and young. But in a few years there'd be no doubt which of the two stamps would brand it. The irreversible one.

Relentlessly she added ten years to her thirty-nine. Forty-nine.

She saw herself then. The grimace over the tea cups she tendered at those alumnae receptions she despised. The ring barbarically embedded into the skin. The hand unconsciously at the loop of beads. The decorative feature of the hat an absurdity against the slackening undecoratable flesh. Worst of all, that youthful immediacy in the clasp of the eyes would be gone: so that the eyes of the young simply passed you over.

And with the years went freedom. You might think your actions were as much a personal caprice as they had ever been. But the others knew better. They could give odds of five hundred to one on exactly the way you would behave. And win. Their certainty was like a curse, unexorcisable.

She studied her face like a mystery.

If you could somehow stop up the flesh where that cast got in, or where the flesh's light leaked out. But you couldn't. Even the subtlest camera couldn't bring off a lie about that.

This, suddenly, was the first time she had ever really looked its fearfulness in the face.

Oh well. She tossed her head in a sudden gibe at her own solemnity. Maybe I'll develop one of those "interesting" faces, for God's sake. Maybe I'll get to look like those cadaverous women who write novels of sensibility or play the harp superlatively well.

She yanked her hair down in a loop on each side of her face and sucked in her cheeks. "Waaa . . ." she went at the mirror. "Virginia Woolf! Maud Gonne!" She actually laughed.

And then she walked back to the desk. The mirror was as far as she ever escaped. She looked puckered in small.

She finished the acknowledgements. She poured herself another drink.

And then she sat in an attitude that had lately become habitual. Her hands were propped against her cheeks as if grown to them. Her eyes, tilted upward, traced the skyline of the objects in the room like a child's crayon. She looked as if she were listening to music, but there was nothing in her mind at all.

Several papers were awry on the desk. She aligned them, page point to page point, in a pattern of exact right-angled triangles. With extreme care she manipulated a pencil lying on the nearest triangle until the perpendicular of its shadow's edge made a perfect bisector.

It took several efforts to shake herself free. She saw that it was nearly dark.

She got up and went to the light switch almost buoyantly. Her face had the expression of an addict's who has kept his promise to himself not to indulge his vice before a certain hour. Light suddenly stripped the room of all its exactions, clothed it with the communicative hum of evening.

She sat down in her father's chair by the bookcase. Her feet rested on the two worn spots in the carpet where his feet had so often rested. She lit a cigarette.

And then, as if this were her addiction, her mind again took up its compulsive argument with memory.

The drinks turned punitive. She saw how sustaining as well as constraining his presence had always been. But of course I never once told him that, she thought. You never tell anyone anything like that while they're alive. You can't give up that mean little advantage you know you hold over anyone who believes he's martyred you. And now his absolute silence had taken him somewhere beyond the soundings of apology, stripped him of even the self-advocacy that a living silence has.

Only once or twice do the living faces of the dead come back absolutely flesh-plain. And then only for an instant. Her father's face came back now. It faded as quickly into the portrait face of the coffin. She knew she had seen it for the last time.

Half-drunkenly against herself, she let herself think for an instant of his betrayed face in the ground. That childish flash of irritation his grin always doused before it quite took fire . . . the young man's gratefulness to the taste of cold water after thirst . . . Where did they *go*? Where *are* they?

And then she had drunk herself sober.

She got up from the chair, spent as if after confession. Her brain felt dry. She had blotted up its suppurations. But the blotter was still there, jungled with the crisscrossed, mirrored-backwards imprints of her thoughts. She could feel the faint weight of it lying in its definite little niche inside her skull. Tomorrow its work would have to be done all over again.

She crossed the room to tidy up the desk.

She was just tired now. Her limbs felt foreign, as if each part of her body had defected from the group. She was tired of suffering even. It no longer flattered or personalized her. She had that smarting excess of clear sight which drinks forsaking you leave behind.

All at once she felt a staggering fright.

It took her completely unawares. She'd been sad enough, but there'd been no hint of fright in her sadness. And this was fright of the absolute kind – when there is no place to hide from it even in drink. No place to hide even in your own mind.

She felt her two selves: her self and its self-watching. All at once they were physically compressed against each other in the tight space of her brain. They couldn't break out. They couldn't escape each other.

For a moment she glimpsed the face of madness which you suddenly see so plain when you've let yourself dwell on something too long, without notice where it's been pushing its self-watching. Her two selves threatened to split apart and plunge runaway with their reins flapping. She was in such an extremity of fear that the one self abjectly promised the other that it would desist immediately.

Fighting for grip, she told herself she was sick of herself for having handled her sadness until it stuck to her fingers. There was one of those moments of balance, as in illness, when it seems purely capricious whether or not strickenness will pass.

The fright passed.

And then she summoned the toughness in her that had never failed to answer its emergency bell. It took charge of her with a kind of savage sensibleness. She surrendered herself to it as pliantly as if it were prescribing for another person.

So what did you do when someone died? You let your sadness make a thorough statement of itself. Once. She had done that. And then you let the whole thing drop.

So what did you do next? You went to a new place for a while. For a complete change. All right. She'd go away for a while.

"Of course." It was as if she'd heard the words spoken aloud. "Exactly as the others would predict." They would find in her old maid's trip something at first laughable, then amended by conscience to pathetic.

She saw their picture of her. Really debating with herself over which postcard views to select from the rack. Always the first to show up for any side-excursion that was planned. Speaking first only to those people she half-hated for their being the sort of people who might have spoken to her first.

They'd count on her coming back to live alone. Or perhaps with a companion spinster who wasn't too well and gave lessons in something lady-like on weekday afternoons. Never to be obtrusive except as her name headed the list of subscribers to any lecture or concert series . . . Until some day, having forgotten her for years, they read of her death and thought: Why, Kate Fennison *must* have been older than that! A flash of anger jolted her eyelids the way an animal's just perceptibly squint with a fresh wave of pain.

Face-to-face with the others, it was different. Then her anger would find itself tripped up by some pitiable incertitude in *them*. Some unconscious testimony of hands when they were quiet, or of lips when they were silent, giving a whole pretence away. Some innocent little vanity that was seen to expose the very thing it thought itself to be protecting. Any feeling you'd never dreamed was present in them seen to have been just below the surface – or one you'd thought to be just below the surface seen to have been buried beyond the soundings of anything but bitterness . . .

73

But now . . . So they pitied her? She cast their attitude. So they had this little mould all prepared for her? Saw already the vagrant little tendrils of individuality bent back neatly around her dry core like a branched object you were packaging to mail? So they'd strip her of every indraft and outdraft pulse except breath, to peek at life until she died?

Well, they could save their pity. Pardon me, but Miss Fennison is laughing.

"Be convener of the Athenaeum Tea? My dear, I'd love to – but I'm afraid I couldn't resist passing the lump sugar to those horse-faced characters in my palm." . . . "Naturally, I'm sorry Miss Ormonde's sick. But whatever gave you the idea I'd be glad to fill in for her at nursery school? I'm thoroughly convinced that every last one of those adenoidal brats is a walking argument for euthanasia."

Yes, they could save their pity. Let them save it for their own dime-a-dozen little lives.

She suddenly relaxed. Her mind gave an almost audible click.

Yes, yes, that was the *answer*. How could she have missed it? The very fetters that up to now had hobbled her own choice of destiny had left her freer than they. They had chosen a pattern while they were still too young to judge, and now they were stuck with it. Now it was stamped all over them like one of those advertising slogans strung incessantly along packaging tape. It was inlaid in them to the core, choked them like a growth of ivy. She still had a whole world of adult choice before her.

Oh yes indeed, she knew now how to take the measure of these pitiers.

Though not with conceit, she'd always had the sense of being an exceptional person; had the feeling that theirs was that type of first-class mediocrity against which the truly exceptional person is more than anything else helpless.

She would go away, yes. But it would not be as they forecast. She would join a circle of her own stature somewhere – the kind of people who cross-pollinated each other with their extraordinariness. Where some extraordinary pattern waited for her too. Where, by the spectacle of her immediate acceptance, she could eclipse and tongue-tie her pitiers as easily and as ruthlessly as she liked.

Her mood was miraculously altered.

She felt that surging sense of what freedom *is*, which only the chronically bound ever know. As if a beam of light revolving in the darkness had all at once lit up its physiognomy with a blinding clarity. Or as the chronically ill may sometimes, with the heightened sense of dream (and in the way a light-bulb filament seems to distend the room with sudden brilliance just before its extra charge extinguishes it), glimpse the transfiguring *ignis fatuus* of an imagined moment of perfect health.

Keys of unusual insight seemed to have been placed, co-operative, into her hands.

She had always thought of living as something quantitative: your length of days could only contain it if every second of them were dipped full of it to the brim. She'd always thought of it as a class you couldn't enter late. As a sort of language you could neither speak nor understand without a grounding in its grammar.

She saw now that it was not a grammared language at all. Nor a quantitative thing. It was not stretched out parallel to the railway tracks of time, so that any part of it you failed to seize as the train came opposite was forever lost. It was a qualitative thing. It repeated its eternal entity opposite each moment. It was available whenever you chose. To the unschooled as well as the schooled.

The word "years" lost its dread. Why, if you were still young (and I *am* still young, she felt then, as gloriously as if recognizing a miracle), just one year – just one – would be enough to contain the whole of living. For how long did any of the big things of sense or sensibility take? Even the act of love? The bigger they were, the *less* time they took. No longer, in fact, than it takes the eye to see or the mind to think or the heart to feel.

And once for everything was enough. It was simple arithmetic. Once was only one more than never, subtracting. But *divide* never (or zero) into once and you found out how many times once contained it. The quotient was infinity.

Maybe that was the reason old people seemed content and so incredibly without dismay. Of course it was. They knew that once for anything was enough.

When the mind is despairing, all coincidence is contrary. But when the mind rides a crest of hope, coincidence seems to be uncannily collaborative.

Where then shall I go? Kate thought now. Coincidence gave her the answer in a flash. That article in the *Clarion* . . . The drinks turned from befuddlers to guide. Her mind went lightfooted to the very place. Paul's!

From habit she took an instant gibe at herself: "Emily Dickinson Rides Forth." But this time there was no real heart in her self-derision.

She thought about Paul, and the first real smile got within

shadowing of her face. The smile of affectionate puzzlement. He was one of those persons who, once you think of them, stick like a burr. You can't leave off the thought until you've tried to tabulate them straight through.

She tried to tabulate him.

The smile itself emerged from its shadowing. It brushed off her face the face that had been drawn on it this last hour.

He had the child's poise beyond poise, but once at least she'd seen him falter. The day they'd said good-bye. Yes, he had. It was not an old maid's hallucination. He'd faltered because . . . she could swear it . . . he'd come to love her almost.

Pensiveness twitched the smile a little askew.

She thought about the kind of people who seemed to gravitate around him. And that was the oddest part of all. He had the least solemnity imaginable, but the sole people he seemed to take with any seriousness were the disabused. People orphaned from something that had once been the big nerve and jugular of their whole life.

If she had stopped to think it through, she'd have seen that Endlaw had more the features of a *cul-de-sac* than of a launching site. But she remembered only that stimulating company of the disabused. They had an ultimate clannishness, a curious naked vitality, which made the insulated sleepwalking of the satisfied seem like a shadowless croquet.

And according to the article, Morse Halliday might be at Paul's right now. That seemed to make the whole chain of coincidence such collaboration as to be almost demand.

Morse is a man of every experience, she thought, and I have done nothing. But that's exactly it. *He's* the kind of person who *doesn't* dismay me. I can't stand tall alone. In the presence of the middling I slump. But with personages, *when* I'm with them, I can stand as tall as they are.

Before, the fixity of one moment's inertness had hypnotized her into that of the next. Now she suddenly couldn't sit still.

She went to the bookcase and took down *Each in His Narrow Cell*. She glanced at the dedication page. "To myself – without whose tireless devotion this book would not have been possible." He had such a horror of its being thought that he took things as seriously as he did!

She turned its pages to the one she knew almost by heart. Certainly she hadn't been the model for this character. He hadn't met her until the book was almost finished. But she was troublesomely certain that she'd inspired these particular lines:

"She would never score any goals for herself, because pity always

76

sent her sprawling. She was forever loaded with the baggage of some lesser person's affliction. She had this fatal compulsion to reduce herself to the other's diminished state, so there'd be no contrast between her condition and his to tax him further. She could never see that that only diminished them both."

Kate felt a fresh gust of that grinding, sacrilegious freedom she'd felt in the hospital.

Had that been Morse's final estimate of her? Oh, how she'd astonish him now if it had! Let any grubby objects of pity try to drag at her skirts as an easy mark now! She had an almost panic urge to get to Endlaw and show off this new emancipating selfishness to him.

The last few years it had got so she abhorred the telephone. She never approached it, if only to bespeak a certain hour at the hairdresser's, without a premonitory chill out of all proportion to the magnitude of her commitment. Now she almost ran to it.

She framed the wording of her telegram to Paul as she went: "Urgently wish arrive today week. Same room. Please evict present occupant if any and oblige – Kate Fennison."

She could sense the flattering amusement in the operator's voice as she read the message back. She felt enormously increased as the thoughtful always do after a snap decision.

Her adventurousness snowballed.

I'll get a new car, she thought, and drive to Paul's. There's very little ready-money, but there's that standing offer for the house. And nothing so shielded you from the discounting glance as being seen at the wheel of a smashing new car.

The window behind her was slightly open. A sudden breeze moved its curtain inward. It touched her back for an instant, like the single catch at breath of a sleeper sleeping like someone dead.

She turned and looked outside. It was quite night now. But the close, communicative, unwithholding April dusk was palpitant as the piping of a frog.

But no voice came to her from anywhere in any kind of answer. The silence of the dead is an infinite rebuke.

Her fingers trembled as she dialed back the operator. Maybe there was still time to stop the wire. She'd never known it to fail that service didn't lag when urgency'd been strongest. But this time coincidence was perverse. The message had gone out at once. She was committed. The whole plan was set in motion.

And then her very thwartedness took on a kind of brackish glamour, near-hypnotic, benumbing even the tiny stroke of assertiveness it would take to send a countermanding wire. She bowed to what she'd laid out for herself as to an order. She had become her own pawn.

CHAPTER 10

Bruce walked slowly through the woods at Endlaw. It was here he'd sought asylum rather than his father's place in Truro. The Truro farm seemed less than ever like home to him now.

He came to the spot in the path where the fence used to cross. When he was a child here, this used to be the pasture. It had had a pasture face. He'd thought he'd remember its every wrinkle. But a dozen years without the axe and the unchecked spruces and grey birch had completely taken over. It had an anonymous woods face now. It had so changed that even when he did spot a familiar clearing, the clearing looked submerged and only patchily faithful to itself. The whole expression of the place had altered.

It had been the same way with the small field beyond the brook where Molly's house used to stand. Young spruce and alders now sprinkled it too. It had scarcely come any more into recognition when he'd stopped and stared at it, that first day driving in, than when he'd almost passed it without recognition at all. That must be the lilac grove, yes. But it held no record, not even the ghostly one, of his and Molly's having sat beside it so often when they were children. He'd had no impulse to get out and visit it again.

The fence wire was still stretched across the path. He himself had stapled it to what then had been saplings. Trees now, they had lipped out over it with growth. It was held fast half-way into their hearts.

He stood there for a moment, quite still.

Today was the first day that the feel of the axe in his hand had tinctured him with a sense of restoration. It was like a hint of returning health. It made him believe that in a moment or so he and the scene would once more fit each other.

His face did not take the ink of his thoughts. Even when he was alone it did not. It did not sigh now, when whatever he'd been waiting for failed to happen.

He stooped and drew the fence wires apart, passing between them.

He straightened up on the other side; and it was then, without a second's warning, that he was seized by something his will had had no part in whatsover.

78

The concepts of "fence" and "Truro" had been floating separately in his consciousness. Suddenly they touched each other like jinn chemicals. And out of them sprang Peter's face. So here-and-now, so exactly as it had looked the day they'd done the Truro fencing, the week that Molly had been in the hospital, that he stood and stared at it.

For a moment Molly's face challenged Peter's. Her face of that next year, when sometimes he'd see her teeth catch at her lips with the thought: What became of the way this second child would have grown up to look, if he'd been born alive? But Peter's overrode it.

His eyes, fixed on the scene before them, saw only the scene behind them. The one in his brain. It had been a morning so exactly in its freshness like this morning now.

The whole memory gripped him like a *dream* you nevertheless know is one of fact. He seemed to be reading it to himself off some relentless hurrying text and at the same time re-enacting it.

He saw Peter walking ahead of him in the hot rubber boots. He struck his own boot so hard with the flat of the axe that the hurt surprised him. He saw Peter's face when he'd put it onto him for scattering the staples. He wrenched his own head sidewise like a sleeper trying to surface. He heard Peter calling him, then fleeing down the road alone . . .

He broke the suction of his trance as savagely as if he'd screamed himself awake . . . and staggered along the path ahead, almost running, to reach the place where he could smash his axe into the trees.

Kate heard Bruce chopping as she drove past. The new car handled beautifully. She was in that first recuperation after grief when you can first deliberately evade grief's ambushes without a sense of guilt. She could hardly wait to get to Paul's. Axes make such happy, ringing sounds, she thought.

And driving past an hour later, Morse also heard the chopping. It was a sound he hadn't heard in years.

It fell so nakedly on nerves the morning had prepared just right for alchemy that he stopped the car and listened. He couldn't drive a car when he was seventeen. And for a moment now he *was* himself at just that age. With such immediacy it was as if the solvent agent of a dream had scaled off every flake of time between.

Seventeen, he thought. In Minnesota. And the clean beautiful axes . . .

My God, a morning like this, only it's a fall morning, only it doesn't point up the fall in everything else then . . . and the axe strikes into the tree on the edge of the clearing on the hardwood slope that you can just see the orchard downward from, the orchard where the dusk will suddenly shift a little that night and it will be a deer . . . but the axe more beautiful like swimming naked than the gun is beautiful like Christmas . . . And the axe conquers the tree so cleanly . . . and your brain, your muscles, have that beautiful cooling system that keeps them just a trifle cooler than your blood . . . and your thoughts sweep in and out of your brain like sailing schooners . . .

My God, everything clean and beautiful and whole as axes . . . and not a shadow on the boy then of the man later . . . Not a shadow of the man with the forest brought inside his head now, only there's no space now between the trees, only they're jungle growths of involvement now, with sap like alum . . . and he's lost his clean beautiful axe somewhere and all he has to cut a path with is the beat-up sickle he's twisted his tongue into . . . that only wounds the forest so it withers standing . . . and the cooling system is cigarette smoke now and tincture of irony . . . and his very breakfast food is shredded wit . . . and there's not a single goddam clearing anywhere you can look downward over and see the orchard with the beautiful deer coming out at night . . .

The sound of the axe stopped. Morse heard the tree fall. He became his present self again.

He noticed the fresh car tracks on the moist road ahead. Perhaps there'd be new people, strangers, at Paul's already.

He remembered Kate Fennison. It startled him that he remembered her so keenly. Was it so keenly that he'd find she'd left her ghosts behind her on the Endlaw air? Would they be standing around in all the old familiar places like garden statuary, visible only to himself? Would he feel a constant bleakness to see the strangers walk through them, unseeing? He almost looked for a place to turn.

And then, remembering Paul – Paul would be there, Paul would be the same, Paul never changed – he went ahead.

CHAPTER **11**

There was no sound of Bruce's axe when Rex and Sheila drove this same road three days later. Everything was dead still. Bruce was driving out, toward town. They were driving in toward Endlaw.

Careless of them all, the morning was sitting for its portrait. This was the first morning spring had really declared itself.

Branch tips of the spruces were tufted with brilliant new green, fresh as mint. Above the road the arms of the hardwood sometimes touched fingers. Their miniature leaves were by turns restless and languid with first shape, wavering in and out of their own shadows. The clean-shadowed air seemed to come from the long throats of running brooks. The brooks were burnished, but not heated by the sun. Wherever there were patches of glistening mud scum on the road it was arrowed with the cuneiform tracks of small birds. The notes of the birds, branched and delicate as their tracks, were the only sound; zigzagging through the silence like a whiter light.

The day remembered warmth. But far off and high on the flanks of either enclosing mountain, there were still ragged patches of snow. Strung out like a clothesline of sheets blown to the ground.

The bright crimson Fiat was new as the morning. For a split second it slewed on the bend before the bridge, hinting the sports car's secret malice.

Sheila bunched the muscles in her calves involuntarily.

"Rex," she said, "don't you *ever* get tired of playing Indianapolis? I'm afraid I do."

He always drove like that now. The moment he set foot inside a car he seemed to start chasing the answer to something that kept just eluding him from one of his destinations to the next.

It was Sheila's birthday – her thirtieth – and she knew quite candidly that she was taking a half-pleasure in the half-sulk that Rex had forgotten it. They were no longer the couple who'd been so sottishly in love five years ago.

The tone of her remark had started with automatic sharpness, then checked itself in mid-sentence, trying too late to twist the remark into a joke. She still had her inspiriting way with others. It was only with her husband, who was so much less than she, that she was now faltering, so much less than herself. Her present look, falling once more into its slot, was that of someone accustomed (but never inured) to living with another whose touchy areas shift location from day to day. You pick your steps by yesterday's map and then suddenly the map's all changed.

Rex brought the car to such a jarring stop that she put her hand out against the air in a mime of self-protection.

"All right," he said. "You drive."

His was the tone of one who carries in him the settlings of a nettlesomeness that the least jar will roil. It was like some chronic physical disorder just short of emergent symptom.

She knew what was coming. He had lately developed this obsessive habit of making a minor quarrel the touchstone of her love.

Things had never been quite the same for Rex since the day he put off his uniform. Most soldiers shed their uniforms like clothing outgrown or a phase of life used up. Rex had put his away as if it were an amputated feature.

And now, at thirty-one, though his looks had physically no more frayed than Sheila's, the years had begun to stamp them *against* the grain. They gave the effect, as hers did not, of currency which has no longer any bullion in the vault to back it up. They – and the cavalier manner which had once gone so well with them – had come to seem anachronistic. Like some festive clothing continuing to be worn long after its original occasion has been forgotten. He kept presenting them as naïvely as ever as a cheque to be honoured. But the tellers in this older company didn't seem to recognize the signature.

It bewildered him. It was as if his body had engineered a double-cross behind his back. Contacts of the kind his mere glance used to command were now seen to have adult locks on them, which only people who had learned their combinations could manipulate. He had never learned or studied anything.

No hint of this shredding bewilderment showed. The others took him to be as compact as his good-looking flesh. But, his eyes being inside it, he couldn't himself watch his own face, to take comfort in its handsome definition. He saw nothing in that very spot where they saw him most flesh-substantialed. And one's *self*, to which the others likewise assign a buttressing compactness, has nothing of the kind. One is only aware of it as a kind of filament, a "field," stretched out over the contours of whatever one's eyes look at and vulnerable at every point.

So Rex had begun to feel nakeder and nakeder. Hard facts, which used to be peripheral to his stride, planted themselves in his pathway, newly self-willed.

For the first time little glances of self-scrutiny began to flicker through him. Now and then he drew a line beneath his life and tried to tot it up. But the good times he'd had, the easy hedonistic goals his looks had won for him, didn't seem to make any kind of total. Piled up, no more than singly, they lacked the property of thickness. He was forced to face the cold-faced fact that he had built almost nothing; and that what little he had built had been built on sand.

It had always been his impulse to meet contrariness with a gesture of annihilation.

Oftener and oftener this last year he'd met this fact of his nullity with the obliterative act of drink. When it or any other like it struck athwart his consciousness, his thought leapt to a drink matically as your mind's finger springs out to touch your when you ask where the fire is and they tell you it's somewhere on your own street.

But here too it was as if treachery had become endemic in everything, even in pleasure. Drinking in the old days had never cost him the smallest coin of his own spirits. Now, almost suddenly, he had to pay for it out of all accounting. In the most punitive coin the stranger to introspection can be charged.

Waking from a stuporous sleep at dawn, he'd feel an utter isolation as if even the day's external climate was different for him alone. Reflexes once automatic nothing now could provoke. His consciousness crushed him not as a weight but as with the singing of wires. Just the bearing of it was nearly intolerable. In his private vision of the day, the day was turned inside out. Only its speechless underpelt showed, like those apocalyptic clouds that curl above the horizon but will not drop their rain. There was this really frightening sense of something imminent holding its breath, at any moment to happen darkly in all things. He had that feeling of *every*thing's being soiled, such as food stains on your clothing can give you, even though they're visible to no one else.

It didn't make sense to him. He'd never had any conscience about drinking. He hadn't now. And yet each time he drank, it was as if the thing turned into a guilt, one of those guilts that become promptly multiplied by the exact measure of its incidence in the past.

The answer was quite simple. Once-innocent pleasures are the things quickest infected by a shame, unconscious enough, about something else. In Rex that shame was totally so. Shame was something he literally could not bear. He simply sidestepped the recognition of it by calling it "anger." But feelings falsely tagged will keep working through you, like a needle in the flesh, until you call them by their right names. That needle was working through him now.

The moment Sheila's remark stung him, he glanced instinctively at his right foot. The slackness of its shoe proclaimed its deformity. He looked at it as if it were obscene. As if a quarrel's first word summoned up all else that aggrieved him. As if Sheila's remark were to blame for this crippling too.

His glance held a double loathing: for being helpless not to carry such unsightliness around, and for his having to rely on such unsightliness to carry him around. But the really erosive, pitting shame connected with it was no more than ever allowed to surface.

He opened the car door on his side and swung himself out onto

...ed the driver's seat to Sheila with a bow and

. "You know perfectly well I don't want to drive.
er . . .? Now get back into this car and don't be

...d tried to make a joke of it. But again she knew she
....He had no idea that he was childish; but as if by
insti...... ...was just those accurate descriptions of himself that he
always c...ose to contest.

He did get back into the car, but not obediently. He was suddenly masterful with affront.

"So she thinks he's childish!" he said. She knew she'd given him a
text. "All right. It's time we got to the bottom of this thing. Right
from the start."

Oh God! It was going to be one of *those*. She didn't say a word.

"In the very first place," he said, "he never *wanted* that stinking
son-in-law's job in her father's office. He was a veteran. The government would have sent him to college. He wanted to study for an
engineer. But, oh, no. She couldn't see that at all. That was the *first*
thing that was childish . . ."

She didn't make her not-interrupting loud enough to be a
sarcasm. She just let her thoughts grate back silent answers to his
words as he went along, in that grittily half-pleasant way you yet
cling to an afflictive situation you know is unworthy of you. One
that you know it's petty not simply to break away from.

"It didn't matter how good an engineer he'd have made. It didn't
matter how hard he was willing to study . . ."

Oh, Rex, *how* can an adult deceive himself so? The very first day
at school . . . starting way back with those kids and that freshman
stuff you should have learned years ago. The very first night, with
a simple problem in algebra . . .

"So what does he do? He takes this job they've wished on him,
just to please her. So she can prune him exactly the way she wants
to, up in that damn Belle Haven . . . hothouse . . . they live in. So
she has him right where she wants him."

This was such utter fable that, as usual in spite of herself, Sheila
was stung into open reply.

"You know, of course, that you don't believe one more word of
that than I do," she said.

But no, she thought, the moment she heard her own voice. You
do. You believe every syllable of it. Now. I've never seen anyone
with such a talent for making up his own memories. If I reminded
you of how it really was at first, you'd quite honestly think that *I*
was the liar.

You loved Greenwich at first, that's how it was. You loved our house in Belle Haven. You loved getting that wedding picture in the *Times*. You loved riding in to New York with father in the brokers' train. You thought the big mahogany desk would fall to you in no time, too. If there was any big cry about engineering then, I failed to hear it.

She was suddenly so sick of having had to swallow so many distortions of a past which in his very company she had witnessed otherwise – so tired and sick of it that for the first time she had a real temptation to something which up to now she'd have considered a meanness unthinkable.

I'd like to see his face, she thought, if I told him I know that whole story about the Merritts and the orphanage. He'd have a hard time squaring that image with this romantic heretic from a silver spoon he's always let me think him. I wonder how he'd juggle himself out of that. I wonder how he'd excuse the way he wounded those good, kind, tolerant people.

But no, she thought again. He's not lying or deceitful. Not really. It's simply that he hasn't any memory in the ordinary sense. It changes whenever his mind changes. And the people in the superseded one become simply strangers, book people. Any memory of him*self* that doesn't jibe with his self-image at the moment – that wildly incongruous orphan, for instance – he's simply dissociated from. No, she thought, it wouldn't disturb him in the least to tell him what I know. He'd be more apt to chuckle – at all the kafuffle that one picture stirred up!

Or . . . her thought abruptly shifted its direction. She remembered Mrs Merritt's picture of the first time they had seen Rex as a child. She felt a stitch of repentance. Maybe "childish" *was* a cruel word for anyone to charge him with.

Rex noticed her eyes tremble. He saw that at last he had engaged her. It softened his outburst, and at the same time encouraged it.

"So, all right," he hammered at his text. "Never mind the job. She loves him, she says. Mur*der*, she loves him! So the sucker falls for that, see? He sticks at the damn job just to please her . . . till there comes a day something's going to give, that's all."

His voice dropped to that inflectionless monotone which denotes that incredulity has taken over from exasperation even.

"So where's she bound she'll take him, for a change? What's she been harping on for the last five years? A God-forsaken place like Nova Scotia! This!"

He swept a contemptuous arm at the trees. Sheila loved the country. He hated it. It was like that bottomless echo-chamber transversing Sunday afternoons when there was nothing in the house to drink.

"And why this cow-path today? Because it reminded her, for God's sake, of a back road they drove along in New Hampshire the first day of their fool honeymoon!"

He glanced to see if this had stung her.

That's his one subtlety, she thought: stinging me. But even that is transparent. For an instant she felt that transparency's terrible bond. If it weren't for me, she thought, there'd be no one, least of all himself, to know what was going on inside him. She felt the curious poignancy of things going on inside people, unapprehended.

A deer stood watching them. It was groomed slick as a flower with alertness, suspended still as stone on its own gaze. Neither of them saw it.

"And *she* says *he's* childish!" Rex said.

Well, she thought, Round One ends up as usual. The slightest word of censure he rubbed off himself as if it were the spit of insult, and somehow managed to smear back on her.

There was only one way to deal with him now.

The dashboard ashtray was brimming with crumpled cellophane and cigarette butts. She leaned forward and tugged at it with her fingertips, ladily fastidious about strength. It didn't come loose.

"Could you get that, please?" she said. She might have been speaking to a servant who had over-presumed on his master's democracy with a personal question.

He disengaged it for her. She emptied it onto the road with a faint grimace of distaste.

"Really," she said, "any habit that *nests* like that is a little obscene, isn't it."

The gambit was a simple one. Fake a petulant distraction from the quarrel by something absolutely trivial and you destatured the quarrel. And, by corollary, your opponent. But he fell for it every time.

She knew the look on his face by heart. The look of a child who, trusting in the steadfastness of a love for him which no misconduct has ever yet outraged, senses for the first time that he may really have irritated himself out of favour.

She felt ashamed. To exactly the degree she'd have felt angered at anyone else who'd snubbed him the same way.

Maybe that's the test of love, she thought. If you still realize what anger you'd still feel if it were someone else doing the snubbing. She remembered Ginny Cutter's snub. I must still love him, she thought, with real surprise. I hate Ginny to this day.

Rex returned to his text. But he was subtly disarmed; just dogged now.

"'And why can't he ever . . .?' didn't I hear her say? Why can't he ever what? Talk like Kaltenborn? Act like Gregory Peck? Dance like Gene Kelly?"

Tenderness that hurts familiarly can as familiarly turn into tedium. Sheila's did then. Shaw . . . Raimu . . . Nijinsky, she thought. You never heard of the real ones, did you.

"Why can't he be President of the United States, for God's sake? Is that what she means?"

She thought she might scream.

"Rex," she said, "let's go on?"

But she knew that Round Two was yet to come.

"Why *couldn't* he ever . . . I guess she meant." Yes, here it came. "Why couldn't the dope see he never did measure up to anything little Miss Perfect . . . ? Why couldn't he see she never loved him, right from the first?"

Ha! She heard a mocking exclamation inside herself. Who measured then? Then, she thought. Then . . .

Once when she was a child her parents had dismantled the Christmas tree after she'd gone to bed and tossed it out back. They hadn't bothered to take off the tinsel. Everything about the tree had been gaudy and artificial but it had made a bright pocket softness in the cloth of the house. The first thing she saw when she awoke in the morning and looked outside was the naked tree. Its flat branches were weaving up and down in a damp January breeze. They looked like some drowned thing beneath the current. The tinsel on them was all matted and awry. And when she went downstairs, the room where the tree had stood looked as raw and bleak as if it had been stripped of a skin. For the first time she had caught her breath at how bare and relentless daylight could be.

Trying desperately not to, she began to cry.

She kept her head down, but Rex noticed the tremor in her shoulders. A sourceless April breeze parted her hair at the back. Her skull was exposed round and small as the skull of a child with its hair parted for braids.

The deer came to split-second decision about their strangeness. It sprang away in undulant flight. They still didn't see it. Nor the snail with the perfect Spiral of Archimedes, $r = a\,\theta$, marked on the back of the house it was inching across their path.

She felt Rex's arm come around her.

This was the final round. No less predictable than the others. Nothing in him of the victor's pose. Nothing whatever. Once he'd found he still had the power over her to provoke tears he was instantly demobilized. What's this? it would go now. You're not *crying*, are you? Now don't be like that, honey? I didn't have any weapon in my hand, what did you take me for?

He tendered her a handkerchief. Like the faithful stand-by as stricken by another's strickenness as the other is by the blow itself – but while the tears last, wise enough not to press consolation beyond attending to the other's small physical wants.

In a moment, though, he'd be as expansive with intimacy as a child. He'd be exactly like the child who's won you over to his idea of an excursion, then starts bestowing on you, so that you may immediately and delightedly concur, little surprise-gift details of it he has thought out. ("Okay?" . . . "Okay?") Now he would be patient and reasonable to a fault. He'd be thoroughly explanatory. Not over-ridingly so or gloatingly, but just as the child is. He'd be full of goodwillingness to make it really clear to her how it really was. Exacting no more than a nod on her part as evidence of her spontaneous agreement.

"Now, look . . ." he said. His hand clasped the cap of her shoulder tight. She felt the muscles harden all along his arm. "You don't want to be like that. You think I don't like to do anything you like to do or go anywhere you like to go. That's it, isn't it? But you got me all wrong, Sheila."

Her crying was under control, but there were little jerks of breath she couldn't quite keep silent.

"Now, listen to you," he said. "You don't want to be like that, honey? I just want to do what's best for both of us, that's all. Now listen. You had this honeymoon ball five years ago, right? And I did too, don't get me wrong. And you think now we've run across a *place* that looks the same – well, the whole *business* must still be hanging out for us there. That's natural. I understand that."

He always picked the most trivial clauses of a quarrel to negotiate peace on. He never gave a second glance at its harsh submerged core, any more than you'd go back at the end of the day and peruse the butts of the cigarettes you'd smoked.

"But . . . well," he explained, "that's really kid stuff, honey. You're sensible enough to see that, if you stop to think, now aren't you? I didn't want you to be disappointed, that's all. I figure when you've once had something a hundred per cent perfect you shouldn't keep trying to bring it back for an encore. The second time, it starts to squirm."

She caught her breath. How could anyone, who was so dead wrong whenever he was serious, be so dead right when he was just talking off the top of his head?

"But, that's okay," he said. "I don't want to be selfish. I tell you what we'll do. We'll go along this road *just* as far as you like. We'll even stay somewhere all night if we can find a place. And then when you see it's just another old back road . . . Well, you'll have it cut out of your system. Now, how's that. Eh?"

She nodded, obligingly. How could you snub *anyone* that innocently confident in a mood of ingratiation?

With her nod, he was instantly re-established. He never guessed that her silence after a quarrel was anything but the silence of acquiescence with everything he'd said.

But she was not re-established. It had been a long time since that had been her pattern too. She was simply drugged and dregged with the perpetual weight of knowing exactly what was coming next with him.

He brought his face closer. Making a gift of it, in the old ingenuous way. That never used to fail.

Now her only thought was: If only he didn't have to keep me "engaged" . . . the whole living time! If not by one device, then by another. He can't let me go for a minute. If it weren't for that I could put up with anything. She felt as if this were one of those dreams that come in a sleep of exhaustion; when you keep incessantly climbing a ladder and incessantly slipping back, but never quite to the ground, because the rungs will never quite let you let go.

His arm tightened sensually around her shoulder again. She found it burdensome. But maybe, with anyone, after five years . . .

And then – she had thought so much about love that all at once the whole thing went bad, as handled grief will spoil and stink. Even the words about it that had passed through her mind left that clinging sweet-rot smell in her nostrils, like the meat that has turned sticky in its tight wrapper away from the air.

She had to get moving again at whatever grinding cost. Calculating the fewest words she could make go the farthest, she smiled at him.

"All right," she said. "Let's carry on." She withdrew the smile, forcing an impishness into it, to her eyes only. As if they might take teasing liberties with him which the lips were afraid to dare. "But have we decided who's going to drive?" she said.

He just grinned – Now, that's my girl – and turned on the ignition.

"You know . . ." he began.

She knew what was coming. He was drunk with magnanimity toward her. In those rare moments he always turned weirdly philosophical. This would be as embarrassing as any other drunken philosophy when you yourself are cold sober.

"You know," he said, "I wish you and I could live forever. I wouldn't give a damn what life was like. But just so there wouldn't be a thing going on – not a damn thing from now to the end of the damn world – that the both of us wouldn't be around for. Together. Did you ever feel like that?"

"I have, yes," she said.

He started the car.

Its front wheel crushed the snail. At the alien sound of the motor the deer, itself far beyond the range of their hearing but they easily within its own, became a statue again. A bird, immaculate as sunshine, hopped from the ditch. Every fibre of it was nerve, but none of its nerves caused it any tiring. It fixed its bright washed eyes on the little nest of cigarette butts in the road. But it knew, without testing, that they were not food. It ate the snail.

Rex drove perfectly carefully, at exactly the speed Sheila liked to drive on country roads. He'd drive like that for perhaps half a mile.

He was crowding sixty when they side-swiped Bruce.

CHAPTER 12

In sudden accidents it seems as if the moment itself slews and splits open like the rocks before Jason's dove. Whatever monstrous force it is that trails and ambushes every tranquil second pounces through the rift, strikes, and just escaping the rocks' closing again, leaps back in one flash.

There was the sow's squeal of brakes, Rex's scream, and then the unearthly bark of wounded metal. And then everything was sideways and dishevelled, but the moment itself was instantly bland and blind again, vibrating only with after-glimpse.

Bruce's car was partly in the ditch. Its fender had scraped a rock, but otherwise it was not damaged. The only blemish on Rex's was a long stripe of abraded paint. Miraculously, no one had been injured, but pallor and shock stripped all their faces to bare maps of themselves, to legibility. Landmarks of chronic thought and feeling were pencilled in like rivers and mountains.

The moment Rex saw that his own car was in the clear he stepped on the gas.

"Rex!" Sheila cried. "Stop!"

"I'm *going* to stop," he said.

She knew he hadn't been going to stop. She'd seen that look on his face too often, of taking to its heels. The scream, though, was something new.

She looked closer at him, but he seemed to be calmer than she was now.

They got out of the car and approached Bruce in the road.

All three had regained hold enough on themselves that now the instinct for self-exoneration was uppermost.

Bruce noticed Rex's limp.

"Are you hurt?" he said.

"No!" Rex gave his foot another quick amputative glance, and Bruce saw then how its shoe had long since shaped itself to chronic deformity. "No one's hurt. But we're just damn lucky. You believe in taking plenty of road when you drive, don't you."

"You think so," Bruce said. "Well, have a look. Whose car had to take the ditch for it? And whose was coming around that blind corner fifty, sixty miles an hour?"

"We could have been driving too fast," Sheila said. "I admit that."

"Well *now*," Rex said. "*That's* interesting?" He smiled at Bruce and delivered Sheila to him with a nod of his head. "You've got yourself a witness. Voluntary, no less."

"Rex!" Sheila said.

"What's your name?" Rex said to Bruce.

"Bruce Mansfield. Do you want to see my license?"

"Not specially," Rex said. "I just wanted to make the introductions. My name is Rex Giorno. And I'd like you to meet my wife, Sheila Giorno. Of Greenwich and New York, as they say." He waved his arm toward her. "Your witness. All yours. It's only in murder trials that the wife can't testify against her husband, isn't it?"

"Rex," Sheila said. "For Heaven's sake. Don't be so unreasonable. You know you were driving too fast."

"I'm not being unreasonable at all," he said in an ultra-reasonable tone. "Just outnumbered. So you two just fix it up between you anyway you like."

He stepped back a pace.

Bruce was completely baffled. At the start he'd hesitated to accuse too squarely – you never knew when the other might be so decent about it as to shame you for grabbing at your pound of flesh. Rex's attitude had relieved him of any conscience about that. But now it was Sheila who subtly disarmed him. It was suddenly like fighting in a civil war. You had to remember that every blow you struck against the opposite camp might fall on a relative.

For strangely-instantaneously, that's exactly what she seemed like: not just any strange woman, but someone who made him immediately and acutely conscious of "you and I." He had a fleeting foreglimpse of himself looking *back* on this moment as "the first time I ever saw her."

He watched her walking alongside his car, looking at it, but with eyes in the back of her head for the way Rex was looking at her.

"Okay then, *you* take over," Rex's eyes said to her – then waited, half-gloating, half-commanding her to falter.

Sheila pointed to the hood of Bruce's car.

"We didn't do any of that, did we?" she said.

The hood had obviously been in some major collision; but the rusty look of its imperfectly tended scars, like that of plants in drought, marked them as old ones.

Bruce looked as if she had touched a scar on his flesh he'd forgotten was still tender.

"No," he said. "That was done before."

"So you've been in another accident lately?" Rex said, taunting with insinuation.

"Yes."

"And whose fault was that?"

Memory slipped in its vivid lantern slide ahead of anger even. It was my fault, Bruce thought. Molly wouldn't have been in the car at all if she hadn't thought she could smooth things over between Peter and me. Or if I'd let her take the minute she asked for, to wash his hands before we left . . . then everything would have happened differently for that one minute's difference. And that's the last way he ever saw me: angry at him . . .

"It was on the ice," Bruce said. "One of those steep hills in Halifax."

Rex nodded insultingly. "And you jammed on the brakes like every other bad driver does."

Bruce's temper cracked. "Now listen here – "

"No!" Sheila interrupted. "If I could just get a word in! I'm simply *too* tired for any fool, pointless bickering. We should be darned thankful there's no blood and flesh lying around. The fault was ours – all right, all *right*. We'll pay the damage." She turned to Bruce. "Whatever you think is fair. And then, *please*, if everyone could just *please*, for the love of" (she whispered it) "Gawwwwwd, shut up!"

Bruce looked at her and a moment happened that normally happens only with friends of a lifetime. Her irritation had had its feet cut out from under it: the vehemence that had turned it outrageous having, by its very excess, turned it comic. To see her seeing that and knowing at the same moment that he saw it too, he had that feeling you get only with people you've known a long, long time – that just such trivial, untaggable interchanges are the most wonderful of all things.

He had to smile, himself.

"Well," he said wryly, "another wrinkle or so in that old crate of mine is hardly a calamity. Yours is the one that really got the pretty knocked off. So let's just forget it, eh?"

"Forget it?" Rex said, just to mock. "When my wife will probably have to have a brand-new car? She can't stand anything the least bit defaced."

Bruce ignored him. "I take it you're on your way to Endlaw?" he said to Sheila. He grinned. "I'm sorry. I was supposed to shut up."

He hadn't grinned since that day of the icy hill. Sometimes people had made him laugh, but no one had ever made him grin.

Sheila grinned too. "Endlaw?" she said. "Where's . . . What's . . . Endlaw?"

Bruce told her. He didn't know why he gave the place such a build-up, enticing her there, foreseeing himself advocate there for all the charm she might not recognize in it. He'd been all set to leave Paul's.

But he enticed her quite innocently. He had no conscious idea of falling in love or in lust with her. He thought he was doing it out of sympathy. He didn't know that he was actively trying to put off never seeing her again.

Sometimes, when you've lost someone, all people thereafter are, for not being exactly like the one lost, exactly alike and nothing. He didn't recognize that Sheila was that first person you meet after a loss like that who again has a compelling personal flavour.

"I think that sounds wonderful," she said. "But if Paul's so independent – do you think he'd take us in?"

"I'm sure he would," Bruce said. "If I asked him to."

Sheila made as if to ponder. "Now if there was only some way we could persuade you to do just that," she said.

She could tease without being silly. No one had ever teased Bruce since . . .

"I'll ask him," he said. "I'll go back with you, if you like."

Sheila turned to Rex. "How about it, dear?" she said. "Doesn't this sound like exactly what we've been looking for?"

Rex shrugged elaborately. "Why ask me?" he said. "You're in charge of everything, aren't you?" He turned to Bruce. "But are you sure you want to let the accident slide? My wife has a good deal of money, you know, and when she gets these tired spells, as she calls them, she doesn't have to bicker. She's only too glad to buy people off."

Another small breeze parted Sheila's hair to the skull again; so synchronous with Rex's words as to make it seem as if they had done it. You don't normally reflect on the sensate quality of the flesh of people you meet for the first time. Bruce thought of Sheila's flesh being sensate.

He looked straight at Rex. "You weren't in high school with me, were you," he said. "No. But we did have a handsome character named Rex Something-or-other. Naturally we called him 'Sex.' And of course he loved it. I'm not sure, but I *don't* think he ever graduated. In fact, I don't think he ever grew up at all."

"Goddam your eyes – " Rex made at him with his fists.

He was the very personification of a cornered animal's flailing courage. It was another of those discordant chapters in his behaviour which continually sent you leafing back through him for some predictive clue you must have missed. With his looks and speech, you goggled to find he had no physical fear of other men at all.

Sheila grasped his right arm. It was equally for restraint and so that Bruce couldn't strike back at one so disadvantaged. She saw the cornered look inside his flesh, and the idea of outside blows falling on it made her sick. She suddenly hated Bruce. She could have struck him herself.

Bruce didn't strike back. He merely caught Rex's other wrist and held it immobile, as if without effort. The whole thing looked like a tableau of arrest.

"*No*, Rex, darling," Sheila said. She laughed like Ginny. "You're not supposed to get mad. You're supposed to laugh. This gentleman is after being a wit. We mustn't be mean enough not to laugh when he works so hard at it, now must we?"

Bruce dropped Rex's wrist. He turned away. Aaaah . . . the hell with her too. He felt that bitter-sweet return to his own inner landscape which the encarapaced feels when once more someone has tempted him out of himself and once more he's been had.

Rex instantly calmed down: Sheila was on his side again: it was Bruce she had snubbed.

And seeing Bruce snubbed, he thought suddenly: I got him all wrong, this is a *good* guy. Suddenly he couldn't bear not to be a good guy with the other good guys the way it had come so easy in the old days. "A drink!" something said inside him, with a great big smile . . . the big warm way you congratulate yourself with a cigarette when some passage in your reading mirrors exactly through its main character a defect you'd thought was yours alone, and exonerates it.

"Look," he said, really laughing, "this is one hell of a way to act, isn't it?" You wouldn't have known it was the same man, the way he made them welcome to every last bit of human generosity possible. "Now *isn't* it?" He saw it working. He was dissolving them both into geniality again. He could still do it! "We're all going to Paul's, why don't we quit this yakking and shove off? But how about a little drink first?"

Sheila sagged. If just once when he'd hit the right note he didn't have to drag in the seed of something disruptive.

"We got two cases in the car," Rex said to Bruce. "What'll you have? Whisky? Gin?"

He made it a party; made it that moment of highest good fellowship when you offer someone his choice between two variants of the same pleasure.

"Rex, dear," Sheila said, "do you think . . . while you're driving? The minute we get there, eh? How would that be?"

"None for me, thanks," Bruce said.

Rex's face fell. It had an immigrant look, as if they'd suddenly pulled a language barrier on him. "Drink!" the voice inside him repeated; but not with the smile now. With the tense plucking command.

"All right," he said. "You two stick to your Wheaties. They'll make you big and strong. But *I'm* having a drink. Right now."

"So go ahead," Sheila said, "if it's all that urgent."

She was almost relieved, if she dared concede it, that he was rancorous again. However winning he could be when he was winning, the tightrope vigilance it took to keep him so was the most taxing of all.

"But *if* you do, Rex," she said, "I simply can't drive with you. I mean it."

She'd never spoken to him quite so defiantly before. She didn't know where she got the courage. She had no idea that somehow it came from Bruce.

Rex never met a charge head on. He simply opened up another front.

"So you'd be happier to come along with Mr Mansfield," he said. "Well, I think that should be cosy as anything, if that's the way you want it. You see no fault in his driving, he doesn't drink . . ."

The funny thing, jealousy played no part in his rancour, now or ever. He no more thought of her being unfaithful to him than you'd think of a relative's, whatever the friction between you, stealing your purse.

"Would you mind?" Sheila said to Bruce.

"It's up to you," Bruce said.

"Fine then," Rex said. "I'll 'go ahead,' as you put it. 'Would you mind?' And if I do land in the ditch, you two sound and sober specimens will be right behind me to pick up the pieces and . . ."

Sheila glanced at her watch.

"It's almost noon," she said. "If you're really going, hadn't you better have your drink and get started?" She kept any note of real irritation out of her voice to make it the more stinging. "I'm sorry, dear," she said, "if I built up your little drink into anything particularly devilish. It's just that I'm still nervous. So let's not be tiresome about it, eh?"

She turned her back to him and crooked one leg over the knee of the other, to take some gravel from her shoe. She paid him no attention whatever when he got a bottle from the car and made quite a thing out of drinking from it straight.

He got into the car, shocking the gravel in the road with his savage start, and disappeared around the far turn like a racer.

Sheila rolled her eyes up to the spotless April sky.

"Noooo-va Sco-tia!" she parodied the *Oklahoma!* tune. But she was too weary to put any spirit into it.

Bruce smiled. "Or how about Mary Martin?" he said. He hummed "I'm gonna wash that man right outa my hair."

He hadn't kidded anyone since . . .

Sheila stiffened. "No," she said. "You don't understand."

And then she relaxed; because she didn't mean, you *wouldn't* understand, which is something quite different. There was, in fact, that most curious of understandings between them: the rare kind that, when it does occur, so often occurs strongest with someone you meet for the first time. The kind when you feel the "Yes! I know!" of your own reaction even before the other speaks.

Bruce didn't understand it. With expensive women before, he'd been made conscious of nothing but his stupid lump of flesh.

Sheila shook her head. "Isn't he . . ?" she said. "*Isn't* he, though?"

The air was cleared of Rex's weather, but Bruce knew that she still couldn't relinquish him as the compelling thing to talk about. He knew, too, that it would be the wrong move to confirm her in anything she might say against him.

Sheila tried to shake Rex off.

"But what are you doing knowing all about Rodgers and Hammerstein way down here?" she said.

She gave him a kind of handshake grin that took the rudeness out of her remark.

"Uh uh," Bruce said. "I know very little about Rodgers and Hammerstein, really. I'm a symphony man. Mahler, Copland . . ." He warmed from smiling to grinning. "Like hell," he said. "The names. But beyond that I don't know a damn bit more about . . ."

"Nor I!" she said. "*Not* a thing!"

She passed from smiling to laughing.

"There's nothing like the good old opera, though," he said, "is there? Especially when the coloraturas get those mice up their girdles. Do they sound like that to you?"

He hadn't tried to make anyone laugh since . . .

"Yes!" she said, biting onto it with recognition. "Yes!" She was becoming a little hysterical. "I remember one time *Rex* and I went to see *Lucia* at the Met. He was so darn funny. Didn't know an *earthly* thing about *any* of it, but he sat there, trying to look so solemn . . . Honestly, I . . ."

All at once, her face changed.

"Oh, the hell with him," she said, half-crying. "Let's go."

CHAPTER 13

In Bruce's car it was still bright morning but a hand-regarding quality had settled into their talk, as if it were the moment of evening when, sitting outside, faces first start to blur.

In each of them that self which is most cautiously animal-eyed seemed to be venturing out of its innermost den. And as it found it could set its feet down with less and lessening caution, Bruce felt curiously flushed with expressing himself beyond his capacity. He was like a tennis player who plays far better than he knows how against a better player than himself.

Each at the pitch of a different parching had sensed in the other someone he could really talk to, and it loosened their tongues like wine.

"You Canadians," Sheila said ruefully. "I have an idea you never quarrel like that, do you?"

"Not like that," Bruce said. "No. We seldom let anything show, escape. Cut one of us open and . . . did you ever see a root-bound plant lifted out of its pot?"

"You're root-bound?" she said. "You?"

"Why not?" he said. "Actually, I haven't lifted myself up out of the pot to look, since – " He halted abruptly. "But . . . yes, I'm root-bound."

"Since when, did you say?"

"That's another thing about us," he said. "We'd never dream of asking a stranger a blunt question like that. We think it's because

97

we're . . . well, I don't know what we *think* we are, we haven't much picture of ourselves at all . . . but it's really because we have no ventilation system. That's probably the most typical thing about us. Actually, we're forever setting up some damn solemn commission to trace what's out-and-out Canadian, and our writers are busy with their little butterfly nets the year round trying to trap it, and what do most of them come up with? A handful of beavers and a Mounted Policeman. Externals like that. When the simple truth is, we have no draft. We're scared stiff of trying a door – any door – without knocking first. We breathe in, but we can't breathe out."

"And what about answering questions?" she said. "Are you going to answer mine?"

"No," he said. "That's another thing about us. We don't answer questions. Don't ask me to answer that one, anyway." He spoke quickly again, before she could interrupt. "Get this straight, though, I'm talking about us as a group. One person by himself, we're altogether different."

"How?" she said.

"Listen to me," he said. "Lecturing! What do you care what we're like?"

"I do care," she said. "Now keep quiet . . . and tell me."

"Well, for instance," he said. He smiled. "We're funny. You came through Granfort, didn't you?"

"Yes. That's partly why Rex was driving so fast just now. We lost time behind a parade of some kind."

"That's what I mean," he said. "They were crowning a fool Mayflower Queen. The Mayflower's our provincial emblem. And the funny thing is that, as a crowd, nobody could see the least thing foolish about it. It's like I say. In groups, we're a mess. But take any one of that group by himself and he'd be all for having a Pied Piper lead the whole fool procession right down to the wharf and into the river."

"Everyone?" she said. "Not just you?"

"No," he said. "Really. Everyone. It's like that with everything. We voted in droves for a Prime Minister with about as much gimp in him as a stuffed owl. Kept him in office for a dog's years – when man to man we wouldn't have exchanged squirts of tobacco juice with him. And that's another funny thing about us. We take no pride in our public figures whatsoever. Whenever we can be bothered to think about them, they just amuse us. And the crew we let speak for us generally! You'd think we were one big Ladies Aid – when, individually, you couldn't find a lustier gang."

She made a startled pantomime of protecting her virtue, and he grinned. Rex never grinned.

"No," he said, "I mean it. Not one damn thing that's supposed to represent us does. The politicians don't represent anything but themselves. The writers, *them*selves. And so on. That's why you Americans never understand us in the least. You think we're as clammy as our institutions. As people. Do you see? . . .I don't suppose this makes any sense, but the Canadian *person* is the kind of guy would never go hard and . . . legal . . . on you, like those hard, legal faces that accuse you in a dream. If you ever did run into a jam with him, it would be like getting into a jam with your own family. And our individuality *is* fast beginning to emerge and make itself felt. But right at the moment . . ."

"And what about us Americans?" she said. "What's typical about us?"

He didn't know why he seized this chance to insult her. He didn't know it was because she was threatening to involve the very cores of feeling inside himself that he had so jealously calloused over.

"I'd have to think about that," he answered. "Or no. It's those cameras, of course. You carry then around like an extra sense. We have them, too, but we don't use them to *claim* everything we point them at, the way you do. You know the picture. The convertible hardtop specimen pulls up alongside the old turnip farmer and gives him the old teeth and tells him to hold it . . . hold it, Pop . . . till he gets him in the range-finder. It'd really do my heart good just *once* to see the old farmer slap his manure-spreader into high gear and let this baby have the whole contents right smack in the sun glasses."

"Well!" she said. "That's flattering. You can be a very pleasant fellow, I must say."

He had to laugh.

"Okay," he said. "I know what a sour customer I am lately."

It gave her the oddest pleasure to have Bruce laugh like that. She was so used to Rex's going immediately injured and defensive and spiteful whenever she took him up on anything he said.

Yet as they approached each turn in the road her sentences, if she were the one speaking, and her attention, if it were Bruce, would grip their teeth until the turn was rounded and she saw that Rex's car was not piled up anywhere on the stretch ahead.

"And me?" she said. "You were afraid that when I asked that simple question I was going to barge right in and photograph your insides?"

"I guess," he said. "Yoo-hoo. Come here, everyone, and see this quaint little Canadian cave I just discovered! We don't like strangers barging around sight-seeing inside us."

"You keep harping on this stranger business," she said, her voice suddenly changed. "And of course that's what we are. You and I, I mean. But somehow – now here's your bold, blunt American! – somehow . . . well, you know the usual performance with someone you meet for the first time. You keep ticking off each other's looks. You kind of keep flirting with each other. I don't mean that in the silly sense, but you know. Your Sunday behaviour. Your best foot forward. All that. Fencing with your party manners, sort of. It doesn't seem to be like that with us at all. And when I say that, I'm not flirting, either. It just puzzles me." She stopped. "You don't know what I'm talking about."

"I do," he said. "It's the damnedest thing. I know exactly what you're talking about." But he couldn't let it alone. "Who knows, it might even turn out we both like those corny old twins – walking in the rain and the smell of burning leaves."

"We do!" she said. "And I like the wash of sun on that old windfall there. Did you ever see anything so absolutely clean? You never get that cleanliness on people or anything else. And you like it too, you can poke fun at me all you want to."

"I wasn't poking fun at you," he said.

They drove for a bit then in the silence that falls between two people when some mutuality – of they're not sure just what, and through what provocation they can't trace – has been tacitly arrived at between them.

They came opposite the spot where Bruce used to go to school.

"Right in there's where our old schoolhouse used to stand," he said. "There's something you should have seen. You and the rest of your fancy classmates at Miss Bentley's – or wherever it was. This old pot-bellied stove that looked as if it was about seven months pregnant and the rows of mittens drying on the zinc underneath. And if you want to know the rivers of Afghanistan and what Portugal imports, I can rattle them off to this day. You know, we were talking about the difference between Canadians and Americans. That hasn't got a patch on the difference between being rich and being poor. Remember what Fitzgerald said? And never mind what Hemingway answered."

He wanted her to know he'd read Fitzgerald. He knew this time that, behind the barb, he was showing off a little. He'd never felt like showing off since . . .

"It was Miss Bainbridge," Sheila said. "And you needn't be so snobbish about your little red schoolhouse. Bainbridge was a bit of an old mare, I admit. But I don't think she did me any more real damage than your Miss Applecheek, or whatever her name was,

100

did you. And I don't care if you are the risen Fitzgerald, money –
no, you're not going to get me to soft-pedal that word – I'm not
the least bit ashamed of it – money hasn't made me a bit different
from anyone else."

"All right," he said. "Money isn't everything. All right, all right,
it isn't *any*thing. But just the same, it's a kind of cushion. You're
rich, you're never right out in the bare open. Everything that
strikes you has those little felt mufflers on it – like piano hammers.
Mind you, I'm not in the least envious. But you yourself. You
haven't the faintest little damned idea of what it's like to have the
bare hammers strike right on the bare wires. You couldn't possibly
understand a pauper like me if you tried."

"You mean that," she said, "don't you. Well, just for the fun of
it – it's a far better game than discussing the weather, wouldn't
you agree? – let's see how close I can *come* to understanding you.
Already. I'll bet I can rattle off your mountains . . . and rivers . . .
and coastline, anyway." They were beginning to echo each other's
turn of speech. "Better than you can, yourself. My great-great-
Spanish-grandmother wasn't a gypsy for nothing."

"Okay," he said. "I'm listening."

Sheila struck the sybil's pose and all at once it *was* fun. Bruce
felt that subtle flattery you feel when someone insists on disputing
with you what you say you're like. He began to enjoy himself. He
hadn't enjoyed himself since . . .

"One thing's perfectly plain," she said. "There is, or has been at
some time, something apostolic about you. I see this youngster
first, and I see him born with what they call a sense of mission.
You can check me when I'm getting warm or cold."

"Don't tell me that kids in Greenwich played 'I Spy' too," he said.

"Of course," she said. "You see? We're no different. Anyway . . .
I don't mean he got a call in the fields. That sort of thing. There
wasn't anything dramatic about it. Or savage. This dedication to
whatever it was he wanted to be was absolutely quiet. But it had
such intentness about it that sometimes, when he was alone, the
mainspring in him would go kind of set. Seized, almost. And yet it
was a comfortable thing then. And a comforting one. And he had
a conscience, I guess you'd have to call it, that big."

"That's a mountain?" he said. "Or a river?"

"A mountain," she said. "This is the river. Right next to the
mountain ran this wonderful sense of the absurd. Not ha-ha
comical. Nothing as ordinary as that. But that rare talent for spot-
ting let's call it the *quirk* in things that . . . well, that's the one
ingredient you can't picture any possible Creator tossing into the
human makeup. If I seem to go on about this, I mean to – because

101

it's a quality *so* rare that if two people ever find they share it in exactly the same way it gives them an odd advantage over the whole dismayingly literal world. This thing would flash out when he *wasn't* alone . . . and it would seem to contradict the dedication we speak of. But not really. It's what gave him balance then."

"Do you have it?" he said.

"Shhh," she said. "Don't interrupt. I'm beginning to see more. I see him reading everything he could get his hands on. And he had this rare talent not many readers have. He could identify so thoroughly with the people he read about that whenever he met their doubles in the flesh he knew them as well and could talk to them as easily as if he had met them travelling. And all this time, this career thing – he used to keep touching his mind against it, sort of, like a talisman."

Or the way a hunter touches his mind against the thought of a drink and the warm meal ahead, he thought.

"Was it writing?" she said.

"Cold," he said.

"Medicine then," she said. "It has to be one or the other."

"Come now," he said, the first trace of bitterness returning, "you've been listening to soap operas. But all right. You're warm. You're so hot you're going to burn your fingers. Go on."

She hesitated.

"I can't," she said. "Unless I skip. The embryo doctor, I can see that. But then . . . something happened, that I can't see, to wash out the whole setup. Was it the war?"

"No," he said.

"No," she said. "I can see that too. War might slash him, but he wouldn't infect. Or wait. He's lost too much time in the war to pick up his career again. Or he hasn't got enough money. Is that it?"

"No," he said. "The government stuffed us into colleges, damn near."

"All right," she said. "So at last he's really on his way. He couldn't be happier."

She made as if to tilt a crystal ball back and forth.

"And there's where I strike this cloudy part. What happened then I can't make out at all. All I can see is what it did to him. That's plain as day. This earnestness about his career, it gets all its nerves pinched off. The appetite for it goes completely dead. It used to puzzle him why this single ambition wasn't in everyone's blood the way it was in his. Now it's something *they* were right about when they puzzled at its grip on him. It's nothing but a big, dead, calcified tumour inside him now. It doesn't even pain.

He walls it off. And that's the grimmest mortar you can ever put your hands to."

"You think so," he said. "You've had experience with it yourself?"

"Maybe," she said. "In a way. There are tumours and tumours." She paused.

"And so," she resumed – but she couldn't rouse the game spirit in it again – "he nails his brake pedal to the floor. He stops himself. Deliberately. He severs all diplomatic relations with circumstance. You can hear the brake grinding whenever anything touches the gas pedal unawares. But he doesn't wilt. Oh no. He goes proud. Copper-tasting proud. And single. And wary-eyed never to let wariness drop into weariness if it would. All in that terrible copper-tasting way. And his sense of the absurd. You'd hardly recognize it now. The eyes and the mouth have put such an edge on it. And the tongue has honed it so . . . I'm sorry. Maybe it isn't as bad as all that. Maybe I just got carried away." She gave up all attitude of the game and looked at him squarely. "What happened?"

He had drawn the deep breath he needed to answer her question as squarely as she had asked it when she opened her purse for a cigarette.

Rich women don't open their purses the way poor women do, glancing first, whatever else their original motive, to see if the dollar bills are still there. The moment Sheila opened hers, he saw Molly and Peter watching him.

The way they always looked at him when he talked this glib way in front of them. Molly, as if the little decorative touches on her dress had subtly betrayed her; and as if she were bent a little in on herself, like someone mending. And Peter, whom almost nothing could subdue, quiet then as a child is quiet when his parents are quarrelling.

He himself had always felt treacherous. Soiled, somehow, as if being drunk with the use of anything like clever words left behind it a soiling like any other kind of drunkenness. He always felt a subtle shame and guilt, as of a traveller returning home from some trip the others couldn't share. He always hated his talking companions a little.

He hated Sheila now.

"It's too bad to put an end to your little guessing game," he said. "But in a few *simple* words for a change, this is what happened. I lost my wife and son. And don't say 'I'm sorry' like that."

"I didn't say anything," she said after a moment.

"And please don't strain yourself trying to hit on the right kind of silence either," he said.

If he meant to anger her he nearly succeeded.

"I'll be quiet how I like!" she said. "I knew it must have been something like that. But can't you give anyone a minute to . . . ? Now, wait. Just wait. I can see how you feel, yes. You've been struck with something exactly the size of the world. And it's as if there's nothing in the world not to have to . . . forgive . . . if you're ever to be friends with it again. I know that. But just the same . . . There's a limit to the kind of lordliness that blows that size give anyone. You think now that no one else's trouble is good enough for you. You've no right to feel that."

"Her name was Molly and his was Peter," Bruce said quietly, as if it were some special explanation.

"And my husband's name is Rex," she said.

She reclaimed Rex almost fiercely; the way you reclaim a child you've been on the point of throwing up your hands about, when someone else says, "No, to be truthful, I can't say our children have ever given us any trouble like that."

They drove on in that knitted silence in which each bristles with defence of a separate loyalty as intensely as if it had already been attacked. Less like strangers than like intimates in a moment of division, each fended for domination of the silence with every reinforcement of this loyalty which memory could supply.

The tracery of tree limbs cut jigsaw sections of light from the air like tablets for them to stamp their thoughts on. Bruce felt the ink-stamp of having been married to Molly in his very grain.

Holding obsessive court on his part in her death, and finding himself, as always, his most hostile witness, he saw her face all those times when its unlocatable delicacy had made it look as if it had gone small.

He saw her waiting for him at the University gates (she never came inside) that raw November day, in the summer coat that, lacking any other, she was trying to pass off as a year-round coat by leaving it unbuttoned. He saw her waving and he wondered how long she'd been waving without his notice; waving to identify herself in case the other boys he was with might pass some remark about her that could embarrass him, thinking she was a stranger . . .

He saw her when the face, with its belittling lie, might have masked as a look of petulance one that was really of desperation . . .

He saw her glancing at his books – proudly, but as if they might be building a new feature into him that she could never touch or be touched by.

He saw her hands, re-searching her purse each time she thought no one was looking the day she'd lost the ten-dollar bill in town, while she waited for the crowded bus that would take her home inexorably without it. He saw her getting on the bus, saw her back-to, and suddenly he had a murderous hatred of its other passengers, thinking of them giving her that challenging stare of the already seated and entrenched . . .

He saw her lips, the night he'd kidded her about the way she mispronounced a word — keeping at the kidding until he discovered that the sound she made when she turned her face away wasn't laughing but laughing-crying . . .

They came opposite the spot where Molly's house used to stand. "That's where my wife was born," he said.

Sheila didn't answer.

And he saw Molly's eyes. The night of the party they'd had for some of his classmates and their wives.

She'd spent the whole afternoon making the sandwiches into fancy shapes and had somehow managed to skimp enough on the household expenses to provide a bottle of really good whisky. And then they'd heard his friends coming noisily from way down the street, carrying on with the evening they'd started somewhere else, already so boisterous with drinking that they didn't even notice her fancy touches on the food — they took it without looking, like a cigarette — and her whisky was nothing special to them at all.

He saw her eyes when she picked the crescent sandwich off the mantel after they'd left, with the one blind bite taken out of it — and he remembering that it was he himself who had asked her to get that old shawl out of Peter's bedroom (Peter waking up, to stare at the dishevelled hubbub in that baffled way of his), and that it was he himself who had draped the shawl over Annette Vardy's shoulders so she could do that just foolish imitation of hers of a Spanish tarantella, and that it was he himself who'd clapped his hands and shouted, "Aaaah, think nothing of it — we'll blame it on the dog," when Annette staggered and upset two glasses half-full of Molly's precious treat all over the rug . . .

He saw, of all things, her insteps, that afternoon he'd gone to pick her up at the doctor's office when she was pregnant the second time, and glimpsed her before she saw him — still waiting her turn and staring at the words on the magazine page as if she were having to translate them.

And her shoulders, the night he came home and their neighbour had phoned, this time to say that Peter had dee-*lib*-erately trampled her flower bed . . .

He saw Peter's face coming at him then.

His lips tightened as if against the blow of it. It was Peter's death mask he saw : his intimate, touch-beckoning, sleeping-face.

As if the first thing that death had snatched away from it was its storminess.

Molly's face branded, but Peter's tore. He could always reach Molly. But had he ever been able to reach Peter at all?

Bruce did something with his eyes and jaws and nostrils then; sent some sort of physical current into them that clamped the shutters of his mind so tight that not a chink let memory through. With grip enough he could do that now.

And then he sat there as they drove along, his mind registering intensively the exact boundary line of the windshield the way he'd sat at his desk those blinded days of last December, with his books open but his eyes threaded fixedly to the words "Patent Pending" on the reel of Scotch tape and the pumpkin-grinner-like face that Peter had scrawled on the cover of the paper clip box and the legend "This is MUCILAGE and NOT INTENDED for joining wood" that ran around the base of the glue bottle . . .

And then he turned toward Sheila and he saw that she was watching the coal of her cigarette blacken down the paper, with exactly the same fixity.

"I'm sorry I was so damn rude," he said.

"Shut up!"

She was almost shouting. What insult just fails to provoke, apology for the insult can often touch off like a blaze.

"Like I said. If everyone would just shut up! You know what people are like with people like me? I try to be decent to them, and what happens? *Their* afflictions give them the whole stage. They come over all haughty with them, like actors. If they have any bitterness about anything they can get bitter at *me*, listening to it. That's one way to get rid of it. Does anyone ever stop to think that to hear they're upset might upset me? Oh no. And if they ever do see they've stepped on me anywhere it hurts, doesn't it *ever* give them a fine feeling right *there*" – she pressed her heart – "to know that the minute they say 'I'm sorry,' wonderful old Sheila will forgive them!"

Her unexpected spurt of anger jostled his personal brooding as nothing else could have. It seemed like such a preposterous self-image for one of her self-assurance to entertain that he was oddly moved.

"Well, do you know something?" she said. "Old Sheila's so damn sick of the whole business, she's so *enor*mously damn sick of it that . . ."

She stopped short. She looked as amazed as if she'd just listened to a tape-recording playback of her own unrecognizable voice.

"You know," she said, "I never sounded off like that to anyone in my life before."

"But you feel better now, don't you," he said.

Impulse, dead in him all these months, suddenly moved again like light.

"Maybe I'd feel better too," he said, "if I told you the whole story about Molly and Peter. The parts of it *I've* never told anyone before."

This was the first time he'd been without a sense of guilt to want to feel better about Molly and Peter. It was the first time it had ever occurred to him that there might *be* another way to feel about them.

And all at once their being in motion made confidence seem easier. His words would not fall all in one spot, a cache for memory to return to later and regret.

"Tell me," Sheila said. "Please."

But it was too late. The landscape of arrival had begun to set in.

"Another time," Bruce said. "We're almost there. But another time."

"That's a promise?" Sheila said.

"I promise."

Five minutes more and as abruptly as a mirage after the last concealing turn in the road, they could see the house and the lake. Rex's gleaming red car was at the top of the long driveway, shining bright and safe in the sun.

The tourniquet on Sheila's breath unknotted. Her eyes looked from the lake to the sky as if they were following the flight of a bird.

"I love it," she said.

They hadn't noticed Rex standing at the corner of the house. He was waving.

Look at him, Sheila thought. Waving. Honestly!

His manner of waving reminded Bruce somehow of Peter's.

And again they were stung separate, again almost hating each other. The feeling came up suddenly in each's throat that by having let the other tempt him even to discuss his first allegiance he'd been faithless to it.

But when the car slowed down for the driveway they were already like a travelling couple with their personal belongings so intermingled in the luggage that nothing of the one's can be sorted out without first having to handle something of the other's.

"How far have we come?" Sheila said.

"Fifteen, sixteen miles," Bruce said.

"It seemed farther," she said.

107

"It did," he said, "didn't it?"

They both half-realized what they didn't dare to mean. That they had, in fact, come nearly as far as the last narrow bridge before the destination of love. And they bent their shoulders to this half-knowledge as if they were slipping into a knapsack.

PART THREE

One day at Paul's, and the stranger was spell-caught – or felt like flight. There were no diversions except the steeping primacy of woods, lake and fields; you were on your own. But you were continuously free to fit together the pure, unalloyed fabrics of Time, Place, and Sentience, as never before.

One day at Paul's, and you sensed the unspoken rule, based on one central fact. Each person is a twosome. Himself and the overriding concern with which he's in such constant dialogue that it becomes personified inside him. This was a place where the privacy of that twosome must be respected.

Mutual gravitations had come about: Kate, Morse and Paul, the one threesome; Sheila, Rex and Bruce, the other. But there was no general congregating. It was extraordinary how these two units managed to live in the same house and collide so rarely.

Sheila luxuriated in the feeling that all the involvements which used to besiege her in Greenwich had been stopped in their tracks at Endlaw's invisible borders. She felt saved from their destruction as eardrums are saved from destruction by the limit to which sound carries; if all the sounds in the world could reach them, they'd be crushed.

She wanted to spend the whole long, healing summer here. Rex did not. But all at once she was in command. For the first time Rex was faced with a rout of his mastery so incredible, so complete, so frightening, that he was willing to settle for whatever scrap of favour total surrender might win him.

There was a small valley between the ridge the house stood on and the woods. Sheila was sitting there now, on an old stone wall.

To walk places here was different than in any other place she'd ever been. You could sit down when you got there without its immediately being time to start back. Her thoughts pleasantly overlaid each other. She feared no disturbance. Rex had drunk too much the night before and now he was sleeping; sleep had lately become his favourite hiding place. And no one else was in sight. Her bemusedness was fixed on a cluster of ferns just beginning to uncurl at the tip.

She didn't see Bruce come out of the woods behind her until a glance of the sun caromed off his axe blade. He'd been blazing up

Paul's timber lines. It was as if Endlaw were an extension of Paul's person. He kept the lines around it as distinct as the lines round himself.

She pointed to the ferns.

"I've been fern-gazing," she said, mocking herself. "They're so much fresher than stars."

"More than that, you can eat them," he said. "I mean, when we were kids, we used to pull them up and eat the 'meat' in a little socket down by the root."

He pulled one and extracted the meat and gave it to her. She had never tasted anything so vividly itself. She was struck with one of those warningless moments when the simplest thing you look at is a miracle. The ferns were a miracle.

"I'm going in town for the mail," he said. "Have you got anything to post?"

"Yes," she said. "A letter to my mother. Would you mind?"

"Or maybe you'd like to come too," he said.

"Well. Yes," she said. "Yes, I would."

"What about Rex?" he said.

"He's sleeping," she said. "He had far too many last night."

"I noticed that," Bruce said. "When he came in to dinner."

Paul always kept enough tables set up that each guest could eat by himself if he so wished. Sheila had come in to dinner before Rex. He was finishing a bottle in their room. And when he did show up he chose the very farthest table from hers, sitting with his back toward her. Flaunting their quarrel, as usual, when his every other weapon had been bested.

Bruce had noticed the involuntary sigh threaten to bring the supports in her face down on themselves, like fire behind a wall; and then her face looking like a weather trying to clear up. And for some reason his own food, eaten at a table separate from the ill-starred one where she swallowed hers, had had a choking sullenness about it.

It unclenched the fist in Bruce, somehow, that Sheila remembered the exact spot on the road where he had promised to tell her about Molly and Peter.

"You promised you'd tell me about Molly and Peter," she said. "Remember?"

"Yes," he said. "But . . . can I? I can tell you what happened. But that's not it. It's the *way* things happen. And you'd have to know exactly what Molly and Peter were like. That's what I couldn't make clear."

"Try," she said. "Please."

He tried. He tried hard. And Molly he could make clear, because she was – well, Molly.

But how could you make Peter plain? He wasn't the kind of child that – well, anything. He tried to tell her about his totally separate faces. His bestowingly communicative one when every feature talked, seemed to keep touching you. And the lost one, with the smashing look in his eyes, that used to make Molly and him feel sick. Just plain sick. And they never had the slightest idea which face would be when. Nothing they tried could get near him when he had the lost face. Patience. Love. Pleading. Sympathy. Nothing. They never even knew if he knew that they loved him . . . You see? You couldn't do it. He just came out sounding like a child in a tantrum. But they weren't tantrum eyes. They weren't crazy eyes. Whatever else they were, they were a bewildered child's eyes too . . .

"Merciful God," he said, "what kind of a stinking setup is this living, anyway – that a look like that can get into a child's eyes? When you're just left to guess what . . . ?"

"Go on," she said quietly. "Bring it up. You've got to. Even if you have to stick a finger down the . . . gorge of your mind . . . to do it."

He slapped the wheel hard, the way you slap a face out of hysteria. And then he was quite calm. He began to draw out the facts as if they were nails.

The facts were quite simple.

Bruce had no classes that morning. He and Peter were going out in the country to get a Christmas tree. Peter was in one of his intensely communicative moods, almost underfoot. He was almost ashiver with obedience.

"Kids don't want to go near axes, do they, Bruce?" he said. "Only fathers have to handle an axe, don't they?"

"That's right," Bruce said.

He went outside to warm the car up and put the axe in the trunk. And when he came back it was Peter's other face that met him. What had happened to roil his eyes like that, or whether it was just some eruption from memory, he never knew.

"Oh, for God's sake," Bruce broke off, "let's leave it. Please."

Sheila touched his shoulder. "No," she said. "You've left it festering there too long now."

Peter's hands were grimy. He'd been helping his father clean the stovepipe that morning.

"Go wash your hands," Molly said to Peter. "Quick. Bruce is waiting."

112

"No," he said.

"Go wash your hands," Bruce commanded. Peter's sudden demolition of what had promised to be such a splendid morning touched him to rage. "Did you hear what your mother said?"

"You make me," Peter said.

Bruce swiped at him with his open hand. He didn't mean to strike Peter in the face, but that's where the blow caught him. The blow must have had more strength behind it than Bruce realized. It made a bright red mark on Peter's cheek.

Peter didn't budge. His eyes retreated a little, that was all.

Molly didn't say anything to Bruce, but she bent down and tucked Peter's hair up under his cap and he heard her whispering, "Please, Peter . . ." in a desperate undertone. "You mind Bruce, and maybe I'll go with you, and we'll all have fun. Eh?"

"That's right," Bruce said ," that's right. Humour him. Humour him. Whenever I try to . . ." He strode to the door. "Are you ready? If you are, come on."

"Just a minute till I get my coat," Molly said.

She got her coat and they went out on the front porch and Bruce locked the door.

"All right," Peter said. "I'll wash my hands."

"Not now you won't," Bruce said. "Do you think we've got all morning to fool with you?"

"It'd only take a minute," Molly said.

"Get in the car," Bruce said.

Peter went to the back door of the car.

"Get in the front," Bruce shouted.

"I want to ride in the back."

"And I said you're going to ride in the front."

He took him by the collar and shoved him into the front seat. Molly got in beside Peter.

She had to gather in the folds of her coat with one hand and close the door with the other. The door had a faulty catch. Bruce knew exactly how to manipulate it. Molly didn't. She had to slam the door three or four times before it stayed closed. Bruce offered her no help at all. He just sat there.

They drove off in complete silence.

Peter had a hole in his sweater. He put a finger in it, trying to make it bigger. Molly kept taking his hand away, surreptitiously, but each time he put it right back.

Bruce knew he was driving too fast. If he'd been in any other mood, Molly would have asked him to slow down. And he would have. She didn't say a word.

It happened at the bottom of the long, blind, icy hill. The car swerved sideways in a flash.

Molly didn't say a word. And Peter didn't either. But he looked at his father – and, if there'd been time, his other face would have come back: this is exciting, eh, Bruce?

There wasn't time. The streetcar was upon them.

Two minutes later and they'd have missed it. The time it takes to wash a kid's hands.

They struck on Molly's side. Bruce would never know whether the catch had been really tight or not. She was thrown out. And Peter with her . . .

"I don't think they screamed," Bruce said. "I don't know. I know they didn't make a sound afterwards. Molly was killed instantly. Peter wasn't. They took him to the hospital, but he never opened his eyes or spoke again." He slapped the wheel a second time. "The inquest summed it up very generously. 'No blame attached to any person.'"

Sheila didn't speak.

"So you see I got off absolutely scot-free," Bruce said.

"Don't," she said, against his tone. "Please. The jury was right. There *wasn't* any blame. No, now . . . wait. I can see why that doesn't make any difference. But don't . . ."

"How, then?" he said. "You tell me."

He looked at her and it seemed to be one of those moments when you can see exactly what people are made of.

"I can't," she said. "I thought if you heard yourself put the whole thing into words you could get on top of it somehow. I thought there'd be something *I* could say. But I was wrong. I can see now what you meant by the way it happened. It's one of those ways when nothing *can* be said." Anger suddenly lubricated her speech. "You know, I think there must be a special department somewhere in control of just those cases where nothing can be said. They put birthmarks on girls' faces. They have charge of idiocy . . . and child blindness . . . and . . . It's their job to plant the truly unburdenable secrets and crosses behind people's eyes. And when they see a blow like yours shaping up, they take care you don't catch it straight, so you can come to terms with it. It's their job to slip in that little piece of . . . grit . . . that makes it impossible to have it out with the thing. You get as far as that piece of grit and you're blocked. Oh, yes. You're exactly the kind they'd have in their books. The kind of person that . . . the way it happened . . . could really get at. They'd watch and wait. And when it was just . . . the way it was with you and Molly and Peter . . . they'd put that patch of ice right there . . ."

114

Others had shown him sympathy, but his trouble had never angered them. For some reason Bruce suddenly felt the car take on the qualities of a house. He seemed to step off the long November street that had been his only pathway for so long – like some street in a strange city where the storm-secret pools of hush floated the withered leaves that stirred breezlessly around the bases of the elms imprisoned in the sidewalks . . . and you outside the pulse of everything because yours was aimless Sunday wandering on a workday afternoon . . . and bearing a separate little bruise from each strange face you met.

"Do you know," he said, "you're the first person who's ever known why nothing could be said. The others all quoted. Time, the great healer. Life must go on . . . that stuff."

"I know," she said. "That pushbutton stuff. Operation Consolation. And Emergency Forgetting. Put it right out of your mind. Quickly, now. Quickly. Well, I could never see what's so damn brave and wonderful about forgetting. Yesterday. Ago. I don't think I'd want anyone to put me into those terrible attics right away. I'd want to stay 'now' with someone as long as my momentum lasted." She spoke very quietly. "No longer than it lasted naturally, though. Not a day longer than that."

"But Peter . . ." Bruce said. "Ten years old . . . I promised him once I'd bring him here. He'd have seen this sunshine."

"I know," she said. "That's all I can say, Bruce. I know. I know."

But thinking: It's still wrong, what you're doing. She knew what he was doing. He was making a career out of never signing a peace treaty with this thing. Rolling up his coastline. Drawing the hard straight core of himself in beyond touch. Refusing the blindfold. Scorning his captors with the look that locks sight's door on them. Stripping himself to one feature – that one burning, eye-narrowed, lip-tight feature of living on because, breathing, you must. Living on, but choosing nothing beyond subsistence, for to choose is to admit the choice's mastery . . .

But that was wrong. That was the very defiance that came to the most ironic ending, that took the course you least foresaw. She knew how they put the grit in that too. You *can't* go into bankruptcy like that. Even the stubbornest heart has to eat. It has its little light bills and water bills. And if it's earning nothing, they must come out of capital. And you shrink and shrink . . . You don't turn solid at all, you just go jumpy and starting at echoes. And after a while the mirror no longer gives you back the one imperious feature you started out with and search for. All you see is a plaintive eye . . . And before too long you lose your audience. People don't come knocking many times without response before they

115

decide that no one's home. They go away for good. You'd never realized how much your scorn depended on their audience at it, but you know it now . . . You've become a nobody . . . And then one day some man who's quite forgotten all the wherefore of your abdication, or never knew it, gives you the look he gives a simple nobody and before you think, you think: That upstart! If it hadn't been for . . . I could have outstripped him so damn far . . .

And then one final day the very inconceivable happens. You lose the last audience of all – the audience in your own heart. For – ah, yes – they know how to turn the platitudes against you too. Time does heal. The very reason for the whole thing suddenly loses its features. No face. No eye. No *ear*. And then you're left with nothing but waste, waste, waste . . . and nothing listening at all . . .

"Don't lean against the door," Bruce said.

His right hand moved to check the catch.

But you didn't check the catch for Molly and Peter, did you? something said. His hand stopped. For a moment he hated Sheila.

She checked the door herself.

"It's all right," she said.

He glanced at her and her eyes looked homeless with fighting not to cry. He didn't hate her any more. He was once more back on the long November street but, with her face beside him, for the first time the other faces didn't leave a bruise.

"Bruce," Sheila said, "I want to help you . . . if that's any help."

And for the first time he wanted to help someone help him.

CHAPTER 15

Kate was nearly happy.

Nights, sometimes, the ghosts came. And even in the daytime, even in the wide, bandaging peace of Endlaw, the old sadness sometimes sprang its frightening trap door.

But in the daytime, with Morse and Paul, her sadness was not ghostly but fleshly. She felt as if, with the kneejerk of some blindfold will, she had leapt from the quicksands of an illness as mesmeric as freezing in the snow, and miraculously landed on her feet. On firm high ground. One week more in Halifax, one day more, and she knew the quicksands would have claimed her.

She found that Morse *had* changed. He was grosser. Touchier. More outrageous. "Aaaaaah, the hell with it" was his most habitual stance. It was hard to tell whether he was readier to be sardonically fisted against life or himself. But he was the kind of man whose given self survives all its own changes.

And he rejoiced to see her. She was sure of that. On first sight of each other, their presences had instantly aligned themselves to their old orbits; felt their dormancies as instantly awakened as if the time between this meeting and their last had not been five years but five days.

And his blasphemous touch on her heartsoreness cauterized her as no suction of coddling could have done.

"You know what you have to watch out for, don't you," he told her. "Once you get the barb out, fiddling with it. Still testing to see if you can still draw blood on yourself with it. All women are great for that."

The case with Paul was different.

She could see no change in him whatsoever. She had never known anyone so consistently his quintessential self. From time to time she thought she noticed little catnaps of abstraction in the face whose symptomatic outwardness used to be as irreversible as a gun emplacement's – but the grin would quickly erase them. Her presence, coming into the field of his, was like an organism coming into its optimum climate.

The noon Paul left for Montreal, the three of them sat out his remaining minutes in the big room facing the lake. The room where they had sat together on Kate's last day five years ago.

The room was exactly the same. The lake hadn't aged a second. The whole thing was like one of those performances wherein the curtain has been momentarily lowered to mark the passage of time and the make-up man works fast. They still had that extraordinary three-way ease with each other that bridges absence with the first returning glance. Time's make-up man had made them no more strangers to each other than the actors'. Like actors they still cued each other.

And yet it was not quite the same play.

"Ryes to the wry," Morse said, distributing the second round of drinks.

"Well, anyway, we're not drinking our wry alone," Kate said. "That's the worst kind of solitary drinking there is."

"I know," Morse said. "But what's come over us? We used to pitch it straight. Now we seem to have to put that wry twist on everything we say. Like a spitball."

"Paul's not wry," Kate said.

"No," Morse said. "Look at him. Grinning. Old Foxy Loxy. You

117

know, it never ceases to puzzle me, Paul, why a guy as whole as you surrounds himself with such a nest of amputees. Oh yes, you do. The old Pied Piper. You know the kind of people this cave beckons. People whose sky has fallen. Whose mainspring has snapped. And still you pipe them in. Is it sadism – do you like to watch them squirm? Or is it fraternity? Have you had some secret loss yourself that makes you feel a brotherhood with other amputees?"

"You're an amputee?" Paul said, sidestepping.

"Of course," Morse said. "Every damn one of us is, in one way or another. I'll show you. Let's tick them off. Kate, what have you lost? In one word, please. Anything that doesn't fit into a single word is no loss at all."

"Well . . . youth," Kate said. "I mean, I can hardly claim anything exceptional about that, but – "

"Never mind the qualifications," Morse cut in. "You had the word right on the end of your tongue. That's the test."

"And you?" Kate said.

"Talent," he said. "You might say that too is the lot of everyone sooner or later, but –"

"One word," Kate reprimanded him.

"All right," Morse said. "And Sheila?" He turned to Kate. "I'll let you pronounce on that. I seem to rub her ulcer the wrong way. I don't want to seem prejudiced."

Kate could see Sheila and Rex sitting together at the side of the lake. They didn't look like two people fused by a mutual gaze at water. They looked like a couple in a train seat, one *accompanying* the other on what may be his sorrowful or dangerous journey.

"Love," Kate said. "I'd say she'd lost love."

"That's a dandy," Morse said. "That qualifies. And Rex – if anyone cares?"

"I don't know," Paul said. "Self-esteem? Self-respect? Whatever you want to call it."

"And Bruce?" Morse said.

They could see Bruce working up the garden spot. Whenever he paused, he still looked thought-stoppingly at the earth instead of thoughtlessly at the sky.

"That's easy," Paul said. "His family. Their *lives*. I told you Letty's sister-in-law tracked down his whole story, car accident and all. So," he added quickly, "we're down to Letty, eh? And, God love her, I don't think she's ever lost a thing. She's one of the few people I've ever seen that time didn't turn porous and leaky. I think the juices she lives by were sealed up tight in her at birth, like a Rolls-Royce engine."

"Oh no, my friend," Morse said, "we're not down to Letty. And don't try to use her for a red herring. We're down to you. Now what have you lost? One word, remember. I got you there. Let's see you try any sidestepping inside one word."

"Identity," Paul said.

"Identity!" Morse exclaimed. "What the hell kind of an answer is that? Say life's whole eternal landscape was spired here and there with little steeples of special individuality, as I like to fancy its being . . . and say I was a junior angel cruising around, way up in the blue. I could pick out Leonardo's and Caesar's and Dostoevski's – and yours, in a minute."

"But I couldn't, myself," Paul said. "There's the difference. Or if you don't like 'identity,' how about 'everything'?"

Morse gave him a mock-scornful stare, as if this was too foolish a suggestion for reply.

Paul glanced at his watch.

"Ten minutes and I've got to go," he said.

He got up and set his glass on the table. And when he did, his face looked as if all at once it had collided with itself. Its sentinels seemed to rush inward to meet some surprise blow behind the gates and leave the bastion of his features standing there unmanned.

"Paul!" Kate said. "You look dreadful. Are you sick?"

The thrust of pain was only momentary and his colour came back. He parodied the boy at Ratisbon.

" 'Sick, sir? Smiling, the boy fell dead.' No," he said, grinning. "It's a slight case of the bends, that's all. I surfaced from all that deep talk too fast." He spoke quickly, to shunt them off. "You know, Morse had something, right there at the beginning. God help us, this is *morning* talk? It's not like smoking your cigarette before breakfast but eating it, isn't it?"

"You wouldn't care to tell us anything *about* this Montreal trip, would you?" Kate said.

If I could! was Paul's immediate thought. Each time he looked at her he loved her beyond what, the time before, he'd thought was the limit. But his boundaries as instantly drew maps of themselves before his eyes. Their ink was stained in now.

"Him?" Morse said. "Enigmatic old Papa Lisa? But *I* know what's behind it. It's the Old Adam. I suspect that's the way he's always fed his libido. À la carte. Any other way he might get involved with someone."

Paul just grinned.

"It's only for a week," he said. "You'll manage. Letty knows your feeding habits. The Giornos have caught onto the rules here: Speak when you're spoken to. And I'm sure Bruce won't

119

crowd you. Did you ever notice Bruce? He seems to have a clot in his speech stream. One minute smooth as anything, and the next minute it blocks the whole main artery."

Kate thought of Paul packing his bag alone. With no one there to take away that sudden and terrible muteness from the personal belongings he gathered up. There was something about packing your bag alone that . . .

"I know we'll manage," she said. "But we'll miss you."

"Not really," Paul said. "What's Boyle's Law for psychophysics? A body weighed in absence suffers a loss of weight equal to the weight of its own volume of . . ?"

"Bullshit!" Morse supplied.

He had a sentiment about Paul's leaving as deep as Kate's and sentiment always turned him savage. Paul laughed.

"And what," Morse said, "if this lovely, pure, clannish amputee strain gets some horrible infestation while you're gone? How do we know Bruce won't let in some hearty bastard – or, grislier yet, the perfect lady?"

"All right," Paul said. "I'll leave the booking up to you. Take no one in that I wouldn't."

"But what's your litmus?" Kate said. "What's your sieve?"

"I don't know, exactly," Paul said. "But I'd beware of anyone that has what Letty calls a 'bold' look."

"You mean it?" Morse said. "I can handle these customers my own way? My God, that's wonderful. I've always longed to pull a flensing knife on some of these patronizing, hidebound specimens that descend on your summer hotels."

Kate recognized the strident clowning so often touched off in him now. She didn't know if she deplored it or not. What had turned him into such a wrecking ball?

"Come on," Morse said to Paul. "Try me out. *Be* somebody, looking for a room."

Pallor, like a flicker of dying lightning, echoed in Paul's face for a second; but he quickly turned his back to them and did the impersonator's thing with his coat collar and when he swung around he was Babbitt to the heels.

"Enright here," he said, clearing his throat. "Warren Enright. Maybe you know the name. Enright Tiles. Appliances . . . Not a bad place you have here. Ground floor room, eh? Bags in the car. It pans out, might stay a week, ten days. Looks like just the change I need. Fresh air, simple life, simple people . . ."

Morse shook his head commiseratively.

"I wish I could," he said. "Myself it's okay. But I run a hotel. Someone suspects. Someone complains. You lose control maybe . . ."

120

"What are you trying to get through you?" Paul said.

"Don't make me put it into words, fella," Morse said absolutely gently. "You've read *Death in Venice*. Well, I have too. Let's just let it go at that."

"Me?" Paul said. "I look like someone reads detective stories?"
Morse smiled.

"It's no good, fella. You see, I wasn't always an innkeeper. I'm an unfrocked psychiatrist. I recognized the signs the minute you stepped through that door. Don't think I don't sympathize. It's just a disease, and fifty years from now everyone will see that. Fifty years from now and you could walk in here with a boy on each arm and no one'd turn a hair, but right now . . . Well, I run a hotel."

"Why, you – " Paul said.

"Go right ahead," Morse said. "Get it out of your system. I told you. I sympathize . . . I sympathize . . ."

Paul grinned: himself. He looked all around.

"He's gone," he said.

It wasn't quite on the note of their old nonsense, somehow. There was something forced about it. But Kate felt the driving urge to show Morse she could imitate the pace of any mood he set.

She moved up to him: the perfect lady, floating on the graciousness of her own smile.

"Good morning," she said, offering him the tips of her fingers. "You're the proprietor? I'm Mrs Wattlebrisket. I wrote to you about coming here, but there was no answer."

She kept two little parentheses of the smile expectant at the corners of her lips.

"Oh, yes," Morse said. "Yes. Mrs Wattlebrisket. You wanted the housemaid's post. Well, we like someone a good deal younger as a rule. But what's your experience? You've done this all your life?"

Kate released a little pear-shaped balloon of laughter. She wriggled a coy forefinger at him.

"Now, now," she said. "I know you. They warned me you'd have your little joke. You know quite well who I am. Mrs Roger J. Wattlebrisket. And I do hope you can squeeze me in. This place is so, I don't know, so . . . and yet it's so *homey*."

"That's right," Morse said. "One big happy family. And that's the way we try to keep it. Now, I know you're a broad-minded woman, Mrs W." —Kate looked modest and arch at the same time – "so if you'll just sit down, we'll run you through this little questionnaire we winnow out the shnooks with. It'll only take a minute." He looked her sternly in the eye. "Such dignity! Have you never, *ever*, winkled that lint out of your belly button with a hairpin?"

Kate recoiled, clutching at an imaginary stole.

121

"Uh uh, Mrs W.!" Morse said. "Watch those dewlaps. They're starting to tumefy. And do you think you could do something about that handshake? It looks exactly like someone picking up catshit with a cloth."

Letty's three peremptory blasts on the horn scythed across the bursts of mirth on their faces.

Morse winked at Kate.

"Let's follow them," he said. "Maybe they're eloping. Wouldn't you like us to see you off, Paul?"

"No," Paul said.

"Thanks," Morse said. "Well, *may* we come, then?"

"No," Paul said. "All railway stations are like graveyards. Please don't move. As Letty says, 'I'd rather remember you the way I saw you last.'"

They didn't move. It was odd the way they obeyed the letter of his words, in whatever tone of frivolity they were delivered. Some iron will they sensed behind them they never questioned or over-rode.

Their nonsense dried up the moment Paul left the room. He was the sort of person whose leaving vitiates the prevailing mood through and through, so that for a moment conversation has, unaccountably, to fall back on the starkest matter-of-fact. The space in the room was full of the moth holes of where his body had stood.

They watched him walk out to the car. He was the sort of person who, silent and from a distance, looks so vulnerably little indicative of himself. He was the sort of person who, whenever he left, left you with the feeling that you should overtake him *yet* and present him with some parting word you'd failed to make the perfect one at the door.

Morse and Kate were twice awkward with each other because, now they were alone, their differing sex broke surface on them like an obtrusive feature.

"Do you notice the way Paul loses colour sometimes?" Kate said anxiously. "Twice this morning. Do you think he might be sick?"

"Sick?" Morse said. "Paul? You think he'd allow a trespass like that? And now just when you've got yourself nicely sutured up after that business with your father, for God's sake don't start looking for something else to bleed about."

His voice changed abruptly. At once pensive and sniffing at its own pensiveness.

"Did you ever think," he said, "there should be some kind of hawker tagging along with Paul everywhere he goes to proclaim what a special guy he is? Strangers never guessing it!"

"That's exactly what I was just thinking," she said. "And I was thinking too . . ." She pointed to Bruce and the Giornos. "Look at them. What earthly use are they making of being young?"

"You're jealous of the young?" he said. "But think how much wiser you are."

"Does wisdom make up for anything?"

"It's a cud," he said. "And what would us ruminant old bison do without our cuds?" He grimaced. "Aaaaah. Paul was right. Talking does leave a nasty taste in your mouth, doesn't it? What do you say we break it off and go fishing? You see the inlet there. We could follow it up to the stillwaters and try for some trout."

"I'd love it," she said. "Yes, let's. I'll go change."

She hurried up the stairs. For once she did not hear her cautionary self whisper "Poor foolish Kate." On precisely the sixth step she had one of those unheralded little sunbursts of consciousness that seem to unload a cargo of life and light at the exact physical centre of the heart. A paraphrase of the words she'd just spoken made a kind of childish roundelay in her head.

"I'm going to change . . . I'm going to change . . . I'm going to change . . ."

CHAPTER 16

Some mornings Rex awoke as if their love was right back at the beginning.

They awoke that morning, touching only where the trespassing positions of sleep had not yet been retracted; but Sheila could feel the cloud of his sensuality bending over her.

Rex felt aggrandized, as always, with physical lust. And as perennially incredulous that the arid peaks of interim living could ever again assert themselves through this transfiguring mist that was always on tap inside you at no more effort or cost than a touch. To look at Sheila's eyes and her hair and her lips, there was something in them just beyond reach. A thump of ravenousness sounded in him, to devour in the only way possible all that was elusive the whole length and circuit of her flesh.

His hands started their conversation with her body, their language expressive beyond any possible speech, always to be relied on for the exact translation of whatever could not be put into words.

For the first incredulous time, Sheila felt nothing of her usual response. His touch was no more kindling than if climax had already neutralized it. She didn't even feel victory.

Springing from the tips of his fingers wherever they touched her flesh, Rex felt the gross glory slide through all his limbs. He was narcissistically half-fascinated by the jungle of coarseness of his own members in their dark thundercloud of body hair; self-touchingly apologetic to Sheila for having been helplessly given them that way. And yet obscurely proud and masterful in the very apology for this, as for any, masculine grossness that must be tempered not to be the equipment of ravage. He was half wonder-struck, as he had always been, that this lubberly growth of his should be the instrument of wreaking such an exquisite refinement of tenderness on them both.

Gently (for in this thing alone was he never reckless or without consideration) he began the first locking movements.

Sheila disengaged herself deftly, as when you invent a mission elsewhere to disengage the confidential drinker's arm from your shoulder. She slipped out of bed and went to the window. She let up the blind and stood looking out.

"It's another fine day, Rex!" she said. "You know, I don't believe it *can* rain here."

"Now just a minute," he said. "Since when have we had to check with the weather bureau before we. . . ? Come back here."

"Let's get dressed," she said. "I can't wait to get down by the lake."

He sprang naked from the bed and made as if to abduct her.

"Rex!" she said, laughing, trying to divert the whole thing into a joke. "Get away from that window. Letty's hanging out clothes right down there. And what if Kate Fennison should come around the corner?"

"Hi, Letty!" Rex called gaily. "Put your old clothespin on this. Wouldn't that be something! Me and old Letty!"

"Rex!"

"Hi, Kate, old girl," he called to an imaginary Kate. "Take a good look at what you've been missing all your life. You know what I ought to do? I should call old Kate up here and show her what it's all about. Seems a damn shame for anyone to go wanting when I've got plenty for everyone."

It was an odd thing about Rex that he was almost never vulgar. Not that he censured ribaldry in anyone else; but he himself simply had no enterprise for it. He didn't even have a favourite dirty joke. Sheila was curiously embarrassed by this uncustomary coarseness now.

"You believe in obliging?" she said.

"Welllll . . ." he said, ". . . we mustn't be selfish, you know."

"I gather you've never been exactly selfish in that respect," she said.

"Nnn-no," he said. "Not exactly. Of course you can't help missing a few of 'em."

These glib fragments of insinuation about his prowess with other women used to sting like shot. And he knew this. He used it as the infallible lever against all her serious resistances. Not in any mean or punitive fashion, but as a child delights in playing some indomitable trump that will make you laugh at the utter collapse of your own cards.

But now her flesh shed his insinuations like any other spatter of words. His rakishness has never been anything but a bluff, she thought. And I've picked up his cards now. *I* have the trump. But she didn't feel like testing its power. She didn't feel anything at all. Not even the joy of deliverance.

Rex sensed his defeat.

"Come on," he said, moving back toward the bed. "We'll do it in Macy's window some other time."

But the gauging glance he gave her betrayed the crack in his confidence. He had never had to check on his effects before. They had always been certain.

She pointed to his nakedness.

"Really, dear," she said, still trying to ward the whole thing off by converting him to its comic aspect, "you *have* gone to great length about this, haven't you. And I *am* impressed. But let's save it for a rainy day, eh?"

"Rainy day, hell!" he said. "When I haven't got lots more saved up for a rainy day . . . well, that'll be the rainy day!"

He started to pick her up in his arms again. Again she disengaged herself, this time less casually.

He sat down on the side of the bed. His face looks shoved, she thought; as if in her new detachment she was writing a description of him. That noose whose slightest tautening used to bring me to heel, I wonder if he knows I've slipped out of it completely.

He did. He sat there, who had never given savings a moment's thought, and knew the robbed miser's agony. The floorboards were up. His life's hoard had vanished.

He began to dress. As always, the first thing he covered was his disfigured foot.

"There's another thing," he said, in an entirely different tone. "Don't you think it's time we started a family? Every man wants

125

a kid. This is some kind of a second honeymoon . . . why wouldn't it be a good time to get things rolling?"

That nearly did capsize her detachment. Here was the final irony. What would she have given to have heard him speak those words . . . five years ago . . . five months ago? She had thought of this child from the very first, roaming lost in the unrealized. Now, strangely enough, the only child that had any place in her thoughts was Bruce's Peter.

She began to pull on her clothes quickly, as if this body-mask could serve as a face-mask too.

"We had a son," Rex said, "it'd be kind of like making the rounds all over again, ourselves. And maybe you could stand *me* better if we had a kid to show for it."

Detachment grimaced in incredulity again.

This was Rex talking? Who had never associated children with love in any way except as love's incongruous accident? Who'd had no more feeling about that contingency of sex than you have for the contingent glass you drink the wine from? He had never been able to understand that love was not a quantitative thing. That what love she gave a child wouldn't leave that much less for him. He himself could give to the limit or take to the limit; but sharing was a poky, puttery thing he was quite uncapable of. He might give a child his bread or his shoes, but never any particle of himself or of her.

This was Rex, of all people, come around to the triteness of vicarious living in a son? Who could no more have abdicated centre stage in favour even of a blood heir than he could have gelded himself?

She looked at his handsome shoved face.

Yes, it was true. This was Rex, who could always slip out of any desperate knot she tried to bind him with, with the single magician's shrug – delivered to her now, bound and captive, by his own attempt to bind *her* with a child.

She glanced at him again. Or . . . she had an absurd fancy that this was just someone who looked like Rex.

He tried again.

"It'd only take a minute," he said – making a stab at the old careless charm that fails like nothing else the instant it begins to imitate itself. "Now, tell me . . . what else could we accomplish in a minute's time – as big as that?"

"Nothing, probably," she said. "It *is* rather miraculous. But . . . 'accomplish'? Isn't that a big word to use before breakfast, dear? Let's just *do* things till we have our coffee anyway. Eh?"

"All right," he said, suddenly angered. "If you want to do something, how would you like to . . . go to hell?"

"Hell?" she said. "This lovely morning? Now, Rex, please. It'd be *so* much nicer down by the lake."

His smile was the momentary one that can sometimes be tricked out of an angry child even though your trick may increase his anger immediately afterward. The shoved look came back, intensified, into his face.

All at once he passed a hand over his forehead.

"I've got the damnedest headache," he said.

She had to smile then.

Of all the illnesses for him to fabricate. Some bright, red, gashing one maybe – but you could no more associate Rex with a grubby, oatmealish thing like headache than you could picture Yogi Berra tatting doilies.

He's trying everything, she thought. Seduction. Binding. And now courting pity for the first fake infirmity that comes into his mind, like a child.

"I'm sorry, dear," she said lightly. "But that's all the more reason for prescribing the lake. The fresh air will do your headache good."

"A hell of a lot you care," he said, almost beseeching contradiction.

She didn't contradict him.

He couldn't believe that her silence was letting that pitch go by default.

She felt nothing but a vague distaste that his nails were none too clean.

It was wonderfully pleasant by the lake. The gentle suction of the water and the stillness and the distances were as soothing as compress on a sprain. She let her mind put on its hat and wander where it would.

And for once Rex was quiet beside her. She had taught herself to luxuriate in these quiet times without speculating how briefly they might last.

She saw Bruce working in the garden. Distance made a robot of him, his motions meaningless. And with himself so seen, the disturbing confidences he had made to her were detached from him and mapped themselves over everything close at hand. She gazed at them on the deep, glittering, sun-scaled water.

Rex moved soon enough.

"Well," he said, standing up, "I guess we've seen everything there is to see here, haven't we?"

Her thoughts instantly drew in their nets and stacked them. ("What time is it?" the visiting child asks an hour after breakfast, and you can tell that the distractions you'd counted on lasting him till nightfall are already used up.)

"What do you want to do?" she said.

"What *is* there to do?" he said. "Unless . . . how's about going over and giving friend Bruce a hand with the digging?"

Nothing could have been more totally unexpected. Just when you were sure you knew him inside out, you found you couldn't predict him at all. Just when he had a *right* to be grudging, he was suddenly magnanimous.

That's it, she thought. He's surprised him*self* with the idea of magnanimity and then instantly warmed up to it. He'll fall all over himself now to be forebearing. He's really trying everything.

"What about your headache?" she said.

"It's gone!" he exclaimed, as guilelessly as if he had indeed just made that startling discovery.

He gave her a hand-up from the rock she was sitting on and led the way up the sloping path. She wondered for what obsessive reason Paul's feet had so often trodden it as to make it absolutely smooth.

"You know, dear," he said enthusiastically, "maybe you're right about the country. It might be just the thing for us."

She recognized the mood. This "dear" was a kind of beaming nickname he gave her whenever his mind thought it had broken out into a clearing. She had a picture of his giving the country's shoulder a quick chummy squeeze.

"Why wouldn't it be a good idea . . . I think it'd be a hell of a good idea . . . to get our*selves* a farm somewhere? I love outdoor work." She had to smile. "And your own boss? Tell anyone you like to go to hell? I know they say farms don't pay. How could they . . . the way these characters run them now? Everyone raising the same thing everyone else raises. But we could go in for something different . . . pheasants, or something. How much did your mother pay for those two pheasants we had last Thanksgiving? Twenty dollars, wasn't it? And how much does a pheasant egg cost? Let's say twenty cents. Now how could anyone go wrong on a deal like that?"

"They get nits in their ears," she said. "Ask Victor Borge. Now there's an idea. Maybe we could rent the first setting of eggs from him."

"All right," he said, "laugh."

But he wasn't really put off. For the moment he had his future unassailably made.

Sheila saw Morse and Kate start down the path with their fishing rods.

Damn it, she thought. One minute later and we'd have missed them. As it was, they'd meet right in the teeth.

She didn't know why, but "meeting him in the teeth" seemed to describe exactly the chancest encounter with Morse. There seemed to be something spoiling inside him in both senses of the word: tainting and belligerent. The first moment in his company and she started to wonder how soon something savage would happen. And that hectic profanity, wrapping a stone in the simplest remark he threw out: how could Kate stand it all the time?

Rex quickened his pace, *not* to miss them. She had the sinking clairvoyance she always had whenever Rex's naïvete was about to lay him open to the swipe of someone's tongue. He would unwittingly say something to stir Morse up. Morse would slash back. And then . . .

Rex launched the greeting entirely toward Morse, as if they were heads of tribes: leaving the women no opening except to smile shadowy acknowledgement of each other's presence. He pointed to Morse's fishing rod.

"So this is the way you writers work!" he said, with a jocosity he could never pilot. "Pretty soft, eh? I've a good mind to take up writing myself."

"A good *mind* to . . ." Morse said. He frowned a moment. Then brightened. "Of course!" he said "It's a sort of pun, isn't it!"

Rex didn't get the gibe at all. He laughed.

But the moment Morse spoke, Sheila's detachment fell flat. She had the instant of falling in hate (with him) that can in its own way be as vivifying as the instant of falling in love. It was so intense it was almost an emotion of ennoblement.

"No," Rex said, "but I always thought I *would* like to write a book."

"Why not do it then?" Morse said. "This very day. No time like the present." He launched into the free association that could be so curiously insulting. "Or are you a disciple of Proust and his *temps perdu*? Tell me, sir, are you the Purdue type, or the Yale?"

Rex kept laughing off his perplexity, over-emphatically, like a child.

"Naaah," he said, "I guess I'd never have the patience to be a writer. But, no kidding, what's your secret? How do you go about it?"

"No secret," Morse said. "Just write what you know . . . if anything. Just get hold of some old truss straps and harness yourself to your desk every day . . . and sit there, as you would on a toilet, until you have a satisfactory literary movement. Keep regular, as the ad says. That's the whole secret."

Sheila laughed lightly. Her platinum Greenwich laugh that no mere coarse-grained man was armoured against. For once riotously thankful to find it a weapon in her possession for the defence of someone less subtly schooled than she in skirmishes like this.

"But that writer's harness," she said. "Isn't it something rather more womanish – like an apron tie? It seems to me that any writer I've ever *seen* is continually overacting his manliness for having been caught out, so to speak, in an apron."

Morse gave her his feral smile.

"My dear Jane Carlyle," he said, "how the hell are we going to keep this conversation going if you insist on delivering curtain lines?" He turned to Rex. "Another thing, chum. A writer has to make very sure he has the right kind of wife. You know how it is with wives. Half of them are a pollywog's nest of jellied sensibility. And it's easy enough to spell out the other half. The basic syllable is 'itch.' Some take a 'w' in front of it. Some – 'b'."

Rex was still in the dark. But he still thought he was a real co-partner in the juggler's act of sophisticated conversation.

"No kidding, though," he said again, "you and I ought to get together sometime. I'll bet I've got all kinds of stories you could use." He winked. "I've been around. I know a thing or two."

Morse shook his head. "Sorry, old boy," he said. "Three's the absolute minimum."

You bastard, Sheila thought, speaking that word for the first time out loud in her mind. You're enjoying this slaughter. One letter and you can change "laughter" into "slaughter." Anyone cornered to act like that, yes. But you're delighting in it for its own sake. There's something sick about that.

Rex's laughter had become wobblier, but he was still game.

"While I think of it," he said – and Sheila knew instinctively that whatever was coming would be tactless to the point of virtuosity – "if we could dig up one of your books somewhere, would you stick your name in the front of it for us?"

"I will," Morse said eagerly. "I will. And I'll put: 'To Rex, who asked for it – as always.'"

It was hard to tell if he was really rancorous or just flailingly drunk. Sheila smiled.

"Darling," she said gently to Rex, "can't you see Morse thinks his writing was an unfortunate blunder? Don't ask him for an autograph. Who wants to endorse his own juvenile indiscretions?"

"Ah," Morse said to her, "but I see you've been reading my books nevertheless. Where else but from my faithfully rendered heroines could you have picked up that Xanthippe accent so perfectly?"

Sheila laughed.

"No, Morse," she said, "I'm afraid I know nothing at all about your work. You see, I have very little taste or time for light fiction.

And whenever one of your books did come out there always seemed to be a Hemingway . . . or a Faulkner . . . or something such that one *must* read . . ."

She turned abruptly to Kate – suddenly hating her too, despite her innocence, for the mere complicity of being in Morse's company and in the hearing of Rex's humiliation.

"And how are you getting on without your father?" she said. "I know how uncommonly devoted you were to each other. And I'm sure you must be . . . desperately" – she glanced at Morse to have the adverb say : desperately indeed, to choose such a companion – "lonely without him."

Kate hadn't spoken a word. Now she let her presence surface for a moment – like a benign First Lady of the theatre discovered in the audience to some charity entertainment and responding to the spotlight thrown on her with a benedictory bow – and then withdrew it.

"I do miss him," she said gently. "And it makes me sad to think he couldn't have known you and Rex. Such a bright young woman and such a" – she just perceptibly hesitated – "nice-looking young man."

Rex got that much. She was laughing at him. Even that starved old maid thought his looks were . . . a joke. A joke!

There was an uneasy silence.

"All around the vinegar jug . . ." Morse began to hum, tapping his foot to the tune.

CHAPTER 17

A flood of anger, receding in Sheila, never rinsed her clean. Its flotsam clung to the basin of her consciousness.

If it hadn't been for Rex . . . she thought now, as they walked away from Morse and Kate. I wouldn't have got into any trouble with them myself. I'd never get into trouble like that with people if it weren't for Rex.

It was the first time she'd ever had such a thought, explicitly. No matter what her own exasperation with him before, the moment he was attacked by anyone else it had seemed unquestionably right for her to defend him. They were using a superficial dictionary to translate him. They looked up "brash" and it gave them "loutish." She alone had the dictionary that gave his valid meanings.

Now – and the thought unnerved her as the detachment hadn't – she wondered if hers could be the false one. She had a sudden dead weariness of having always to run interference for him. And as if the two appliances of age and dismay had been plugged into the current of her mind at the same moment, so that its lights dipped almost to blackout, she saw the future with him like some winter that lasts and lasts like a cooking failure you can't get eaten up.

The supervising April sun, localized in this one place, leaned down from the sky to houseclean the dropsical earth.

It blew its drying breath gently onto the house and the trees and the lake and the road. Growth moved imperceptibly upward as if springing back from a light footfall. The sun polished every blade of green with the glister of a child's eye and turned things around face-to. It touched eyes and hands, assigning them the task of opening up the closets of the heart and mind to the fresh linen air.

This was that once in the year when the death mask of each thing's self-blinding privacy is suspended. That once in a year when the soundproofing between the tenses is lifted and you can listen exactly to yesterday or now or tomorrow according to your state of mind.

Bruce was expertly clouting into fragments each lump of earth his spade turned. His eyes were dense and somehow wistful as a round stone with preoccupation.

But, fluent in the earth, he had the true countryman's rock-bottom sturdiness and masculinity that no other can match. Men like Morse, seasoned in glibber fields, might worst him in a fist fight, out-endure him, out-venture him, out-blaspheme him, be like flint where he might have to cry . . . and yet, beside him, stay the petticoat.

Looking at Bruce, Sheila felt Morse's taunts thin to nothing.

It didn't surprise her that Rex greeted Bruce with an almost storming intimacy. After a snub he always greeted the next person he met as if here was the one whose nothing less than constitutive friendship his eyes had just been opened to.

"Look," he said, "you've been banging away at this all morning. Let me take the spade for a while. Have yourself a breather. I love this kind of work, y'know."

He reached for the spade as if he'd just discovered his life's calling.

"What about your shoes?" Bruce said. They were heavy shoes, stylistically rustic; but the solid ground, facing down their idiomatic pretence, made them look as ridiculous as pumps. "Do you want to change with me?"

"Okay," Rex said, as brightheartedly as a child exchanging garments with his pal. "Fine."

Then, the moment he stooped to undress his broken foot Bruce saw his hands go irresolute.

"What size do you wear?" Bruce said quickly.

"Eights."

"Oh God," Bruce said, taking him off the hook, "I couldn't get my big toe into eights."

Rex straightened up. "Aaaah," he said. "It won't hurt these shoes, anyway. That's what they're for."

It came wrong for him to use his good foot on the spade, and he couldn't use the broken one without fumbling. He didn't want them to see that.

"Look, Bruce," he said, "you're working uphill this way. I'm going to the other end of the field and work down."

Bruce and Sheila kept a mutual, though not a tacit, silence until he was out of hearing.

"*Your* shoes," Bruce said then.

She moved back from the loam to the clean sod as if he had accused her.

"Cigarette?" he said.

"All right," she said. "I don't usually smoke in the morning, but all right."

She cupped her hands lightly next his to shield the match flame. There was an odd wariness between them, in exact antithesis to the wariness of suspicion. They might have been those two characters in a play who the audience realizes, long before themselves do, are slated to fall in love. The grip on their cigarettes – though neither realized that, either – was constraint's invariable reflex to grip something, anything, corporeal.

"Are you getting bored here?" Bruce said.

"Bored?" she said. "No. You mean, because I'm not charging around *doing* things? No, I don't see it that way. Most people think nothing ever happens unless they're trumpeting around giving all the verbs a whirl – Places! Camera! Action! I don't. I mean it. The only events that matter are the ones that take place inside you. And nine times out of ten when they come over you you're still as a telegraph pole."

She did mean it. Real events weren't verbs at all, they were phrases. She thought of them as heralded by a little premonitory dazzle, like when you first turned the television set on, and then some striking picture of truth or feeling falling into place. The most eventful lives of all might well be those that had the most little phrase-dazzles like that in them, though not a muscle was moving.

And what flashed them on? Hardly ever the rat-a-tat and the verbs. Some line on a page. Some glimpse. Some glance. Some echo in the mind. Some quality of stillness . . . The way this April sun demonstrated all geometry in its shadow patterns on this ground.

"In Greenwich this morning," Bruce said, "what would you be doing?"

"You'd really like to know?" she said. "Or is that a trick question? I know your sentiments about Greenwich."

He'd really like to know.

Well, to give him the whole damning picture from way back:

Their family had always had enough money to maintain itself at the tenth remove from anything noisy. Their house had once had its picture in a *Previews* brochure. Her father was maybe just a bit the ghost of Brooks Brothers Past and her mother had maybe just a bit the Dresden air about her of a Mary Petty drawing. But, God love them, that didn't mean they were in any way formidable. Nor was the set they moved in anything like the squalid rich's, with its hectic shenanigans and fashionable adulteries.

They had travelled a lot together. She was the single room adjoining the double, the table setting waiters were always adding to the two-seaters or taking away from the four-seaters in all those summer hotels. It was a miracle she hadn't turned into "the Rossiter girl." Or something more strident: the Colonel's Daughter. But some miracle had saved her.

Her memories, though. They weren't like old orchards, as his probably were. They were varied enough, but they all seemed like the same memory in different costumes.

So what would she be doing in Greenwich this morning? What everyone else was doing, probably. Phoning someone. That was the thing. Get the pendulum swinging. Arrange to drive somewhere. Eat somewhere. If all the luncheons she'd ever eaten were laid end to end . . . And talk, talk, talk. Chiefly about petty exasperations. But know about things. Be amusing. Interesting. Deft. Even the girls with the impossible faces knew exactly how to capitalize on them. Recognize all each other's allusions, that was the thing. *All*usions? *Ill*usions? Which was it? She was never quite sure. Like Rex. He always said "deteriate." . . . She, of course – self-caricaturing – was the sensitive one in all this merry-go-round, but you still couldn't escape it . . .

She stopped. "You're not laying any charges?" she said.

"No," he said. "Not at the moment."

They stood there until standing began to seem like an activity.

"Won't you sit down?" Bruce said.

He motioned to the rock behind them.

Sheila perched on the rock's slight promontory. "The Lorelei!" she said, flashing in and out of the siren's posture.

She had a really inspired talent for tangential absurdity. Rex never got it.

Bruce had to laugh. In a way he had never laughed with Molly. Molly didn't quite get things like that, either.

He sat down beside Sheila; close to her, yet dividing the rock between them. It was as if actual touch would release information of the sort that lawyers motion their clients *not* to confide in them.

But, on this rock, Sheila no longer felt the lassitude she'd felt at the lake. There was a resurgent sense of all the things there *were* in the world – things which not an hour ago, with Rex, had shed their flesh to the skull. She and Bruce gave each other an odd feeling of consequentiality.

"I'm glad you're getting the use of your laugh back," she said. "It's one of your most important limbs."

He chortled like Santa Claus. "How's that?"

"That's terrible," she said. "Please, Bruce. Let's *don't* start throwing our quills again? I told you I wanted to help you. I meant it."

"I'm sorry," he said. "But . . . I've been thinking. You got the impression that I have a problem, didn't you? I haven't. I've had a – well, I've told you what I've had. But it didn't leave me with any problem. When you have problems you don't know what to do next. I've found the answer to that right here."

"Where?" she said.

Their bodies were still guardedly not touching, but they had both leaned forward in that particular stance which even from a distance proclaims the locking of minds.

He unclasped one hand toward the field and the woods.

"Right here. Working with my hands. I'm right back where I started from. Where I belong."

He meant that too.

In the last few days he had really come home. He had breathed again, as if he were standing in a breeze of it, the spirit of how it used to be here. When no one was more important or trying to be more important than anyone else. No one gaining height by standing on someone else's face. When one man's trouble was everyone's, like the weather . . .

All work but this left its own particular tarnish on your hands. This was the only place you could come back to with whatever little you had left and be able to feel sound and whole again, with no questions asked. It put no poultices on you, but you didn't fester. And while you worked you could lay down your wounds, like your lunch pail, somewhere in the shade beside you and the ground sat by them and took care of them. You must still pick them up again when the work was done; but you found them clean, not clogged with dust and grime. It was the only place where exhaustion made you feel cleaner at night, not dirtier. Because you'd been putting your muscles to the use they were meant for. No other workers felt tired that same clean way. No athlete, with his silly toy muscles. No pencil men. Or think men. Or manipulators. He'd seen these last in the examination room with their clothes off; the cords like string and the arms like jowl flesh . . . Yes, he had thought it straight through. This was the only work that made you feel you were plugged into life's main artery. That you were not just one of those . . . air plants . . . with no roots in any basic soil. You collaborated with the sun and the rain. Growing the stuff for your own tissues, chopping your own heat. You felt like a tree . . .

And when you came right down to it – when something had *made* you come right down to things – why the hell was a life like this supposed to be the dead end of all ambition? Could anyone tell him what amounted to so goddam much in what everyone else did? What had the best of them to show for it in the long run? A bunch of tics, over and past. Nothing. Creating a mess of dead things, grabbing them back and forth out of each other's hands to see who could get the biggest fistful. Even if you trafficked in what they called the finer values, how much sediment did you leave when you were over? None. Maybe if you could write Shakespeare again . . . or something like that . . . but what was the sense of the second-best? What was the bloody *sense* of the second-best – let alone the nth best? Stopgapping big holes of nothing with nothing, that's all they did. Like barbers, every one of them – cutting the hair that grew again, to be cut again, to grow again . . . Housewives preparing for this taste or that, this food or that – and what was there to show for a meal when it was over and you were hungry again?

The whole thing was just one great leaky sieve. They just kept pouring their energies down a bloody sluice. And little *or* big, nobodies *or* famous, not a bit of them stuck to its sides. They didn't *dare* to stop and *look* at what they were doing or it would drive them crazy . . .

"But all that study . . .?" Sheila said. "You can turn all that into waste?"

"Without a qualm," he said. "I haven't a twinge of conscience

136

that I'm wasting anything, running out on anything. Because I've lost the whole feeling I once had about being a doctor."

There was nothing quite like that feeling he'd had then: as if this were the one job without challenge the most important in the world, and yours by command as freeing as love's. But not any more. Call it a necessary job now, if you liked – though you knew quite well the word "necessity" had no damn meaning – but he could let someone else do it now. He didn't feel any more stunted outside it, or as if he'd feel any taller, inside it again, than if it were the manufacture of hairpins.

Somehow since last December physical pain had lost its stature for him. That's when it's bad for a disciple of any kind . . . when his particular devil loses its stature. Pain, he had come to see, was just a wrinkle. And seldom the most painful one, as the sufferer himself so often knew. Doctors were merely wrinkle-smoothers, like all the rest. They couldn't make the only real cure. They couldn't cure the meaning back into that word "necessity."

The other students used to kid his intentness sometimes and call him Old Galahad. But now that was all changed. Behind their student blasphemies about their calling he could sense a discipleship he now lacked altogether. So now he could let someone else do it.

"And before you start thinking cowardice," he said, "it's not cowardice, if I do say so myself. It's not because I've had a blow and can't take it. Look," he interrupted himself, "there's a soap opera on the radio about now. Letty says it reminds her of a calf with the 'scours.' If you'd rather go tune in on that one . . ."

She gave him that face of patient exasperation which can at the same time flash round the outline of a singular empathy. Then she did a quick mime of the stenographer reading back her shorthand. " '. . . a blow and can't take it.' That's as far as I got."

"All right," he said. "It isn't that I can't take it. I could go back and pick up the threads tomorrow. But that wouldn't be courage. I know, I know. That's the one crazy wonderful thing *about* people. That they do pick themselves up and have at it again, whether it makes sense or not. But courage, to be courage at all, has to be 'blind courage.' It wouldn't be courage with me. I'd just be dancing the ritual steps to an empty little courage ballet I could see right through. I can't see any damn value or virtue in that."

Oh hell, he thought, why don't I keep my mouth shut? You had something all worked out inside your head. In texture grey and smoky maybe, but contained in a little round ball nevertheless. And then you started talking. And it started to unravel. Forking out and ramifying like the communications maze underneath a city. (He made a gesture almost violent.) And smacking at it, it was like a tarbaby. You got stuck up with it from head to foot.

"All this bloody thinking," he said. "Squirming around in everyone's head like a skullful of worms. Sometimes I wish they *would* drop the bomb – and level the whole business. All at once. Start with new seed."

Listeners to the venting of a private vehemence usually bridle a little, as if they were a stand-in for that vehemence's object. Bruce looked shamefaced that Sheila didn't look that way now.

"Bruce," she said, "can't you see what's happened? It's all so simple . . . but so hard to put clear. Don't you know that when you lose the biggest thing in your life it's the next biggest thing in it you turn against? A man's house burns and he takes an almost . . . glittering . . . satisfaction in letting his barn burn too. You've lost Molly and Peter, so naturally it's your career you turn against. In a way you're jealous of it on their *behalf*. Always have been. It's a little the same with this work here. If you leave your beginnings you always feel guilty toward them too. And so you want to prune yourself back to the roots, go back to them. You want to repay this place . . . the only thing you can repay now . . . for ever having left it. You think that's just cold reason. But it isn't. It's simply the unreasonable way all serious people punish *themselves* for the knocks they get. And what's the classic punishment? Solitary confinement."

"But –"

"Hush," she said. She was revelling in this. She could never talk to Rex about the patterns *behind* appearance at all. "If you don't trip me up, maybe I can put you straight on this 'necessity' business too. This 'nothing matters' argument."

Admitted, there were no loopholes in his argument about that. None that the eye could see. But it was one of those conjurer's tricks just the same. You didn't *stay* convinced about it. No, certain things did matter. It was merely some sleight-of-hand too quick for the eye to catch that proved they didn't.

And here was the point. You might believe the proof that they didn't; but it was the only belief that didn't bring a *command* with it, to act on it. Just the opposite. The nagging command was to act against it. And who was to say that this command was not a sounder authority than logic? What Einstein in the behaviour department, with some $E=mc^2$ for the heart, might not one day prove that?

"And you *aren't* really acting on your belief, Bruce," she said. "Only as far as it suits you. If you followed it straight through, you wouldn't even comb your hair. You wouldn't get out of bed in the morning. And, oh, Bruce, you don't want to be like the people who do act on it, do you? They don't have the . . . whole . . . look of people toeing the mark to an inner truth. They just get that cramped look, as if they'd signed a contract the *other* party is gloating over . . . You *can't* act on it, Bruce. You're wrong. The earth here won't bank you up the way you think. After all, what does earth do? It makes whatever's in the seed sprout. Maybe I could bank myself up here. I'm an ordinary person. But you can't, Bruce. You really are a Galahad. Bury yourself twenty feet under the earth here, and the old ambitions will still sprout. And loneliness is so bad for you. A taste of it does most people good. But you should never touch the stuff. You're like an alcoholic. One taste of it and you can't leave it alone. Your laugh is what – well, God forgive me, waters you and keeps you green. When you're alone that sinks right into the sand. You're one of those people who has to get right down and put his head together with himself when he's alone. You can't let yourself mark time for a minute. You feel a conscience if for one minute you're not in harness to *some* mode of living . . ."

"You think you know me pretty well, don't you," he said.

"I do," she said. "I told you I did. I'm int-yoo-hoo-it-eeve" – she clowned the vowels – "haven't you noticed?"

Again, he had to laugh.

"But take a little while *out* of harness, Bruce. Just let things settle. Don't harness yourself into that straitjacket you're talking about now. Please?"

He felt curiously warmed, the way you do when people really sweat over arguments to defeat your own arguments against yourself.

"You say you're just an ordinary person?" he said, his tone a blend of quizzicality and the chiding that is nevertheless fond.

"Of course," she said, as if nothing were more self-evident. "You're not. You're an all or nothing guy. You keep holding yourself up against this searching light all the time, the way they test eggs. I haven't got a bit of that. I just take what fare comes along. At its face value. No whys at all. Or hardly any. I never measure my own little universe against any final check. I don't ask it to make any total. Not that I'm a turnip, mind." She caricatured the frank, open face. Her tongue felt that chattering freedom which comes when you recognize how pent up you've been and how receptive is your present audience at exactly the same time. "I'd hate to think my mouth fell open *at* any of the performers," she said. "All I ask is to 'get' things – but I do ask that. I have no sense of my own significance whatever – but I'd hate not to know how to snub anyone who presumed on my insignificance. Listen to me! I'm out to tie Tallulah!"

He grinned. "Go on," he said.

"Other than that," she said, "I'm extremely ordinary. I have no particular talents. And I don't particularly hanker for any. I was the dowdiest child." She did a lank dowdy child. "You should have *seen* me. For a long time I was scared stiff there was nothing left for it, I'd have to be brainy. Luckily that original grub did break cocoon into a fairly personable woman." She did Bea Lillie doing a personable woman. "And I'm thankful for that. Those poor people – and please don't think I'm as smug about this as saying it makes it sound – those poor people with the faces not odd in any interesting way but just . . . peculiar. That no one can possibly credit with having the normal share of tragedy or ecstasy behind them in the normal way."

He didn't have to look at her to know that she wasn't miming that.

"But I'm in no way exceptional. I'm never stuck for words, but that doesn't mean I'm never stuck for certainty. And back to you. Maybe nothing has any lasting value, you say. But that doesn't bother me especially. If anything's worthwhile *while* it lasts, that's all that matters. The way I see it, what can 'forever' do for anything, anyway? It's just multiplication. And multiplication is just a lot of adding. And you *can't* add a satisfaction, a moment, to itself. Can I still go on?" she said. "I'm loving this."

"Please do," he said.

He gave her the smile that's a deeper step into the province-of-laughter's capital than laughing.

"Okay," she said, "where was I? Oh yes. I'm ordinary. I'm not like you. I'm so ordinary that when *I've* had a bad whack I *welcome* anything that tricks my mind away from the real state of affairs. If I'd lost both eyes and some tactless soul said 'We're taking a drive to see the autumn leaves, why don't you come along?' – *I'd* go. And be glad for whatever good the fresh air, anyway, did me. And this sophisticated – isn't that a ghastly word? – this sophisticated business you're always holding over me. I'm not sophisticated in the least. I like clever people, yes; but not half as much as the people who are – well, exactly true to the way they happen to be. And the clever people I like far and away the best are the ones you catch out sometimes in an old-fashioned sentiment – or an old-fashioned principle – it'd kill them to know was showing. I can't even enjoy a comedian unless, so help me, he has a 'good' face.

"That's one thing about Rex," she interrupted herself suddenly.

140

"You almost never hear him poke fun at anyone. Not even the thoughtless way all of us do now and again. Unless he's desperate."

When she mentioned Rex's name their bodies straightened up, as if in alignment with some quite different posture of thought. They glanced at him.

Even the length of the field away they could see that the original thrust of his movements had gone slack. He was reminding of the child who gleefully contracts to move mountains for you; then discovers himself committed not to a flash of accomplishment but a grind; then tries, by varying his approach to it, to turn the work into play; then sidles away from it altogether.

"I wonder how long he'll be able to stick it out up there by himself," Sheila said. "He'd go completely nuts in the country. On his own, like you."

Watching him stricken with distance, an echo of the old fondness came back. Retrospect seemed to leaf through a snapshot album of him, identifying the circumstance when each likeness had been taken. There had been so many different likenesses, in so many different circumstances. And in so many of them the sun had been shining.

"What happened to the foot?" Bruce said.

"The war," she said.

"But why doesn't he have it built up?" Bruce said. "There are some wonderful new prostheses that would correct that limp, you know. I'd like to have a look at it sometime."

"Dr Mansfield."

She smiled. How little he knew Rex. Rex, whose flesh was his temple, tolerating a prosthesis!

Bruce leaned forward again.

"Yet you say *you* wouldn't feel stived up here?" he said.

"Stived up?" she said, mock-frowning. "What's that?" It might have been some phrase in a foreign tongue.

He was brought up short. The current between him and Molly wouldn't have snagged on that old rural expression. They had shared a whole country of communion like that that Sheila would never know except through translation. Her adjustable accent could learn its way around in that country like any other accomplished actress's; yet how many times would she reach out and touch only backdrop, where Molly had touched the living core?

There's a trapdoor over memory. Of a milk-glass transparency, but just solid enough to support your weight. This was one of those trifling things which unexpectedly spring that trapdoor and drop you physically right back to your beginnings.

For a moment he was back in the breath of his youth's snug

dominion. Where hands knew the only subtleties and eyes told the only stories. Where tongues were so clumsy that faces were so marked with the overflow into them of messages the tongue could not discharge, nor could they, that you carried these faces, whole, inside you all your life. Like tablets of braille . . . For a moment he was as far away from Sheila as if time had made a switch with space.

For a moment he had a picture of Molly's hands giving the rack of dresses another turn after she'd glimpsed the prohibitive price tag on the one that really took her eye . . . For no good reason he thought of the time Peter had run away. They had found him on the railway tracks and, in punishment, paid him no attention walking home. He had trudged a little behind them, small with guilt and not saying anything about his hands being cold, because he'd got his mittens wet and hidden them in his pocket. Until Molly could stand it no longer and had turned and said, "Aren't your hands cold?"

Surfacing again, he said to Sheila: "It was just an old country expression. Forget it." And then, quickly: "You think you can have money and be ordinary at the same time? That's hardly an ordinary point of view, is it?"

They were fast slipping into that bantering way of speech which people something more than half in love use, distrusting any other, while they still believe their love is just liking with the volume turned up.

"Bruce," she protested, "I do wish you'd get that money business out of your craw . . . as if I were a woman with a past. I'm innocent! I wish you could step inside me and look around. And wouldn't it save a world of gab if people could do just that with each other? You wouldn't see a bit of money. Rich man, doctor, Indian chief . . . that doesn't describe anyone. You're yourself over and above what you are in that sense, or do. The way you talk, money's something like smallpox. But it hasn't pitted me, Bruce. It hasn't got into my blood stream. Most cases, it doesn't. You just . . . well . . . pass it, like those coins *you* probably swallowed and passed when you were a child."

Again, he laughed. This time in a stroke sharp enough to snap the suction in their swamp of earnestness completely. They had the sudden closeness of people coming up out of a joint gravity not with the signatories' mien but with a start of amusement. They were abruptly conscious of the day; luxuriously shipwrecked in the sea of sunshine.

Up to now their bodies had held their tongues. Now they too had their say. Now they began desire's paradoxical argument of flesh

142

opposite flesh. And, at this, the bantering became more defensive still of what it masked; yet, by the same paradox, steered its path toward the very subjects it would find most precarious to cope with.

"And what *does* stived up mean?" Sheila insisted.

"The way I've kept you hemmed in on this rock with my sour gripes," he said. "Something like that."

"They weren't sour gripes," she said. "And I haven't felt hemmed in." She looked at the field and the lake. "I love it here. Or has love come to be a four-letter word with you too, the same as rich?"

He sidestepped her question.

"What's a rich girl's idea of love?" he said. "I've often wondered."

Sheila let out a quick breath, but not to answer him.

"I'm afraid the short happy career of farmer Giorno has come to a close," she said.

Bruce looked up and saw Rex walking toward them, trailing the spade. He knew better than to comment. The rough ground warped Rex's shadow like a funhouse mirror.

He dropped the spade at the edge of the garden, with no thought whatever that any excuse for quitting should be offered. It was the first time that Sheila had ever consciously wanted not to be in his company.

"Look," he said to her, "what's the matter with us? Why didn't *you* think of it?"

Sheila put a rummaging look on her face.

"Me?" she said. "Think of what?"

"We could do some target shooting! All these beautiful wide open spaces . . . What's wrong with us? I'll go get the gun!"

"That gun!" Sheila said to Bruce; her mouth wry, but her smile a humouring one. "He even had the customs officers hefting it and squinting down the barrel!"

"So what?" Rex said. "So I notice he didn't make any trouble about the liquor and the cigarettes, did he? He was a swell guy! I'll go get it. I may never have another chance like this in a lifetime."

He was a superb shot. He had no use for actual hunting, where conditions were outside his control, but he would spend hours at target practice. Trudging back and forth to check his shots with the same surprising and inexhaustible patience he had for tinkering with cars.

It's the one thing he really excels at, Sheila thought. He's showing off for me. He's trying *that* now. The Juggler of Notre Dame.

"But, dear," she said, "do you think it's safe? We can't shoot that way – there's the house and the clothes line. Or that way, for the road. Or that way . . ." She pointed toward the inlet. "We don't

143

know where Morse and Kate are." The view had seemed so unobstructed, and now suddenly there was almost no direction in which you could fire a shot that mightn't injure something. "That gun is dangerous," she said. "It carries so far."

"Oh, dangerous, hell," he said.

Sheila turned to Bruce. "Maybe Bruce hasn't got the time," she said. Her tone was almost that of a parent winking excuse out of some child's game to another adult, over the child's head.

"No, that's okay," Bruce said. "I'd like to try a few shots. I'm no earthly good at it, but –"

"Sure you are!" Rex said. "I'll bet you *are*."

He went for the gun. Bruce and Sheila didn't pick up the thread of their talk again. Until he returned, each maintained a separate abstraction, as parents do waiting in the car for the child to come out of the little corner store with whatever bauble they've humoured him to stop for.

Rex selected the targets: three sentinel pines in a perfect row on the edge of the woods. One for each. He had three tin cutouts, the size of saucers, which he tacked on for bull's-eyes. He paced back a range of fifty yards from the pines and beckoned them to join him.

"You think I could hit one of those things from here?" Sheila said. "I'll be lucky if I hit the tree."

"All right," he said. He began to strip off his jacket. It was a white sports jacket with a bright red breast pocket in the shape of the fencer's stylized heart. "I'll button this around the tree trunk. You can aim at the pocket, but we'll score you if you can hit the jacket anywhere at all. How's that?"

"You paid seventy dollars for that jacket," Sheila said. "That's how it is." She couldn't help glancing at Bruce's faded denims.

"Okay," Rex said, laughing. "I'm betting you my jacket, my shirt, you can't touch it."

He directed the shooting the way a child casts and coaches some imaginative play of which he alone has the master plan. Altering the position of their hands on the gun barrel a centimetre. Shifting their cheeks a centimetre closer to its stock. Bursting with generosity in the bestowal of these instructions, though at the same time exonerating them beforehand from the slightest censure on his part if they shouldn't be able to implement his tips. Bruce and Sheila summoned the face of participation and then let it relax according as Rex's attention was focused on him or her. Their glances kept asiding over the shoulder, one to another.

Who does he remind me of? Bruce kept thinking. And then he remembered. Peter. Peter, exactly.

His first shot, they could see Rex's bull's-eye jump. A gleam in his face registered it like a recoil. Sheila had aimed deliberately between the trees, to miss the jacket. It looked as if Bruce's shot had gone wide too.

Three rounds each and Rex could no longer wait to tally up the scores.

"Come on," he said. "Let's go check."

"But there's no point in us all going, is there?" Sheila said. "We'll trust you, dear."

"But don't you want to?"

His face looked doused. It is right at what should be the exclamatory peak of the game that the child is oftenest betrayed.

Rex had three bull's-eyes, Bruce had hit the tree twice but had no bull's-eye, and Sheila had hit nothing at all.

Rex fired next. And then Sheila, still aiming between the trees. And then Rex could find no more bullets in his pocket.

"That's all right," Bruce said. "I wouldn't have hit anything anyway."

"No," Rex said stubbornly. A surge of fairness is the child's final effort to revive the spirit of the thing. "You might have hit dead centre and beat us all. I'll go get another box of shells."

"No," Bruce said, "please don't bother. It doesn't matter in the least. Honestly."

"No, sir," Rex said. "We've all got to have our turns."

He had taken a few steps toward the house when he did come across one more bullet in his pocket. He tossed it to Bruce.

"Here," he said. "Have a free practice shot while I'm gone. Fire at anything you like. We'll still give you your target turn when I get back."

Bruce and Sheila saw Letty driving in from town. She stepped out of the car, visoring a hand over her eyes to see what all the fusillade was about.

Sheila giggled.

"Bruce," she said, "did you ever spend any time on Letty's medical theories? She was telling me at breakfast this morning that her sister-in-law's got a sack of gallstones as big as a tobacco pouch. She thinks she should have an operation before one of them gets out into her duck!"

Their laughter went off as if from a spring.

Rex heard them laugh. He almost stumbled, as if a blow had caught him between the shoulders. His face stared at itself the way faces do which have never been able to touch off or join in that kind of laughter with the one they love. Its skin went as lost with indraft as the skin of hands.

145

"And the story she tells about the faith cure," Bruce said. "It seems this couple that was both stived up with rheumatism come to hear this evangelist and went right home, the simpletons, and throwed away their crotches!"

"Now wouldn't the evangelist love that!" Sheila said. "And, come to think of it, it might be the answer to a lot of things, eh?"

They laughed again, the same way.

"And her aunt," Bruce said. "That the undertaker did such a miserable job on. Did you hear about that? 'I tell ya, Bruce, if I hadn'ta knowed her, I wouldn'ta knowed it was her.'"

They kept laughing.

Rex kept hearing them. And he was swamped by the desolation which has for its face ice trampled in a wheel rut to look like splintered glass. It was one of those moments, like the one hard on the heels of death, when the nature of all desolation is seen by the stricken to have been instinct always, orphanage grey, in the sound of the wind or the roots of trees.

CHAPTER 18

Sheila had seen nothing but the victor's poise in Morse and Kate as they turned away. It would have astounded her to know how riddled that was by the licks she herself had landed. Morse's scalp smarted physically. And Kate was toppled. Sheila had had only to mention her circumstance to have that circumstance strike its own defeating blow.

I *am* an old maid, she thought. I was a fool to think I could drink that away. For the first time Kate realized that freedom is a cutthroat country. She almost shrank back to her Halifax self.

And then they both reacted with a surge of spirit.

For snubbing is an excellent tonic. You go along stooped into the harness of your present self-image; its very actuality, however grating, lends it actuality's peculiar validation. A snub is the only thing that can make you stand straight again and take a straight look at yourself, make you question that validation.

Morse leading the way, they walked in single file down the path to the stillwaters. Each was so preoccupied with his own self-facing that they scarcely spoke. And when they did their words were more like the automatic tacking, not to collide, of two people working together with concentration in a small room. The drinks, having passed their climax and gone, left behind them a clarity as stripping as knives.

The woods glinted with April. And once field and lake were out of sight it seemed as if its boundaries were infinite in all directions. Morse and Kate found themselves inside a dome of pristine cleanliness where earth-breath and tree-breath were like a gentle acid wash. Their simple animacies, elsewhere a background unfelt, here tingled in them as entities. Sheila's snubs had loosened the lint on them and the wash of woods air rinsed it away, leaving each facet sharp and clear.

The path left the thick woods and followed the twist of the brook. Alders and hardhacks lined the brook. Until they reached the first stillwater, dark and pond-like and muted with sudden depth. Here, for some distance back on either side, the banks were like cleared field.

Stillwaters issue the peculiar drawing invitation of conundrums. This one spoke to them as compellingly as a voice. They relaxed into the fisherman's "gaze," as Sheila had into the dreamer's.

They cast their lines there and watched them as fixedly as if it were their own thoughts they were fishing for beneath the enigmatic surface. The sun, for the first time confident in its own warmth, blessed their faces and the backs of their hands. The woods, dark without doomfulness, stood between them and time. And now their thoughts slipped the stranglehold of pre-judgement and broke ground and leafed out into speech as if with the fluency after repentance.

"Tell me," Morse said, "why do I bring out the bitch in women? Like a magnet. Is it the bastard in me? Or whatever the masculine of bitch is?"

They had been fishing and talking. Now they were talking and fishing.

"Bitchiness has no masculine," Kate said. "It's exactly the same for both sexes. Do you bring it out in me?"

"No," he said. "A funny thing. You haven't got it. You or Paul. But – well, take Sheila. Take the three women I've been married to. Helen, Janet, and Natalie. The Three Furies. Something brought it out in every damn one of them."

Helen was this kind, he said. Exactly when you yourself were on the top of the world she'd choose – and he did mean choose – to be irritated by nothing at all. Tell her your book had just gone into a second edition and the next minute she'd be grimacing at a run in her stocking. *Couldn't* he get a hammer and drive in that upholstery tack? This was the third pair it had ruined. On the other hand, go to her with anything that had got you down and she wouldn't exactly take its side but she'd make you *argue* yours, for God's sake . . .

Janet was worse. You couldn't get anything off your chest to her, either. She wasn't a fighter. Oh no. She'd just get oh so speechlessly hurt. Living with her was like picking your way through a maze of invisible feelers. Right when you'd be slugging it out with a page that wouldn't come and needing a lift, you'd hear that sigh. "Oh, great. She had a sigh that . . . My God, it was like nerve gas!"

And Natalie. Natalie was a sniper. An ambusher. Her tongue had a finer bore than Helen's or Janet's, but she had an aim that could hit a chink in you a millimetre wide. That's what she was, a chink-hunter. Her specialty was remarks like: Well, I was just going by what you said on Monday. Is it different for Tuesdays, Thursdays and Saturdays? . . .

"And if I ever have another wife, God forbid, I'll give you odds she'll be a bitch too. A jealous one, or a lying one, or one that teacups or liquor bring it out in . . ."

"This bitchiness you see all around you," Kate said. "I wonder . . . if that's what it really is. You can find examples if you look for them, yes. But you'd be surprised how trying people can be . . . when the truth is they're simply trying to be decent. In a clumsy bewildered way. Ninety per cent of that decency goes to the grave with them, unrecognized. And strip off *their* skin sometime, and see how many blood blisters you'd find. I think I can understand Natalie aiming at your chinks . . . with weapons even . . . if there was no other way she could get in to you."

"You see," he said. "You haven't got it. You can't even comprehend it."

"I was bitchy enough with Sheila just now, wasn't I?" she said.

"Oh, that," he said. "But the point is, you haven't got that stockpile of ammunition the others have. Your only weapon is the boomerang . . . that comes right back and bruises *you*. You're sorry already."

"Aren't you?" she said. "I mean, for the way you baited Rex?"

"That juvenile psychopath . . . ?" he said. "I should be sorry for that? Or, I suppose, *you'd* call him psychopathetic."

Kate had a sudden strike . . . and their glances leapt at each other. There were fish here all right!

Her line plunged swerving, then tautened straight outward, describing with the water that most beautiful of acute angles. Her reflex was to reel in the line immediately. Morse clapped his hand over hers on the rod.

"No," he whispered. "Not yet."

She played the trout, testing its hold and then nodding at Morse, and then testing it again. Their sprawling thoughts fisted instantly with concentration. She raised her eyebrows: Now?

"All right," he said.

She flung the trout out onto the bank. Its body flapped and arc-ed glistening like their excitements. Morse took it from the hook expertly and broke its neck. Kate touched the dead fish.

"I wonder if it hurts them any," she said.

"You would," he said. "No, it doesn't. No nervous system. It's when there's a nervous system that maybe it hurts a little to break your neck getting off the hook. Don't mind me," he added quickly, "I'm all symbollixed up this morning."

"You've had experience throwing a hook?" she said, making another cast.

"Not exactly," he said. "I just cut the line. The hook's still there." He looked around him. "You know," he said, "I can't figure out what drew me back here to the workshop of my first novel. Is it the criminal returning to the scene of his crime or the dog to his vomit? Maybe friend Sheila got the mood wrong, but she sure as hell got the tense right. I *was* a writer."

"But *why* did you cut the writing line?" Kate said. "Why *aren't* you writing now?"

"It'd take all week to answer that one," he said.

"I've got all week," she said.

All right. She'd asked for it.

Writing was a mug's game. What hope in hell did you have of trapping thoughts and feelings in a net as coarse as words? It was like the ancients trying to enclose the bird with a wall. "And this infernal time business." He began to look almost frenzied. A writer needed ten lives. And he had only one. To do it right you'd have to experience all things first, then learn how to tell them, then tell them. But there was no time for that. You had to keep the three operations all going at once. Tolstoi thought the only thing he'd missed out on was a yacht race. My God, how foolish could you get? . . . How fast could anyone speak or type? Say a hundred words a minute. Never mind the hours spent writing it in and rubbing it out in his brain, or the long white days when not one word would come – just say he had it right at his fingertips. If he typed, or spoke, without a second's break, for seventy years, he couldn't *physically* get more than a grain of the whole truth down. If he had the sense Proust hadn't, he knew that. A penny compared to all those billions in the national debt . . .

"Can't you see? One man, one little hen scratch. It's so impossibly hopeless."

"But surely," Kate said, "you don't have to take everything atom by atom. An ounce of suggestion . . ."

"Ball!" he said. "That foolish thesis doesn't even rate the plural."

Granted that with the microscope your tool you engraved no more than a single comma of infinity on the head of a pin, how much better did the telescope serve you? What good was a bloody relief map if half the truth was in a blade of grass? When every damn thing in the world was *sui generis*? What good was an *outline* of the heart if the infinite subdivisions of human feeling defied the microscope even?

"You might as well type out the alphabet and say: There. That takes it all in."

"But I don't care," Kate said. "Those inexpressible volumes you're so dismayed about. You do have a knack of writing them between the lines."

She'd often wondered how he'd look if the pleasure something gave him showed before he could hide it. For just a moment he looked as if his mouth and his eyes were suddenly moved to make friends with each other.

"And how can you say you've cut the line," she insisted, "when you're still so intense about it?"

"All right," he said. "There were other reasons. This one, chiefly. If you want to find out what bitches there are in the world, get married. If you want to find out what *sons*-of-bitches there are, write a book."

To start with, there was no device quite like it for winnowing your friends. You'd be surprised at the limits to which some of them could carry their indifference to its fortune. If it fell among vultures, you'd be surprised in how many of their gardens the cock crew too. You'd be surprised how gleefully how many of them came to you, disguised as amusement peddlers, to relay this scandalized comment on it or that . . .

His mouth and his eyes began to grit against each other once more. She didn't interrupt.

"And then you make the acquaintance of those charming types who just wait for a writer to have his entrails exposed to hold their little torches against them. And, make no mistake, a writer's guts are exposed. There it all is, in black and white. Irrevocable. Absolutely bare-assed . . . You know, I used to be so naïve. I really thought the four-letter words were 'mean,' 'sham,' 'cant' – those. There was a fair amount of sex in my books, sure, because I had the idea there was a fair amount of it in life. I really was naïve. I couldn't see why it should be any worse to say screw than to do screw. I couldn't see why it should be any more shameful to name certain organs than to possess them. And how do these pietists figure it's so sinful to follow or mention these instincts God gave them? What's their idea of God anyway? Someone that breaks his child's leg to begin with and then beats him because he limps? And what's all this ruckus about good taste – when what's good taste in one longitude is anathema in another? . . . The funny thing, these very critics had children. I gathered from that they must have had sex too. But I was so naïve. It seems the way *they* do it, the man slips behind the pantry door with an egg cup . . . and then he passes its content out to the woman, who is veiled to the chin . . . and then she retires behind some suitable arras and completes the operation with an eyedropper."

Kate's knot of listening was split wide open with a sudden clap of laughter.

"You fool!" she said.

It was exactly the right thing to say. His expression looked as if the thumb had been lifted off it. She was astonished to find that she could temper his mood in any way. She had believed no one could. I'll temper his bitterness, she thought. I'll make it my job. I can do it. I know I can.

"Aaaah," he said, "we're scaring the fish away with our bloody chatter. Which do you want to do, fish or talk? We can't do both."

"Talk," she said.

They reeled in their lines. The sun had become so warm that their jackets had taken on weight. They took them off and spread them on the ground and sat on them.

He continued in the same gritting strain, but she could see that his bitterness was sieving away through a dozen punctures.

Write about murder, he said, which anyone might think was rather worse than sex, and nobody was in the least offended. No one accused you of being a murderer yourself. But just mention sex and you were a whoremaster from way back.

Ah, those charming types that his outspokenness had upset most. All those bewitching ladies. (He began to play it for laughs almost.) Such models of consistency. One who'd been brought to bed with childbirth two months to the hour after her wedding vows. Another with the overriding concern that her innocent daughter shouldn't get hold of his corrupting books – which daughter happened at that very moment to be so pregnant that her smock was literally bursting at the seams. Those venerated types with more slaughter to their tongues' credit than Belsen. And a *great* many of those splendid matrons with the mountainous busts that he was damn sure had never had an ounce of milk, of human kindness or of any other kind, in them . . .

Oh yes, these critics were a choice gallery all right.

A politician who could give pointers to an eel . . . And guys who'd make change in a collection plate: put in a quarter and take out two dimes. Not to mention the sweatshop manager with the enchanting habit of scratching his fat behind and then slyly sniffing his fingertips. And the flint-faced Uplift type who could easily double for Black Pete and scare off any child of God *or* of man, certainly the gentle tolerant Christ Himself, within miles . . .

"But surely," Kate said, "you're not Gulliver. Pygmies you despise like that – surely you shouldn't let anything they say bind you down and silence you? You wouldn't *want* their kiss of death, would you?"

"You despise them," he said, "yes. But once you've found in what hundredfolds they exist . . . you'd rather clam up than put your guts out on the counter again for their narrow little eyes and grubby little hands to maul over."

"Excuses," she said, drawing out the word just teasingly enough to turn the gibe into a mollification. She was amazed that it worked.

"All right," he said, suddenly capitulating. "Excuses. I admit it. And by all the rules I should hate you for seeing through them like that. You're my Hickey. You know Hickey, don't you, in *The Iceman Cometh*? The guy that makes other people see their self-delusions for just what they are?"

"Oh yes," she said. "I've had some dealings with Hickey myself."

"But somehow I don't hate you for it. Somehow I don't mind telling you the real reason I've quit. Do you really want me to tell you what it's like when the writer's iceman cometh?"

"If you'll tell it," she said. "If you don't try to write it."

"Who's going to write it?" he said. "That's the whole point. I simply can't write it . . . anything . . . any more. The old engine just won't turn over. Got your tear ducts unplugged?"

"Just tell it, I said. Stop watching your tongue."

"How can I?" he said. "A writer's tongue gets so damn coated." But all right. He'd just tell it . . .

He'd never had a quick engine, but when the starter did turn her over she'd go like a charm until he shut her off. "Now when I step on the starter there's just nothing. Not a sound. Check the battery. Not a spark." He was not so much speaking as reading off his mind. Something that constant rehearsal in his thoughts had lettered there like the inscription on a headstone.

That staggering multiplicity, that's what used to be the bad thing. Truth may be behind the very door that one more push you didn't make would have opened. The feeling that you were alive with antennae . . . that with the right stimuli for straight men you could trap significance in every line. So many tumbling ideas

152

so hard on each other's heels that you had the crazy wish that you could press your forehead against the paper and stamp them off like stencils before they vanished . . .

"When it's like that, you think *that's* dismay. Well, sister, that's just a boy. Wait till the starter won't turn her over at all. Wait till your writing's lips go dry as chalk."

Kate kept just the right strain on her listening, playing his spate the way you do a child's confidence; knowing that the slightest miscalculation between too eager and too flaccid an interest will cause him to roll it up again as suddenly as he's spread it out.

"All of it still out there somewhere – but now you can't get your hands on a bit of it. If your fingers were thumbs before, they're prostheses now. It's like trying to dip up triangles with a cup. And anything you do get down is wrong. You know it's wrong, because that master page inside you stays white . . . white . . . white. Now there's one sweet colour!"

"That's writing it," she said.

"It's not," he said. "You wouldn't dare write it that strong. That's telling it. Truly."

It spared you your heart, but it took out your bone. And no one cared. Why should they? How much more did it matter to them than if a guitar player had lost the finger that held his pick? But to you yourself – there was no other damn dreg in any other damn bottle that could hold a candle to that particular bit of yeast lying there dead.

"I suppose you think that's overwriting it?" he said. "Well, listen to this, sister."

You lived the rest of your life as if you were dipping it out of a well with not a trickle seeping back in. It was like a piece of food you left on your plate. The gears of your mind clacked against each other like thresher bars when no grain's going through. You felt as if you had one of those pieces of shrapnel inside you that aches on an overcast day . . . And now time shoved its face right up against yours. Not Time with a capital T, but *your* time. As finite as a bloody weekend. You're dying by weekends, and it's still out there unsaid. Time's slicing you away like a bacon slicer. It's a tide eroding you. It's an inexorable snow piling up on your shoulders. You went through the motions of living, but it was like the farmer who still fenced his fields and kept his barn shingled though he'd had no stock for years. And then, finally, the fences in your mind began to collapse. Had she ever seen those derelict old fences teetering and sprawling around an abandoned pasture?

"And not a single word of what I've said would have hit the mark if I'd diluted it or tourniqued my upper lip. And I don't give a sweet goddam how overblown this sounds, I'd thank someone to shoot me. Old fox hounds that still stir at the sound of the horn but can't get onto their feet – they shoot *them*, don't they?"

"You don't want to be shot," she said quietly. "Not any more. You're feeling better about the whole thing already. Now aren't you?"

He looked curiously abashed.

"Yes," he admitted. "The funny damn thing, I am. It's the way you listen that does it. I've never had anyone listen to me the way you do. You know how other people listen. They have these little sacs behind their ears they let fill up and then dump out when you're not looking, like ashtrays. When you listen you translate what I say back to me for what it really is. I talk and I shed. And somewhere along the line my mind finds itself in a new suit. Did you ever wear new shoes home from the store and have the salesman put your old ones in the box? You know how the old ones look when you open the box? That's what your listening does for me. I can see that old shoe look about all that food-spotted clothing my mind's been wearing before."

"Yes," she said. "That's my big virtue. I'm a born listener."

He looked at her tone of voice.

"I'm sorry," he said.

He really did sound sorry. She was astonished.

"Okay," he said. "We won't say another word about me. We won't mention ideas of any kind. They've all got mice nests in them. I get sick of this damn spade talk myself – digging under the crust and shifting and sifting all the earth beneath. We'll just talk pleasant morning talk like everyone else. Just let it skim along the surface like a cork on the current. Make our tongues check their luggage and travel light, like everyone else's, eh? Not sack it around in their hands the whole damn time . . ."

"That's all right for you," she said. "You can do that. You've had such a furnishing with people and places you know how to coast on any level. I can't. My mind's the only part of me that's ever been anywhere or done anything. And when I'm not holding up my end with *that* I come over all wrists like the bright country lad facing the strange silverware."

"Nuts," he said. "Experience doesn't furnish anyone. Either you're born furnished or you're not. You were. So . . . *I* know. We'll talk about you for a change. You can talk about yourself, surely. Anyone can."

"I can't," she said. "Because my self's not continuous, like yours. You've never been alone enough to understand that. How, the minute you *are* alone this door inside you opens and you see your

154

self standing there, waiting. That's the only self I ever see. The minute there's the hum of being with someone else it vanishes. That's the only self I can talk about: *to* myself, alone."

"Try," he said.

"You're not a listener."

"Try me."

She had never talked about herself. Like being loved or getting married or having children it had simply come to be another of those things which They did and she didn't. She could see what talking about themselves did for Them. It was like a stream of running water that kept them free of pond scum. But fluently as she could hear herself unburdening herself to Them when she was alone, to their faces she was stage-struck. She would come to the brink of it; and then in increasing thrall to some subtle whisper that forbade it right *now*, turn the discussion back with her own self. Until, finally, herself became a confidante so intimate that to have sought any other would have seemed like treachery.

And so that final carapace, the conscience about slighting one-self, hardened and hardened. Until They came to take her reticence so for granted that to have talked about herself then would have seemed like a startling *act*, as embarrassing to Them as confession.

Now, it was suddenly different.

Whether from the light-headed suction of April in this book-running woods . . . or from the gentle undulance of new-leaf and breeze-hush lapping like light in the trees and beneath the dusty layers of her hitherto plodding breath . . . or whether from Morse's looking at her with that grappling immediacy which strangers sometimes give you for not having their glance modified by the knowledge of your accepted shape in others' minds . . . she felt an odd release.

She felt herself thaw and liven and become almost tearfully meritorious. The way you do when at last real disease is turned up to account for the symptoms you've always kept silence about because there was no evidence to dispute their being imaginary.

"I'm waiting," he said.

"Look the other way then," she said. "I'm like a child. I can't recite if anyone's looking at me."

"All right," he said. "But no dawdling around. No reneging in the middle – 'Aww, I caaan't' – like children do."

His taunt touched her. No one had ever asked her, let alone taunted her, to talk about herself before. But it was as if touched in the alternative sense of being angered that her response came. She had been living witness to the paradox that people with nothing to lose are oftenest the least likely to venture. She might have passed her whole life without this instant of recklessness.

But she had it now. The one when you do begin to talk about yourself. Gaining momentum with each sentence. Tasting a brand-new delight in the art of astonishment, outrage. Dwarfing without mercy the listener's problems with your own. Drunk with the discovery of venom in yourself for things you'd always thought you'd had only forbearance with. Watching the listener crumble and go crestfallen at the spectacle of your spirit burning in its own fire. The ecstasy of unaccustomed rebellion coursing through you like the ripples of a caterpillar. Ending dishevelled, but with the defiant flag of the one with nothing to lose flying more victoriously from your mast than the flag of any other kind of victory . . .

"All right," she said. "I won't dawdle. I'm no child. I'm forty years old. And the rim around my fingernails is getting a stiff, glazed look. The skin there looks like a punctured blister. You talk with a fine literary frenzy about shooting old hounds, because your hands can't write any more. You ought to be me and wake up in the night sometimes and think about that glaze around your fingernails. You'd see how much writing talk would come to you then. You're a man. You can stride. You can swagger. You've done that. You can grab for things. You've had everything in its right *season*. You've been married. You're We. You've had all that, and you've published too. And is there a twinge of thankfulness in you that you're not one of the people who can never get published at all? Not one. You should be me. Can I grab for anything I want? Have I ever published anything? I don't mean words. Have I ever published *any*thing? Looks, flesh, love, life, children . . . *any* damn thing? I'm an old maid. That's what I am. A spinster. A virgin. Doubled. In spades. And my cuticles are glazing over – "

She gave a short scornful laugh.

"But I embarrass you. Oh yes I do! You're the big rough extrovert. Old Man Frankness himself. Nothing shocks you. Nothing embarrasses you. But this does. This is bad taste, even in your book. An old maid advertising her scrawny little deformities? It just isn't done. It's the one thing the *voyeur* in people looks away from. You couldn't be more embarrassed if you were a mother, and her child had broken wind in the middle of her ballet recital – "

She gave another relentless snort of laughter.

"But it'll do you no good to fidget like that. You got me started and I'm going to finish. I had no idea what hellish fun it would *be* to get rid of all this. It's like that habit boys discover. I think I'll make a habit of it. I think it's a habit already. This soon . . ."

"I'm fidgeting," he said, "because you won't let me look at you. May I look at you now?"

"No," she said. "Not yet. I don't think it would halt me now. I can sort of hear myself cheering myself on. But this is too much fun to take any chances with. All right. I took care of my father. You never took care of anyone. I watched him die. For years that was the only show I had a ticket for. I sat in the same seat for years and watched someone die. You don't know what it's like to watch someone die."

Her face went fixed, like someone's smelling a flower.

"You're not listening," she said. "You're skipping, because you've read me somewhere before. The Daughter Who Looked After Her Father. That scarlet placard. She's the best joke since the Elizabethans used to put out larks' eyes and watch the crazy way they flew. You're skipping because my kind of loneliness reads dull. It has no body to it. It doesn't register on any dolorimeter. People laugh, and you think all's well with them. You don't know what a living thing loneliness is – breathing along with you, breath for breath. Until it gets to be like a *scent* in things themselves. And mark this: it's the things you actually do or don't do that mark you, no matter how little they're like your true spirit. If you're forced to live like an old maid, you're marked like an old maid . . ."

He looked at her.

"God, Kate," he said. It was the gentlest oath he'd ever pronounced.

Her look back at him pierced straight through his looking at her.

"You think you can skip," she said, "because you know the ending. None of us ever comes out alive. And I hate to distress you with a second coming after you'd had my obituary all phrased – but I'm the exception. I never realized that until I began to talk. And do you know how I managed it? You wouldn't understand, but every time you reach out for something and then remember it's off bounds, there's a little husk – I can see it, a little grey husk exactly the shape of a Christmas snowflake – that drifts down out of the air on you. Only I didn't let these husks pile up on me myself. I held up this sort of canopy over me – I can see that too, a big square white canopy – and they fell on that. Whatever kind of arms held it up – you wouldn't know the kind, the invisible ones that spoke out from I think it's the blood – ached and ached. But they never let go. I wasn't crushed. I'm still alive . . ."

Her hands gripped each other.

"Of course there was nothing I could do about time. I had to pay its tax whether I was using its services or not. There wasn't anything I could do about my fingernails or around my eyes or . . . But that's all right. I'm still alive. I didn't let go. And nothing can make me let go now. I don't fool myself. I know I can't enjoy the fruits of youth in their season any more. But I know exactly what personal stock I still possess. And I can bargain with that. I can go out into the market and buy the very most it will buy. I intend to price myself up for every cent I'm worth. The hell with this going around putting pots under the places where loneliness leaks through. I'm going to fix the roof."

He looked at her and he remembered a girl he'd seen in a bombed lane in Normandy. No more than fourteen, he'd have said, watching her lead a small brother by the hand. When she saw him she turned bold, trying to look seductive, believing that by an act of will she could take on whatever age she liked – but her true face showing through any face she put on, because she was hungry. He had never been so keenly conscious of the writer's scavengery, peeking at wars.

He moved over to provide an extra sitting space on his jacket.

The morning turned its face away. A small April cloud distracted the sun, the sun's shadow distracted the brook. The cloud passed. And then the sun was preoccupied with the brook, the brook with the rocks it eddied around, and the leaves and the breeze exclusively with each other. In no other place or weather could he and Kate have been so totally alone.

"Come here," he said. He motioned her closer to him.

"I'm not finished," she said.

"Come here."

She moved over onto his jacket in the manner of obedience without capitulation.

He held out his hand like an object. "Touch it," he said. She looked frightened. "Touch it," he said. "You say you've never touched anything. Touch my hand. What better thing than a hand to start with? If you're going to bargain you've got to find out what's worth bargaining for and what isn't. It's very easy to build up the wrong notion altogether about things you've never tested. For all you know, this touching business might turn out to be a complete bust."

She touched his hand.

"Not like that," he said. "Like this."

He went over her hand with his own, as if he were smoothing on an invisible glove.

"Is it any different," he said, "from touching anything else that might be of exactly the same shape, texture and temperature?"

"It isn't like I thought," she said. "It's coarser. But . . ."

"But is it something or nothing?"

"It's something," she said. "It's . . . it's induplicable."

"All right," he said. He lay back flat. "Now touch my face. And my hair."

She touched his face. Then hesitated. Her face broke clear of its subjection to her eyes. She had to try hard, not to cry. She gripped her own hands together in her lap.

"Damn you!" she said. "Why did you have to be gentle with me? You're savage with everyone else. That's what I was all set to bargain with. How can anyone bargain with gentleness?"

"It's not gentleness especially," he said. "It's just that old anachronism our generation still hangs onto. What did we call it – feelings? I did a piece about that once. How it had got bred out of the next generation somehow. The new bunch know too much too soon. Nothing's rare to them any more. Everything's an everyday thing. Even other people. They've lost wonder. And somehow the more wonder they lose, the more fear creeps in. Fear casteth out love . . . Have I given you time to get your bearings?"

She shook her head.

"It *was* gentleness," she persisted. "I won't accuse you of pity. But it was gentleness. And that was the one snare I hadn't counted on."

Her defiance was gone now, and the threat of tears turned into a memory of itself as brackish as if the tears had been the foolish puddle of a drunk's.

"You knew the one thing that would trip me up, didn't you? The one thing that would make my arms let go. I guess I wasn't so bright after all, not to let each little husk fall on me as it came. They're all down in a heap on me now. And I guess they've knocked me out. Because I really don't care. But just for the record . . . if you *had* been savage, do you want to know the very first bargain I was going to try?"

"I didn't mean to trip you up, Kate," he said gently. "God knows I didn't."

"I was going to ask you to marry me," she said. "No, wait a minute. Nothing romantic. A bargain pure and simple. A contract. For one year less one day. Or however the expression goes. I had a certain dowry to offer. I'd make you an excellent straight man. I know I could get you really writing again, not writing *back* at people the way you do now. I'm forty, but I have a year or so yet before that's really disfiguring. Before it's a joke to be getting married for the first time. I know how to dress. I'm not ugly. You wouldn't have to be ashamed of me . . . And me? I'd be Mrs Morse Halliday and they could put that in their pipes and smoke it. I'd be We. One year – or six months, if you thought my first price was too steep – and I'd set you free again. But that wouldn't matter.

I wouldn't be Miss Fennison any more. No one would *look* at me the way they used to . . ."

Morse didn't speak for a full minute by the clock. And when he did, his face seemed to have faded out and in again in the way that movies denote a lapse of time.

"And just for the record," he said, "who'd have got custody of the child?"

"The child?" she said. Again she looked frightened. "There wasn't any thought of . . ."

"That's funny," he said. "Haven't you heard that children are the things that really keep you from shrivelling up? Like a few green berries among the ripe ones? I never had a child, myself. I was afraid I might pass the writing pox on to him. And God knows hereditary writers are the unluckiest bastards of all. They don't even have the disease good and proper, they're just a little dumpy with the vaccination . . . Naaah, that wasn't the reason. I'm just talking. If there'd been a decent place to bring him into . . . but this bloody world with its chromium guts. Or else I simply didn't want to sow myself to that big crop of question marks a child is once it's out of your groin and you lose all control of it. . . . No, come to think, I haven't published any flesh or blood either. I got as far as discussing it once with Natalie. But Natalie was the kind that couldn't let five sentences go by, whatever the subject, without lighting a little match right under your scalp, and. . . . Aah, the hell with Natalie. Who'd have got custody of the child?"

"I'd have taken it off your hands," Kate said.

"Like hell you would have!" Morse said. He thought. "You know . . . with you . . . I think he might have been quite a guy. I can call up quite a picture of him. Hardly any question marks at all. He'd have had enough of you in him . . . like a compass . . . so he could reach wide but touch small. So he'd never be mean. And . . . he'd have had the sense I've got to know what a fool thing bravery is . . . but I think he'd have been the kind to stick with it the whole fifteen rounds, just the same, until the great big fouling lout of a world was booed right out of the ring. How do you see him? My eyes and your mouth? Or your eyes and my mouth? And what is it kids always have the same as the father's – the fingernails? Like hell you'd have taken him! I'd have fought it through the highest court in the land!"

"He'd have had your eyes," Kate said, "*and* your mouth *and* your fists. . . . But I'd have seen myself in him *around* the eyes and the mouth, I think . . ." She caught her breath; then turned it into a caricature of catching her breath. "And now will you please be a gentleman and forget that Miss Fennison threw all her clothes off in front of you? Sometimes Miss Fennison gets touched in the head. And afterwards her head aches. She'd rather not talk any more about it."

Morse abruptly turned clown; but this time not insultingly.

"I won't be a gentleman," he said. "Kate doesn't like gentle men. And the hell with this Miss Fennison. Who is she, anyway? Never saw her. She's nothing but a bogus . . . thought-up . . . bogey. Shoo, Miss Fennison. See? She's gone. Just Kate and me here. The real Kate. And do you know something? It wouldn't surprise me one damn bit if I loved her from the soles of her feet to the tip of that alder catkin she doesn't know she's got stuck in her hair."

He drew her head toward his shoulder, to pluck the catkin free.

"Morse!" Kate said.

"Mind you, I'm not sure," he said. "But if it's not love it's something so damn close to it that . . . All right. Let's *make* sure. To me you're utterly unlike anyone that might be almost exactly like you. That's test number one, isn't it? Other women, I've never been more than a visitor in them . . . but with us I have this wonderful feeling that it doesn't matter which of us is which . . . that what's one's is for the other to take. That's test number two, if I'm not a fool altogether. And . . . oh hell, I never could write a love scene. Who can? Natalie said I made all my heroines sound like comfort stations. It *is* odd, isn't it, that the one thing that makes sense in the world – I mean, love – can make a sensible person sound so foolish talking about it. But get this straight. I like to talk with you. Eat with you. Drink with you. And, god*dam*, I'd love to sleep with you. Physically – do you understand? Physically. So . . ."

"You *are* a gentleman," Kate said, "aren't you! You really do know how to help a girl restore face."

"Will you stop that?" he said. "Can't we both stop our bloody fencing? Can't we just *give in* to a simple fact when we see it? All of a sudden you're the only woman I ever knew that I'd like to give in to everything together with. And what else can you call that but love, the hell with the syntax?"

Kate rubbed her hands as if what she'd said about them were paint she was trying to get off before it dried.

"I lied about my hands," she said. "Can we pretend that? I lied about them."

She gave in completely to his touch where touch had never before been deliberate. And then she was lying beside him. And then he was above her . . .

The first bullet zissed through the leaves and whined over their heads.

"Jesus!" Morse sprang to his feet. "That was a bullet. What the hell – "

161

"No!" Kate said, grasping at him. "Lie down flat. If it's someone shooting . . ."

They lay flat on the ground. A second shot followed. And a third. And then there was a pause.

"It must be that fool Rex target shooting," Morse said. "He had a rifle that night they came. Doesn't the damn fool know how far a gun like that will carry? We've got to get out of here."

They waited a little longer like people waiting for the lull in the storm to confirm itself before racing to the house from the sheltering tree.

"I think we ought to make a dash for it now," Morse said. "You're not afraid, are you?"

"No," she said. She wanted to go, quickly. They had grabbed up their rods, but the trout was left parching on the bank.

"Crouch as low as you can," he said.

They ran, crouching, down the path until the whine of bullets started again, well behind them. They stood straight then, and again the morning fell about them like a cloak. But it had been pierced full of spy-holes. And Kate's shame at her self-exposure had settled again on her with such a weight that she almost stumbled under it.

"Wait till I see that crazy nitwit," Morse said. He touched her cheek. "But, don't forget. Tomorrow we're coming back here again. Same spot. Same thing."

"No, Morse," Kate begged him. "Please. In the name of all touched old spinsters who ever made a show of themselves, can we please . . . please . . . never mention this morning again?"

He gave her no answer but a startled pause – and then an enigmatic shrug, with one finger to his closed lips in a gesture that she could not read with any certainty as either humouring or derisive.

CHAPTER 19

In the bedroom, Rex stood chained to himself. He had no more thought of returning with the extra shells than if some intervening disaster had rendered his errand absurd. When word of a death is brought in, you don't go on with your charades.

He looked at his face in the mirror. Where *was* everyone? Sheila. Everyone. All the people that face used to be the passport to. He studied it closer and he saw that the face his mind had kept seeing as his was gone. You had this feeling that you could choose how your own face looked, but you were wrong. It went its own way.

His eyes went a little wild. Sheila wouldn't have believed them. It was strange how she could read Bruce's greater complexity with such precision and be so often wrong in the sureness that she knew Rex through and through.

The gears of his flesh began to grind. He knew what was coming. One of those attacks – that Sheila knew nothing about. That launched themselves with such silence and stealth.

He felt the orchestra of dismay begin to take their places in the pit of his head. In the time it took him to draw the window blind, something dropped an eyelid between him and touch. The very objects in the room became their own corpses. He moved from the mirror to the bed.

He lay on his side on the bed, huddled in the shape of a question mark. One eye was pressed against the pillow. The other he covered tight with his hand. But it was only in appearance the cataleptic mask of flesh asphyxiated with grief. He lay like someone bludgeoned, but it was not stun. It was the ungrammared agony of him who has never shipped any oars for that dead sea which comes to everyone, when the breeze of others' attention veers from your sails to their own – come there now and transfixed there in the very eye of a hurricane loneliness.

He was encircled by an absolutely naked hush in the things around him. That terrible escapeless hush when sounds are without echo, objects without shadow, words without inflection, touch without touching. . . . The sun comes out, but it is still there. Move, run, its boundaries move with you. Shout, and it is still there, unpierced. Put your head in your hands, it gets in behind your hands. Close your eyes, it gets in behind the lids. Lie down to sleep, it springs up from the pillow into the dark of your mind. It was exhaustion so that when you lie down exhausted you still have the feeling of having to stand up exhausted. It flayed the very casings off his thought and sense.

Flensed of its casings his mind's eye saw in the dark of his skull like a cat's.

It fragmented into a swarming hive of headlights – one for each of the locomotives of flash-thought that began to race along the infinite rails of his brain, himself a passenger on all of them. Sometimes leaping from one to the next as they shot past each other. Sometimes glimpsing in their glare all the bright destinations that might have been his if some diabolic switch had not shunted him where he was now. The locomotives swerved and slewed on the crisscross tracks of his brain but, like the galaxies, without collision. Until all together they jumped the tracks and shot straight outward . . . to crumple, one by one, against the impenetrable wall of his skull.

And then his mind's eye was one single white light again, trying to identify this scrap of wreckage or that. The dark smoke of them rose up like fog curling up bereft from rotten snow, to cloud his skull tight; like the smoke of all the butt ends of all the cigarettes he had ever smoked and the dregs in all the glasses he had ever drunk from, packed tight in a little socket between his eyes. And his skull shrank again to exactly its physical size: the size a soap bubble may be blown to before it bursts.

He didn't move a muscle. It was the gritting fixity of someone turning on the self to which he is as inescapably shackled as convex to concave, with a burning hatred of everything about it. Inside and out.

And then, in a single reflex twitch, as if to distract it from shouting out its secret, he shifted his crumpled foot.

A squid's ink of the shame he called anger mounted inside him. Denting his consciousness just short of puncture with its true name. His consciousness put its fingers into its ears not to hear that name pronounced.

And then, falling back unnamed, the shame coated all his other feelings like a verdigris; paralysed them like those predators that go with unerring aim to the exact pregnable spot at the back of their victim's neck. His foot seemed more like a face than his face. It seemed as if all these years he had been walking on his face. He still lay there without a physical tremor, his forehead drawn taut as if in some shocking scrutiny, his jaw muscles set, his teeth clamped tight as if onto a rope.

And then this ferment began its dreadful transubstantiation. Into the flesh of fear.

He had never been a coward in any sense. But it was in just this capricious way that the transubstantiation had first made itself manifest. In fleeting fears.

Driving along the street sometimes it would seem as if the approaching car turned suddenly monstrous and inimical in every line, certain to smash evilly into his side. For seconds after it had passed, his foot would tremble on the gas pedal as if he'd just taken a long dizzying drag on some frightful cigarette. His hands would feel as useless as wings on the wheel until the dark cloud of *imminence,* that was visible to himself alone, lightened. . . . And sometimes there'd be this senseless fear of what might be alurk behind anything opaque. Lifting up the car hood

164

to see if the battery needed water, he would feel himself tensed for the possible shock of finding all the cables broken, the block split in two, and the gasoline through some will of its own exploding in his face. . . . He hesitated sometimes at the threshold of the most familiar door, fearing that when he opened it he'd find the ceiling fallen or a fire blazing in the sofa cushions . . .

At first these flashes had been only momentary, and at first touched off only by things that did hold some dangerous force in leash. Objects in velocity (the train from Greenwich to New York). Water under pressure (he might turn on the tap to shave and for a second expect the pipes to burst with a brutish clang). Fire, electricity, gasoline . . . Only the gun was exempt.

And then the flashes began to stretch out. One morning he might waken to feel that the whole day was on a hair trigger, and that only by the wariest threading of himself through avoidance after avoidance could he navigate the trembling hours intact . . .

And then, still later on – this fearfulness or its ghost began to appear on the face of things that were altogether harmless.

Passing the Flatiron Building, he would suddenly take the sidewalk's farthest edge because it seemed as if the building's mortar were going to crumble between the bricks and the whole structure topple toward him in one of those long swooning dives that toppled buildings make in spectacle movies. Or, walking up their Belle Haven driveway (if Sheila hadn't met him at the station), one of its trees might suddenly seem poised to split from top to bottom across his path with some black centrifugal lightning . . .

And now, just lately, this menacing cast had begun to spread to people. Where of all places before, the sun of a mutual beneficence had warmed him safest. Now, he might suddenly read in their faces, behind their outward expression, that look which gives no quarter, that sickening transformation which the child shrinks from in the adult when they join the company of a second adult.

Strangers accosting him, if only salesmen . . . a voice on the telephone whose identity or purpose he couldn't immediately place . . . even the most familiar face hailing him from a distance . . . any of these might strike in him the instant chill that this was someone coming to "get him." That the moment was at hand for a *showdown* on some accusation against him of whose nature he hadn't the slightest inkling. Up to now he had lived like a child, poised on the springboard of each moment to leap into what might be exciting or different in the next. But now he might feel the chill cackle of apprehension merely to think of testing a new garment for fit. An unexpected letter, and something inside him would go white as the page until he'd sent his eyes darting over its content, frisking it for what weapon he didn't know. At the touch of any strange situation whatever, something inside him would ball up like an inchworm you touch with a blade of grass.

None of this showed. He was a far, far better actor than people took him to be. And whatever else inside him ran or crouched or balled up, some basic courage still stood its ground.

But it had got so his breath walked more and more on the tight-rope of emergency. It got so this dark-predictive face of existent things found its way even into the objects of his dreams. Not in the surrealism of nightmare that waking rescues you from, but with exactly its same undistorted daytime chill – so that neither dream nor waking was an escape one from the other.

Outside the window blind, a roomful of prodigal April sunshine held itself ready to pour in. But his was the weather of November's close – when unshed rain clings to wool like frost and the liver-spotted hymnal with the Roman numerals on its frontispiece moulders in the attic and the woods you walk in give you no woods feeling, only the stark multiplication of each insensible tree.

And now, lying there right now, for the first time the menacing face that had hitherto been only occasional in this thing or that became the face of *everything*. He lay there crouched beneath it, tense in each last fibre of consciousness for the moment when some terrific suction must suddenly blow every door in the house open . . . or as slight a detonator as the dropping of a spoon touch off some splintering thunderclap of elemental sound . . . or one extra charge of this dreadful current cause Shape itself to disintegrate. His throat muscles were taut with alertness for a matching scream.

And now the transubstantiation took another form.

The quintessential perfume of loneness and apprehension had been like a vapour so attenuated that even the naming of it with noun or the description of it with adjective would make it sound too falsely substantive. Now, as if under such pressure that it changed its state, it condensed into physical pain.

Pain had once been as alien to him as caution to a child. But once struck with it, it had turned out to be the one thing that blossomed with imagination.

His head felt tight, as if he had never exhaled. Nothing was sharp or declarative. But blunt little toothaches of ache were inserted against his brain. A kind of smoke of ache flooded upward into his skull, as if from a vial where the words that used to mean nothing to him – bruise and discouragement, disappointment and stain, dreg and frustration and gone – and the taste of brass and the sound in seashells and the touch on rope – were all being brewed together. And the content of one vial, so pure it was almost an odour again, was poured over the top of his head and seeped down through it: the essence of the word "unnamable." You could never explain why this was an ache no physic could reach. (And whenever he said his head ached, Sheila mentioned aspirin!) It was the kind of sickness when that part of you which *feels* the sickness is itself sick.

And then it seemed as if crews of tiny faceless men began to set up their frightening engines inside his skull.

Little networks of spider-rope were stretched in every direction. Nothing quite attached anywhere, or quite touching anything else – but everything tightened to just within its breaking point. The ropes chafed against his thoughts, though never quite enough to rupture their skin. Little telegraph systems were set up, and the ache ceaselessly tapped out the message of its own tirelessness along them. The circuits sagged but never quite snapped. Little battering rams were pressed against his temples, but never quite split them open. Weights that themselves ached for being suspended by their own arms were not quite attached to his eyelids. Every nerve in his head was tied up and suspended in the position of prisoners who can't quite touch their feet to the ground. A million little suction cups pressed everywhere there was blood, drawing it upward against a downward pull, and whitening it. Two blunt thumbs pressed against the arteries in his throat without quite choking them off . . .

He pressed his own fingers viciously against his scalp as if to bring the pain's maddening just-out-of-reachness to a head. But just beneath the flesh at every spot he touched, individual pulses of it began to beat no less elusively than behind his eyes.

And then the system of ropes and weights and wires was extended downward to his heart and along the corridors of his breath.

His breath dragged the weights back and forth with it and his heart felt drained and sore with them.

And then his breath and heart themselves became a kind of shipping station. Each inhalation and each systole carried back to his head a little trainful of sensations that had no property except that of heft, and unloaded them there. Until his head had not a pinpoint cavity of open space left in it.

But there was no stopping these inexorable trains. Still they came. And their baggage had to be jammed in denser and denser and squeezed down tighter and tighter and tighter inside his skull . . .

Sleep . . . he beseeched something.

If he could only sleep . . .

He knew it would do no good to get up and move about. He couldn't give this thing the slip that way. It would shift from foreground to background, but as long as he stayed conscious it would stay dried on his brain.

But, sleep . . . he knew this like some incredible statistic . . . sleep without dream could wash it out. Could cut the crisscross scaffolding from under the network of pain so that it fell down and dissolved in a merciful exhaustion, trembly but transparent. He would awake with space in his skull again and the traffic in his heart and breath completely cleared. For weeks after, perhaps, it would be as if this had never happened.

Sleep without dream . . . he implored something. Sleep . . .

He slumped for a moment, absolutely yielding. The extent of his suffering was so great it seemed almost a flattery.

But sleep was wide awake and just moving off whenever he tried to lay his head down on it.

And then the grinding anger began.

This stillness, these fears, this crew inside his head, goading him, goading him, because they knew he couldn't get at them . . . oh, he'd like to give them one big surprise. He knew how he could do it too. He'd like to send a bullet through his damned head. Oh, that would finish them, wouldn't it? That was one stillness he could damn well smash this one with. Smash every one of these things still. Smash them . . . Smash them . . . *Smash* them . . .

Or would they only scatter . . . and come back like maggots to ache-eat his brain away even after it was dead?'

He moved then. He tore his hand from his face. He drove his foot against the bed board. He started to scream.

But the scream got no farther than a sob in his shoulders.

Sheila came up the stairs slowly. She carried the gun and Rex's ruined jacket. Her last shot had gone fair through the heart, aim as she had between the trees.

With each step her face seemed to drop one more garment of expression and put some article of its work clothes back on. By the time she had reached the bedroom door, it was a mask of: Well, you and I again, but let's not go into that.

She took a long breath and opened the door, her first glance prepared to locate Rex's face and her next to look away from it until one or the other had spoken first.

When she saw him on the bed, sound asleep and breathing quietly as a child, her face looked tricked. She was always cueing herself for the wrong scene. How could anyone just lie down and go to sleep in the middle of the day? she thought. I wish I had the secret. But how like him, if he felt sleepy, to let his promise to bring back the shells go hang!

She tiptoed to the foot of the bed, looking at him all the time, the way you keep trying to read a sleeping face. It wasn't at all chilly in the room and she didn't know why she did it, but she sighed and bent down and eased a fold of blanket up over his lower extremities. He didn't stir. For such a restive person, she thought, I never saw anyone who slept gentler.

More and more as she read his face it seemed as if she came across passages that were inexplicably touching because they gave – gave *away* – just the opposite impression to the one his waking face strove for.

Sleepers look denied. Your own wakefulness seems to be a sneaking advantage. Every mutual rancour in the past seems to have been your own fault. It seems that as soon as the sleeper opens his eyes everything can get off to a fresh start. She felt half-penitent, as if in spending (on herself) the waking time he'd been asleep she'd been spending something that was half-his.

She let herself down quietly into the chair by the window, dropping the footfall of her gaze cautiously on each object she saw outside, as if it might arouse him.

She knew how automatically the waking face could shred your mood toward the sleeping one. She promised him that, thus fore-warned, her face would wear no jarring cast when he awoke, to force his own into the clamp of any matching attitude. Nothing but peace.

CHAPTER

A naked rain was falling when Paul arrived at Windsor Station in Montreal. Rain at Endlaw plucked at the leaves like robins at cherries. Here, it brought to a polish the cruel strangeness in the streets he glimpsed outside. It seemed incredible to him that travel had once been his basic urge.

The crowds in the lobby, with the hurrying eyes equally intent whether on something or nothing, jostled him as he walked to the exit. With no one to meet him, even the bag of personal clothing he carried looked as estranged from him as if it contained the props of ventriloquism.

Bruce Halliday. He repeated to himself the new name he'd taken. One familiar enough to him in sound and association that he could wear it without detectable or surprisable awkwardness – yet nothing like his own; and so, with strangers, his shield. He'd thought it would give him absolute cover, absolute immunity. It did nothing. He had stepped onto a seesaw that for the next few days would swing back and forth between wholeness and dissolution like a pendulum. This was the first high point in the arc of dissolution.

He'd counted on these strangers (then featureless) as a vacuum in which he could operate with perfect anonymity. But it was not so. Suddenly each of them presented an individual face. Just to look at anyone, to have him look at you, is to know him a little, to be involved. Wherever there are actual faces you can't escape engagement. Your public part is forced to the surface. Just the presentness of the present moment made it nothing like as manipulatable as it had been in prospect.

Never before had strangers affected him the way they did now.

Looking at them, it seemed as if they knew exactly who they were. A single sharp definition for each of them. And skimming him with the most casual return glance they seemed to challenge him to the definitive statement of himself. In one single sentence.

He could find none. Only a cloud of phrases and clauses. He had counted on their facelessness to support him. Now (though he knew this to be imagination only), he felt as if it were himself who was so faceless as to attract stares.

With friends, his indistinctness had never worked that way. In that context, however unfailing his talent for submerging his own identity in empathetic parallel to theirs, he had never been a chameleon. What his indefiniteness had cost him in height it had seemed to gain him in area. His noncommittal grin had somehow come out as authority; his equanimity somehow a manlier thing than wrestling. Himself lacking index, they had nevertheless seemed to look themselves up in him, as if he were a dictionary to their own subtleties. And however separate he had kept himself from absolute communion with them, their company had nevertheless been as stabilizing as the iron bars that are dropped into molten cement. It had drawn his mind's attention away from itself long enough that the guarding part of it could, with the strength of enough rest, put down that outlaw part which sometimes threatens to uproot the whole consciousness and draw it away somewhere like a labyrinth of trailing vines.

But here, with these strangers, where he'd been sure he'd find himself freest, he felt himself the most invaded. Here, out of context, with nothing for them to add him up from except his appearance, and each of them seeming to challenge him for the single sentence he couldn't discover, he felt absolutely lost. He was invaded by an absolute loneliness. For the second time he saw what a self-delusion his self-sufficiency had been. It was nothing.

And here, in this homesickness, among these strangers, Kate's face sprang up behind his eyes, and again it struck him just how much he loved her.

Hers was the face that turned up the quintessence of everything you looked at with her to its perceptible limit. It was the face that would give you the most exultant feeling in the world, for knowing that you loved it, to see its lips trembling not to cry. It was the face that had, in absence, that partitioned-off light about it of a dream in which you were young again.

When he went back to Endlaw, with this sickness shoved out (as suddenly he felt it would be: you can never really believe that pain is something stained into your flesh, that there is not *some* persuasion it will bow to), he would ask her to marry him . . .

He gave the cab driver the hospital address. Inside the cab his face again felt at once as insulated from the passers-by as a public figure's in a procession, and as exposed.

And then the cab driver's face engaged him, its individuality. He could see that this was one of those people who can't rest until they've established some point of resemblance between themselves and whomever they meet. And despite all his resolution to walk through these days with his real self in abeyance, Paul was helpless not to respond. He must help him set up that fancied correspondence.

A stern-busted matron in a club-woman hat stepped off the curb against the light. The driver honked his horn at her. She gave him a haughty stare.

Paul studied the driver a moment. Yes, that's how he'd figure himself: an inspired clown.

"When they do that," Paul said, "couldn't you rig a little gadget on your horn that'd pop out and goose them?"

The driver's grin came on like a light. There was the point of similarity! This was a comical guy, just like himself. Paul ceased to be a fare, became an ally. He began to tell him all the other wacky things you ran into in this game. He slowed down a little, as if Paul was someone on whom he must register himself while this one and only opportunity lasted.

They approached the hospital.

"It's none of my business," he said, "but I hope it ain't nothing serious brings you here."

171

"No," Paul said. "Just a check-up. I don't think they'll turn up anything serious."

"I hope not," he said.

He really did. Paul had that quality of person which, with its opening sentence, however unexceptional, intrigues you like the opening sentence of certain books. Strangers always wished they could have more time with him, to find how he came out. They didn't want anything to happen to him.

The driver swung off the street into the hospital driveway. He treated Paul to a little flourish of driving expertise, landing him within inches of the entrance steps. He delivered the buddy's parting shot which he'd been grooming these last few moments.

"Now watch out them nurses don't get their hands up your Johnny shirt," he said.

"If they do," Paul said, "I'll take *their* temperature with *my* thermometer."

The driver threw back his head and roared. Touché!

He gave Paul his card. "Any time you want a cab," he said, "just call this number and ask for Ingersoll. Know how I got that name? I can tell the time o' day within five minutes if I ain't looked at my watch for hours!"

"Good luck!" he sang out to Paul when Paul was halfway up the steps.

His familiarity invaded Paul more than the first strangeness had done. There *was* no way you could take even your sickness into the wilderness and wrestle with it, uninvolved.

The rain had stopped. White uniforms of nurse and interne shuttling from building to building flashed cold as knives. (Home, an April night after rain, everything would be the colour of wood or leaf or wild rock; nothing the colour of fabric or educated stone.)

Paul felt a chill, as if every sickness that had ever been cast out of its bodily habitation here still lingered in the corridors like a homeless guest.

He felt unfleshed, diminished to nothing but his voice; as if the rags of your sickness were the only aspect of you these lordly, white-staring therapists could see. For a moment he was less conscious of his sickness's invasion than of its loyalty. At least, having chosen him, it punished him as an equal. Kate. For a moment his tongue reached for her name and a shower of her broke over his brain . . . .

Inside the rotunda, the lights were on full; and to glance back outside it was suddenly night.

Twosomes watched and waited for the elevators. Their street clothing looked suddenly out of place on them. One waited for the elevator that would take his sickness to the clinical rooms above, where it would be processed in a final nakedness; the other to see his sickness off. A single glance and you could tell which was the sick and which the solicitous. Something masked the sick with a fearful best behaviour. They were like children out of their depth. They stepped back more than the necessary pace to give anyone in authority passage past them. And suddenly out of that wariness that tried to pass itself off as lethargy, they answered too dutifully any question that was asked them and with too extravagant a smile.

The woman beside Paul addressed her husband, who sat there in acute embarrassment at being exposed in the company of his sickness, in a quite public voice.

"I imagine," she said, "that one there with her hair in a bun's the one takes your name and everything, ain't it? Now you tell 'em all about your kidneys too. And don't worry about things home. It won't hurt Harve one bit to give us a hand. You done enough for him, Lord knows!"

Somehow her remark had an effect of consolation on Paul.

In this climate of abject divestment he felt a returning flush of integration. His autonomy straightened up again. He would *not* be invaded. He would not allow his sickness to be a lever in anyone's hand to scatter his wholeness. Again, he willed it to have been a trifling one, with no real roots in him. He held this willed picture over the reality the way drugs hold their hands over the eyes of pain.

And when it came his turn with the woman at the admitting desk, whose immaculate bun was like the centre of gravity of her extortionate poise, it was he who took subtle command of the interview. Instead of using a stabbing glance with each question she directed, as she did at the supplicant meekness she was so accustomed to, she disposed of his questionnaire as unobtrusively as if it were a particle of phlegm one of them was disembarrassing himself of while the other held a mannerly inattention. When it was finished she gave him a sudden off-duty smile and escorted him to the elevator personally.

The nurse who settled him into his room, likewise so used to chronic mastery over the abated and the abashed, he likewise conquered. And the glib-eyed interne who took his clinical history and gave him the first routine examination.

He slept and woke. He could sense the incessant trooping of anxieties in the corridors outside. In all the corridors of the world people were baffled about the next step to take . . .

But lying rested in his bed he had a sudden access of euphoria.

The picture his will had forged became authentic. His sickness *was* without root. This master doctor could pluck it out without there having been any real invasion by either the pain or the cure. And then he would ask Kate to marry him. She was the one person with whom he could feel both invaded and free.

But the following day the pendulum arc-ed back. When they took the cardiogram (making him dance up and down at one point like a puppet) and gave him other prescribed tests, he felt like prey. And again when he first encountered Dr Lennick.

Dr Lennick sat beside the bed, his stethoscope dangling about his neck like a mayoralty chain. The cut and cloth of his suit spoke urbanity from every fold. He was not wearing the usual white, annulling smock. His very tie-clip and cufflinks had the confidence of features. In such immaculacy, he looked as if this were a Sunday call quite divorced from suffering's weekday raggedness; as if he had brought to it nothing professional but his ineradicably professional hands.

Paul had counted on his being a much older man, his face easefully lined with the marks of listening. Himself in mussed pajamas, he again felt stripped and homesick.

Until the doctor opened conversation.

"Nova Scotia," he said. "That's the province for fishing, isn't it? . . . and hunting, in the fall?"

At once Paul took his cue. This was the doctor-fisherman type. The hunter-doctor whose costly gear and togs his guide would find in no way ludicrous, because this one could shoot and tote and lace the rum into the black tea after the long day's tramp as primordially as himself.

"Yes," Paul said. "The salmon run's started in the Granfort River already. There's a mill creek they come into just below the town, with a little stillwater" – he saw the word strike an almost sensual gleam in the doctor's eye – "and . . . well, I've taken fourteen, sixteen pounders there before now."

He knew he had awakened the doctor's keenest, if kindliest envy. He too was a specialist, practising at will in the very field to which the doctor could only look with longing. They were back on even ground.

"What kind of fly?" the doctor said.

Paul grinned.

"Well," he said, "each man to his own sorcery, you know. Actually, I concoct a little lure of my own with a bit of pheasant feather and a sliver of pimento."

The doctor grinned back.

"Just unbotton your top," he said, in a sort of aside. "You have pheasants down there? I didn't know that."

"Oh yes," Paul said. "And it's funny about them. They're so bloody beautiful you almost hate to bring them down – but yet when you do you feel like having a drink on it, you know?"

The doctor nodded. Paul could sense that almost mystical rod-and-gun fraternity between them. The stethoscope was dotting his chest with spy posts; but his first foolish longing to disown his heartbeat, as if it were a witless companion prattling just the wrong comment about you to rupture a moment of fusion, vanished.

"I've never hunted pheasants," the doctor said. His voice was almost wistful. "A deep breath now . . ." he said in another aside.

He conducted the whole examination as if it were an aside. Again Paul felt clothed and confident. His sickness too seemed like an aside. He had ceased entirely to feel like prey.

The doctor sought further details about his pain (when? where? of what type? for how long? of what severity?) – and this time Paul held nothing back – but he didn't pounce on any answer and pursue it. Paul could sense him folding up his mind, to leave. He felt like a prisoner who's braced himself for a third degree and been asked nothing but his name and address.

"Is it only when you do something strenuous you get these pains?" the doctor put his final question. Still like an aside.

"No," Paul said. "Lately they often come right out of the blue."

That had been his first shocking discovery: that your body could strike you for no reason whatsover, like an animal you'd trusted to be entirely tamed with food and affection suddenly baring its wild streak.

The doctor had a clip of papers with him. He glanced at the top sheet. Paul supposed it was dotted with facts about him that could be joined to form a likeness like those concoctable by drawing from number to consecutive number. But he no longer felt exposed. For the first time his alias gave him complete cover.

"Well," the doctor said, rising, "your tests should all be in tomorrow. I'll look them over and we'll see if we can't get you back to your fishing as soon as possible."

Home. Paul's mind held its hands over the little brazier that this word alone could light in his mind. Home. Where it didn't matter whether you came back with the trophy or the scar.

But now he had no fear that it would be the scar. With this man in league with him against his sickness, it would surely be routed.

The doctor turned at the door.

"A sliver of . . . what was it you said you used?"

"Pimento," Paul said, smiling.

Dr Lennick himself took Paul into the laboratory and showed him the photograph of death. Paul knew what it was, from the doctor's face. He didn't have to hear the word "thrombosis."

You see a juggernaut approaching in your mind, you throw a deflecting thought in its path. Paul's first deflecting thought when he looked at the cardiograph tracings was: It's nothing like the pictures artists draw of death. No *kind* of form. Nothing but a ragged alternation of stalactite and stalagmite, the shape of icicle teeth along an eave.

The doctor explained its detail, while a group of white-coated technicians shuttled to and fro in the room. Their own mortality not yet confirmed, they islanded Paul in the hush of the one kind of realization that suddenly pencils in your boundaries as if with the hand of a lightning cartoonist. You couldn't fool death with a false name, was his second thought.

For a moment his face had the look about it of the hands of someone on whom a joke has been sprung so dismaying that he doesn't know whether to laugh or to cry. And that other, make-do look (as if the whole face inhales) that meets the one occasion for which there *is* no look: when the bland flux of things suddenly discloses the mindless fist, strikes with it, and then hoods it again. For a moment his eyes had the catch in them of one whose glance falls on the sky some November dusk when the coming evening's prospect has no texture save that of the pendancy of curtains and the gravitational rootedness of chairs, or of one whose hand continues to rest on the telephone after receiving a staggering wire.

But for a moment only.

His face as quickly exhaled (so, when the homebound train is just pulling out as you reach the station platform, do you turn and bend again to the weight of the suitcases you were carrying the homecoming presents in); and once again he was simply and absolutely stage-confident in the role of the man who's just been told he is soon to die.

He picked up the message the photograph directed at him. He had no fear of it. But he didn't read it through. He wouldn't read it through until he was alone. Alone, he could match anything's eye with the level of his own.

"How long?" he said to Dr Lennick, his tone a challenge to complete candour.

"Well," the doctor hedged, "we don't like to talk in terms of any specific time, you know. We can't, to tell the truth. The heart's a funny thing. Perhaps the most capricious organ in the whole body. Sometimes, no matter what its defects, it will bear all kinds of strains with hardly a complaint. And sometimes a comparative trifle will . . ."

It was he who looked confused – as if he didn't know whether this unaccountable affection for Paul was friendly or paternal or filial or what.

"But you're *thinking* in terms of some specific time, aren't you?" Paul said.

The facial inflection of having good-naturedly scored a point came as easy to him as an actor's. He felt total mastery of the situation.

"All right," the doctor said. He shed his professional mask. "I'm giving you some nitroglycerin tablets . . . and if you don't overdo . . . it could be years." He hesitated: he could never remember having felt so sick to know that never yet had he been mistaken in a case of this kind. "Or it could be tomorrow."

Paul sat on the bed in his room and began to read the message through. Off the walls and the floor and his hands and his feet. Engraved there in a script so remorselessly legible it was without grace whatsoever.

He read the part that had all the words in it starting with "n", the most remorseless of all letters, the one that infects every syllable it helps to form. (Take it out of "alone," and you still had "aloe.") No and nothing and never . . . .

He read the part where it said: "You will suddenly be nothing." He tried to think what "nothing" would be like. He couldn't.

He skipped to the postscript:

But you're lucky. This ending will be clean. No rot. No wilting face in the fetid capsule of bedclothes for them (who?) to try to mourn at the end but fail to, because their mourning likewise has wilted into a fret. And, it went on, knowing how close you are to the freedom of death, you can tap that knowledge for the freedom to act in all the ways that life constrains.

He tested this. He put some shapes of recklessness out on the window ledge of his mind. But they wouldn't lift their wings. And he knew there would be no mutinous behaviour of any kind. You wondered why people, certain of death, loosed from the straitjacket of caution, never turned their remaining days into an exclamation point of all the madbrain impulses they had hitherto stifled. Now he knew why not.

You couldn't grasp the fact of death. You could no more (both blessing and curse) *realize* that "I am going to die" than you could

177

stand up sticks in a rushing current. The rushing current of the actual moment so persisted in its sentience of unlimited future, so held you from leaping far enough outside its magnetic field to observe it, that you went on doing exactly as you'd always done . . .

He looked out the window. Everywhere there was movement. The April sun touched each glinting surface. But somehow remotely here, inaccessibly; more like a winter sun back home touching the glaze of a sled-runner track. A high April cloud was ceaselessly dissolving one shape into another. But it too was like a winter cloud back home.

The message itself clouded over. He could make out the great fixed capitals of KATE and NEVER – but in between, the lines were so quickly shingled one upon another that to decipher them was like trying to separate layers of smoke . . .

He stood up then. His mind straightened with him and threw back the crouch out of its shoulders.

He tried by a swamping attack of will to pile-drive a stick into the current's bed . . . to know for one moment at least, eye to eye, flesh to flesh, the message's very core. This had always been his key to victory. If he could stare out a thing's core into a flash of constitutive feature he was never, from then on, in any way its suppliant.

But this thing was different.

This was not a noun, with a noun's face. It was a faceless verb. He couldn't tell if it was transitive or intransitive. All he could grasp was its *ad*verbial shadow.

And, oddly enough, this was gentling, as all the final trickeries are. You were slewed around, with eyes in your back – facing all that had or hadn't happened to you : a gallery with subtly shifted emphases, at once totally communicative and totally deaf; but numinously distinct in some opalescent light like the sun's light drawing water over a high wall of trees in the primaeval secrecy before a change of weather.

And you felt as if you were dreaming the whole thing, in a dream that yet knew it was not a dream. (He wished he could have dreamed it long ago . . . been informed of it in the way that only dream's sixth sense can inform exactly. So that, awakening, he could have known exactly what it was like but also known that it was not yet fact. You shouldn't have to face the likeness and the now of it in the same breath.)

Again and again he stressed himself in waves of concentration against the ineluctable note of the verb, the way you try to flush the just-elusive memory of a name. But it would not come.

Reverberating? Was that its note? No. Muting? No. Cueing? No. Hinting? . . . Lurking . . ?

He gave it up. He couldn't do it here, where the monotone of strangeness hummed like invisible tuning bars between the lines of the message and its meaning. Home, he thought. There I can capture it. Where the trees and the house and the sky will help translate it for me. Each in its own particular hand, as familiar as a wife's.

And then, suddenly, without conscious bidding, there was a pulse-thump of recognition and the verb's name flashed across his vision like a bulletin.

The verb was "notify"!

That was the way it went! You drifted along, with all perceptions swaddled in a cirrus of hopes and forgetfulness and hearsay and excuses; then all at once you were precisely *notified*. Of *everything*. And you stood there with the implacable registered letter in your hand and there'd be no more swaddling cirrus ever again.

"All right." He said the words aloud. Let's have no more of this literary dying. Who do you think you are, Robert Jordan?

All right, then. You've been notified of everything, so align your compass with the facts. With that clear a direction anyone should be able to hold a steady course. He set his compass then and there, its North his old familiar star: no one must know. He had lived alone. He would die alone.

He finished packing.

His hand was on the doorknob, to leave, when the pain arrested him. "Just one more thing," comes the cross-examiner's question right when you think you're in the clear.

It pencilled a hot white wire across his thoughts, bleaching them as vertigo bleaches appetite. He saw that pain *was* the one inquisitor that struck at the nerve centres of the will in a way neither imagination could conceive nor memory reconstruct.

He staggered back and lay across the bed. He didn't call a nurse. He tried to bargain with the pain: Let me off just this once. Please. Don't kill me here. Not here. Home, home, home . . .

The pain came closer, and closer, and excruciatingly closer . . . hunting down spots inside him he didn't know he had so close . . . until he was nothing *but* pain, and the only concreteness in his fleshly mask the teeth clenched over it . . .

And then . . . that claw of it went in no deeper than the last one anyway . . . And this one not quite so deep . . . Or this one . . .

And then, listening to the pain as much as feeling it, he heard it going away. Gradually, grudgingly, sulkingly at compromise with total victory . . . but it was going away.

He didn't move a muscle. He lay there and listened until he was sure it was out of hearing.

And then he got to his feet, moving very cautiously, and once again will found its familiar toeholds.

In the lobby he called the taxi stand and asked for Ingersoll.

"Well," Ingersoll said, "did they fix you up?"

Paul grinned.

"You mean the nurses?" he said. "No, they wouldn't even shake hands with it."

CHAPTER 21

"Good morning, Letty," the postmaster said. He reached for General Delivery. "Warm."

"Hot," Letty corrected him. Her voiceful hands clasped and unclasped the latch of her purse. "Never remember 'em havin' to close the woods in April before. They're like tinder."

The postmaster flipped through the letters.

"Morse Halliday?" he said. "That's yours, isn't it? I been out sick for a week, but wasn't he here once before?"

Letty nodded. "Yes. He's the one writes books. Maybe you heard of them."

"No? No? Can't say I have."

"I don't *see*," Letty said, "how a man like Morse kin set down all be his lonesome and make up them rigmaroles. When you couldn't hire him to tell a lie to anyone's face."

The postmaster shook his head: it took all kinds. His hand paused again.

"Rex G-i-o-r-n-o?"

"Jonah," Letty pronounced it for him, gathering up the letter. "That one!"

"And Mrs. Rex Jonah."

"Oh, *she's* nice."

Letty's hand worked in a quick visit to her hair.

"Is Paul back yet?" the postmaster said. "I seen him boarding the train, was it Thursday?"

"No," Letty said. "I kinda looked for him today. But they tell me the Digby's boat's broke down agin. I suppose he'll have to go round be Halifax. All that extry travellin'. And he hates travellin' so." Her voice went at once soft and authoritative, as wives' voices do when they quote from the catalogue of husband foible they've compiled with such affection. "It's funny, he used to love it. Now he hates it."

"I thought there was another . . ." the postmaster said. "Ah, here it is." He pushed the last envelope in the pile across to her. "Bruce Halliday," he said. "Father and son?"

"No," Letty said. "Ketch any o' them with children! They're too wise."

The postmaster smiled. He hadn't heard the word used in that sense for years.

Letty puzzled. "No," she said again. "We got no Bruce Halliday. We got a Bruce *Mansfield* . . . maybe you remember him . . . but . . ."

"Well, take it anyway," he said. "It must be your Halliday it's meant for. There's no one else that name around here."

Letty picked the letter up. She could feel some hard thin object inside it.

"Where's it from?" she said. "I ain't got my glasses."

Letty could read a little, but it was like translating with only a skimpy dictionary and no knowledge whatever of the construction and grammar. Whenever she came across the blind letters of a strange word she felt like someone in the presence of the law.

"It's date-stamped Montreal," the postmaster said.

"Oh then, it's from Paul," she said. "He's wrote to Morse and" – her voice turned soft again – "I wish you could see how absent-minded he is sometimes, he's put down Bruce's name on it."

"It's from the Renfrew Hospital," the postmaster said, "according to the stationery. Is that where Paul is?"

"Oh no," she said. Her hands clasped each other. "No, I don't *think* so."

But who knew? Something might have happened to him. Could he be in hospital there, so *sick* he got the names twisted? She had such a sudden clap of misgiving she felt half-undressed. She wanted to get outside at once. She glanced almost with anger at the originating address in the letter's corner. Half the trouble in the world come from printin' things. It wasn't natural.

"There's nothin' for me, are they?" she said quickly.

"No," he said. "Nothing today."

Her question was ritual, and his answer unvarying. But each time he gave it her heart sank a little. Each time no one wrote to you it made you a little older. The half dozen letters she'd had in her lifetime she'd puzzled out until she knew them by heart. She kept them in her trunk, like treasures.

It took Huldah to show Letty how worked up she really was over Paul. Let her have something on her mind and Huldah was more aggravating than ever. She inflamed her today.

181

"I see your fancy friends in town sometimes," Huldah said. "Mostly going into the liquor store! Letty, I don't see how you stand all that drinking and carousing around you."

"Who said anything about carousin'?" Letty said. "They drink some, yes. But – " she shot Huldah a meaning glance – "sometimes I wonder if that's any worse'n settin' around with a face on ya that'd reach from here to next week."

Huldah was not to be deflected.

"And I seen the Mansfield boy on the street one day with a strange woman," she said. "I suppose it was the Giorno woman. Now isn't she married?"

"You know she's married," Letty said. "But does that mean her and Bruce can't be civil? That musta bin' the day he was showin' her the old Fort."

"Humph!" Huldah snorted. "It didn't look like he was showing her any Fort, the way they was chinning up to each other. That's another thing, Letty. How can you stand to watch them all carry on that brazen . . . well, *bulling*, if I *must* say the word, is all it is . . . with each other? I don't think I could keep my tongue still."

"Oh, fart!" Letty exploded. "God give them privates the same as anyone else." For a second she saw Harry quite plain, bending over her. "And privates's something I guess no one'll ever be able to hush up. I don't make it my business, anyways."

Huldah ignored her.

"Letty," she said plaintively, "*why* don't you come in here with me and Jim? You might as well do it first as last. You know Paul's not as young as he was once. And the way people are dropping off nowadays, he may not always be there either."

"I'll resk it," Letty said.

As usual, Letty felt her spirits rally the moment she turned the corner for home. Her anxiety persisted, but in a quieter key. Paul seriously sick – it was unthinkable. Somehow that stood between her and its being true.

For weeks no rain had fallen; and yet this was exactly like an April morning after rain.

Starting grass and diminutive leaf (whether high in the trees or low in the minuscule forests beneath) had a rained-green freshness. Close to, the air was clear as bird notes; but far-off, something not quite as thick as a haze in it made the trees look like an incredibly light-aerified oil painting of themselves. The sun came out full, making all things distinct and equal, with its warmth. Everything exhaled. The ferns uncurled their tips like a long green breath. The water in the brook ceaselessly chased its own sequins of laughter. And she saw the first small white butterflies blurting and stuttering their immaculate diagrams over the benisoned road.

She rolled down the car window, to enjoy it the more.

And when she did, the same kind of April breeze that had touched Paul so evocatively at the hollow of the throat touched hers. It too a sudden messenger.

She'd had hints of its tidings before. Evenings sometimes, when she would sit at the kitchen table and watch the sun's brook-glaze, totally pacific toward the coming night, green-burnish a leafing tree. Then she might feel its ineffable challenge to grasp each fact and memory in the world, an ineffable pang at her helplessness to meet the challenge.

But this thrust now was different. It held prophecy. This was the first mood in her life she'd had no say in, herself: its entire declaration came from without.

She searched herself for that inner face, variable at will, which in other moods you take such company staring at. But the light had got into the camera: it was completely bleached out. There was nothing anywhere inside her but this blind statement the breeze had delivered, like the statement of windowlight on the floorboards of moved-from houses, with their curtains down and their carpets rolled up.

For what she saw, by sense clearer than if it had been by word, was that nothing contested a thing's being true against you. Fact made no choice, no decision. It simply fell. If you were standing beneath it you were struck, as with a senseless falling plank. She saw that, within itself, the hodgepodge of reality took no sides at all between green and grime, butterflies and phlegm, spring and death . . .

And she saw that as you got her age things did end. Her life had gone so smoothly for so many years now, without a reckoning of any kind. She hadn't been charged with a single major break. But one day that great unseen record system would catch up with her, her file would be pulled out and stamped with all sorts of irrevocable cancellations.

Things did end. Huldah's words about Paul came back to her, She thought of the letter again. Paul . . .

The road blurred and she knew she was crying. One hand brushed angrily at her tears. She was always angry at tears in herself, even when she was alone.

She summoned a muscle in her breath that she had never had to call on before, to shrug this mood loose. It was just strong enough to do what she asked.

Early that morning Kate heard Morse drop his razor in the bathroom. She heard him curse.

These last few days her mind had been stapled at every point to the memories of the stillwater. As, she had premised, his would be too. Hearing him vent this petty and divergent anger she could have struck him. Had his honouring of her plea been nothing more than pure indifference?

They were sitting in the living room now. (Living, loving, leaving rooms, she thought.)

It was pleasanter to be indoors than out. Outdoors, the great blazing tree of April was too dwarfing. The light was too pure, the green too lavish; sounding and resounding until they shocked themselves into a silence too predictive of the evening, when the day's stringent and immaculate beauty seems less like beauty than like a drawing sadness for all the things that have, or haven't, happened in it. Inside, the light was domesticated. It spilled into the room with the levitating of shadow pattern and the coolness of of slant and stripe. The room was grottoed and idled as if its canopy were fern.

This was one of those days (in such a place) that seems to stamp even the most recent orientation between two people with the growth-rings of years.

Last night Kate had dreamed about her father. He'd been showing her the Karnak films, the prehistoric tombs of stone. She'd watched him in two places at once: running the projector and in the films as well. She'd heard the tap, tap, tap of his excavation pick inside the tombs . . . until it turned into the sound of Morse's typing, and awakened her. One eye was still back on the dream.

There'd been a subtle change in Morse these last few days. He'd kept to his room almost continuously, typing. He had the air of one who's happened on some secret panel.

She looked at him now. He was not in his usual sprawl: the abdicating player scorning the whole game. His mind was no longer crouched to spring at provocation; but bolt upright, with grasp in its eye.

He looked as if he'd never be old. The old are marked off from the young in one main way: in them some physical mucosities (the eyes' lubricant, the mouth's inside . . .) offend, which in the young do not. Morse looked as if he'd stay unstained as bone to the day he died. He did look like her father, she thought.

"You know," he said, "I think Letty had a qualm or two about leaving us alone this morning." He chuckled. "Did you notice that long hard look she gave the room? As if lust was going to spring out of it the minute her back was turned, like a Pandora's box?"

He might as well have thrown the morning of the stillwater at her again in as many words. There was no dodging mention of it now.

"Are *you* afraid I'll attack you?" she said bitterly. "After the other day?"

His mood took on grip.

"Look," he said, "you're fishing for a gentleman's answer to that one, you won't get it. I'm not faking this gentlemanly amnesia another minute. I don't wonder you're embarrassed. You really played the Little Match Girl to the hilt, didn't you? But the point is, it didn't embarrass me. I didn't see any Miss Brill. You're no foolish virgin. All I wanted was to put you straight on this sex business – that doesn't amount to much more than a damn good sneeze anyway. You'll see. Would you like a drink?"

She had really thought she might strike him. She found herself laughing.

"No," she said, "I don't want a drink. But you go ahead, if you want one."

"No," he said. "Drinking and writing don't mix."

"You're writing again?"

Her tone was deliberately offhand. She felt every bit of him on the hook, but she'd learned that the only way to play him was with a slack line.

"Yes," he exclaimed. "It's the damnedest thing." His speech tumbled out as if he'd just been delivered from some racking sickness. "I'd been just moving around carrying myself sitting down inside myself – on my own guts. And then . . ."

– Did she want to know what that was like . . . what it was like when a writer wasn't writing? The solid in you separated from the liquid, to form that paralytic guy sitting on your guts. And then you found they'd cut the cords on the little hammock that held your brain up and your brain had slipped down below your eyes. They'd cut your heel cords too and the hammock strings under your heart and they'd taken the balls out of your voice. The only thing they hadn't cut was the one nerve that smoulders when you watch yourself sitting helpless on your own guts. . . . You were like one of those *days* that have no talent – that you try to drink away or sleep away but keep awaking to, dead sober. You couldn't force yourself to write. You could prop the words up on the page, yes; but they wouldn't join hands. You knew the minute you put the paper away each letter in every word dropped down as dead as the spaces between them. That's what it was like when a writer wasn't writing.

"And then . . . whatever it was you did to me . . ."

He came over and sat beside her on the couch. He passed his hand over one of hers and touched her hair as if he were testing them for something enigmatic. Her body was tongue-tied.

He took his hand away and studied it as if it held a text.

"I was carrying myself around exactly like that, see," he said. "And then . . . whatever there is about you . . . that special sort of air, I guess it is, that one person can be for another to breathe . . . I warn you, it's the fanciest damn thing you ever heard. Anyway, I began to inhale you. And my lungs were astonished. An old bastard like me inhaling a woman again! Only it wasn't like any of the others I'd inhaled. Cigarette smoke, the others. Lung cancer. They should test Natalie on a mouse's back. This was absolutely fresh. My lungs began to spread the word all over me. And that paralysed guy sitting on my guts, he stirred. And then he stretched, and then he expanded right out to my skin. I was one man again . . ."

Again he touched her hand.

"I hadn't been able to write a word. And all at once everything I looked at was like a letter addressed to me. You're a letter addressed to me. The day itself had my name on it. Do you know that feeling? I tried out a few words and they said, 'Yes! Yes!' . . . amongst themselves. They were still saying it the second time I looked at them! That's what it's like to be writing again. And I loved you so very much!"

For a moment Kate felt unreal. Every detail in her sight became a tableau. The door casings and the window sashes. Rex spread-eagled beneath the car he was tinkering with. Flashes of light that glowed between the leaves as yellow-bright as electricity.

These were not like his words at the stillwater, that she had doubted the next hour. She had to have a minute before she could look them in the face.

"What were those first words you wrote?" she said, to gain that minute.

"I remember them exactly," he said. " 'It was April and she was there with him like someone helping drive back an animal through a gap in the fence, and he knew that together they could drive any damn trespassing thing in the world back behind the fence and he loved her so very much.' "

"And pity had nothing to do with it?"

"Pity!" he exploded. "Pity! Where's the peck of pickled pities Peter Piper picked? For God's sake, Kate, are you still frigging and parrying around with that nonsense? Do you have to play it so deaf? Do I have to take out a beginner's licence and court you coy – like a kid? I'm a sensible, grown-up man and I'm telling you I *love* you. Can't you hear me?"

"All right," she said. "I hear you. And I believe you."

You could no more disbelieve him when he was that serious than you could doubt rain. He hadn't the ounce even of patience that lying takes.

"And I love you," she said. "Do *you* hear?"

"I do," he said gently. "And I'll remember."

He put his arm around her and, as if she were making one great leap across herself, she sprang into the ranks of the women who had someone to love them. She'd been drawn on the map of existence with invisible ink. But now her country was marked in a shade of its own. And if that dimmed, she had only to take one step across the boundary into Morse's country to be safe and in colour again. Her face and hands were rescued. Their youthfulness would be present again by proxy in the unlacking flesh of the child. She felt as weak with salvation as if a great plummeting weight had missed her by a hair.

(She saw a car drive up the road and stop beside the driveway. Two men in uniform got out. They looked around, then tacked some sort of placard on each enormous elm that stood there. She saw Rex draw himself completely in beneath the car. She saw him crouch – yes, crouch – there, until the men had driven off. But she didn't really interrupt this splendid selfishness to wonder why.)

Morse's tongue was already unfolding plans, like the darting hands of children bursting with helpfulness at a picnic.

They'd be married in Granfort tomorrow. The first thing in the morning . . .

No, she said, you had to get a licence first and then they made you wait another day or two.

Well, they'd damn well have to guarantee that nothing happened to her in those few days . . .

And, anyway, they ought to wait for Paul oughtn't they? They'd want Paul here.

Yes. All right. But one week at the latest. And going into it this way, at their age, with every eye in them open, just before it was too late, they could make the next few years the vintage years of their lives. They'd stay here the whole summer, where an hour went as far as a month went anywhere else. They'd start the child.

They'd start the book. She had him pregnant with the book already. He'd repay her service in kind.

"Did you love me . . . at all . . . that first summer here?" she said.

"I don't know," he said. "I mean . . . the tinder was probably there, but no one dropped the match. I remember one morning it did come into my head to cross wires with you to see if there'd be a spark – but you and your father had gone to Blomidon."

"I remember that morning," Kate said. "He wanted to see the rock formation there."

She had a small chip of amethyst quartz to show for *that* morning. Again she felt the hair-breadth salvation.

"This book you're pregnant with," she said. "Is it far enough along it has features?"

"Yes," he said. "The characters are still in embryo, but I can see their story gene. And that's the hardest thing to isolate in people. There's such a cloak of accidental, obscurantist growth around it in their factual lives. You have to strip all that away before you can see their story gene – and make a culture of it, pure and simple. Before you can fit them into a book."

"You're borrowing from living people then?" Kate said.

"Certainly," he said. "How else can you make it sound like anything real? You can't make *up* a recipe for people. Who could make up anyone like Paul if he hadn't seen him? Or you?"

"My God!" he broke in on himself, "what a headline! Writer Bores Fiancée to Death on Betrothal Morn. Endlaw was the scene of a pretty murder on Monday last when . . . The murder weapon was ingeniously concealed in the writer's mouth . . ."

"Now cut that out," she said. And then: "Do I dare ask you that question that makes a writer wince? What's your book about?"

"You may," he said. "And that's funny too. I could never talk about my books with anyone before. But with you I can. You know, I *caught* this book from you. Only I didn't know it then. A book is like the spirochete . . . you can have it in your system for years without knowing it. Do you remember the morning you said that what characterizes people is what troubles them? Well, that's its theme."

(She saw Rex walking toward the elms. For some reason he suggested the hunted who curbs his pace just short of the run that would give him away. She had never noticed his limp so pronounced. She could tell the exact second he came within reading distance of the placards. His whole body seemed to subside in the manner that's so alike in exhaustion and relief.)

"Morse," she said, "have you spent any time on Rex? It strikes me he's afraid of something."

"No," Morse said. "I haven't that much time to waste. He's got no story gene. No chemical properties, only physical. He triggers nothing, disposes nothing. He'd be useless to me."

For a moment the edges of Kate's openness curled slightly inward on themselves. She saw that what Morse couldn't use as writing grist he had no use for otherwise. The kind of sympathy she had for Rex he wouldn't understand at all. It's always something of a shock to find the one you love has certain qualities that can't be rendered into any likeness of your own.

"Rex *is* afraid," she insisted. "And lonely. Did you see his face when Bruce asked him and Sheila to go fishing? Saying no, he had to fix the car, but sure they'd coax him? And then they didn't?"

"Their fishing!" Morse said. "That's the euphemism of the month!"

"All right," Kate said. "It was just a womanly parenthesis. Go on about the book."

He chuckled. "Now isn't that request a coincidence!" he said. "I happen to have the synopsis right here with me." He reached into an inner pocket and brought out two folded slips of paper. "My harp," he said, passing them to her.

She started to read:

"Cast: the troubled. Sect of psychical amputees, not unlike batch have here, that bloody great world – never looks where putting bloody great paw down – has crushed mainspring in. All congregated in place as focusing, April as intensifying as this. Not for mutual comfort – wounded actually hate each other – but simply because carrier belt dropped them all same compartment. Carrier belt sorts all people out according weight. These heavier than happy ones, somehow. Or purer. In chemist's sense. Their individualities cameoed. Disenchanted know exactly who they are every minute of day. Can stand up straight inside themselves in only truly erect posture human can achieve. World comes sucking up to them again, with licorice pipe in outstretched hand. Consolation prize, smooth things over. They look straight through it. World's so used being forgiven because bigger. These people surprise it. Bigger than it because can stare its bribery down. Not heroes, make plain. Too much pride to be heroes. More stature than heroes. Heroes accept licorice pipe. Brandish it in stiff upper lip. Get sticky all over with it . . . North these people set compasses by man like Paul. Their Pope. His contempt toward world with shifty consolation prizes so supreme no bitterness even. Invulnerability of totally unarmed. Can grin back at world without having make grin derisive. Can truly fart in face licorice pipe without this being *gesture* even. Straightest man living."

That was the end of the first page. There were only a few lines on the second.

"But what happens?" Kate said.

"You mean action?" he said. "That finger-drumming most people distract themselves with so they can't hear what's going on – the ocean currents – inside them? Not much of that. I know. Everyone sets great store by action. People are always moaning about the things they haven't *done*. But wouldn't they be a damn sight better advised to bemoan the fact that if it hadn't been for the din of what they'd done – *that* opiate – they might have heard who they were? And if you're looking for what everyone's wearing and at just what angle the whatnot stands, you won't find much of that guff either. Why should I waste my breath on that? Someone has a gutful of loneliness, it's on the point to say whether he has his ass planted on a cane-bottomed chair or a tilter? We're sitting here with a gutful of love and it matters whether I have on these tan slacks or a pair of bloody *purple* ones? Whether you're wearing that polka dot affair or zebra stripes with a fool bolero?"

She turned to the second page:

"Whole book study in only saving kind of insolence. Devise ultimate test of insolence in case of each. Dynamites everything to surface. Electrolyzes each ion in solution to its pole. Gives book its orgasm. Point: separates men from boys."

"Well," he said, "how does it strike you?"

Kate took a moment to shape her reply.

It took only half her moment of silence for Morse to sense her reservations. Demolition began to flash and smart in his eyes.

"Well, clumsy old me again," he said. "Now I've knocked you speechless, be damned if I ain't. Old butter fingers." He started that hateful free association. "Butter brain. Stutter brain."

She made a movement of protest. He held up his hand.

"It's all *right*," he said. "I under*stand*. Here you were, just sitting here taking the April airs, and I spring this bloody great art piece . . . fart piece . . . on you without warning." He was talking so fast she couldn't interrupt. "I honest to gracious me never dreamed it would bowl you over like that, though. Just the bare skeleton. Just in the rough. In the buff. Off the cuff. Guff . . ."

"Morse!"

"Geeee! Before I'd even worked it up. Quirked it up. Murked it up. Just the plot. Clot. Blot. Just the thesis. Jeessis!" He shook his head. "Stupid bastard. I might have known. Just the way I took these little old ordinary characters and put my little X-ray machine . . . Jack O'Lantern . . . behind them and there's all their bones spelling out a bloody passion play! Or maybe it was the words themselves that beaned you? Was that it? The old ten-pounders like 'stature'? Did I say that? I'll *bet* I did. I always do when I get carried away. Or maybe it was the little nuances. Nances. I have a set of jeweller's scales I weigh them on. Troy weight. Coy weight. Maybe you drew one o' them little nuances down into your lung."

His voice sank almost to nothing.

"All that bloody sweat over blokes that come out sounding as if they needed to be wormed. Writer: A screw. Dictionary meaning: Small twist of paper. Know thyself. Screw thyself. And carry off the Prix Goncourt, or any other Pricks you want to name."

Kate held her silence another moment. And then she said quietly:

"I'm going to fool you, Morse. I'm not going to take you up on that at all. You have this habit. You show people something you've done. They don't applaud soon enough to suit you. And what happens? You don't turn on them, you turn on it. You hurl it as far as you can send it. That's not independence, Morse. It's simply tantrum. I'm not going to apologize. If I have to start this soon picking my words with you or watching my pauses, where's it going to land us? If you were a child I'd say, 'Now you pick that right up again.' You're not a child. So all I can do is sit here until you feel like picking it up yourself."

He gave in so abruptly it startled her.

"Allll right, allll right," he said, in mimicry of the child's capitulation. "I'll pick it up. I'll pick it up."

He looked at her, completely puzzled.

"But how is it you can disarm me so? Is that what love does? I'm asking. All at once I don't know the first thing about it. I thought I was in love with the others once. But they never disarmed me. Not even at the very first. They armed me to the teeth." The free association gave its last tic, like that tick of a stove cooling. "But you're not out to emasculate me, are you? Maybe I'd better swaddle them in one of Letty's tea cosies and bullet-proof it."

"I'm not out to emasculate you," Kate said. "And I'm not out to disarm you against anything but yourself, your characters. You shouldn't take yourself out on them, Morse. Write with your knuckles, if you like. But do you have to put on those *steel* knuckles? Do you have to make the truth smart so? I know, I know. People's bones are like Carmen's cards. They never spell out anything but *la mort*. But their flesh spells out things too. It has a kind of *happy* insolence . . . against its own bones . . . that's just as incorruptible as the other. You forget that. And for some reason the characters you do pick to write about are always good people, basically. Couldn't you give them a little break?"

191

"Of course I write about good people," Morse said. "Nothing's evil but meanness. And who can get any effects with meanness? The world itself knows that. It knows that for its really diverting effects it has to twist its gimlet into the periwinkles with the tender spots. They're the ones that really dance on the air."

"I know, I know," Kate said again. "*Don't* I know. I know what the taste of the world and the truth about yourself can be. You stated it perfectly in *Each in His Narrow Cell*. A cup of ditch water with the alum and steel filings in it. But . . ."

"You want me to stick little sprigs of uplift into everything," he said, "like cloves in a baked ham? You really want me to retool for the silver lining trade? You want me to do it gentlemanly? Gentleman lily?"

"No, no, no," she said.

She thought a minute.

"What I'm getting at . . . There comes a stage in every human plight when it's balanced on a little pinnacle. One nudge is all it takes to send it toppling into that iron-grey business of yours. But it can be nudged the other way too – into something quite different."

She thought harder.

"I mean . . . Say someone has a stubborn sickness. He's tried so many cures that failed that now they mention some new treatment he isn't even curious. His body will be blind to it as well. He'll be damned if he'll offer it one more overture for it to turn its eyes away from. Now you'd make that into a fine iron-grey story. Look at the way he trumps each card his sickness plays with that fine iron-grey endurance inside him. Insolent to the very end. And that would be that . . . But *I'd* have some new drug discovered just when he was most hopeless. Ten chances to one it might not help him, but they'd persuade him to give it a try. He's still uncurious – but exactly when he should start feeling better, if the thing's to work at all, he does start feeling better. And maybe this next feeling only lasts an hour – but going home from the doctor's office that day in the bus, there's a kind of sun comes out on everything he looks at. Even the handbag of the woman sitting beside him is somehow a touching thing for her familiarity with it. All at once the driver is such a fine, courteous fellow that he writes down his name to commend him to the bus company. And the smile the couple gives him back for smiling at their handsome child seems to add ten inches to his stature . . ."

"The movie version," Morse said.

"No," she said. "I don't *mean* it that way. If I could just think of a better example . . ."

Again she concentrated. And suddenly she thought she had it.

It's someone's last summer to live. He knows it. You know it. One hot still afternoon you watch him vulnerable in sleep and you hear the seconds playing Russian roulette with his breath. Each time they press the trigger harmlessly the odds mount that the next time they will chance on the fatal chamber. And then he's awake again, once more defended with consciousness; but you catch him staring at the veins in his own hands, wondering where inside him the message comes from that will one day stop the circling of this blood that has either to move or go blind. Everyone has places he has always wanted to revisit and knows he never will. With him you know exactly which those places are. You know he thinks about them constantly. His mind may be roaming there the very moment death surprises him. So that his mind dies in one place and his body in another. And that's the most terrible divorcement of all. So you vow you'll turn the very certainty of this summer's being his last into a kind of victory. You'll make this summer absolutely his. You'll buy a car and you'll take him all those places . . .

Morse started to speak.

"I know," she said. "I know what you're going to say. Five miles out and he'd be tired – and querulous. And twenty miles out you'd catch yourself saying, 'Well, after all, this wasn't my idea of a holiday, I was just doing it for you!'

"Or when you got there the places would be so changed, so different from his memory of them that even that would be stolen from him – and every time you glanced at him you'd see him struggling with his face, trying to shift aghastness on it into the look of saturation he still remembers any passenger owes his host . . ."

"Or," Morse supplied, "that would be the summer they'd take *you* to hospital. Nothing critical . . . but he'd be left with strangers, and day by day he'd watch the time for the trip run out. There'd be no one to see or know or care that he'd had to fold up the idea, all by himself, and put it away forever. . . . Or that would be the summer the paving gangs would have the road torn up. You'd have to turn back . . . Or you could get the car, but the first trip you'd make in it would be to his funeral."

"Oh yes," she said. "There are hundreds of things that could topple it that way, your way. But Morse, it *could* happen the other way. The one other way. You could buy the car . . . and the places would still be there, unchanged . . . and you would catch the saturated look on his face when he *didn't* know you were looking at him. . . . And he would come back tired . . . but tired from *doing* something . . . not tired that awful way from doing nothing. . . . And he wouldn't stare at his hands, he'd have the living picture of those places in his mind to look at – and he'd have been there and back, and now home would be home again. And his mind and his body would die in the same place. . . . And don't you see? That ending could be just as true as any of the others. It wouldn't be any sell-out either, to sentiment or anything else and . . . Don't you see a little *bit* of what I'm trying to get at?"

"You didn't buy the car last summer, though, did you?" Morse said gently. "You didn't go on any trips."

"No," Kate said. "I didn't. But – "

"Or how would this example suit you?" Morse put in quickly. "Say you had this writin' feller and the gal he loves. And what does she do but spot the steel filing he'd always thought was in the world right in his own eye? Takes it out on her little hankie point and shows it to him: There it is, see? Draws the grey frost out of him like you thaw out an axe bitt on the top of the stove so it won't chip when you strike a knot with it. Makes him see that he and his books have always mated the wrong way – biting and kicking each other like a stallion and a mare. Makes him see that he's always been a bit of a sow's ear – and a sow's ear can't write a silk purse . . ."

– Yes, you could have her show him that the world's not quite such a bastard after all – what does it take away that matters in the least compared to what it leaves? The sense of recognition. Show him that the one true insolence is not the grin or the fart, but the sigh between two people who recognize precisely how things are. That two, not one, make up the unit of that insolence. That the one splendid posture is not that of the man standing alone in his insolence – that's bound to crumble, its air's too dead, too parthenogenetic – but that of a man and woman in love conquering the whole bloody racket with two simple words: "We know" . . .

Was it just baiting? Or did he mean it?

Kate never knew. For right then Letty's car drove into the yard.

"Quick!" Morse said. "The duenna! We've wasted the whole damn morning with our tongues. Let's see what the lips have to say."

He gripped her tight and gave her one great fixed staring kiss. For a moment each somehow became the other, in what's the one supreme holiday from self.

Letty handed Morse the letter. He opened it. The only content was a tie-clip. Snapped to a piece of cardboard. The cardboard was stamped: LEFT IN ROOM.

"That tie-clip's Paul's!" Letty said. "I remember . . . it was all

194

skewgee the day he went away and I straightened it for him."

He doesn't care a fig about appearance, was Kate's first thought; and yet there must have been something about that one tie-clip that made him choose it rather than another. You hardly ever had to buy your own tie-clips, you got them for presents. No one ever bought Paul a present.

"He must be sick," Letty said. "All alone there."

"No," Morse said. "If he was still in hospital they wouldn't be sending this along. He must be on his way back home. But – " he pondered the address again – "Bruce Halliday. I don't get it."

All at once it seemed to Kate as if the morning picked its cloak of shadows up and left, washing its hands of the day. She looked at Morse.

"Well," she said, "I guess this puts your approach one up on mine, doesn't it. The evidence does seem to mount up on your side."

She couldn't help the snub in her voice: as if his speculations on the way things topple were to blame for Paul's sickness itself.

"Any mail, Letty?"

It was Rex, suddenly in the doorway. They looked at him the way you look at the very last person you want to see when events have taken a turn so sobering that no one feels like talk at all.

Letty passed him his letter and Sheila's.

"Bills," he said. He turned to Morse. "Boy, you should hear that old motor purring now! It was the carburettor."

"*Was* it," Morse said.

"What are those signs the men put up?" Kate said quickly, to stave off any further reference to Paul. She didn't want him in on that.

"Oh, they're only fire warnings," he said. "On account of the dry spell."

At first sight of the fire rangers he'd been struck atremble by one of his reasonless premonitions. They were policemen, coming to get him. Now he was as expansive with relief as a child.

Letty had turned her back. Her hands were mindlessly twisting ravellings of thread off the upholstery tape of a chair. Her breath was making uncontrollable little engine puffs that sounded like snickers.

"What's the joke, Letty?" Rex said.

He went over and turned her head around in a great show of playfulness. She was crying. Her face was so shockingly changed that Kate almost gasped. Twitchings of nakedness and exposure shattered it in every direction, like a windowpane struck by a rock.

"Why, Letty," Rex said, "what's wrong?" He turned to Kate and Morse. "What's wrong with *Letty*?" They didn't answer. "Now, come on, Letty," he said. "Cheer up." He winked at Kate and Morse. "You're going to mess up all that pretty make-up. Now come *on*, Letty."

Kate stepped toward Letty as if to protect her. Letty made a quick movement as if she were ducking away from her own face. She ran, bent over like that, out of the room.

"What's *wrong* with her?" Rex said. "I didn't think the old girl had a drop of fluid in her, did you?"

Morse raised an eyebrow at Kate. "You still maintain his story gene is worth investigating?" he said.

"That's still important?" Kate said. For different reasons they both seemed almost equally obtuse. Any of that business was still important now?

It was scarcely fifteen minutes before another car pulled up beside the driveway. Again Kate saw Rex stiffen; and again her sympathy was very nearly re-engaged. This time it was Paul who stepped out.

A gleam Kate couldn't quite decipher struck in Morse's eye.

"Look," he said, "I've got an idea how we ought to handle this. Let's have some fun with him." (Fun? Kate thought.) "Now when he comes through the door . . ."

He explained to Kate what part he wanted her to play. He gave Rex none.

CHAPTER **23**

Paul had reached Halifax with no two notes inside him combining in any chord.

That *was* literary dying in the hospital room, he thought. All those dramatic "messages" and stage lighting. All that imagination. Here, in the long rainy day's wait, where the placard of Hotel Regulations was like the skin of the soul of all travelling pinned to the wall, and the wheeling gulls scooped up scraps from the soulless harbour water with their terrible precision, there were no messages whatever. The battery of his imagination was absolutely dead.

He'd always thought that death would be less like a shrinking to zero than an expansion to infinity. He'd thought that, if you knew you were going to die, there would be a gauze of sudden meaning standing out on everything; that things would finally tell you all about themselves. But nothing told him anything. His vision was so clear it was like a glass-patch of ice on a tickingly-frozen moonlit night – but *so* clear that it destroyed its object. Nothing had any quality save the taste of utter tastelessness.

He felt nothing but the stillness of the unconscious stillness at the dead-centre of everyone and everything staring at the stillness inside him: the stillness that nothing – sound, glance away, movement, not if he were to sit there and break the joints of every finger one by one – could shatter.

From time to time, in this strange room in this strange place, his mind's breath gave an involuntary knee-jerk of sigh; but the sighs could lift nothing from the mind's floor. Not for an inch. Not for a second. He fabricated a grin; but the grin loosened nothing else's still, staring lips.

To be by himself had always given him an insulation impenetrable. Now, for the first time in his life, he knew the unspeakable nakedness of having the stillness at the heart of all things stare at the stillness inside him right *through* the wall of being alone.

And then, once more, he summoned up the thoughts of home – the one image which never failed to start the nuts that were seized on their bolts in his imagination. Home, the one blessed wall this staring could not penetrate. The one blessed spot where all the hushes of absolute familiarity would blot this stillness out completely . . .

In the cab that brought him from the station in Granfort, he was helpless not to prompt the driver's favourite spiel. They talked about his children and the long dry spell. But he asked to be let out at the gate. And he saved his first glance at the house until the car had turned and gone back out of sight. Until he was alone.

He looked at the house. And caught his breath.

It stared at him.

It looked factitious, not inevitable. It might have been one of those houses you drive past in a strange village, all uniformly barren for your not knowing what special bond with its occupant demarcates one from the other and redeems its little flower garden or its painted lawn chair from an underlining of that barrenness.

The house was a stranger. He looked at it and he saw just how much a house would do for you if you were going to die . . .

A picture from another day flashed into his mind.

One morning he'd been hunting through a swamp the treeline bordered. The rain of the night before had stopped, but grey stalactites of it still hung, sullen and unshed, the circuit of the horizon. The sickly mist of it, beading on his gun and everywhere, brought out the entrails smell of his woollen clothing . . . and, sodden black in the rotted fence boards and in the twice-killed grass (starved to death and *then* drowned), it gave to them the look of things that had never once dreamed, as other objects never ceased to do, in the sleep of inanimacy.

There, beside one of those little rain-brooks with the clammy soul, he'd come across the carcass of a calf, strayed or butchered. Its staring bones were absolutely clean except for the shanks – where the matted hair still clung, parted slick as pencil lines by the rain to the glistening white beneath.

And suddenly between the partings of the hair he'd thought he'd glimpsed the very face of Death. It drifted outward from the thing it emptied, yet still stayed locked inside; its single feature the gaping zero of a Bowery mouth . . .

A flock of robins perched above him in the elms. Their brook notes struck against the very valves of spring. And now he saw Death's face clearer in the stintless sunlight than ever in the rain.

Differently, but clearer. It was nothing but that cross-eye of anachronism in everything your vision reached for. The people you looked at were people of another time; the places you looked at were places of another country.

And if that staring still followed you, even when you were home, where could you escape it?

The moment knocked his mind down; then passed over it, and on. (That was its mercy: it held no rage. It didn't bring its fist down, grunting, for lunge after lunge; one great blow and it was done.)

And when his mind got up, first onto its hands and knees and then onto its feet, it had a self-possession altogether new. The stubbornness returned: He had lived alone, he would die alone.

He hadn't noticed Letty. She was digging greens in the field. She dropped her knife into the pail and came toward him.

"Paul?" she said. "Are you all right?"

"Why?" he said. (How could she know?) "Don't I look all right?"

"When that letter came . . ." she said.

"Letter?" he said. "What letter?"

She told him.

His mind instantly gave up its self-scenting, became instantly alert. They knew about the hospital. They knew about the false name. Already he was sketching out a second cover.

"Don't worry, Letty," he said. "The whole thing's a bit of a joke. I'll tell you about it later." It *was* a joke – of a kind. And that's the way he'd have to play it. It was the only way. "But right now, will you do something for me?"

"Of course I will," she said. She'd do anything for him.

198

"I've decided to close up shop here, Letty," he began.

He'd decided it on the instant. Intenser than ever, the original stubborness returned: He had lived alone, he would die alone. Above all, it became obsessional that no one must discover what his final secret was, invade his wholeness with that look they gave the doomed. And if he kept these people near him, they'd be sure to happen on it. He'd had his warning with the simple accident of the tie-clip. He'd have to get rid of them immediately. Yes, Kate too. All right. All *right,* then, was his mind's stance now.

"I've decided to get rid of them all," he said. "And this is where you can give me a hand."

He felt acutely the Judas, to be playing on the privilege she considered it to help him – when her own betrayal was in the cards. But there was no other way.

"And it would save so much – well, of their chewing" (again he felt the stitch of Judas, to be using her own diction as a snare of alignment) "if I could simply tell them that you don't feel like working here any longer."

He winked at her, feeling more treacherous still.

"Would you back me up on that?" he said. "They know I could never get anyone to replace you."

"Now, Paul . . ." she began, first rendering him the abashment due his compliment.

And then the full implication of his words seemed to explode in her hands. They looked as if they'd been knocked senseless against her apron. She put one hand to her mouth to steady her voice.

"Certainly," she said. "Tell them anything you like. But you didn't mean . . . ? It's no trouble to look after *you,* Paul. You're no trouble."

"No, Letty," he said. "I can hold down the fort perfectly well by myself. And you need a good long rest." (Once he'd had to shoot a dog and the difficulty was to get it the gun's length away from him, it was so used to tagging at his heels.) "There must be lots of places in town you'd find it far more pleasant than it is for you here."

Letty took a deep breath. He *wanted* her to go.

"Well," she said, "Huldah and Jim's always bin coaxin' me to come live with them." She'd do anything for him.

"There you are then!" Paul said. He picked up his suitcase. "Did it rain while I was gone?"

"Not a drop."

"That's funny," he said. "It rained and rained in Montreal . . . and in Halifax too."

Letty turned toward her pail. But as she bent to the ground again

199

all the fresh tender greens seemed to have disappeared. The only ones she could find had coarse bitter blossoms at the centre.

Carrying his suitcase up the driveway, Paul seemed to step into the ground mist of another mood. Suddenly he missed himself – his former self, alive with its ignorance of death – achingly. As if his former self were a neglected brother, and this the empty house you were coming back to on his funeral day. He felt the nowhere of everywhere – the long "o" in every syllable of the senses.

All right, he took the bit again. All right, then.

He'd already settled on his tactic for the questioning he faced. (He didn't worry about his promise of explanation to Letty. He knew she'd never remind him of it.) He'd stall at first – never had he been so grateful to his reputation for stalling – and then take his cue from whatever way the inquisition went. He was sure he could outwit it.

The moment he stepped inside the room he recognized the atmosphere of conspiracy. Morse had obviously been its instigator, Kate his reluctant accomplice. (Rex was just sitting there, like someone half-recognizing his insolubility in present company but yet so eager to prove himself soluble that he can't leave.) They gave him no sign of greeting, except for the glint of it in their eyes. Paul felt the first inner smile.

"Mr Halliday, I presume?" Morse said. "Mr Bruce Halliday?" He gave Paul a stern magisterial stare.

Paul nodded.

"Give him a drink," Morse said, without unbending.

"I'll get it," Rex said.

"I'll get it," Kate said.

She poured Paul a drink. Morse had broken out a bottle of his best.

"Saaay," Paul said, running his tongue over his lips after the first swallow, "that's good stuff."

The liquor warmed his stomach in a flash, but the stillness was in no way routed. If you couldn't escape it at home, with friends, *with a drink* . . . where else could you?

And then Morse launched into the format of his gag.

"We were working the day watch out of Missing Persons," he began, like Jack Webb. "My name is Thursday. April the twenty-fifth. My partner's name here is Kiss Me Kate."

He wasn't quite bringing it off. His concern about Paul was too great (Kate saw now) for the reckless savagery that concern always touched off in him to be in unfaltering charge.

But Paul fell on his cue at once. That was the only civilized way you could counter a blow's hick rudeness; play-act some nonsense on it. He leaned against the door jamb in a truculent slouch.

"Sit down," Morse said sharply.

Kate tried to maintain the same gruff stare Morse did; but from time to time an involuntary pattern of pleading anxiety would turn face upward in her eyes. Rex just sat there, baffled. He tried to get into the act by imitating Morse's stance, but no one paid the slightest heed to whether he was in line or not.

"The suspect was last heard from in Granfort," Morse said. "And then we got this lead that someone answering his description had turned up in a Montreal hospital. Only the name he used there was Bruce Halliday. We ran that through R and I and this time we came up with a package." He thrust the tie-clip at Paul. "Is that yours?"

Paul shook a reproving finger at Morse.

"Now, now," he said. "You know I don't have to answer no questions without I have a lawyer."

For a moment the whole performance turned shoddy. Was this another feature of his new estate, that everything people did, even their particular choice of clowning, seemed to be beneath them? Would even death turn out to be beneath itself?

"I'm a lawyer," Kate said quickly.

"But didn't the judge unfrock you one dark night?" Morse said.

It was a mark of his unsettling concern that even his coarseness was off key. It was plain now that he was the one who was hooked by his own jest and Paul the one who wouldn't let him off it.

"I want a word with my client," Kate said.

She went out into the hall and beckoned Paul with her.

"Paul," she whispered to him, all acting abandoned, "are you sick?"

It was the wife's clandestine aside, the only corrective she dares to a line of behaviour her husband can't see he's running into the ground.

Paul looked at her. Her face was so close, so open to him. On its tiny space was written in the face's inimitable shorthand everything in the world he would ask for. He almost made the drowner's grasp for it. For a second it seemed as if the stillness, deciding it had gone too far, was making overture.

And then his pride was stung back sharper by its overture than it had been by the blows. No, thank you, he said to the stillness; suddenly made stronger by ignoring its hand right now than he knew he'd ever need to be to ignore it again. No compromise, he told it. Let's stick to the bargain.

"I never felt better in my life," he said, without a word of lie. Between attacks there wasn't a trace of physical distress.

He stepped back into the room. Kate followed him.

Rex had left. The moment he was stranded in a room with Morse alone, any contact hooks they threw out to effect a junction fell so far apart that even the chairs seemed to stiffen. It was as if Morse were one of those opponent's counters in a child's game which, landing on the same space as his, sent him all the way back to Start.

Morse took a new tack: the cop turned benign.

"Now, look, son," he said to Paul. "We're not in this business to persecute you. If you're sick – or in trouble – we want to help you. Hell, kid, we love you – can't you see that? Now why won't you give us a break, yourself a break, and sing? And let me warn you," he added really gently, "that nothing you say will be held in evidence against you."

Paul's heart suddenly opened. (If there was no cause for secrecies in the world . . . If everyone could tell everyone everything . . .) Then closed.

He poured himself another drink and sat down, grinning like himself; and all at once they were gathered in one spot again from their separate stations in the joke.

"All right," he said to Morse. "I'll sing. You remember the bees? You remember saying you could identify me anywhere in the world by the cockeyed things that happen to me? That I attract?"

Morse nodded.

"Well say I went to Montreal. Say I took it into my head to see if this purity drive against the nightspots there was having any success. Just looking, you understand. Just for scientific interest. What do you think would happen?"

"That's easy enough," Morse said. "The first place you went to would prove to be a brothel right out of Hogarth. And two bawds would get into a hair-pull and, chancing into the line of fire, you'd be crowned with a flying pisspot."

Kate laughed. Her fears were so relieved she'd have laughed at anything.

Paul laughed too. Morse's nonsense had given him his second cue.

"No," he said. "Not a brothel exactly. But you're psychic. Say there were two cocky young reporters at the table next mine who kept needling the bartender. Say he suddenly flew into a rage and heaved a bottle at them. He being no Annie Oakley, who do you suppose would catch it right on the *os parietale* and be knocked out cold as custard?"

"You!" Morse cried. "You! Naturally!"

He was so relieved it never came to him to cross-examine Paul's story for plausibility.

"And say the newsmen, all at once great buddies, insisted on hustling me off to the hospital to have an overnight check for possible concussion. Well, you know me. Anything that just might find its way into the papers. Do you think I might be tempted to use another name?"

"Damn sure you would!" Morse said. "An old partridge wing like you. And then . . . yes, yes, yes . . . it *couldn't* happen that way to anyone else . . . you left your tie-clip there . . . a bloody friggin' tie-clip . . . it couldn't be anything else . . . and . . ." He shook his head at Paul with a steady summarizing grin; almost idolatrous with the affection any cockeyed thing that happened to Paul touched off in him. "You crazy old bastard!" he beamed. "My God, I'd liked to been there!"

"But just a minute," Paul said, to clinch it. "Mark you, I didn't say that's what actually happened. I was just citing a hypothetical case."

"Hypothetical, hell," Morse said. He grinned again. "You crazy old coot. And here Kiss Me Kate had you half-dead with heart attacks or cancer or God knows what."

"Oh now," Kate said, "you were just as worried as I was. You know you were."

"All right," Morse said. "You old clown, I was."

Paul knew he was safe. He drew a deep breath.

"So what happened here while I was gone?" he said quickly.

"What happened here?" Morse said. He was bursting with it. "Well, don't think we haven't got a story for you too! And the hell with the suspense. In two short sentences, us two old cods got so choked up with April, I asked Kiss Me Kate here for her hand and what do you know? She was kind enough to grant me not only her hand but everything attached thereto. Now, what do you think of that?"

His eyes watched Paul's, the glee in them ready to feed on Paul's surprise. Paul saw the hand that sought Kate's and, in that simple movement, took her away from him before his very eyes, to the farthest country possible. He had to speak, not knowing how.

"Well, bully for April!" he said, drawing the words out as if in bemusement. "Bully for you!"

He knew they were looking for something more, but that was everything he could manage.

"It's all set up," Morse said. "We're going to be married in Granfort next week and you're going to be best man and I'm going to write the first damn novel here this summer that ever had a navel – that's where you tie off the cord of truth – and you're going to be stuck with two of the stickiest bud-sticky old lovebirds since David and Wallis, Part One."

Paul's face went completely sober.

"I'm afraid not," he said. As if ever so reluctantly some news he'd been planning to break gently had been flushed out of him by the very eagerness it must decapitate.

"What are you talking about?" Morse said. "Afraid. What the hell kind of word is that to use on a morning like this? And look at your face. It looks like that right one – or is it the left one? – that hangs down the lowest. What kind of a look is that for news like ours?"

Paul smiled.

"I'm afraid," he said, "this time it's simply a case of 'Morse proposes, Letty disposes'."

Morse turned to Kate. "Can you translate yon elliptical old coot?" he said. Masquerading as irritation it was really the lingo of fondness. "What's Letty got to do with it?"

Paul told them.

He'd known it would be difficult. But he'd had no idea how like a traitor to them he would feel. As if every word he spoke, whether he was to blame for it or not, threw the ranks of their trust in him into confusion.

But Paul, they cried, seeing the whole embroidery pattern of their summer's plan yanked out into the blind kinked thread of ravellings. But, Paul . . . But, Paul . . .

Their protests flopped about like fowl with their heads cut off. For once they strove for no "arrangements" of their speech, with gesture or inflection. Even Morse's key was C natural.

It staggered Paul to find they'd counted all that much on spending the entire summer with him; it always comes as the greater shock to find you matter more to your friends than you'd thought, and steadily, than to discover that you matter less. And this made his own stand that much harder to maintain. Because they weren't really fighting back. They kept speaking as if there must be some mistake. He, *Paul,* for whatever reason, couldn't really mean to discard them . . .

"But, Paul," Kate said, come to simple pleading. "Couldn't Morse and I stay anyway? I could look after the three of us. I'd love to. Wouldn't you like that?"

For a second his mind leapt to the picture (a long picnic summer, with the picnic improvisation about it making Kate belong almost as much to him as to Morse); and then as quickly tapped itself on the back, back to reality. He'd have to use his second weapon.

"Yes," he said, "that would be fun. If it was certain I'd be here myself. But perhaps this might be a good time for me, too, to make a break. The break I guess I should have given thought to long ago."

To say "I should have . . . long ago" is to make the most dampening comment you can let fall before a family group. If you had . . . long ago . . . then this present interweaving with each other would never have come to pass exactly as it is. They see what you imply, if you do not: that you'd be willing to exchange all this for what might have been. And their faces wear the blunted look that goes with keeping even protest silent, so not to bare the implication more divorcingly still. Paul saw that very look on both their faces now.

And then, within the instant, Morse shifted to the typical. Let any sentiment of his meet block and he turned on it as if it were some despised physical nagging he couldn't get his hands on to throttle.

"Well!" he said. "If you have other plans . . . in *that* tone of voice . . . far be it from us to – of course we'll leave. And thanks for picking such a splendid day to turn us out into. You're very thoughtful. At least Kate isn't pregnant and your stern upraised finger isn't pointing her out into a blizzard. At least we won't perish."

It was a definition of Paul that he was the one person Morse had never used this sarcastic banter on. And it was as embarrassing to have him do it now as if two brothers who'd always gibed at party manners had one of them sprung party manners on the other.

Rex, appearing in the doorway, spared Paul an answer.

Rex had been roaming around outside, feeling as vaguely disowned as a child on Sunday. Until he spotted a pair of Letty's underpants ballooning on the line. They were in the style of a time long past – homemade of flannelette, with ruffles at the bottom of their sausage legs.

He stood in the doorway now, holding them up before his waist. He wriggled his hips, chanting "There's no business like shooow business." They would surely explode with laughter, and their laughter would at last admit him.

He might have been someone unfortunate enough to have an exposed birthmark the way Kate and Morse kept their glances off him.

"You'd better put those back where you found them," Paul said quietly.

The members of Rex's decapitated laughter twitched all over his face.

"They *are* funny-looking things, though," he said uncertainly. "Aren't they?"

205

They'd have to admit that much. If he couldn't make them laugh, surely he could make them smile. They didn't smile. Two prongs of headache suddenly calipered his temples.

"Listen," Morse said. "You think it is a riot that people look funny when they cry. You like springing jokes. Well, here's one for you. Paul's closing up shop here. Turning every damn one of us out without a moment's notice. Now why don't you be a good little Chicken Little and run and tell Bruce and Sheila their summer sky has fallen? I'll bet they'll laugh their heads off."

"Morse!" Kate said, frowning. But Rex was too captured by the bombshell of Morse's news to catch his thrust.

"No kidding?" he exclaimed to Paul. The caliper was released.

Morse and Kate swung toward Paul's reply as intently as Rex. It was now clear to Kate what Morse's tactic was: Rex was his tool to force a final "yes" or "no."

"No kidding," Paul said.

"And listen, Chicken Little," Morse began, suddenly really savage. "Tell them that Foxy Loxy is throwing a big ship's party before we all clear out . . ."

But Rex wasn't listening. He was already off, like a child so eager to bear a startling message that you can't restrain him for the details of it.

"Did I say anything about a ship's party?" Paul said quizzically.

"No," Morse said. "*I'm* Foxy Loxy. You're Turkey Lurkey. But we're having one just the same. It's the conventional thing at the end of a voyage, isn't it?"

He spoke stridently, but somehow ineptly with heartsickness, as if he were parodying a parody of himself.

"Only this won't be a masquerade affair. Just the opposite. We'll play the old Truth game, that's what we'll do. You know it, don't you? Anyone free to ask anyone else whatever he likes? Anyone refusing to answer has to forfeit a piece of clothing? Big joke, see, that's the way it starts off. But you'd be surprised. Temper, temper, and before you know it, the whole damn party's stripped to the skin one way or another."

Paul's mind slowed down and came to a full stop, like the motion-blurred teeth of a buzzsaw when a stick of cordwood is jammed against it.

"You see," Morse said, "I need to catch the absolute pitch of this setup we have on view here. I'd thought I had the whole summer to do it in. I want to use it in my—Kate, tell him about the novel of the century. But who needs a whole summer? With a little luck, one evening of the old brass-knuckled Truth game should do it very nicely."

"And what makes you think the others will play?" Kate said.

"They'll play," Morse said. "A little alcoholic narcosynthesis beforehand. In Seagram's Veritas, you know. You watch me. They'll play."

"But Morse," Kate said, "that sounds like such a brutal game. Someone will be sure to get hurt."

"Now, Henny Penny," Morse said. "What's a little X-ray burn?" He turned to Paul. "Will you play, Turkey Lurkey?"

"I'm game," Paul said. Again he caught the whiff of shoddiness. He stood up and turned to leave the room.

"Where do you think *you're* going?" Morse said.

"You've heard the expression *pis aller*?" Paul said. He grinned. "Well, this is just the reverse."

He was rewarded with the kind of chuckle-through-distraction he had bid for. But it seemed to him as if he must quit the room at all speed, before the chuckle died, lest one of them should say "Listen. What's that?" – pointing toward the stillness that ticked louder than a clock inside him.

CHAPTER **24**

Bruce and Sheila had walked toward the brook in all innocence.

It was the sensual woods-spell that drew them there; but in the mind's pact of camouflage with itself to disguise the heart's truth they were approaching, it told them they were simply going fishing. They were unconsciously gormandizing on this atmosphere of sensuality, thinking they could protect themselves from what it kindled by labelling it something else.

Yet each still carried on his shoulders the pack of his past.

In Sheila's were the days of her childhood when she was always two continents away, one and a buffer, from anything like the world where becurlered women with the waking-stained faces swept morning litter from the sidewalks in front of their graceless houses . . .

And of later years in a moneyed world where rub-off from the stylized team-play of speech and feeling became almost sinewy on her, like a Nassau tan . . .

And then of the years with Rex, when she'd become more tired than from anything else for being tired *of* him and sometimes she sat and stared at her own hands as if they were the undecipherable parts of someone else

Bruce's pack could not have been more different.

His childhood days had had a different kind of cleanliness: of eye directly on original tree, mouth on bread with the oven heat still in it, muscle against the natural weight of natural things, lungs taking the first breath out of the rested air that came trooping through his bedroom window in the morning, and at night the ear of sleep directly against the deliciously emptied ear of silence . . .

And then the days of the years when muscles hugged each other for their own sheer jubilance and he had this new and proudly modest centre of gravity in his groin and the doctor ambition sometimes like a glowing nugget in his heart and sometimes like a balloon that lifted his heart in its basket clean outside him . . .

And then the war years when his muscles lifted gun steel and his eye was on blood, but coming back with his own blood and muscles unalloyed as ever and his consciousness still wedge-shaped and tipped with the same ambition, like a diamond drill . . .

And then the years of study when his eye was again on blood, but now to understand it, and he and Molly were an impregnable island . . .

Until the day of the accident when the invisible enemy team had sprung up against him to score, score, score . . . and now the betrayed and blameful eyes of Molly and Peter stared out of the calendar that hung in his heart with the date that never changed, meeting his heart's eye in whichever direction it looked . . .

In the cleared field their packs had been protectively divisive. But in the woods the circumstance their minds had pre-manipulated with such confidence outflanked them. It set up an obliterating alliance with the senses. And at once.

The first turn of the path beyond the field left Time behind. The first drooping branch they stooped to pass beneath brushed the packs off their shoulders like dry scabs. Where the past was grimed into their consciousness the April woods-air rinsed it clear. Their feelings' only content was the naked Now of each other: male and female. For they had reached that point, at last, when all the vagrant currents they had set up in each other cried out for definition in the pooling of their flesh.

And in a kind of helpless yielding to the woods-spell, which gently made its message clear in every leaf and breeze, they finally acknowledged to themselves that, yes, they had come here to make love. Their eyes were quick with it, their breaths trembling with alertness; but they scarcely spoke. Their faces took on the regal stupor, almost, of people committed to a public destiny.

They came to the spot where the fence crossed the path.

208

Bruce held the wires apart for Sheila to crawl through. As she straightened up a barb became entangled in her hair.

"Wait!" Bruce said. "You're caught."

He held the soft hair, sun-coloured, the very colour of her substance, in his hands; and, the surgeon's knack gentling them, began to extricate it from the barb as tenderly as if the least yank on it would draw blood.

"Absolom!" Sheila said, making the joke of it that people, somehow touchingly, seem compelled to make when suffering any ministration with their necks bowed down. "Maybe it would be simpler to cut off my head."

The hair came free and she stood up, giving him the special smile that is half the smile of rising and half the smile for small favours that can be so much more recognizing than the smile for large . . . and his hand felt the loss of her hair and her hair felt the loss of his hand and it was suddenly unbearable.

He put his arms around her and they clung to each other, each drunkenly with final admission of the truth trying to siphon the other into himself and stamp himself on the other at the same time.

Bruce broke the kiss in two like a kiss of farewell when the train blows for the station. He looked about them for the place to lie down. The arm-sweep of a beneficently conniving breeze showed him the spot. On the soft-needled ground between two great murmurous pines.

He touched her breast and that leaping note of appetite, with the salt-pinch of pure sadness in it, struck; longing distended in them like a horse's nostril. They were on the brink of that one redeeming moment in man's life : when, just for that one moment, and by just a gift of his nature in no way subject to luck or skill or fortune, he can be as great as anyone or anything. The purses of love and sense became identical and spilled out that content which is of all things the least to be configured while the catch stays unsprung . . . They could suffer no wait, to bare themselves, except where these pulses clamoured.

And then the stroking . . . and the mercilessly merciful long deliverant stroke. The tide that is more and more like itself as it rises to the flood, mounted. And then the exquisite turbulence of the clamping holding against the dashing apart . . . when coarseness and tenderness switched voices, as did the verbs "come" and "go," and all cried out together in the final proof that struggle is all because even this was helpless not to make a struggle of itself though he gave, gave, gave, and she let him, let him, let him . . .

And then, flesh convulsing through itself with the beautiful moist tremor-music, he spilled himself that broke from himself, from the roots of every nerve and muscle and hair, into her, and she was in every one of her senses split straight down the centre . . . and closing again to try to capture his self and hers in the supreme flux when there was no knowing which of them was which . . .

And then, without a second of anything's lasting exactly as it had been, even under these standstill trees, time began to pay out through their hands again like a rope and a slight shadow fell between every two things, making each thing once more its own preoccupation . . .

And in the draining tide that is nothing like itself in the ebb, their separate selves emerged again like brook-rocks in a dry season, like flues still standing after the houses have burned down . . . and they lay there with their heads sprawled sideways like broken-necked dolls or victims of a crash.

And then the memory of the thing was nothing like the thing remembered. Their faces (in the way of faces, which use their own capricious judgement on what is worth recording and what is not) bore no testimony to it. Each resumed the distinctive steeping that made it individual. The woods-face itself was quite neutral now. And degree by imperceptible degree the packs of their pasts settled back on their shoulders. They readjusted their clothing with an almost studious diligence.

But now they were freed forever from the one great scrambling curiosity about each other. And they were gentler with each other and loved each other more for the act's eternal trickery than if it had kept its promise never to subside. More than anything they felt a bedrock candidness.

Bruce lit them both a cigarette and they exhaled the smoke as if they were blowing out their thoughts against each other.

And in that moment (as when in the fall you pick up something off the ground and universality comes at you fresh and clear from the cool breath of the grass) the most ordinary things were suddenly freighted with the extraordinary. They were almost scrupulously not touching now, but their eyes gently lionized each other's: this new and constant foundation their feet had touched down on after the landslide of desire. They had the splendid sense of being king and queen of this one hour anyway.

Sheila spoke first, as soberly as if she were just discovering the truth of some profound lesson.

"The very first time I ever saw you . . ." she said, "I didn't see you, I recognized you."

"And we're going to get married," Bruce said intently. "You know that, don't you?"

He felt suddenly masterly, almost lordly, about the future. His flesh began to write a kind of poetry and to take the poet's burning pride in it, wordless in him though it was.

She'd be there with him when the great night trucks went by and shook the house . . . when everyone else seemed younger than you were or older . . . to decide with you what clothes to take, and to help give them the necessary bravery, whenever you had to go away among strangers . . . there, when there'd be no reason for doing one thing rather than another or for being in one place rather than another, if she were not . . . . Her saving face would always be there, as proxy for all things . . . to greet and to share . . . to hurt, maybe, but never in that naked way you hurt yourself . . . to forgive and to be forgiven by . . . . She'd be there, to put meaning between the bare lines of him . . . no farther off than the next room no matter how much farther off she chanced to be . . . someone to whom his name and his face would not be just a scrambled hieroglyph, but reading . . .

She'd be there in all the springs like these . . . and in all the summers, when the trees were drugged with August heat and the drug of love sprawled in their bodies so that the voice of all the other senses was soaked up in the voice of touch alone . . . and, when they were old, in all the falls when the incommunicable memories in every blazoned tree and branch pinned each leaf to its twig with the gossamer ligaments of its beauty and sang in a note just beyond the ear's detection in the mosaic-ed air . . .

Those were the falls when the sense of nothing's being altogether present in itself but only in the echo it sent, thin as pain-shadow, pinned the lonely man to his own unfulfilments. But she'd be there with him, with the still voice of touch between them to make it as different from that as fall-chill outside with a fire burning in the grate from the chill fall outside and house-chill too within . . .

"That's if you really love me," he said.

"Oh, Bruce," she said. "You must know that! The *trees* know that!"

He'd be there in all the ways that Rex had never been there at all.

"But, Bruce," she said after a moment, quieter. "There are so many things . . ."

She could almost see them, like big physical question marks. The shape of ears. Feel them trying to stump her for the answers.

"Rex," she said, "for one. What about Rex?"

"All right," he said, his sureness mounting. "What about Rex? You don't love him, do you?"

"No," she said. "And this is the odd part. A week ago I didn't love him either, and I didn't care that I didn't love him . . . yet

211

I still didn't want him to catch me not loving him. Now I don't care in the least . . . not even in that way."

"Well then?" he said. "Tell him you want a divorce."

The word was like a smear on the air. If she could only be free of Rex by some clean surgical stroke, Sheila thought. She felt no guilt. She'd be cutting his harness too from that yoke that so seemed to gall his flesh whenever they tried to pull together in it. But that abortionist's touch about divorce: "scraping" marriage away with its unsanitary instruments . . .

Bruce, the peasant always in him, found it scarcely less a fetid word. But he plunged his hands into it the way a doctor must into pus or phlegm, finding it quite possible to eat with the same hands afterwards.

Sheila took a deep breath.

"All right," she said. "I'll tell him."

They talked no more about it then. There'd be plenty of time – there'd be the whole summer here, if they liked – to plan. They didn't feel like planning now. They felt like nothing but to take their ease, like bathers, in the lapping sea-swell of each other's presence. It was half an hour before they spoke with purpose again.

And then Bruce gave her the kind of teasing look that's solely the franchise of one who's just known the other's flesh.

"But, let's face it, Sheila," he said. "You won't find being a doctor's wife any bed of roses. Phone ringing in the night and . . ."

He watched for the exclamation in her eyes when they turned his words over and caught the premise behind them.

It came.

"Bruce!" she said. "You are going back to it then!"

"Yes," he said simply. "You made me see. It's as plain again as it ever was. And, my God, thank you."

He didn't know until that moment how truly she loved him. Not until he saw the tear-glint dancing every which way in her eyes for his having decided, after her persuasion had given up all hope, to do the thing that was best for him. He had never seen a face so multilingual in every feature.

"Oh, Bruce," she said. "That's the perfect news. The best . . . best . . . best . . ."

He felt a surge of the old purpose give him back his grip. Medicine his meat again and she his drink. All the sullen weights that in the long days past had hung by their own separate gravities from the hooks of each of his senses now took each other's stress in the way that cantilevered bridges give the effect of a great floating lightness. He couldn't speak.

And in the silence that now fell between them as easy as speech,

Sheila had time to hold his words against the light and test the other codicils behind them.

Yes, there were things about being a doctor's wife that . . . Did doctors work so constantly with flesh and blood that after a while all its terrible poetry was lost on them? Were they apt to turn into the noun for their calling, like lawyers or bankers or other professional men? That was the one saving thing about Rex, the perpetual uninitiate. Not a scrap of him had that awful distance about it of identification with something you couldn't share . . .

And, yes, there were lots of things about marriage itself that . . .

You saw your partner's personality with its skin off, and that could be as shocking as to see the physical face without its skin. There were rawnesses about marriage like eating uncooked meat. Seaminesses, like a salesman hawking his morning throat clear in a hotel bathroom. However well you knew a person in any other context, he still maintained enough of the *stranger's* consistency to make a single attitude toward him possible. But in marriage one partner was forever hitting on some facet of the other so startlingly incongruous with the rest of him that it brought you up as short as when an announcement in one language suddenly interjects the proper name of another tongue . . . and your single attitude was shattered into fragments. The merest trifles were forever reminding you that the two of you were *not* one. And there were the eye-flashing moments when one would seem to shed the whole shared context with the other and hate like a stranger . . .

She shook the thought off and gave *him* the teasing glance.

"You're sure you're not just marrying me for my poverty?" she said.

"Positive," he said. But he looked sheepish. "You certainly led me up the garden path on that business, didn't you?"

"No," she said. "I didn't do the leading at all. You were simply so mulish about rich girls that it made me just as mulish to defend them. To let you go right on thinking whatever you pleased about me. And then, yesterday – why yesterday and not before I haven't the slightest notion – but yesterday the whole thing seemed so childish."

Yesterday she had told him the facts.

Her father had been rich, yes. Greenwich-rich. And somehow once a man like him had ever been that kind of rich he became a sort of juggler; he could still keep up appearances, no matter what he'd lost. But it was a stopgap action, pure and simple. Everything had been thrown into the breach . . . the house, his life insurance, everything. It had come down to small ammunition like that. And when he died and all the pluses and the minuses had to face each other in a simple balance, without the juggler's hand, there'd probably be less than nothing left. Her mother had two small annuities in the clear, and that was all.

"I'm sorry," Bruce said. "But – I couldn't help it, that damn money did stick in my crop."

He wanted her all to himself. And money made three.

"All right," Sheila said. "I understand. But will you promise you won't hold it against me any more?"

"Not on your life," Bruce said. "I'll hold it against you every chance I get!"

It was the coarse cleansing joke of the married, when the man's tenderness must, in instinctive man-fashion, break wind. They laughed together and were married.

And then Sheila sobered completely. She picked up a pine cone and studied its scallops, as if that would help her to bring out what she had to say next.

"My money stuck in your crop because Molly and Peter never had any, didn't it?" she said.

"Partly," he said.

He waited for the faces of Molly and Peter to turn toward him as they always did whenever and by whomever their names were spoken. But for once they did not.

"Will you find it hard to tell *them* about us?" Sheila said.

For a moment he made himself quiet. But this time it was like one of those Armistice Day silences when no amount of will can put your mind directly against the object it seeks beyond the paperweight-snowstorm motes of hush; when, ironically, it is that terrible latent hush in the nearest object your eye fixes on that claims you.

His mind could turn Peter's and Molly's faces toward him with its hands, but now they were faces blind with allegiance to their own primal silence. They were faces with their own ghosts no longer behind them; and the thing that actually claimed his eye was a leaf which lay hushed with being exactly the way it was, on Sheila's skirt.

"No," he said. "Not any more."

It was Sheila's living face that was turned toward him then. And he saw its ghost behind it. In the way that only in love do you ever see the flesh and its own inseparable ghost together.

Sheila touched his hand with the cone.

"You know, Bruce," she said eagerly, "they *like* me. I can sort of feel the way they're looking at me now. Maybe you think their mouths look like Molly's did that night of the party. But they don't. I can't explain it . . . but they can see that I'm such an insider with *them* – more, in a funny way, than you are – that . . ."

214

He saw their faces then, looking at Sheila.

"You don't have to explain it," he said. "I know."

He took the cone from her hand and touched her hand with it. And the spine of love branched through and stabilized them both. It seemed as if their two equations had yielded a value for x that would unlock every equation in the world. And each felt that, in place of the two selves he'd had before, one for when he was alone and another that clicked front whenever anyone came on him unawares, now he had only one, indivisible, unsurprisable, and constant . . .

Rex coughed, coming down the path.

They sprang to their feet; and as if at a signal, the woods struck their sets. This play was over.

"The fishing rods," Sheila said. "Get them, quick. It's Rex."

Bruce got the rods.

"Do you think he'll notice the lines aren't wet?" she said.

"I thought you didn't care," Bruce said.

"I don't," she said. "I mean, I just . . ."

Barely through the fence again, they saw Rex coming toward them. He was hurrying, his limp more conspicuous than ever on the uneven ground.

He didn't give the lines, or anything else about them, a glance. Most people have a miniature third eye, of suspicion, that never blinks. Rex had none. Kate and Morse had snubbed him, and now Bruce and Sheila were his brother and his sister.

"Paul's back," he said. "And wait till you hear the rest of it!"

He was so guileless, so innocent of the secret that they shared against him, that Bruce and Sheila felt more cramp at taking news from him than if it had been money. He knew nothing about her father's losses either. Somehow the family never told him things. They'd kept it from him this whole last year. She felt ashamed.

"Where *was* Paul?" she said. "Did he say?"

Remembering too late that she had almost never asked him a deflecting question to which some part of his answer hadn't been a blow. Already, in his presence again, she felt cross-purposes begin to drag their feet.

"In the hospital, I guess," Rex said.

She saw the familiar sheen on his eyes for his being the centre of attention.

"The *hospital*?" she said.

Rex saw their faces fall. This was his reward. He could let his own face fall and the three of them would all be drawn together. Somehow the only time he didn't feel left out with Sheila lately

215

was when he brought her word about things that had taken some unsettling turn.

"What was the trouble?" Bruce said. "Anything serious?"

"I don't know," Rex said.

Nor really care, Sheila thought. For him, its being Paul the sorry news concerned didn't dampen its exclamatory worth at all.

But it made all the difference to her. And, she knew, to Bruce. Paul sick. Maybe critically. The whole day suddenly went off its feed, and April's jarringly innocent dress became all at once something almost foolish.

"And listen to this!" Rex said. "He's closing up shop here. Kicking every one of us out. Right away. Isn't that something?"

Sheila's quick look at Bruce sought from his at her a directive *how* to look, but got only its own question back. Home base was slipping out from underneath their love. They felt its going like a physical lurch. There'd be no time, no calm, to plan anything now.

"You're sure of that?" Bruce said to Rex.

"Absolutely. He said so. Right up and down."

Bruce grimaced. "Yes," he said. "That's something."

The path was too narrow for three to walk abreast. Rex and Bruce walked ahead and Sheila trudged (she was in that state of mind when all the simple verbs take on their wryer forms) behind.

Details of the landscape, dead as the landscape on a postcard, by their very blindness flagged her eyes down. With Rex's mind so caught up in his news, his lame leg seemed to be following (no, tagging along) after the other like a kid brother the older has momentarily ceased to clout home. (She felt the commentating dryness of the fishing line beneath her hand.) And the folds of Bruce's shirt kept drawing (no, caricaturing) knife slits between his shoulders. Foolish ironies sidled unbidden into her mind. The consort must always walk three paces in the rear . . . Turned out of Eden . . . But her mind's mouth was too set to grimace at them even.

Rex kept up a steady chatter, trying to set up an absolutely equilateral fellowship of question and answer amongst them. He could never tell the difference between news that joined and news that split.

"Where will you go, Bruce?" he said.

"I don't know," Bruce said. "Exactly."

"Look," Rex said. "Why don't you come back with us? Awhile in the States and I'll bet you'd never want to see Nova Scotia again. You've never been to New York, have you? I'd show you all round New York and – it wouldn't cost you a cent, either."

"Oh, Rex," Sheila said, "do you have to . . ?" She didn't know what.

216

"Well!" he said. "What's got into her ladyship all of a sudden?"
But he wasn't in the least annoyed; just brimming with the confidence that shows itself in kidding. He winked at Bruce. "Did you say something to cross her this morning? She's pretty touchy, pal, I'm warning you. You have to watch your words. It doesn't take much to ruffle her feathers. Now isn't that *true*, darling?"

Sheila looked away from him, at the trees. But the faces of the trees were no longer in league with her. They were obdurate as tombstones.

Bruce dropped back a pace.

"Will you tell him?" he muttered to her, sleight-of-hand. "Or will I?"

"I'll tell him," Sheila said.

CHAPTER 25

It was always like this when they packed. To Rex a suitcase symbolized the next adventure. To Sheila it was like a little coffin of the visit past; the layered clothing like a group of yesterdays with their arms folded in death. The bedroom was taut with these conflicting atmospheres.

It was still more taut when she began to break her news.

She started with the money business first: to create in him the climate of astonishment, dismay him, with that; and then she wouldn't have that climate's first vigour to contend with when she sprang her second disillusion. Surprising herself that she could be so heartless, she felt nothing but impatience to have the whole thing over and done with. She begrudged even the effort of tempering the manner of her telling to his reception of it. She was in that cruellest state of apartness when even the due to familiarity asserts no claim. She simply didn't want to be bothered with his reactions.

"So there goes your stinking heiress that gets her feathers ruffled up so easily," she wound it up, almost striking the dress she was packing into place.

Surprising herself that she could be so nasty, she'd used this grating roughness to command the air against any less manoeuvrable atmosphere that might develop.

He'd heard her through without a word.

Defiantly, to make him speak, she looked directly at him. And

. . . yet once again . . . she'd envisioned it all wrong. The astonishment was hers.

It was quite plain why he hadn't spoken. It was not dismay, but *un*dismay that he'd been saving up: to surprise and present her with in one big smile. He was smiling it now: the smile of a man for the wife who's always thought her youthful looks must be maintained at all costs because of *his* vanity about them, when he actually welcomes her first grey hair as an equallizing factor. My God, he was going to *rally* to her. He was going to put his arm around her.

And then, desperately before this of all atmospheres could become established as the prevailing one, she told him about her and Bruce. Omitting only the adultery. In a few short, simple, brutally matter-of-fact sentences.

And again he astonished her. He believed her.

He believed her immediately. She'd been certain that she'd have to hammer it home, persuade him that she spoke the truth. A year ago, a month ago, he'd have found it absolutely incredible that she could help loving him. That he hadn't absolute dominion over her. But now she knew he had seen in a single flash that his one dominion (and everyone must have one such or die) had crumbled.

He didn't do any of the typical things she'd expected. He didn't storm at her, or strike out at some substitute target. He didn't even try to explain her magnanimously to herself, as if she were the ingenuous self-deceiver. He didn't say a word.

She glanced at his suitcase. He had piled things in, in a stack, just as they came. He hadn't fitted the small pieces in with the large to complete each layer. There was waste space everywhere. He could never fold a jacket properly.

And then she heard the choppy breathing in his nostrils, unsilenceable for his mouth's being clamped tight. She had never in her life seen Rex cry.

And then he sat down on the bed and he was shaking all over and trying to strike back the advancing sobs, all-hated but half-luring, with those helpless little blows of the hands against the side of the bed and his thighs and each other.

Rex, she thought. In simple wonder. Five years ago – five months ago – what a victory this would have been! But now she felt no thrill of victory whatever. Nothing but a kind of unthinkable irritation: of the sort you feel when someone comes to join you in impulsive mourning for your dead just after your own has exhausted itself . . . and you sit there knowing you owe him the posture of sadness in your lips at least, but helpless not to keep your glance off the ball the neighbours' children are throwing dangerously near the kitchen window.

She kept on packing. *Sotto voce,* in a kind of respect for his crying. But that was all she could manage.

One corner of her suitcase tipped down into the depression his weight made on the bed. She drew the suitcase toward her. Its lid fell sharply, it seemed viciously, across the back of her hand.

"Owww!" she exclaimed. "You blasted . . ."

She knew this was violence beyond anything she really felt. She knew, surprising herself again, that she was merely using this exaggeration of her petulance to give his tears the snub, the devaluation, that only petulance can.

Rex's shivering stopped. He looked up from under his face like a child momentarily forced out of his sulk by some minor calamity to the one he's sulking against.

"Did it break the skin?" he said.

"No, no," she said. "It just took a jump out of me, that's all. The damned thing."

There was a kind of no-man's-land silence while Rex put his snubbed (and now self-snubbed) crying back inside him and, as it were, cleaned up after it.

"You say you want a divorce," he said. "That's what you said, wasn't it? Did you mean that? Did you mean . . . right away?"

"Yes, Rex," Sheila said. "Let's *not* have to drag this thing out. Yes, yes, yes."

At last his docility cracked. A little spot of wildness sprang to life in his eyes and danced there like a dervish.

"*All* right!" he said. "You just go right ahead. All *right*." And then he said the two words over and over, with absolute equality of emphasis on each. "All right, all right, all right, all right . . ." As if he had every punishing thing that had ever happened to him by the throat and was choking it black in the face with this grinding assent. He had such a headache he could scarcely think.

He got up from the bed and moved toward the window, exactly the way an actor walks to a stage window and then turns around to deliver the slow deliberate speech that clinches the play's theme. She wouldn't have believed that Rex's feelings had any of the theatricality about them which all deep feelings have. They'd always seemed like an artless child's.

He turned exactly like the actor. But what he said had no connection with the play. It came tumbling out in one wild and uncued leap from everything that had gone before.

This wasn't recrimination. Or self-pity. None of the things she was used to.

This was simply that moment come at last when (if you are like Rex) the forces gathered opposite you have so grouped themselves

219

in vectoring of energy and angle so classically the maximum against your weakest point that, senseless as it seems, the only *affirmation* you can counter with, at last defiant even of your own pride, is to flaunt the one great blemish in yourself it's been a lifelong purpose to conceal.

He spoke in a kind of glittering, reckless glee. He had at last taken the giant step into the burdenless country of the confessor. His words, fantastically bald of any preface, drooped from his lips like those little animals from the lips of the characters in a fairy tale.

"All right," he said. "All right. You damn well fooled me on that loving me business, didn't you. But let me tell you something – I can fool you too. I fooled you good and proper – about this goddam foot. I fooled everyone." He looked at his foot as if it were something famous. "You thought that was an honest-to-God war wound, didn't you. You thought I really did step on that booby trap, didn't you. Everyone did. But I didn't, Sheila. Oh, no, I didn't. Do you know what happened to that foot? I did that to myself!"

Sheila was quite literally stunned; as if she'd been struck by a great passage of time contracted into a round hard pellet. As if years had passed in the moments since he'd started to speak. She watched the little animals drop from his twitching lips and she was in a play in a dream when the other actors shout at you but no one has shown you the answering lines.

"I knew that tin can was a booby trap. We were always on the watch for things like that when we mopped up those deserted houses. I *told* them I just kicked the can before I thought. That's what you always do with a tin can, give it a kick. But I didn't kick it like that. I knew it was a booby trap. I was all alone and I lay down flat on the floor and I just tapped it with the toe of my boot. Until it went off." He looked as if his mind was turning pelt side out. "My God, since then . . . or sometimes. Sometimes when I look at that . . ." His eyes scorched at his foot. "Nights sometimes. When I dream. I see tin cans with all sorts of *crazy* things inside them . . ."

She had a sudden piercing glimpse of the shape an unmentionable secret can grow into. Like those abortion-faced grotesqueries, curdling in their own macabre logic, that you see sometimes in the suffocating spell of nightmare: the fist opening and a little snake nestling in its palm; the intestine blossoming clammily, to the cheek's amazement, in the centre of a cheek.

"Rex," she said. "Rex . . . I . . ." But they still hadn't shown her the lines.

He sat down on the bed again and talked toward the floor, his eyes darting nervously around the whorls in the carpet pattern in a compulsive nerveless aside.

"A tin can," he said almost tonelessly. "A booby trap. And who was the booby? I was. A tin can! I'd have laid down my life for you, Sheila. And what did I lay down? My goddam foot . . ." His voice rose. "That's what you won't believe, Sheila. I did it for you. I wasn't a coward. I wasn't scared of getting killed. I didn't have sense enough to be a coward. But I'd get thinking of maybe never seeing *you* again. I couldn't sleep thinking maybe I'd never see you again. I knew the war was almost over. I knew it was only a matter of days maybe. But what if I got killed the very last damned day? It would be just my luck. I thought, what did it matter if I grabbed this way out now? You won't believe this – but I was sick, I was *crazy*, I loved you so. I was. I was kind of crazy that day. I'd had a letter from you with that snapshot – do you remember? – taken there by the bird bath behind the house . . .?"

Bird baths, she thought foolishly. There were things like that and things like this. Her mother had snapped that picture of her just to finish out a film. If the smallest deed were banded, like a bird, her foolish thought continued, what end of the earth mightn't it be reported from?

He struck his fists against the bed.

"I was crazy for a minute there when I did that. I just *had* to see you again . . ."

At the end of a terrible confession you somehow count on what you hadn't known was your expectancy right from the start. Secrecy has built up such a terrible authority for the deed it hid that the breaking of it seems to be the open sesame to everything. A kind of universal passport. You are all open, awash with an enormous roominess you expect the listener to rush into without a pause. It seems as if the agony of concealment has miraculously not been waste; it has been transmuted into a burning solvent force to cancel out all other discords. You forget that only you are drunk with this, that the listener is sober.

Rex expected Sheila's arm to come around his shoulder. He didn't feel it there. He looked up, to see why nothing came running from her toward him.

She knew what he expected. She knew she could take back her own confession about Bruce and make him believe the recantation as instantly as he'd believed the truth not half an hour before. And then – give him a week at most, and in his memory-less way this whole monstrous scene would be discarded on the scrap heap of the past and virtually forgotten.

. . . Or did she know the first, least thing about him? Did she even believe she did? Or was it only when you were still in love with someone that you thought you knew him inside out?

Of one thing, though, she was dead certain. This cry had sprung from him without a motive. It was none of his familiar snares, to trap her. It was not even a scorched-earth policy. It was nothing more or less than an explosion of innocence.

"And what did they do?" he said. "They gave me a pension! Sheila, I've been taking *money* for it." He shivered. "My God, I wish I *had* stepped on that booby trap. I wish it had blown me off the face of the earth."

A diabolic sentence limned itself for an instant on the blackboard of her mind. "I wish it had." No. No. She rubbed it out in a panic.

"Rex," she said gently, words once more at hand, but only the conventional ones, "you should have told me all this long ago."

"You'd have hated me," he said.

"No," she said truthfully. "No, I wouldn't have."

She wouldn't have, then. But now . . . She had often wondered how two people no longer armed with love ever kept on in the bell-jar of marriage when there was some *physical* reminder of past disgrace constantly before them. The scar on the wife's cheek where the husband had struck her once with his fist. The little bluish line on his inner arm where he had once tried to slash his wrists . . .

"I guess you don't think much of me now," Rex said. "Or have you been listening to a word I said? You'd never know it."

"Yes, Rex," she said, "I've been listening to every syllable."

Yet once again she was dumbfounded at her own detachment; astonished to find that she was merely searching for words that would dispose of his confession with the minimum fuss. She spoke slowly, out of respect to it, but the respect too was only conventional.

"But, Rex," she said, "I don't think that has anything to *do* with what we've just been talking about. I wish I knew how to say this, that you won't misunderstand me, but . . . No, I don't think I think any the less of you. No. As far as that goes, I imagine plenty of soldiers did the same thing you did. But, Rex, that's not the point at all. We were talking about people loving each other. If you tell someone you don't love him any more, it doesn't mean you don't think much of him. They're two entirely different things. And if I were you," she added, "I wouldn't even think about the pension. After all, you gave them three years of your life. That should square off anything they've given you."

He saw what she was doing. She was picking up his secret and passing it back to him. He saw that you couldn't unload a killing

secret like this by telling it. The other faces didn't absorb and eva-
porate it. Their sudden guardedness splashed it back all over you.
So that now you bore it twice: inside again as always, and on the
outside too.

The pattern in the carpet turned suddenly terrible. The little
point of wildness that caromed around in his eyes really frightened
her. He was suddenly almost screaming.

"Where's that bottle?" he said. "You're always sticking every
damn thing away somewhere."

"I threw it out," she said. "It was empty."

"Well, then," he said, "let's beat it the hell off to Morse's party.
He'll have half a dozen."

"Do you feel like a party right now?" she said.

His head was vibrating on his neck. He was saying the first thing
that came into his mind.

"Why not?" he said. "Don't you? You say you've lost your money.
A party'll cheer you up. You're getting rid of me, too. You can cele-
brate. Morse says now it's an engagement party. Him and Kate.
Well, how would it be, for a great big switch, if I got up and
announced our . . ." – he fumbled – "unengagement?"

Ah. She felt a sudden fervent gratitude toward him. This was an
attitude she recognized. This blind storming away from realities.
She knew the lines for this play.

Another time, it would have tripped her up that he didn't know
the word was "disengagement"; that he didn't *have* many words
would have struck her in the way of a child's not having many
clothes. Another time, she'd have been thrown into disorder by
that crazy unpredictable fairness of his in venting no rancour whatsoever against Bruce . . . remembering, as she did, in what tone of
negligence she and Bruce had dismissed him.

But not now. This attitude he'd fled to now gave her the least
taxing of all responses to maintain: reasonableness rebuffed. She'd
make sure she gave him no pretext to let himself off it.

April's evening breath came through the window and for an
instant lifted the layers in each of them apart, like the leaves of
a book. She closed the lid on the suitcase.

"All right," she said. "If you're in the mood for drinking to our
unengagement, let's go."

CHAPTER 26

They all toasted Kate and Morse. But Kate's happiness smarted a little under its check-rein. Why must this big moment of her life, which could have but one celebration, have it under these conditions?

It was such an uneasy party. Each of them had one eye on his behaviour and the other on some private uproar inside him. Rex's fairness toward Bruce had turned into a kind of insolent good-fellowship just short of taunt. Bruce and Sheila, short-circuited with consciousness of each other, sat self-conscious as enemies. Frost-spots of interior stillness bleached Paul's face from time to time. There was no general crisscross of communication. All attentions were focused on Morse, in simple protection from the constraint of having to direct them at each other.

The very uneasiness of the party was exactly to Morse's liking. He was merely biding his time until the drinks had dissolved the umbilical thread of each to his private tension. Then these tensions would float loose and collide in the general atmosphere. Then he would spring his game.

At first they sat there in that lull just before speech loosens; when the ear is so taken up with the sinuous hubbub the drinks have started inside you that you don't notice you're being obtrusively quiet. It seems as if the hubbub is loud in the outer air also; your face begins to dissolve (and the consciousness of it as the solid mask it presents to another eye); and your own eyes glance fixedly at inanimate objects as if all at once they were going to disclose an animate face.

There was scarcely a word spoken. But Morse hadn't long to wait.

Bruce picked up the weekly paper Letty had brought home from town. His gesture was almost in the nature of a stifled yawn.

The others might throw in their lot with the liquor as with a reckless friend. He always managed to keep his distance from it. Drinking tended to make Kate forgetful of unpleasant things, Sheila mindful of them. It heightened Paul's wariness, and stupefied Rex. It started Morse reading compulsively off whatever outrageous cue card popped into his head. But it merely made Bruce better acquainted with himself.

"Did you see this?" he said. "This case came up in court last week?"

The moment he spoke, Sheila had that certain presentiment you sometimes have about the extraneous remark: that it will lead straight to the present occasion's sorest spot. The more precarious the occasion, the greater your certainty. She felt a profound annoyance with Bruce for his very innocence of any such design.

"Where will you and Morse be living?" she said quickly, across him, to Kate.

"We don't know, exactly," Kate said.

"Euphoria, USA," Paul said.

But the innocent blunderer is never to be deflected.

"This arson case," Bruce said. "Apparently the guy burnt his house for the insurance. And what do you suppose put them on to him? His wife was away, it says, and the adjuster got snooping around in the shed and came across a letter the guy had written to her . . . all stamped and everything . . . in a feed box! He hadn't sneaked another thing out of the house before he burned it, but he just couldn't bear having to write that letter over again. There's a story for you, Morse."

Morse shook his head.

"No," he said. "To write anyone you have to be able to get right inside his head. Murderers, yes. You can do it with them. Liars, yes. *Some* kinds of thief, yes – but I couldn't get inside that guy's head. There'd be the precise moment when he'd have to put the match to the kerosene rag or whatever the hell it was. I'd lose him then. There'd be the precise moment when he cashed the insurance cheque, if he got one. I couldn't understand that either. How he'd figure he could live with himself again on that foundation. I couldn't see that. Could you?"

"Well, no," Bruce said. "I guess I couldn't."

"I knew a pianist once," Morse said, "quite a celebrated pianist, shot two fingers off his right hand for the insurance on them. Or anyway they tried to prove he did. *He* said he was standing with one hand over the muzzle of his gun, taking a leak, rabbit-hunting. Honest to God, taking a leak. As it happened, he was a queer of some proportions and that type doesn't usually go much for hunting . . . but there's exactly what I mean. I could even gather the queer business enough to write it. But the thing about the fingers and the insurance. No. Could you understand that part, Paul? You understand everything."

"Well . . . no," Paul said. "Not exactly, I guess. I mean, not so you'd have any idea whether you were right or wrong about it."

Sheila glanced at Rex.

Neither case they'd mentioned had duplicated his. But she knew that the likeness had been close enough for him to see how his own would strike them. And she saw, too, why Morse's attitude had cut him deepest. Morse was such an anarchic man. You didn't expect him to have strictures against any kind of conduct. But he'd disclosed one toward this.

"Well!" she said, laughing her light dispatching Greenwich laugh. "The only thing *I* can't understand is this uncommon relish you're all exhibiting for jury duty."

"Uh, uh," Paul said quietly. "I've seen a jury in action."

"Yeah!" Rex said, skipping Paul's remark and linking up with Sheila's. "You're hellish angels all of a sudden, aren't you!"

He'd had enough to drink already that it didn't occur to him they might wonder what explained his vehemence. He turned on Morse.

"And how come you know so damn much about queers?" he said "Have you been playing around with them?"

Morse was quite unruffled.

"I didn't say that," he said. "I said that in a certain sense I could understand them. I remember certain inclinations when I was twelve, thirteen, yes. All kids that age are fairies to a man. I don't think it's so much a case of loving the older guys as being in love with their laying the girls. That's all I was going on. But it gives you the idea. Or take writing about women. You don't *know* how they feel . . . but listen to them shrewdly enough and read those blab-sheets forever hanging out on their telltale faces and check your guesses during those ecdysiast moods they so dearly love . . . it gives you the idea. I have no ideas whatsoever about the arson business. Have you?" His tone came to a point. "And, incidentally, where you were brought up – " (Did he know about the orphanage? Sheila thought. He must. Rex must have told him. It would be just the crazy thing he would do, tell Morse of all people) "– didn't you experiment with each other? And didn't you enjoy it?"

Sheila saw Rex flounder; but Morse had decency enough immediately to turn his back to pour another round of drinks, leaving the question a rhetorical one.

"Which reminds me," he said briskly. "Anyone here ever play Plain Speaking?" He described the game. "There's nothing like it to perk up a sagging party. We seem to lack a parcheesi board or any interesting sixteen millimetre film, so why don't we give it a try now?" He passed the drinks around. "It can be a little rough, but . . . are there any sissies here?"

Sheila thought about Rex's foot.

"Isn't that clothing forfeit a little childish?" she said.

"You mean childish?" Morse said. "Or too indelicate for milady? Say exactly what you mean. That's the basis of the whole thing."

"I meant childish," Sheila said, smiling. "Who'd ever question your judgement in matters of taste?"

"Good girl!" Morse said. "That's the spirit! That's the spirit! Okay, then. No stripping, if you say so. No rules whatever. We're all out of order, anyway. Perhaps irreparably. So let's dispense with the rules. Just a simple old-fashioned rhubarb."

Bruce and Sheila exchanged glances. They had scarcely addressed each other in any other way all evening. But this time their glances didn't quite mesh. His half-conscious thought got in the way. Once money and sophistication had given your tongue a cutting edge like that, could you toss it away on the disarmament pile of love if you wanted to?

Rex threw back his drink in one swallow.

"All right," he said, to be daredevil first, and thus commit them all. "Let's go. Let's get things moving."

He was now so high that in the liquor's mirror the lettering of caution was turned square round and looked as strange as Russian. He swung immediately to Paul.

"Why didn't you ever pick up a wife?" he said. "Haven't you got what it takes?"

It was the cornered dog biting wantonly now, at anything within reach. You crazy fool, Sheila thought. Paul would have been on your side. All right then, go it alone.

Paul grinned.

"I've got what it takes," he said. "But maybe I was never satisfied to take what I could get."

"Attaboy, Paul!" Morse said. "Now it's your privilege to shoot one back at Rex."

Paul thought a moment. Then grinned again.

"I'm sorry," he said. "I guess I'll have to pass. At the moment I can't seem to think of anything in particular I want to ask him."

It was a quieter snub than Morse's, but Sheila knew that, drunk as Rex was, they were all mounding up on him just the same, as the growing cold turns a runaway child's lips blue whether or not he feels it consciously in his tantrum. Her detachment began to falter all over again.

The next few rounds were harmless banter; but it wasn't long before Morse could see the first playful boxing blows turn into the revealing jabs of spite he'd counted on.

Kate herself Sheila liked thoroughly. But she began to hate her almost for her tie with Morse.

"I'd like to ask Kate something," she said; still in a joking tone but the barb beneath it. "How old are you, Kate? And don't you think you're taking quite a risk to marry a man who's already failed with three wives . . . and two books . . . and is old enough in experience to be your . . . father?"

"I'm forty," Kate answered calmly. "And I think you and I have quite different ideas of what constitutes failure in a man." She had felt the first wifely sting of hearing her husband assailed. "As I see it, the only failures are those of spirit. And even if Morse were a failure, I'd find that no reason not to . . . stick with him. I'd feel it was my function to revive his spirit, if possible. And here's my question to you. A year from now we hope to have a child. Which of us then – you or I – will have more to show for marriage?"

"Make it two years," Sheila said, "and we'll see."

She saw Rex start. He gave Bruce an annihilative glare.

Morse's outrageous cue card flashed up.

"And don't talk as if Kate's such an old model there's no getting parts for her," he read from it. "And don't think I'm too old to father a child. Not in these days of synthetic testosterone anyway."

"Which is like everything else," Paul put in. "What you buy is so often better than what you make yourself, isn't it." He could almost always draw the fangs of an exchange like this with some preposterous joke.

Everyone laughed except Rex. Two years from now, she'd said. She must have meant a child with Bruce. A child . . . a child . . . a child . . . The word hurtled back and forth inside his skull. The calipers closed against his temples.

"How about another drink?" he said. "That's the next question, isn't it?"

"Haven't you had enough?" Sheila said. He was beginning to slump and blur.

"No?" he mimicked her, "I haven't had enough?" As blazingly as if in questioning the companionship of his liquor she had aspersed his closest friend.

Morse gave him another drink.

"Ask my wife what she told me this afternoon," Rex said, in a sudden smashing recklessness.

"What did you tell your husband this afternoon?" Morse said.

Sheila hesitated only a second. "I told him my father had lost his money," she said.

"No," Rex began, "I didn't mean . . ." But his head had begun to weave and, with it, his concentration.

Morse looked intently at her. "Interesting," he said. "Most interesting, if true."

"True . . ." Rex echoed vacantly, with the drunk's private smile.

"Well, poor Sheila!" Morse said. "You'll pardon the expression, but when will I ever get such another chance to combine the literal with the commiserative? Bruce," he said, "you look so sober it's damn near a mien. Doesn't this startling intelligence about Sheila affect you in any way?"

"Not particularly," Bruce said.

"Liar!" Rex cried. "Liar . . ."

They ignored him. And he drifted away from himself. To emerge again, from then on, only as that uncanny prompter in the drunk's ear recalled him.

"Nevertheless," Morse pursued it with Bruce, "and I speak as one pauper-born to another – you must have feelings of some kind about rich women. Say you were in love with Sheila. Wouldn't that silver spoon – present *or* past – still get in the way of your lips?"

Bruce tried his hand at using the joke as a sword. His adeptness astonished them.

"You know," he said, "if I hadn't been brought up never to strike old men, you might find something in the way of *your* lips."

Morse was geniality itself. "Thank you, sir," he said. "My question angered you. That answers it exactly."

"Bruce won't answer, won't answer!" Rex chanted. "Sissy. Sissy. Ask him what he and Sheila . . ." But it trailed away.

Sheila's lips drew back in a rueful grimace. Which Bruce misread completely.

He took it to be a smile such as certain mothers accord a simple nastiness in their child. Mildly upbraiding but half-intrigued, nevertheless. More exasperating than the nastiness itself. He had a funny qualm.

So long with Rex, had more of his grain penetrated hers than she realized? It happened so often in the contagion of marriage. Girls once honest even in trivial matters came to relate the tricky deals their husbands put across as if they were engaging peccadillos. He'd seen others, prim to the bone, become nearly evangelical about their husbands' smut. Wives renounced their own political faith, however rabid, and became the most taunting spokesmen for their husbands' . . . And look at Kate. The way she'd fallen in step with Morse. And . . . he and Molly. He and Molly had certainly grown into each other's views. Suddenly in this airless, hothouse talk Molly seemed like the fresh-breathing night outside.

Kate sat there, half-hating everything Morse said; yet thinking proudly-foolishly: If the Athenaeum Club could see me now!

And Paul heard his love for her louder or softer as his glance fell on her or away, like a code-stutter in the death-stillness inside him.

229

"Does nothing ever get in the way of those profane lips of yours?" Sheila said quickly to Morse. "Have you no conscience whatever about what you say to people, or about them? And, please, if we could just have a plain answer to that. Don't you think, Kate, that maybe you'll find his vulgarity a mite sickening . . . find it a trifle wearing to get an epigram – of sorts – every time you ask him a simple question?"

Kate's circling glance just perceptibly lingered on Rex. His eyes were drooling now. He was barely present. His face was prepared for interjection, but in the lag between impulse and speech the conversation would take a different turn and outdistance him. His glass was almost unattended in his hand, the drink's surface precariously aslant.

"No," Kate said. "I think I prefer an articulate husband rather than not. And I think that if you knew Morse at all, you'd find that he's anything but a clever cynic, that he has a good deal more conscience that most."

"Conscience makes Noel Cowards of us all," Paul said.

"I wonder if maybe the whole thing isn't quite simple," Bruce said to Morse; and this time it was his incisiveness that surprised them. "You mistake being rude for being tough. They're different things altogether. Writers and actors are always getting them mixed up."

"Maybe so," Morse said, still perfectly affable. "And don't think you offend me. A writer gets hardened to . . . pricks . . . of all kinds. But let's get back to Poor Sheila's – or Portia's, for short – let's get back to Portia's question about conscience. I'm glad you asked me that, Portia. You've hobbled me with your plain answer rider. Nothing is plain except surfaces. Plane surfaces. Nothing whatever is simple – except maybe wrestlers and senators from Alabama. But to be as plain and simple as I can, the only thing I have conscience about is Truth."

He held up his hand. "Uh uh. This is no claim to virtue. It doesn't mean I couldn't be fifteen kinds of s.o.b. . . . fifteen kinds of liar, in fact. That's beside the point. But Truth is the only thing I really have any *conscience* about. It's the only thing that makes you feel good for any length of time. No, no, not that kind of good – but good, sound. It's the only thing that doesn't carry its own bacteria. Everything else breaks out – give it time enough – even love, give it time enough – with its own little sick spots, like the spots squash get in the spring." He spoke at top speed, taking the hairpin bends in his mind on two wheels. "So find the Truth, I say, face it, and anyone that skedaddles around it – slug him."

His tone went cajoling.

"Now, Portia," he said, "let's hear what, if anything, you have any conscience about."

Sheila didn't have to stop and consider. Everyone has one obsessive theme pocketed and reservoired somewhere inside him. He had tapped into hers.

"I have the most conscience," she said, "about saying things or doing things to make another person feel guilty. If there's anyone I despise in this world it's the guilt-maker. The guilt-seeder."

"Guilt-seeder," Rex echoed, in a vague snicker.

Her words rolled up into a speech.

"I know. It's an absolutely respectable kind of murder by inches. Make the other fellow blame himself, think less of himself. It goes on every minute of the day, and nobody ever dreams of putting it alongside dope-pushing. But that's where it belongs. They're exactly the same thing. Put that little germ of guilt under the other fellow's skin where it can get at the nerves. For that's what it feeds on. The tenderest little nerves. Parents do it to their children. Preachers, judgers, right-knowers of any kind —they all do it to the people that don't see things exactly as they do. I've never known anyone that absolute conviction about anything didn't make crueler in some way . . . But that guilt-pushing, that's what your Truth characters are doing all the time. And I say, the hell with them. If I were ever a preacher, do you know the only two texts I'd take? 'Forgive them for they know not what they do,' and 'Let him among you who is himself without sin cast the first stone.' "

"Stone," Rex echoed, hearing the sound of his voice only as a sound in his thought.

His eyes had closed. His mind away, some of the old handsomeness seemed to creep back into his unguarded face, as youthfulness does sometimes in death. He just barely held onto his glass, like a child that goes to sleep with a toy in his hand.

"I hate that cry of the pack," Sheila said, "whenever it scents anything a little different. Get him! Get him! I hate that. Yes, you and your Truth. I've seen things that are done in the name of Truth. The truth is, that all the damn truth in the world wouldn't make up for a single night-time of someone's lying awake heartsick and bleeding inside from the guilt-pushers."

Morse clapped his hands.

"Well spoken!" he exclaimed. "A bit beside the point – unless you're making some private point to yourself, as I suspect you are – but well spoken nevertheless!"

He turned to Bruce.

"And you, sir," he said. "What do you have conscience about? There's a theory that you blame yourself for the death of your wife

231

and child. Now we might ask Portia what becomes of her case when a man does his own guilt-pushing. And do you still really remember them enough to keep that conscience gouging you?"

Every face has a kind of respiration rhythm. If Morse noticed Bruce's face getting short-breathed, he gave no sign.

"It's interesting, if you still do. Because I can't really remember my wives at all. Certainly not with any conscience. They're no more than like dates . . . on which certain things happened to me. Helen some Tuesday, Natalie some Friday . . . a long time ago. But perhaps I'm polygamous and you're monogamous. *Are* you monogamous?"

Once Bruce had promised to meet Molly and Peter downtown after classes and take them to a show. And then forgotten it entirely. He was in the trolley with Jeff Morton, talking the medical shop talk that made all other exchanges in the car echo like stupidities, when the car turned the corner by the theatre and Jeff exclaimed suddenly out of conclave: "Wwww-atch it! Wwww-atch it, sister!"

Bruce's glance followed Jeff's to the street and he saw Molly and Peter standing there. One of Molly's small hands was clutching her hat and the other was holding her skirt down against the wind. Their "good" clothes had gone less and less protective of them, with waiting . . . less and less a friendly feature. Peter had that assaulting docility about him he so often had in crowds. He kept looking up into the face of everyone who jostled him, to share apology . . .

Plainer than he had seen her then, Bruce saw Molly now. Bending against the gusts of those cruel little street winds that slap you in the face when the person you're waiting for is later and later and you've changed your position a hundred times to let the blind purposeful strangers pass. And Peter, with no one looking down at the tie he'd looped way out over the top of his sweater, because it was new . . . That was the very corner, at the foot of that very hill, where the car had skidded and . . .

Anger in the others sharpened the precision tools of cultivated speech to a finer edge. Angered blind, Bruce instinctively stripped for action to the rugged idiom of his youth.

"You're hellish smart where the skin's off, aren't you!" he blazed. It was half to Morse and half, retroactively, to Jeff. "Well, you . . . don't . . . know . . ." he threw each word separately, like a rock, "anything. You've never done anything, that's why. You just loll around on your ass and shoot off your face. You wouldn't know an honest feeling if you fell over it. Nobody knows anything about *any*thing unless he's been poor as piss . . ."

232

His anger was suddenly a so much more ringing friend than any tepid personal alliance that it spread out to indict everyone in the room. The recoil of it drove him back into a corner alone.

"I always had conscience about being some use in the world, that's what I had conscience about. You're no damn good for anything. And do you know what I think about the whole bloody caravan of you?" For a second his glance relented, exempting Sheila and Paul. "I wouldn't give Letty's little finger for your whole damn carcass. Yes, Letty. And you can kiss . . . my . . . ass . . . and scratch my hole and . . ."

The language he was using brought him to. He braked the sentence to a dead stop.

"And take my cock for a jumpin' pole!" Paul finished it.

He spoke in the bemused murmur of nostalgic recognition, slurring the offensive word like someone slurring an oath in a television play. He alone could deliver a shocking line without the slightest effect of vulgarity.

"Gracious me," he said. "I haven't heard that tender little couplet since we used to hurl it at each other when we were boys."

"Nor I!" Morse cried, "nor I!" – his bellow of laughter rousing Rex even. It was impossible to anger him when your own anger was grist to his mill. "But I remember all right. It used to be our favourite defiance too. So you see, Bruce, we weren't such different boys anyway. What's wrong with *you*?" he said, turning to Kate.

Both Kate and Sheila were shaking with pent-up giggles, the sight of one's struggle with them fueling the other's. Bruce's outrageous bomb of coarseness, hurled with such startling incongruity by one naturally so grave and fielded and detonated so expertly by Paul into a blast of air-clearing humour, had caught them at exactly the right pitch of tension for the hysteria content of their drinks to topple them into helpless laughter.

Paul assumed a grin of innocent perplexity (What did I say, to bring this on?); and Bruce was sheepishly disarmed. Morse indicated the women with a flip of his head (crackpots!), purposely striking the same stance of incomprehension as Paul's, to play along with the thing. For the first time, good feeling went the rounds.

Morse's next tone with Bruce was almost conciliatory.

"You may not know," he said, "that when I was young I had just as much claim to this . . . insight through poverty . . . as you have. And I know exactly that superiority in his bones – no, in his stones – that the man with the axe has. Haven't I told you so, Kate? Well, *look* at those bloody simpletons!"

The women were still in that state of hilarity when you strike a sober face to answer a rational question and then just your own seriousness sets you off again. Morse shook his head, turning back to Bruce.

"And, by and large, you're right. You say poor as piss, but you don't mean that, of course. You mean that benign poverty just short of pinching. It may twist you, but it wrings the watery part, the diluent, out of you too. The melody of being has only four or five big notes, and I grant you that poor people catch them clearer – the others can't hear them through the orchestrations. I grant you the grain of their pleasure has far richer complexity than the rich man's. They share that brotherly, bedrock sentience the others never know. All right. That's part of *your* truth. But if you cling to that part of it so viciously you'll defeat the other part. You'll never be any use in the world. You'll never get in position to be of any use. What government would ever come to power on a platform of keeping everyone just poor enough to be ideally sentient?"

He turned to Paul.

"So what about you, sir? What's your sentence for good behaviour? 'My conscience tells me . . .' Would you care to complete that one in twenty-five words or less?"

"I can do it in four," Paul said. "Laugh and let live."

He was completely serious: a manner so rare in him that it always commanded instant seriousness in his listeners. Kate's face and Sheila's sobered as if a brush stroke had wiped off their giggling.

"Mind you," he said, "I claim no absolute value for this little maxim. Who talks about absolute values when the best brains in the world can't riddle out space and time even? When there may be intellects and senses on some other star that make our eons as an evening gone . . . our little psyches as millimetric as a grasshopper's? When, such is the mind's odd function, the more we learn the more it's just to learn how really insignificant we are? When the only rational action is suicide? But we're funny grasshoppers. We have laughing . . . and loving . . . and self-objectification. We can watch ourselves and watch ourselves watching ourselves . . . and so on. Did you ever stop to think what crazy, wonderful things those are to be found in grasshoppers like us? They're literally *unimaginable* without example. And here's my point. These funny characters know they're fools to think that stuff like courage and tolerance and compassion can be called the good things with any reason. But I'm kind of glad we're the kind of fools that do. That's what I believe in, I guess – the fool's consciously foolish belief. So why be intense about anything? As I say, laugh, love – and there's the truly funny one, because who doesn't love the bad as often as the good? – and let live. End of filibuster."

He was grinning again, but thinking: And the fool knows that all these silly antics for grasshoppers – one man makes noises with a horn and the others clap their hands together – amount to nothing, yet why does everything inside him go still when he knows he has to leave it?

"But you skipped the chapter about sex," Morse said. "That old forehead-wrinkler is a laughing matter too?"

"Of course," Paul said. "Lord knows that's the most laughable of all. The intensity about that. It's good manners for a man to stand up when a girl comes into the room, but it's nasty if his member imitates him. Could anything be more comic than this whole great mythography that's been built up around an involuntary little Jack-in-the-box like that? Think what a different turn the whole thing would have taken if we'd happened to be so designed that we carried our genitalia in some quite unconcealable spot – say, the centre of the forehead. There'd be no more of this mytho-graphical flapdoodle and hush-hush about sex than there is about blowing your nose. Intensity of any kind . . . to think anything more important than anything else, any man more important than another . . . with all the time our funny little stomachs distilling a little hydrochloric acid and our lungs a little phlegm and our livers a little bile and our kidneys a little urine and our gonads a little semen . . . it's all so laughable *sub specie aeternitatis*." He grinned again. "You see what laughable verbiage you get into when you try even to take the joke of it seriously!"

Morse turned to Sheila.

"Sheila," he said, "I'd say – although you never can tell – that you and I were the intensest ones here. Do you think we can remember this little sermon?"

"We can remember it, certainly," Sheila said. "But it's like Paul says. Reason hasn't any troops."

They spoke to each other like friends, as if the bad feeling between them had altogether thawed.

Kate felt a great lift. She was delivered from her partisanship. Take his side against Sheila's she'd had to, but it had gritted so acridly against her sense of fairness, put her in that dreadful spot when the one you love is pitted against the one you like. Now, not knowing the secret sores where blows had fallen, it seemed to her that Morse's game had turned out far less brutal than she'd feared; that the tide of this omened party had been miraculously reversed. That with each's credo stampeded out of him, they'd stumbled on enough resemblance in each other that now the party had a common circulation, and from now on would bask in that oddly binding blandness which follows the type of quarrel that's enriching. Life is almost constant discord, she thought – but the lulls like this can be wonderful.

Rex shifted in his chair and Sheila leaned over to ease the glass from his flaccid grip. But he'd kept just enough pressure on it to guard it; as, in what looks like the profoundest sleep, the child sometimes will his toy. He opened his eyes, instantly alert.

"Where do you think you're going with that?" he said, sobered with truculence.

With Rex's presence emergent into the atmosphere again, each was subtly precipitated back behind his own fences.

"Nowhere," Sheila said. She was all at once unutterably tired. "Nowhere. Forget it."

"You think I'm drunk, don't you?" he said. "Well, you needn't worry about me. You don't have to watch me. If you want to do something you can fill it up."

He held his glass out like an alms cup. No one responded to him in any way.

Something meshed in his mind. He'd half-heard their conversation and their laughter, as in an unlocated dream. Now he related it to the waking moment. They'd been laughing without him. Maybe at him. Right here. They paid no attention to him. Well, they'd pay attention to this!

"Did you ask Sheila about her and Bruce?" he said. "Like I said?" He spoke as if he were spending every last bit of distinctness he could muster in these few sentences. "Well, I'll tell you about her and Bruce. She wouldn't take her clothes off in the game. Ask her if she's that fussy when they're back in the woods. She and I are through. Finished. She told me. She wants a divorce, so she can marry . . ."

A great involuntary sigh suddenly surprised and collapsed him. The glass fell from his hand. His eyes followed it rolling along the floor as if it were some small benign wonder. And then they closed like the dead's.

Kate glanced at Morse. She saw the feeding in his eyes again. Grist. And again she half-hated him.

Sheila went over to Rex and took his arm. "Come on," she said.

He lurched to his feet without opening his eyes. She put an arm around his waist and yoked his right arm up across her shoulder. The other dangled at his side. Their first step together he almost toppled her.

Morse moved to help.

"Never mind," she said.

She glanced at Paul. But Paul, knowing his heart (and for the first time hating it for its proscription of what her glance asked), could only enact a well-mannered blindness.

Bruce got up and yoked Rex's dangling arm up over his own shoulder. He crossed his other arm over Sheila's around Rex's waist. Rex offered no protest. They made their stumbling way with him toward the doorway and the stairs.

At the doorway Sheila turned her head towards Morse.

"Oh yes," she said. "Thanks for the party." She was too tired for more than the gesture of sarcasm.

"My pleasure," Morse said.

She glanced non-stop across Kate's face to Paul. "And have your laugh, Paul," she said.

When they laid Rex on the bed he nestled out of his sprawl into the foetal sickle she knew so well. He gave another long collapsing sigh.

"Do you want me to take his clothes off?" Bruce said. He bent to untie Rex's shoelaces.

Sheila glanced at Rex's foot. "No," she said. "I'll take care of that."

Bruce straightened up, hesitating a moment. Then he put his arms around her and held her against him. But her arms were still trembling from Rex's weight, Rex's body was still between them, and more than her face her hair looked as if it could find no clear answer to anything. My God how many years had it been since morning? Some nights fall asleep, but this one seemed to be lying awake, staring.

Kate picked up Rex's glass. Liquor dregs staled its sides. She had an impression of the room's having talk splashes dried all over it the same way. She felt the indescribable blues of winding up a visit with bad blood rankling in the air.

"Well," she said to Morse, "did you find out what you wanted to know?"

"Indeed I did!" he said. "That last break especially . . ."

He turned to Paul. "You see," he said, "these characters here are roughly the models for my new book." (Oh, shut up that *talking*, Kate thought. This is a *living* matter.) "Not that any novelist worth the powder to blow him to Hollywood ever sticks to facts – but the facts help. And now I have the facts about Bruce and Sheila. I had each of them statured by an insolence against his own lonely fate. Now they've fallen in love and we see how said stature meets that test. Kate got me fooling around with a theory that people might gain a stature just as great through the common insights of love."

He turned to Kate. "But I'm afraid, darling, the cookie still crumbles my way. They're sure as hell in love – but did you notice any stature it conferred, any identical vision for that matter? With all that old money stain on her that all the perfumes of Arcadia could never . . . or however it goes . . . and all that old earth grit in him . . . it'll be the weirdest, most cross-eyed, whittling marriage you could imagine. You see that now, darling, don't you?"

She did. And with a kind of fright she saw the writer's gloat that far outshadowed any sympathy toward the living circumstance. She saw the grit in love that she would always have to swallow along with the love itself. Was Bruce right? she thought. Was it only Letty's kind who lacked that cruel streak?

She looked at Paul. No, Paul didn't have that grit. Her father hadn't had it. For a moment she wished that somehow Morse could turn into Paul.

And Paul heard the stillness louder than ever.

CHAPTER 27

The rifle shot broke Paul's stillness. He was writing in his notebook.

It came in that no-man's-land of the night which you hear at the temples when you think you're the only one awake in the house. His eyes went automatically to his bedroom clock, as if Time itself had exclaimed. The clock said ten minutes past three. He couldn't fathom what the noise had been. It sounded like something splitting. The night splitting.

When there was no following sound he almost disbelieved it. He went to the window and looked out to see if it might have been a sudden crack of thunder. But the April night hummed velvet with equableness. Its swarming molecules of darkness were a pointillist roil of absolute quiet. It didn't know what storm was.

And then he heard Kate and Morse moving about. He slipped into his shirt and pants.

Bruce was dreaming. It took an earthquake to waken him. The sound of the shot came into his ears, then into his dream; but he didn't stir. And when it broke the sound barrier of his dream it turned into the noise of a window falling.

In his dream he was reliving the night of the day he and Peter had gone fencing. The day of the skeleton and the whipping. He was sitting on Peter's bed again, and again he heard him say, "Bones make you feel funny, don't they, Bruce?" And again he winced.

He left the room, and it was just as he turned to go downstairs that he heard the window fall. He knew that Peter had let it fall on purpose to bring him back. He went back.

And then there seemed to come a sequence altogether new.

"I'm sorry I threw the staples, Bruce," Peter said.

Bruce sat down on the bed again.

"I'm sorry I spanked you," he said.

"No, no," Peter said. "You spank me every time I do things like that, won't you, Dad . . . *Spank* me, Dad."

His night-face seemed happier than Bruce had ever seen it. As if the trigger-spring of his driving restlessness had been finally cut.

Bruce had a dream-flash of sudden understanding.

Was that it, then? Peter had called him "Dad." Could it be that a child would rather have a father than a pal? ("Wait . . . Wait up, Bruce.") Whenever he punished him, did he break their adult partnership and really set him free? Peter could cry then. His guilt could be paid for all at once and absolved. He had worried about failing Peter. But that wasn't the point at all. What had bothered Peter was an adult shame of failing *him*.

He kissed Peter good night.

"Okay, son," he said. "I'll spank you sometimes."

Peter nodded, smiling.

"Dad," he said then, "how come you knew I jumped off the roof?"

Jumped? My God, Bruce thought. Is that what happened? He didn't fall, he jumped. Are we that far apart . . . that he was driven to jumping off a roof to shock me back?

And then the dream-sight, shifting just a degree and yet an entire revolution, showed him the most liberating shaft of hope he'd ever had. Because Peter's hadn't been a question, really. It had been a statement: "How come you *knew* . . ?" He isn't lost, Bruce thought. He isn't lost. He hasn't the slightest doubt that no matter *what* he does, wherever I am I'll know it, and that wherever I am I will come . . .

"Bruce! Bruce!" It was Paul shaking him awake.

Morse too was dreaming. And of all the dream-spaces inside the skull-spaces inside the space of the night his was the most chaotic.

New writing mash had thrown the distillery of his mind into hurtling activity. So that when sleep took over from consciousness, the tempo had simply accelerated; until all control mechanisms stripped their gears. Ideas and images slashed at his captive but inexorably compelled eyes so hard on each other's heels that he couldn't quite claim any of them before the next succeeded it.

His models: Paul . . . Kate . . . Letty . . . Paul . . . Sheila . . . Kate . . . Paul. . . . Countless permutations of them in every possible grouping and circumstance alternated with each other on what seemed like a mirror that tumbled and revolved; that from second to second caught a beam of light which flashed out from it what these people were proofs of, or could be made to be proofs of; a dozen possible translations of each according as you took one or another of the possible meanings of the constitutive verb, transitive or intransitive, in each . . .

And then the mirror stopped revolving so abruptly it was split apart . . . with a sharp cracking sound . . . and for a moment he saw, behind it, a still life of them all. Fixed as statues. Standing together in their one definitive frieze.

The next instant he was totally awake. One of the most surprising things about him was that he slept light as a cat.

In Kate's dream the shot took no disguise. She'd heard that same sound the morning of the stillwater.

She was dreaming the thing almost exactly as it was happening. Except that the gun was pointed toward Sheila. And that when the sound dislocated her dream it was Morse she saw fall.

And then, in the last moment of the dream's light, before her eyes awakened to the room's darkness, it was her father she saw somewhere . . . with lazy little fountains of blood he seemed to be unconscious of arc-ing from a hundred tiny wounds all over him.

Morse's room was opposite Paul's at one end of the upstairs hall. Kate's was opposite Bruce's at the other. Sheila and Rex had the big double bedroom on the third floor. Letty slept downstairs, off the kitchen.

She wasn't dreaming at all. The only one of them physically weary and with no drinks air-castling in her brain, she slept like the dead. The shot translated itself into a single lantern slide before her eyes and then withdrew it. She saw Harry's tombstone fall and split and when she looked again the name on it was Paul's.

She dreamed no more and heard no more until Paul roused her for the clean cloths and hot water.

Sheila hadn't slept all night. Now, at three o'clock, she was half awake and half in a doze. She knew that she was lying in bed beside Rex, that he too was awake, and that she had pretended sleep for fear he might start conversation. But at the same time she had one foot in a dream with him.

240

In the half-dream they were back in Greenwich, packing to come here. Every other minute he'd leave the packing and go over to the window and look toward the Sound. They were racing speed-boats at the Yacht Club. They'd accept hours of his help putting their engines right, but they never asked him to join them when they raced. Each time he came back from the window to his suit-case it was empty, no matter how near the top his garments had filled it the moment before. He could make no headway at all.

Now she had both feet so far inside the dream that this irration-ality posed no question. And all the while she herself packed she had this feeling that she was forgetting something she should take. She couldn't, for the life of her, remember what it was; but she had this feeling that it was something of the first importance.

The dream fell dead with the shot. And when she saw Rex's blood – in the instant before she didn't scream – it came to her in a flash what she'd forgotten. Yesterday. Yesterday was her day to bleed. She hadn't bled.

At half-past two Rex stumbled awake. His dream had never varied.

He had been walking all night. Without a moment's rest. Past Grand Central Station. Past the railway stations in London. In Paris. Up the hill from the railway station in Greenwich to the Belle Haven Road. When he came opposite their house it turned into an orphanage. Past their house. And along the road from Granfort. Up the rise before Paul's house. Into the woods. And out, and past the railway stations again. They were orphanages. Past all the public buildings he had ever seen. Post offices, Hospitals. Museums . . . They all turned into orphanages. And down the hill from their house to the Sound. Down the sidehill to Paul's lake. Running down the ridge in France, for cover in the trees . . .

His foot walked beside him. It was naked. He walked on a road he didn't know. It went up and down, up and down, between rocks on one side and cliffs on the other. There were no houses on it. Only strings of telephone wires almost out of sight above his head. And past the railway stations again and up the hill to Belle Haven again, keeping his eyes closed so that their house couldn't change. It changed behind his eyes. And then past the railway stations again and down to the road he didn't know. Everyone else was inside. There were no trains running at the stations. No automobiles. All the houses had their backs to the road . . .

He couldn't lie down. Each time he stopped to lie down there were tin cans all over the spot. He walked past the railway station that turned into an orphanage and up Paul's hill onto the path into the woods. He tripped over two fishing rods. The fish hooks embedded themselves one at each temple . . . and he stumbled awake.

His head was splitting. Trawl hooks of ache were in past their barbs in his eyes and everywhere behind his skull. All the other particles of his body were trembling without movement, grasping at each other for stability but their reaches just failing.

He lay awake beside Sheila. The liquor still blurred, but he was sobered enough to think. Sheila didn't move. He supposed she was asleep.

He loved her to agony. He breathed as if to draw her inside him with each breath but, unable to hold the breath, having to breathe her out again. He lay there breathing her in and breathing her out.

He lay there and heard the silence go aaa*shshsh*, aaa*shshsh*, aaa*shshsh* . . . with relentless systole and diastole.

And then the terrifying imminence he sometimes awakened to in the dead of night began to gather in the underpelt of everything.

He waited for the pressure of the darkness against the windows to smash them in. Now . . . This moment . . . The next then . . . The next . . . He waited for the scream the walls were just containing. For the ceiling plaster to leave the laths. If anything moved, it would happen. If anything moved a hair . . . He waited for his breath to burst. Now . . . The next one . . . The next one . . . He waited for his heart to break. This beat . . . The next . . . The next . . . He waited for each systole of the silence to split the silence wide open with a crash of thunder and a blinding light . . . He couldn't stand it.

He got up, moving with extreme caution so the ceiling wouldn't fall or the walls scream, and turned on the light. Would the bulb splinter? The bulb didn't splinter. He wished the light would open Sheila's eyes. But it didn't. (She was watching him watch the speedboats.)

And then came the stage of demolitionary anger.

He saw the rifle standing in the corner. If he picked up that rifle and sent a bullet through his heart, it would show them a thing or two, wouldn't it? Sheila. The pain. Every cursed one of them. She'd wake up then! They'd pay some attention to him then! He'd make every cursed one of his hurts see that he didn't have to take it, he could smmm*ash* it . . .

He picked up the rifle. He pulled back the firing bolt. He did it with no real intent to carry the act through. He'd made no move to load the gun. But it was beautiful to play with the vision of how it would be. She'd see then what kind of torment he must have been in, to . . . She'd be sorry . . . Oh, wouldn't she be sorry!

He'd heard how you could do it. You leaned your chest against the muzzle and pulled the trigger with your toe. He looked at the foot that had no toes. He winced.

And then he held the gun off from his heart with one trembling hand and reached for the trigger with the other. Maybe just the click of the firing bolt would awaken her. She'd see just exactly what kind of a state she'd got him into. She'd get the surprise of her life, wouldn't she?

Bruce hadn't bothered to take his free shot the morning of the target practice. He and Sheila had forgotten all about it. The cartridge was still in the barrel.

Rex pressed the trigger and his was the moment of utter surprise when the silence split. He staggered and fell.

CHAPTER

"Get out!" Sheila screamed. "Get out!"

It was the first time she had screamed. She had not screamed before, not to bring the others. Quicker than the first cry gathering in her throat had been the thought that she and Rex could heal this wound, like animals with their own tongues, if no proud flesh from the others' gaze got into it.

But the others had come rushing. They stood there, their eyes pouncing in exclamation.

She had thrust the gun under the bed, but not quite soon enough. They saw her do it. She had wasted the first minutes after she heard them on the stairs, to draw a sock over Rex's broken foot. The gun was loud in the room. It encircled itself with that horripilant voice of objects that have just drawn violent blood.

Sheila snatched a handkerchief from her suitcase. She bent down and pressed it against Rex's wound.

There wasn't much blood, but it was blood broken in anger. And that made Rex and Sheila strangers to the others for being actors in a thing that had been carried just too far. The others could view the roil between them without shock as long as the skin of it stayed smooth; but once the skin of it was broken and the blood of it came outside, they drew back. Paul could see a shadow of the courtroom look in every one of them.

They stood there in a terrible chatter of not saying anything, of not knowing what face they should put on what they were thinking. They believed it was Sheila who had held the gun, that she'd tried to kill her husband. What did that make her? They didn't know.

There was a tiny hole in the window, a pinwheel of crack spoking about it like starlight, where the bullet had gone through the pane into the night.

Morse moved. "Sheila!" he said. "What . . .?"

Her eyes burned him. "Don't *you* ask what happened!" she said. "Don't you dare! You don't *know*, do you!"

Then her eyes went to Bruce. "Or you!" they said, though her lips didn't move. If you hadn't read out that newspaper story in the first place . . .

Bruce knelt down and tugged gently at the handkerchief in her hand.

"That's not the best thing, Sheila," he said. "We need something antiseptic."

"Don't you *touch* him!" she said.

Bruce blinded his mind against everything past by fixing its eye on nothing except what must be done right now.

"Paul," he said. "Tell Letty to get some boiling water as quick as she can. You've got an electric kettle, haven't you? And some clean white rags for bandages."

"There's a roll of sterile gauze in the pantry," Paul said.

It was the voice that bows in only as the hands can help and then bows out again, exacting no attitude. The word "gauze" might have sounded in the same way terrible as the word "gun." But somehow Paul made it sound like a syllable of comfort. Sheila's eyes turned, seeking, toward him.

"All right, Paul," she said. "Will you get that, please? And, for God's sake, will the rest of you leave us alone? Can't you leave us *alone*? Haven't you done enough, for God's sake . . .?"

"Bring the gauze," Bruce said. "And bring that little bag in my room. I've got some instruments and stuff in it."

"I don't want you to touch him," Sheila said. "I want to take him in to town. To the doctor there."

Morse and Kate made the movements you make when you can neither stay nor go. Kate had never seen Morse's movements stammer before.

"Well," Bruce said to Sheila, hearing his own words as if it were someone not exactly himself talking to someone not exactly Sheila, "as far as any danger in the trip . . . you could. The wound's not serious, I can tell you that. But there'd be questions. There's a rule doctors are sworn to. They have to report . . ."

We "should," he thought. I "should." Report Sheila! For a thing like this! It was like a stake through his mind. His mind was in a ball of not knowing where it stood on anything.

"I don't care," Sheila cried. "I don't care. I'd tell him it was an accident. I'd tell him we were packing the – " she couldn't say the word "gun" – "and . . . you'd tell him it was an accident, wouldn't you, Rex?"

Rex had been lying with his eyes closed. In a kind of ecstasy.

This was beautiful. He knew he'd never really meant to shoot himself. (That belief would come later.) But this was beautiful, the way it had turned out. With Sheila thinking that. It had solved everything. For them both. Yes, for them both. It had brought them back together closer than they'd ever been.

"It's all right, dear," he said to her. "Let Bruce fix me up."

With Sheila entirely his again, Bruce was entirely forgiven. He signalled Bruce not to mind anything she said. Sheila had to surrender.

Bruce nodded to Morse. Morse put his arms under Rex's knees and Bruce grasped him expertly with one arm under his good shoulder and the other down his back and they lifted him onto the bed. Kate quickly placed the end of a pillow under his wound before they lowered him. Sheila went over and brushed her hands across the spots where they had touched him as if she were a child rubbing off a hateful kiss. She bent down and kissed him.

Bruce examined the wound. The bullet had struck just below Rex's left armpit. It had merely creased the flesh. The bleeding looked like stigmata.

Sheila couldn't stand still and Bruce's love for her moved with her, spatially, like a pain outside him; but its projection to her could not quite achieve its mark. This was the first time he had had to member in the family of her deeds a chilling one he could in no way understand or love. And having her turn so against him, without a hint of why, planted a stubbornness in him never to *ask* her why. His dream of Peter seemed like the only oasis in this whole feverish night.

"Well," Rex said, "that's the first time I ever missed a target that close."

It purported to be the hard-bitten comment the situation prescribed. But he could scarcely keep a cheer out of his voice.

"You . . ?" Bruce said.

They all saw then how it had really happened. And when they realized that Sheila hadn't realized they'd taken her to be the culprit, a sudden circumferent breeze of tenderness went from them to her. More somehow for her ignorance of the suspicion than for her innocence of the deed.

"Why don't you have a drink, Sheila?" Morse said suddenly gently. "It'd do you good."

"Yes, Sheila," Bruce said, the stake drawn from his mind as if it were a weight of tons disengaged. "Why don't you go downstairs with Kate and let her fix you a drink? You need it."

Kate moved toward her.

It was then that Sheila sensed what they'd thought. She looked at Bruce. Yes, he too. She didn't mind that he could think her capable of murder. But (she saw Rex watching the speedboats) for him to have thought she could shoot Rex . . .

She felt a glinting deadly calm. She spurned their tenderness as if it bore the stink of weasels. Paul was coming back with the things Bruce had sent him for. His footsteps sounded on the stairs. She looked at Morse.

"We'll excuse you, you know," she said, "any time you have to leave. I think I can promise there'll be nothing more to see."

Morse nodded to Kate. They left the room.

Paul put the things onto the bedside table and himself turned to go.

"No, Paul," Sheila said. "Please, you stay."

No one else's presence could so deaden the vibration of the words she and Bruce weren't saying to each other. But even as she vowed to keep silent, the first notes of hysteria tricked her into speech.

"Isn't it lucky we had a doctor . . . of sorts . . . in the house!" she said.

Bruce bit his lip. Again the stubbornness not to plead and the dream of Peter stiffened in him like a spine. He pruned the ragged edges of the wound and sterilized and bandaged it. He didn't speak until the job was done. Rex hadn't flinched once.

"If that should start to bleed again . . ." he said.

"It won't," Sheila said. "And Rex never infects."

Bruce and Paul walked to the door.

"Paul," Sheila said. "Would you bring me a drink?"

"Of course," Paul said.

"Do you want a drink, Rex?" Sheila said.

"No, thanks," Rex said.

His headache was gone. The imminence was gone. He didn't need a drink. He didn't need a thing.

Paul and Morse and Kate convened downstairs, savouring the peculiar clannishness which follows joint witness to a shocking scene. Bruce was in his room. Letty sat by the kitchen stove, keeping the fire. In times like this, that always seemed to her the indicated ritual, even in summer. In town she'd always been the one who "stayed at the house" while the funeral was in progress at the church.

"He was stoned, that's all," Morse insisted. "He didn't know what he was doing. Did you ever seen a drunk drop his cigarette on the rug and stare at the smoke? He doesn't know it's burning. Or stick his fist through a window? He doesn't know glass will break. He doesn't know it'll hurt."

"No, Morse," Kate said. "There's much more behind it than that. He doesn't seem drunk. Now. He really meant to put himself out of his misery. He's been in some kind of turmoil right straight along. Do you remember the fire signs? I swear he was terrified when those men drove up."

"Nuts," Morse said. "That numbskull wouldn't have sense enough to see a forest fire might be dangerous."

"I didn't mean that," Kate said. "I meant *until* he found out who the men were."

"Aaah," Morse said. "You and your excuses for that character. *Would* a forest fire be any threat to the house itself, Paul?"

"Not really," Paul said, grinning. "Not if we fought it on the beaches and in the fields . . ."

"And watch us do it!" Morse said. "Sure, sure . . . we all came here to abdicate. Turning our backsides on Life and all its treacheries. But what'll you bet the first puff of smoke the whole lot of us wouldn't hit the road like lemmings? If only to save the bloody cars."

"Well," Kate said, "we're leaving in any case, aren't we? So let's not fret over academic questions like that tonight."

Paul felt abandonment as complete as if it were physical. One who speaks of leaving is already half-shadow. A sudden gust of longing in his eyes (he had forgotten that eyes confess more than you can command them not to, like the bleeding of a wound you never notice until another's notice draws your own attention to it) was as snagging as physical movement. It drew Kate's eyes to his face and startled her with its unaccountable intensity. The miracle of expression, she thought. Whether the face itself changes or not. How separate we *would* be – how much more separate than if we were without words – if we were without that. Paul's stillness had almost gone. He had never wanted so much to live. He had never loved her so much.

It was on the tip of his tongue to tell them they could stay.

But Morse's voice got in ahead of his.

"And what a blessing – backhanded though it was – that Paul did warn us out," he said. "You see, I had it all wrong. I thought I needed more time to study these people. But the fact is I know too damn much about them already. The more you find out about people the less you know about them. I learned that tonight. So bloody much of them's beside their point. You can't prove anything by people, I've found that out too. Not even if you follow them right through to the bitter end. There's always some damned *accidental* thing to upset the whole applecart. I learned that tonight . . . Or you can prove a hundred different things with the same people, each contrary to the others. So don't try to prove anything at all. Just give the facts."

Kate sighed. He was launched into another talking binge.

"It's like this. You break up a clump of rhubarb into ten parts and transplant the parts and you get ten new clumps of rhubarb. Identical. Break a man up into ten parts and transplant the parts and what would you get? Ten entirely different men. According as each was the seed of a different self. According to which got the rain. The rain of accident. The bloody blasted reign – that's r-*e-i-g*-n – of accident. So here's the switch. I want to draw the line under these people as of this moment . . . and then get the hell out of here before I hit on something else about them that'll throw a monkey-wrench of surds and minuses into the whole damn business."

"You call blood a surd?" Kate said.

There was bleeding of every kind upstairs – she could still feel that terrible precariousness in the air's cohesion, as if after a blast – and his only interest in this haemorrhage could lie in what it illustrated!

"Among other things," he said. He chuckled. "You know, I was in the midst of the weirdest dream when our cowboy fired the shot that was heard around the ward. We were all wheeling around in a fool kaleidoscope of possible dénouements. The shot sort of knocked us all into a deep frieze. Either spelling. Trimmed right down to the actual here and now, we were. And that's what I'm going to concentrate on. Actuality, as of this moment. That's the only thing you're safe writing about. There's no such thing as future truth. Nothing is true unless it happens, until it happens. New truth doesn't follow from old. It *is* new."

He looked at Paul. "What do you make of this . . ?" He rolled his eyes toward the ceiling.

"I like what Letty said," Paul said. " 'Poor Rex. His *grand*mother would have stuck up for him anyways.' You know the kids that . . . only their grandmother? Not even their mother?"

"That one never had a grandmother!" Morse said. "I tell you he's fortuitous, through and through. This business tonight was pure accident. He was just blind drunk, that's all. But I'll say this for

248

him. He's shown me what accident can do. That was my big mistake. I thought the whole thing was like in algebra. You know algebra. You solve your equations for x and y and then it's duck soup. You can substitute those values in any *other* equations that x and y turn up in. But not in this business of life and love, if you'll pardon the expression. Not there you can't. You could solve every past equation that ever existed, you could get the value of every past variable . . . and still you couldn't substitute those values in any future equation. Occasion. Because. you'd always run into that damned arbitrary monkey-wrench. That accident. That z . . .

"Oh, hell," he broke off, "let's have another drink and cut all this head cheese. I remember an old uncle of mine that always asked for a sour pickle whenever he had head cheese for dinner, to cut the fat. Let's have a drink."

Paul poured him another drink.

"Look," Morse said suddenly to Kate, "I seem to be doing all the talking. Do I bore you? It'd be a hell of a neat poetic boomerang, wouldn't it, if after all your hassle to get me writing again – to persuade me to turn the dark clouds inside out – if after all that you married me and discovered I was nothing but a crashing bore!"

"You don't bore me," Kate said.

But how could he come from a spectacle like the one upstairs and not be in some way stilled by it? (As Paul was, joking or not.) She knew that people of the world, especially of his world, got like that. Artless people, sheltered people, drew a bouquet of affrightment from the simple generic names of things like Suicide, Murder, Lawsuit, Disgrace . . . To Morse these were no different from any other grievousness, except in decibel and degree. She felt chilled.

"And now you've drawn your line under us," she said, "what do we all add up to, as of now?"

"Well, now the dust is settling," he said, "I can see there's been no damage to my main plant at all. I'll have to separate Bruce and Sheila again. You can see that coupling's off forever. But I'm afraid my thesis still holds against yours. Their constitutive insolence, they've merely lost it in a subtler way. They've fallen in love with their own wounds. Sheila thinks no more of Rex than she ever did. But she's in love with bearing him now. And Bruce loves Sheila not a bit the less, but I suggest he's found out that he loves his own ancient sorrow ten times more."

"My, we *are* death on heroes, aren't we?" Kate said, with the purposely ambiguous smile that can either disarm the remark or hone it.

"Not altog*ether*," Morse said. "Not quite. I've decided to spare

249

a couple. This old clown here –" he nodded at Paul – "and myself. He's a hero for sticking to the grin and the fart to the bitter end. And I'm the guy that brandishes the truth about things and puts the bullying world to shame."

He looked at Paul again.

"But there's my big snag. I've got to have some foul blow you're grinning against. And I can't invent one that fits. You haven't got a care in the world, have you?"

"Why don't you make me impotent?" Paul said, grinning. "Then you'd have the critics searching around for symbols like crows in a horse bun."

Morse's eyes synchronized as if from shock.

"Cripes!" he said. "That's perfect. That's *it*. Now why couldn't I think of that!" He banged the table so hard the glasses jumped. "I'm sorry, fella – and don't check now, Kate's here – but you're gelded as of this second!"

"But what if your readers get us confused and think the eunuch bit's autobiographical?" Paul said.

"Hell!" Morse said. "Who cares? Any writer that chickens out on risks like that isn't worth the name. Or I could have my picture on the dust jacket in full erection. Maybe I could dub in that old crowbar of yours to remove any last doubt." He was in one of his soaring, irreverent glees.

Is he simply foul-mouthed, Kate thought, and nothing more?

"And what about me?" she said. "Where do I fit in?"

Morse looked at her.

"Gad!" he mused. "It's perfect! You don't beat it away with me, you don't escape at all. In the book. Somehow you hit on Paul's cross and, presto, you're trapped all over again in your old compassion syndrome. You look at me and say, 'I could not love you half so much, loved I not pity more.' Or words to that effect. And cleave to Paul like a limpet. It's perfect!"

Kate started to protest. Morse held up his hand.

"No," he said. "Not another word. I've finally got it. That's it. The gangplank's up. I'm going to press. The topic's sealed. So bids for a new one will now be heard." He made as if to ponder. "Who's your favourite movie actor? . . . Which do you think is more important, heredity or environment? Are most people's megrims due to circumstance? Or is it just their blue genes?"

His nonsense, Kate thought, isn't like Paul's at all. It's like the bountiful exuberance of someone a plum's just fallen to, that somehow sets your teeth on edge against accepting it. Paul's nonsense tonight was no more a symptom of callousness than gravity would have been. She could sense the deeper tide of stillness underneath it.

"I wonder if people *are* half as unhappy as they think they are," she answered Morse. "Maybe they're like those sleepers who fancy they've never bobbed an eye all night."

You could be so wrong about yourself . . . about everything.

"Bruce!"

It was Sheila's voice – a voice in the extremity of having to call for help on the very name it finds hardest to pronounce, impossible to judge the tone for. Rex must have started to bleed again.

All through the house the old vectors of feeling, dropped like a hand of cards when shock first struck, began to reassemble like cautious animals.

CHAPTER 29

"I can handle one of those bags," Rex said to Sheila, all enthusiasm. "They're too heavy for you."

He had slept. He felt fine. The others had but one thought: get this day over with.

"No," Sheila said. "Not with your . . . I can manage."

She came down to the second landing with the first two suitcases. She had the waifish look of women doing things their muscles aren't meant for. Bruce stepped out of his room. They had been as keyed to each other's movements as if connected by an invisible wire. Neither had slept.

"Let me take them," Bruce said.

"It's all right," Sheila said. "I can manage."

"Let Bruce take them," Rex called. "He doesn't mind."

Rex, the victor, was all benevolence now. He mistook their sodden quiet for a face of meekness they'd put on in deference to his crisis.

Sheila put the bags down. In pure resignation. She had come to the point when surrender seemed the only positive thing left. She was perversely sustained by the knowledge that whatever she'd always struggled against she'd now obey to the letter.

Bruce picked up the bags. He and Sheila didn't speak. It had not been lettered out between them that, after today, they would never see each other again. But when their glances met they were the glances of two people who have each heard the same bad news from a different source.

Their states of mind were identical. Neither could think any thought about the other straight through. So much had come at them so fast that they crammed it all away to be fathomed later.

The detonations of love and memory and stubbornness and repentance stunned them. One second's feeling contradicted the next's. Their half-thoughts got in their own light. The barrage that's in any good-bye, let alone this one, paralysed them. Just to get through the next hour, physically, was the single over-riding challenge.

Bruce took his own bags down while Sheila went back for the rest of theirs. He would drive close behind them as far as Granfort in case the rough road opened Rex's wound. At the cross-roads there he would take the turn to Halifax, they the one to Digby.

The summer job he'd turned down at the Medical Library might still be open. If not, he'd find something. Something he could throw himself into so hard he'd have no time left to think.

He had jolts of anger against his present numbness. It was like the dropsied lids of a summer rain that hang unyielding as a fall's, until everything becomes stupid and incommunicable, nothing but the intolerable catalogue of its own physical properties. But he couldn't shake it.

He came back and picked up another load of Sheila's things. He and Sheila dodged each other's movements like two people super-stitious about passing on the stairs. One suitcase had a small triangle of cloth sticking out at the side. The skirt Sheila'd been wearing yesterday. He had an impulse to cut off the bit of cloth and keep it: at first, the garment is of all things most evocative of the wearer's presence and most powerfully. But, with the cruel literalness of stupor, he knew how very soon that power would begin to fade.

His fourth trip back from the cars, the landing was bare.

He would forever after think of good-bye as a long stretch of hallway where no suitcases stood. In the spot where they'd been the robbing sunlight had taken the eye of Time away and put its empty socket there instead.

Sheila was coming down the upper stairs, with Rex behind her this time; but it was as if she'd already gone. In her left hand she had a shapeless package wrapped in brown paper. It must be the mayflowers she had gathered yesterday. She had never seen may-flowers before. She had planned to press them.

In her right hand she carried the gun. She was so nearly insen-sible she could have picked up a snake. Rex had a jacket draped over his wounded shoulder as proudly as an investiture shawl.

"Maestro Sandeman," he said, glancing at it. It did suggest the figure on the bottle. His "drinking" jokes were the only ones that ever hit the mark dead-on.

They almost smiled. He kept watching their faces. In one hand he was carrying Sheila's purse. He gestured with it, effeminately. He was determined to make them laugh.

He was quite convinced there'd been nothing really serious going on between them. Just a bit of spring fever. When it really came to a showdown last night there hadn't been much uncertainty which way the cat jumped! Naturally they felt a trifle sheepish now. But, hell, they needn't think he was the kind of guy would make a roaring stink about it. He'd acted like a damn fool too – but now everything was ironed out, hell, forget the whole thing.

He kept at the clowning all the way out to the cars. Making jokes about the shooting even. "You could have lashed me to the fender like a dead deer."

They didn't laugh. But the more they didn't laugh the more benevolent he felt toward them, for what he took to be a lip-pucker of their consciences.

Sheila put the gun into the trunk beside the suitcases as carefully as if she valued it. She put the package of mayflowers into the little cavity beside the spare tire.

"What *is* that, anyway?" Rex said.

"Nothing."

"Well, it couldn't be much less, could it!"

There was a short space when they stood there in suspension. That last hiatus when the present moment still faced their way.

"Is that everything?" Bruce said, glancing at the trunk.

"Yes," Sheila said, "I think that's everything."

Bruce closed the lid of the trunk. The present moment turned away. Its back's minutiae had that strange unrealness of the backs of people studied in the seat ahead of you in church. His movements and Sheila's were like the fumbling responses of the litany.

"Well . . . so long," Rex said.

He gave Bruce a hearty handshake.

"So long," Bruce said.

Sheila opened the car door for Rex.

"Hey!" Rex called, in a last exuberant joke. He had fallen head over heels in love with his own forgiving. "You don't get me in that car until you've said good-bye to Bruce. I'm standing right here to make sure there's no funny work."

Sheila came back and shook hands with Bruce. But there wasn't any funny work. Even touch had been painted over by insomnia and clamour.

Each knew that every face hereafter would be featureless for not being the other's. But the feeling was not nerved. It was more like the chilling touch of garments you've put on for some precarious journey. Their reflex selves at once took on the grimaces of smooth behaviour. Much more proficiently than if their feeling selves had been informing them.

"Good-bye," Sheila said.

"Good-bye," Bruce said.

Each half-groped for one haunting summative phrase, some imperishable nugget for the other to find when he sifted through the ashes of this moment later. But for the life of them neither could find one.

Kate, Morse and Paul had made themselves scarce until the last possible second. They came out now. And again embarrassment itself lent that added proficiency in the slick behavioural grimace.

"Well," Paul said, expertly splitting *here* from *gone* before they started sagging one against the other, "*bon voyage*. And don't sit on any strange toilet seats."

He made it quite transparent why he'd picked the feeblest joke he could think of : so that each could laugh at humour's giving up the ghost against the general tension. For an instant, laughing, it seemed as if each might throw down the broken shards with which he propped up his hurting singularity and they could all piece together a fluid union.

And then the car doors closed, both motors caught, and "now" began to be "ago."

Departures weld those left. Kate, Morse and Paul walked back to the house as if they were one individual having said good-bye to another.

But with Kate and Morse themselves to leave so soon, the parting was robbed of its afterlight. Its sets were straightway struck to make way for the sets of the next. And for the moment they felt that curious disembodiment, almost to the point of seeing their own faces as physically pinched, which people whose chief alacrities reside in thought's analysis of feeling feel between peaks of engagement.

"Are you all done packing?" Morse said to Kate.

"Practically." She turned to Paul. "Would it be too late to transplant lilac, Paul?"

Lilac grew so tall and dense along one side of the house that in places bush-stalk had become tree-trunk, and the patches of light on the ground beneath were forest-light.

"It's late, yes," Paul said. "But you can't kill the stuff."

"It'll be too late when we get to Simsbury," Morse said.

Morse had a house in Simsbury. It seemed a quite capricious place for him to live. His comment was that Simsbury was the poor man's Woodstock – without the writing sects' sex or the writing insects' incest.

They would first go to Halifax, be married there, and then dispose of Kate's possessions. She'd made a quick sale of the house, at sacrifice prices, to buy the car. Now she must take another such loss on the car and the furniture. She and her father had always kept things to the limit of their usefulness and so got their worth. She felt a little chastened now, having to part with her chattels for what they'd bring, like gambler's garments.

"And don't tell me," Morse said, bantering, "that you're one of those women who has to have a slip of every bloody plant she sees."

"Never you mind," she said. "You go finish packing. Come on, Paul. Where's the spade?"

She wanted to be alone with him. There was nothing Paul wanted less.

"I'm warning you," Morse said. "If you're not ready to go by eleven sharp, I'll damn well leave you here, lilac and all."

Kate half-knelt beside Paul. That special cone of intimacy which shapes itself around two people working in the earth enclosed them. Paul loosened the ground about the lilac shoot. Kate was holding it by the stalk.

"Just keep a little upward tension on it," he said, "so I can tell where the roots are. I want to get as much earth with them as possible."

He hadn't had a single warning from his heart in all these last days' turmoil. How could pain come from nowhere and go to nowhere? It was the only violence that was mute.

He tried to keep his eyes from trying to steal the lifelight from Kate's face and hands and hair and store it in his brain.

Look away, he told himself. Look away from everything until they're gone. Count ten. Do algebra in your mind. Think of something astringent and absurd: I love your hair, said the Hare to the Bear . . . What foolishness to think you could store away that kind of light in any case. You couldn't capture any kind of light. Enclose it in your hand and it turned to darkness.

"Paul," Kate said. It was the opening syllable all at once gone cold in every nerve with something's being now or never and this being now. "Paul, I don't know."

She gave him the troubled smile that's half self-fondness for your liking so much the one you turn to.

"Don't know what?" he said. (I love your smile, Said the Wile to the Guile.) "Is that stalk free now? I didn't tell you to *yank* on it," he added, mock-muttering. "Just try it."

"Who's yanking on it?" Kate said.

She was suddenly touched to the laughter most precious: at a shapeless nonsense. What fun we could have together, she thought – the kind of fun Father and I used to have – over nothing. Morse has to have something *palpable* to laugh at.

"No, it's not quite loose," she answered. "There must be a root that goes straight down beneath it." Then, soberly again: "I meant, I don't know . . . about Morse and me."

He knelt down beside her to feel beneath the lilac for the root still holding. They were so close he came inside the polar field of her hair. His love for her danced uncontrollably like a line of clothes in the wind.

"I mean . . . since last night," Kate said. "Since Rex . . ."

She was merely sitting beside the task now. In the attitude of one who takes a hand at first, purely that with movement he may slip his burdening subject in without its seeming to announce itself embarrassingly loud . . . and then drops out, simply to talk, while the other need give answer only by the gestures of his chore. He can say "yes" with the way he tilts the spirits level. He can say "no" by the way he takes the shavings from the plane.

"There *is* a root right there," Paul said. "But there are so many others clustered with it it's hard to tell which stalk belongs to which."

The way he gently dug the earth back with his hands, to trace the root, said, "Yes. Go on."

"He was cruel about Rex, Paul," she said. "And I can't stand that kind of cruelty. He had no feeling whatsoever about the whole thing except for the story in it. I'm afraid he has no use for anyone once he's wrung the story out of them. Don't you feel that, Paul? But maybe not. He's not like that with you. For some reason you're the only one that . . . But I'm afraid he'll have no more use for me either once he's wrung the story out of me. He tells me the only inspiration he has to shine is to make *my* eyes shine. He says my listening is the only fuel he needs. But I have this terrible fear that even in that . . . that any minute he'll decide I'm not an audience worthy of him. I don't know."

Paul located the root.

"Do you love him?" he said. "Do you know that?"

"Yes," she said. "I love him."

"Well, then – " Paul cut off the root with the spade – "for God's sake, don't stipulate any conditions, Kate. The world is full of people left with nothing in their hands but a bunch of dried-up terms they've set. Maybe what you should do is learn a little cruelty from him. If you don't – well, you've seen these people who sort of suspend their own living until every claim on their sympathy has been discharged, haven't you? Then it's too late. And of course making love, if you don't mind me saying so, is often the greatest thing in the world to outmode conscience . . . anachronize it. So if it's Uncle Paul's advice you want . . . Marry him, Kate. Take him on any terms. And make him *see* about people like Rex. There's your challenge. If you could really bring that conversion off and make him the writer he promised to be before he took to alum, wouldn't it be worth any risk? Here," he said. "Steady that again, will you? I think it'll lift clear now."

She put her hand on the stalk again.

"Toss for sides?" Paul said, making as if it were a baseball bat. She ignored this.

"I don't even know about having the child," she insisted. "I thought that that would . . . but . . . now . . . I don't know."

Paul put a hand to his cheek as if he were stifling a sigh there. It left a smooch of mud. The smooch commented on his colour.

There's something wrong with Paul, Kate thought. He's sick. I *knew* it. What would it be like for him alone here, she thought – with no one who spoke his tongue ever at hand to interrupt the narrow-minded, egocentric, one-themed, boring-neighbour monologue of his sickness? She saw her father's face knuckle-white with the leeches of time at it while he slept unguarded in the afternoons. How could you leave people like that?

Paul was easing the root clump gently out of the ground. He looked up at her, the corners of his eyes mock-frowning again.

"I'd *love* to know why it is she has to keep *yanking* on this thing," he muttered.

"Paul," Kate giggled, "you darn fool. I wasn't *yanking* on it."

For answer he gave her another cautionary glance, brushing her hand away (just to touch it). If we lived together, she thought, we'd have so darn much fun. We'd always have some kind of nonsense "going."

Paul got to his feet. He held one hand under the root clump of the lilac and supported the stalk with the other. A wind had come up. Patchy at first, as if the air were slapping out its dust rags in the sun; now, more determined. Paul turned his back to it, sheltering the leaves of the plant.

Kate glanced at her watch. Five to eleven. Time had almost run out. And the footing under their voices seemed to be scattered by the wind. Her heart felt as cold and shivery as if the wind were a cold one. She was in the twin dilemma of knowing it was now or never to say a final thing which in itself tortured her with doubt whether it should be said at all or not. She half-said it, the safe way, in a joke.

"Paul," she said, but the joke came out shivery too, "what if I hid here in the lilac bushes? What would you do with me if Morse did go and leave me? Would you turn me in?"

He read her feeler exactly. He thought: She wants me to know how desperately uncertain she is that she wouldn't rather be with me. My God, if I reached for her I could have her. Kate. She's making the decision mine.

All his life he'd been liked, but never in the way of a partner, a preferred partner. It gave him such a sudden glorious feeling to see himself in that light now that his clothes felt shabby on him. For the first time in his life a straggler's. He should have been dressed for this!

And then the whole black suffocating bile of his secret came up in his throat. The bitterest choke there is. When you can't even tell someone there's something you can't tell. He was abruptly conscious of his seedy heart. And for the first time savagely. You'd probably die smack in the middle of the honeymoon act, he told himself. That's exactly the kind of crazy thing that happens to you. Ask Morse.

"Yes," he answered mock-darkly. "I'm afraid I'd have to turn you in. You see, I'm Secret Agent Number B2647. That's why I've been so enigmatic all along. That's why I couldn't tell you there were things I couldn't tell."

He's clowning, Kate thought. But he looks dismayed, just the same. She misread his dismay completely. He wouldn't want to be stuck with me under any conditions. She let her smile put a period after the whole thing as a joke that had run its course.

There was a moment when they stood there in tableau. Each waited for the other to make the first scene-shifting move. To fill the gap, Paul bobbed the bush at her suddenly, as if it were a presentation bouquet to the Queen. She really laughed. And again she had the desperate urge to test her doubt on him.

But you couldn't reopen a thing like that. Not with someone who stood holding a lilac shoot precariously in his hands. If he would only help her a little . . . absently edge some earth back into the hole with the toe of his boot . . . anything, to take the patience out of the way he was balancing the plant. But he didn't. He just stood there, holding it loudly.

"Well," he said, felling the moment with one quick business-like emphasis, "we'd better get this thing in out of the wind." The edges of the leaves were already blighting, as with fire. "I'll wrap it in a damp bag and put it in the trunk."

She thought: There'll be no one here to start him laughing at himself whenever he's tempted to think he could *possibly* sound business-like.

He turned toward the tool-shed.

"And for heaven's sake," he said, "when you plant it, try not to keep yanking at it."

"I won't," she said. But the joke was dead. "Do you want me to fill in this hole with the spade?" she said. She felt as if they had suddenly become a slow-motion movie of themselves.

"No," he said, "that's all right. I'll do that afterwards."

He'd been like that with every offer of help this morning. Like those people who won't hear of your lending a hand to clean up after the party, so that every second you linger on makes it seem as if they were having to hold the gate open between one minute and the next.

She walked behind him to the tool-shed. One thing turned foolishly in her mind: Why should it be so peculiarly embarrassing to tell people they had food on their chin – or a smudge on their cheek? And in Paul's brain the word "Kate, Kate, Kate" train-wheeled so blurringly that he couldn't stake down a single thought between its revolutions.

Kate stood beside her car and Morse beside his. The moment of leaving, as it always does, seemed shot with treason; their travelling dress like the badges of it. The wind, a near hurricane now, had taken charge of the day. They had to brace against it constantly, to keep their balance.

Paul blessed it. It outruled the loitering good-bye he'd so dreaded. There was no question of any overtoned remarks. It would plaster them back against you the way it did your clothing, or else make off with them like crazy kites. It left no choice of any stance except the bluntedly straightforward. Their good-bye was as darting as one in a driving rain.

For one thing more Paul was thankful: they were leaving singly. People leaving you in the same car begin at once adjustment of the seating space between them, consigning some small article from one's hand to the other's, already dedicated not to you but to the sharing of the trip ahead, even as they wave.

Morse grasped at a lull in the wind, to get in the parting word.

"Now, look here," he said. "When we get settled we'll write. And then, by God, you're coming to see *us*."

"We'll see," Paul said, grinning.

"We'll see!" Morse said, the old exasperation and affection for one last time in deadlock. "Look at him. He hasn't the slightest damned idea of coming to see us."

"Won't you come, Paul?" Kate pleaded. "Really? Won't you *promise* us you'll come?"

"Name one single damn reason why you *couldn't*," Morse said. "No. You *can't*, and you know it. What's wrong with us, anyway? We wouldn't poison you or anything."

"I know," Paul said.

"Well, then . . ."

"We'll see."

"We'll see!"

And then the wind, rising again, made vocal intonation hopeless. And they were forced to make their very abdication to it, their very tonelessness, an eloquence of everything unspoken.

"Well . . . good-bye, Paul," Morse said.

"Good-bye, Morse."

"Good-bye, Paul," Kate said.

"Good-bye, Kate."

When you go out to welcome someone, the ground seems to rise up to meet your feet. When Paul turned back toward the house the ground seemed to shrink away. He had a sense of stumbling, as when you miscalculate that final step at the foot of the dark stairs.

PART

Sheila drove slowly.

The wind had not yet risen. It was one of those mornings whose streaming light seems less to be falling on objects than issuing from them. Newness sprawled over everything. The pure sleep-washed air, fresh as a child's eye, experienced itself as cleanly as running brook water. Breathing it was like drinking.

Once in motion, the drug of her sleeplessness had dropped from her like a scale. Now she was in that following stage of wide-awakeness so charged with clarity that everything she looked at became as challenging as if pain and sleeplessness had made her an artist. She felt the exaction on her of each detail's being precisely as it was; an indescribable beckoning to her to know its essence through and through and so erase its excommunicate otherness, yet never yielding up that last punishing bit more than sight could quite devour. This smarting claim on her was everywhere she looked, like the lash of tiny wires.

The light sparkled dryly on the dry chips of leaves that pathed so cleanly beneath the light-breathing saplings wherever the ground hollowed down and away from the sides of the road. It flashed wet-diamonded or blading wherever a flourish of dew still clung. It buffed the dead-white of the fallen trees' immaculate bone. On the ground beneath the living growth the blasted remnants of other seasons lay as if on a light-hallowed battlefield. In both these diagrams of life and death was represented every linear or curvilinear pattern possible. Bird notes sounded high above as if from the morning's gladed throat itself.

They reached the swamp. It had the midnight quality that all swamps have, even in the morning light – with its quick coarse grass that nothing would eat springing through the grey matted grass of last year.

And then they were at the brook. Its plaited surface had a central arrow of current that thrust into the stillwater just below the bridge, constantly puncturing the lather of foam scum lying there and send-ing silver, bubble-cellular coins of it sailing downstream in the light – round and then ovoid and then shaped like amoebas – until, charging the bank in a single straight line, they broke themselves back into the air. All along the bank tufts of dead twigs and grass clung like nests in the bushes, marking the high-water level of last fall's floods. The bushes looked stony-hearted, outside consolation.

And then, beyond the brook, starting to leave the woods, she saw the blessing-white once of the dogwood blossoms . . .

The challenge kept mounting.

She wanted to put on a burst of speed to outreach it and to escape the sight of Bruce's car. But she stuck to her cautious pace on account of Rex.

"Are you comfortable?" she said.

"Sure," he said. "Fine, fine. You're the only woman driver I ever did feel comfortable with, you know that?"

He felt perfectly comfortable. He felt as restored, as expiated of all his shames, by his childish act last night as if it had been something majestically immolatory.

"You're quiet," he said.

He had given up trying to force laughter on her as a token of his generosity. This was a different tack. He was inviting her to a sober, commiserative talk.

"Am I?" Sheila said. "Well . . . I'm going to have a baby."

She'd had no idea of blurting that out so soon. But his bid for a quiet talk – anything but that! – had jostled it loose.

"A *baby*?"

The lighted cigarette was halfway to Rex's lips. It was as if all at once it became an insupportable triviality. He threw it out the window as far as he could send it.

And then his eyes made a slow sweep upward to the news, grinning wide and proud with it. He just kept looking at Sheila, speechless, as if she were something half-fearful for being made so beautiful to him by something he himself had wrought. He was almost comically the father in one of those scenes grisly with sentiment in the television play.

She'd thought that never again would surprise at him take her by surprise. But again it had. Could this be Rex? Really wanting a child? Not just to trap her (he knew there was no longer any need for that), but really wanting the child itself? She waited for his unconsciously despoiling comment to follow.

And again he surprised her.

"Are you sick with it?" was the thing he said. Really gently. "Is that what makes you so quiet? My God, it never dawned on me . . . it's wonderful . . . but I'd hate like hell to have you sick."

Rex genuinely thoughtful! Now, surely, at last, she *had* heard everything.

"No," she said, cutting the wheel hard to make the sharp turn, "I'm not sick. And please let's not – "

She braked the car to a gliding stop and the sentence was never finished. For there, in the dead centre of the road, stood the deer, watching.

Bruce came to a jerky halt behind them: Had Rex begun to bleed again? And then he saw the deer himself.

A deer standing watching you is the stillest, livingest thing there is. Sheila had never seen a wild deer before. Its very stillness was electric with life, it was framed there in the morning's immaculacy with an airiness of such unearthly grace that it seemed hardly corporeal. It seemed like something her eyes had drawn on the air. It seemed as if the whole morning had been arrested, and forever, in its posture of the moment; like those people in a fairy tale at the moment the spell (or the curse) is cast.

The deer stood there and stood there.

And then just when this whole tableau-fixity had begun to seem infrangible (if nothing had so far caused the deer to move, what in the following like-frozen moments could?), the first test-breath of the wind carried their scent to it. Its head went upward in a flawless exclamation of intentness, to challenge their own. (Sheila sighed, almost with relief.) And then, with such exquisitely smooth translation of statue into motion that there wasn't an instant of accommodation one to the other, it was arc-ing across the undergrowth between the road and the treeline as if its feet didn't quite touch the ground between leaps; as sure-pathed as the light and as collisionless through the maze of scraggle.

In one last transcendental parabola, it vaulted a windfall at the treeline and was gone.

It was then that Sheila had her vaulting insight. Of the rare kind that comes only when the mind has been conditioned just so to be triggered just so by the present spectacle: when something in that spectacle turns the tumblers of the heart's combination the one way in a million that will make it fly open.

It was not that in this moment's illumination she was pointed away *out of* distress. That need not be the case. It need only be the seeing of your *way*, final and clear. And that is what it was with her.

She saw, in this sudden light, the charactered – rather than the caricatured – face of stoicism. It was nothing like the falling in love with her own pain that Morse had predicted. What she saw, instead, was how little, how very little, happiness mattered.

She saw that there would always come a Copernican revolution in your life, when with your weighing eye you saw that happiness, your happiness, was not the earth the sun revolved around – but no more than a tiny planet of no more lustre even to yourself than the planet of another's happiness. That there would always come a time when whosoever's gestures that were now the wands of love, and its bludgeons, would become no more than unaffecting mannerisms. Bruce's no less than Rex's. And that the ones you'd known the longest were by far the most binding.

Sentiment, released as if by intoxication, slipped its curbs as completely as the drunk's.

That time would come when they had the child. The child would be exactly the way it was, and it would be for its being exactly so that she'd love it. Beyond everything. And if any factor had been different – if Rex had been in any granule otherwise – the child would not have been exactly *this* child. It would have been as if they'd taken this child's life. And she and Rex . . . how little did it matter, in the end, who your mate was.

For that brief moment, without its being happiness at all, she had somehow never been so happy.

Rex had been as quiet as she. In a few more years, the light continued to disclose, he'll lose that anarchy of his completely. He'll be as much of a piece as anyone else. Maybe the *child's* loving him – the way that children sometimes did love parents who themselves loved like children – would make an adult of him.

She had expected, now, to have him strut. Instead, a curious shyness made him fumbling. He looked at her as if he were looking at himself.

"Well," he said, "we can tell him he saw a deer." And then, trying desperately to better this little joke, he added: "And we'll stop in town and pick you up some sour pickles."

"No," she said. "I haven't any abnormal cravings yet."

She started the car.

If the child shouldn't love him . . . , she thought. In sudden savagery against it. If it kept asking him those cruel child's questions about his foot . . . if, with the child's uncanny insight, it kept putting its finger on all his shallow spots . . . For no clear reason, she had the picture of a child she'd once seen at a county fair, extorting quarter after quarter from the father whose money was so hard come by that he always knew to the penny how much change he had in his pocket . . .

She was defending him against the child already, the way she'd defended him against Morse. The memory of Morse rose in her like a sting. It should be Paul I remember, she thought. He was worth the others put together. But you forgot Paul, like a fine day.

And then, in that crazy generosity of his, Rex said: "Gosh! I wonder if Bruce got a good look at the deer. Maybe we blocked his view. Maybe he didn't see it at all."

"He must have seen it," she said. "He didn't make any move to find out why we stopped."

She wasn't quite yet in conversation with him. Not quite yet rutted back out of that trance of impatience with him for not being Bruce. But her tone had begun to be answering rather than fending.

And somehow the detail of the trees had ceased to punish her. they didn't cry out for *ap*perception now. They were steepingly content with simple notice, and perception of themselves. And somehow the loss of Bruce was already a yesterday's verdict; a yesterday's sentence that somehow she'd got through the first worst night and the first worst morning of serving out.

Bruce saw the deer.

But his mind's leap was backward. Through time and time again until it left him standing looking at the first deer he'd ever seen. One morning on the road to school. He saw it clearer than the one before his eyes. His deeper eye was back completely on that wide, wide day.

That was a different time. And deer were scarce here then : a deep woods secret. They never came out into the pastures even. In all his father's years of hunting he'd never caught a glimpse of one. Many moose, but never a deer.

That was a different time in every way. The whole settlement lived in a kind of eternal and unaging present then. The trees and the fields no less than the people. There were no specialized and worldly knowledges to put one man ahead of the other. There was no ghost from the outmoding future then, to cast its shadow on the present and corrode it like a machine. There was no consciousness in anyone or anything, not even in the rocks, of Time's outmoding its very self. All things lived on the plain of a replete and self-renewing now, which stayed as young to the adult as it did to the child.

On an April day like this there were no ghosts of any kind; no more rust in the shadows than in the light. And the children, never noticing the blossoms of the wild cherry and the dogwood or the white blossoms of the bunchberry that starred the edges of the road, felt a spreading aeration by them just the same.

He was on the way to school with a group of boys. A group of girls were walking ahead. Molly was among them. She walked modestly because her gingham dress was so proudly new. The light sparkled on the gleaming sides of the lard kettle that held his lunch. There was an orange inside it, like a gold nugget. Oranges then were such a luxury they were as exciting as a trip.

266

At first he saw only the deer's head in the bushes. He thought it must be a calf's. And then the deer stepped out full into the road in a sudden magic of self-identification. It stood there just long enough for his heart to exclaim: It's a deer! And then it leapt and vanished into the thicket on the other side of the road.

His heart leapt with it. That he and the wild wandering deer should have come to this same spot at exactly the same moment, it was a kind of miracle. He'd seen a wild, secret, beautiful thing that not even the grown men of the place had ever set eye on.

But, more than that – and in the same leap of the heart – this was the first moment he knew as surely as he knew the orange nestled in his lunch pail that he was going to be a doctor. He would be like Dr Armstrong, who could make you feel so safe you cried, the moment his horse's head showed over the hill from town.

He looked at Molly to see if she had seen the deer, and waved to her. She nodded and waved back. The boys ran to catch up with the girls and they all chattered together.

"Let's come down at recess and see if we can find its tracks," he whispered to Molly.

"All right," she said. "Yes!"

At recess he took the orange from his lunch pail and put it in his pocket. They found the deer's tracks in the mossy place around the spring where the lady's slippers grew, and he said, "I've got an orange. Let's sit down on the rock and eat it." He peeled the orange and gave her half. And sitting there on the sun-warmed rock, looking as if at the tracks of grace itself and tasting the orange and watching Molly eat her half as daintily as if it were a diamond, to make it last and not to get the juice on her new dress, this was the first time he knew he loved her. And life then had no long, complicated words in it at all . . .

The deer sprang away and his mind resurfaced.

There was nothing legible on the flesh of his firm-fibred face. But his eyes flickered a little as with the pupil-wing of pain: Peter had never seen a deer. Children didn't seem to see deer any more. Of any kind. Their hearts no longer seemed to leap in just that way. They got to know the long and complicated words too soon . . .

He had never thought of other kids like that before. Since Peter's death their faces had been nothing but the shrillest masks, for lack of Peter's face behind them. But now – by what sudden light he never knew – he had a different picture of them altogether.

One Peter only there had ever been, would ever be, but could the other children help their not being Peter? Not being Peter seemed a cruel and unconscious cross they bore, that somehow showed them to him as assaultingly bereft.

And then it was that his mind took its vaulting leap ahead. With the slip, like fingers into gloves, into a single socket of purpose, he knew as surely as he'd known his destiny, that April day so long ago, what he was going to do now. He would be a *children's* doctor – yes, yes, a children's *psychiatrist*.

Remembering Peter, he would try to save the ones who held their bodies like a weapon. He'd take that smashing look out of the eyes so homeless even within their own lids. He'd make them see a deer. He'd make it so their hearts could leap again as a child's heart should. He'd give them back a few years' freedom anyway from the long, complicated, staining words . . .

This was no rush of sentiment. It was simply the heart's hard-headedness when it finally straightens up with one long hard despising look at the pygmy captors which have strapped it to the ground. He stepped on his morbid self-embroilments, one by one.

The first test-breath of the wind nudged him. He thought of it dividing Sheila's hair. For a moment he remembered how she could domesticate his fervours, make him grin at them. For a moment the spine of this one threatened to crumble.

He took a long breath, not quite stepping on the thought of her. But he lifted it forever to one side, like a child from the edge of a thoroughfare.

And then they'd all gone on, leaving no trace of themselves anywhere except Rex's cigarette.

Rex's cigarette had landed on the platform of a fern that grew up through the alder cuttings. Privately smouldering, it had eaten along itself almost to the end when the breeze nudged it. It brightened for a moment and then fell, dying, onto a dry leaf beneath. The surface of the leaf blackened and crumbled back-ward as if from the polite and hesitant nibbling of a tiny arc-shaped mouth; but there was no flame. A splash of dew lingering on the leaf nearly halted the arc's advance.

And then a second breeze nudged the leaf against a tuft of dry grass. There was the first little yellow rag of flame. The grass burned itself to death as instantly and absently as an idle thought rising and falling. But where the tip of its flame had reached, a dry alder twig turned red, and a third breeze, almost a gust, following just at the moment when, without it, the twig would have turned black again, the twig began to burn. The gust held it burning just long enough for it to gather its own confidence, to catch the *message* of fire.

The message began to spread, from dryness to dryness. Little tongues of flame began to speak with fire's *voice*. Whenever one flame was defeated now by a tuft of green or a patch of dew, there were others to try other paths. Within an hour any one of them was able to defeat the green or moisture in its way. They became surer of themselves, and surer; more purposeful. They cracked open the wood and let its hot hissing soul loose like a nest of snakes. Heat became strong enough to strike blows.

Within another hour, the breeze had become a steady gale. It drove the flames before it with its own surging voice, until they lost their mind completely and charged the woods-line along its whole front with a manic, blazing roar. . . .

The two cars reached the corner at Granfort where the dirt road joined the highway.

"Give Bruce a toot," Rex said.

Sheila pressed the horn. For a second she thought she couldn't stop pressing it. But she only gave it three short signals.

Bruce signalled back. She saw his face. Two women with shopping baskets were chatting at the corner. She would never again see two people so totally strangers.

She swung out onto the highway, and turned toward Digby. There wasn't a cloud in the sky, but the daylight seemed to dip. The grey pavement looked inexpressibly tired with its own length.

"Do you think I could drive a little faster now?" she said to Rex.

"Sure," he said. "I'll be fine, now we're on the smooth road."

"You tell me if anything starts to hurt, won't you," she said.

"I'll tell you," he said. My God, this *was* his day.

She drove faster, straight into the wind. Thankful for the vigilance the steering took and for the roar of the wind against the car, so that she couldn't hear herself think.

She still wasn't quite ready for what she heard herself think. No season like the one with Bruce would ever come her way again. She knew that. But she also knew that she left it with a feeling of escape.

Bruce turned toward Halifax. The hills and valleys of his senses were suddenly levelled when Sheila turned the other way. His consciousness took the imprint of the letters on the corner bill-board like a *tabula rasa*. GRANFORT – FOUNDED 1782. Every single soul living in the world then was dead now. Dead . . . Gone. Live . . . Love . . . Lose. Ago . . . Ago . . . The memory of Sheila's face stamped the word "ago" across everything.

And then there came the moment – one definite, particular moment – when her face stamped itself with the same three letters. Finally believably. And, over and ago, she became somehow simpler – easier to deal with than in her complicated presence. In memory she became a short word : like Molly, Peter.

The wind was behind him. He drove faster, to escape the long complicated words. He wouldn't willingly have turned back to her.

CHAPTER **31**

Paul stepped back into the kitchen.

The house's retina was thronged with fleeting after-images of the ones gone. Friends or lovers leaving a house suck its tide out after them, like the moon. He felt that first crushing burden : he alone was responsible now for perception of its objects and its surfaces. The dry wooden skewer of lonesomeness in his chest was worse than the steel one of pain had ever been.

Letty watched him missing the others. It is serpent's tooth enough to watch someone you love take special pleasure in the kind of people you can never hope to be like. It is sharper still to watch him missing them while you're still there. This was the second time this morning she'd been made to feel her place.

Rex and Sheila had breakfasted in their room. When she went to get the tray, Rex said, "Just a minute, Letty. Sheila, will you see if there's a ten-dollar bill in my wallet?"

Sheila looked. "No," she said, "there isn't. Letty," she said quickly, as if to head him off, "I'd like you to have this perfume as a little gift. Maybe you won't like it, but it's my favourite." She took out the stopper and dabbed behind Letty's ears and then behind her own. "Do you like it?"

"Oh, yes," Letty said. "It smells beautiful. Thank you."

But Rex was not to be headed off.

"Let's see that wallet," he said. Sheila gave it to him. He explored inside. "Well, here's a five," he said, ". . . and two twos . . . and a one. You don't mind a little chicken feed, do you, Letty?" He passed her the bills.

"What's that for?" Letty said.

"Just a little tip," he said, "that's all."

It was like a slap. "Oh, no," she said, fumbling for the door-knob, "I couldn't take that."

The other three had looked her up to say good-bye. But she didn't go out to the cars. She knew she didn't belong there. And now Paul, with that faraway look on his face . . .

270

She was holding a woman's umbrella in her hand.

"Someone left their bumpershoot," she said to him, trying to make him smile. To be truly funny she had only to be natural, but her *idea* of being funny was to use a "comical" word. Paul winced. "I found it standin' in the hall," she said. "I took a quick look around upstairs, but I couldn't see nothin' else they'd left."

Paul looked at the umbrella. Umbrellas don't speak their owner's tongue, like clothing. Its utter lack of any such inflection made him feel keenest yet that they were really gone.

"It must be Kate's or Sheila's," he said. "What's the store label on it there? American or Canadian?"

Letty passed it to him with a thump of fright. She couldn't read long words like that.

Paul shook his head. "No," he said, "that's only the brand name. Maybe there's a label inside."

He pressed the spring, to open it.

"Oh, don't open it!" Letty said. "Not in the house. It's bad luck."

He put it down. Not smiling. Not even shrugging. And again she felt the subtle little slap.

He didn't joke with her about her superstitions. He never joked with her that nimble clowning way he kept jokes going with the others. The instant their backs were turned, he put all that away, like the pieces of a game back into its box. He never let them catch him with that far-off look on his face. But he didn't care how sober she saw him. And he knew it wouldn't do him any good to talk to her about them now.

"What would you like to eat?" she said.

"Oh, anything," he said. "I'm not hungry."

"Would a picked-up dinner be all right?" she said. "I've got a lot to do."

She was restless for the conversation of her hands with the house's clutter. Everything must be made neat again before she went away. She couldn't ever go to bed and leave a dish unwashed. (What if someone had to have the doctor in the night?)

"Sure," Paul said. "Anything."

Sure, anything. Again she felt the little slap.

She watched him climb the stairs to his room. How much longer did she herself have here with him? Good-bye: it was a bitter thing. But she didn't mess in it the way the others did. They ravelled off its outside casing, as they did with everything, and rubbed their eyes against the harsh inner weave. She merely lifted up her arms a little, testing good-bye's weight on the backs of her hands. Her hands could lift it. She went to work.

271

For the first few minutes Paul sat at his desk as motionless as someone holding himself rigid against an uprooting gale.

His elbows were on the blotter and his hands pressed against his face in that cataleptic stance against the soundless unallocatable suction of "gone." His physical eyes had the fixity of smelling rather than of seeing, as if the objects they were staring at gave off an hypnotic bodiless odour rather than an image. That mind's eye which in abstraction stares out over the head of everything at nothing was like those objectless rays of longing from mouths. The hands of his mind were paralysed. His mind kept tracing over and over its changeless content of the moment, the way you pencil a word over and over when the next one won't come.

For a moment he had the most paling of all frights: Was it mistaken to think that bearing anything was simply a question of will? Were there certain circumstances that could turn their volume up beyond the *limit* of bearing?

And then with that long sigh which is almost as hard to lift as the head (awake enough to know it's dreaming) from the mesmeric nightmare, he lifted and broke himself free.

His thought was immediately clear, a precision instrument. His mind's eye telescoped its beam downward to synchronize with the beam of his physical eyes, and his eyes began again to manipulate things like hands.

He prepared to die. He started to sort out the papers in his desk.

The mind is normally the heart's lawyer. Now the situation was reversed. His mind listed the residuum of his lifetime: his body, his notebooks, and his house. His heart advised him as impersonally as if he had hired it what to destroy and what to bequeath.

Destroy his body by overtaxing it, before it betrayed him into one of those long wasting sicknesses, naked to all the prying eyes.

Destroy his prattling notebooks, like diplomatic secrets when the invader is at the gates.

Bequeath the house to Letty.

He wished there was some money to go with it. There wouldn't be; the small annuity he'd eked along on would die with him. But if you had a house to call your own you could always get *some*-one to come live with you. If you hadn't, you were forever tacking to another's breeze. He could spare her that. He'd have the lawyer write his will tomorrow.

He started to destroy his notebooks. They'd once proposed to encapsulate the lessons of a lifetime. He glanced at an occasional line; they were no more than a coreless scattering of tangential chaff, whether nonsensical or serious.

Solitude opened his veins and his life seeped away into the sand. Sometimes known as Paul's Disease.

By clock's time . . . by joy's time . . . by dread's time . . .

He didn't know why, but he tore out each page individually and crumpled it before he threw it into the wastebasket.

Faces with their blinds up . . . or like pianos with no music open on them.
Sartre, less existentialist than existencilist. Stole the whole thing from Popeye: "I yam what I yam cause I yam!"
Each man switchboard of uncompleted calls.
Dear Mr Pater: Were you aware scientific fact that farts too will burn with a hard gem-like flame?

Occasionally he aligned the loop of an *e* or made a better *m* of one that looked like an *n,* before he crumpled the page; but the lines themselves were merely the pencil drawings of thoughts with their eyes left out. They brought back no shadow of the moment of which they had been the sole content at the time he had set them down. They looked as archaic as your own hand-writing on a self-addressed envelope coming back to you in the mail. This little guano island that was all there was to show for his whole life's consciousness . . .

Word game: Words, sword. Rose, sore. Love, vole. Live, evil. Life, file. Death, hated. Stud, dust . . . Ah yes, but: Penis, spine. Our cage, courage. Earth, heart . . .

The wind, still growing in sound and strength, scoured the leaves of the lilac trees against the house. The invisible wind erased at nothing on the smooth transparent window glass.
The notebooks disposed of, he began to crumple the jottings that had been for the novel (maybe) he'd one day write.

His Achilles heel the first keel laid in everyone.
Title: But for the Grace of God.
How crisis can alter people – or can it?
Incident: Time stripped for bath, armful clean clothes to carry bathroom, no place balance bow tie, clipped it pubic foliage, forgot there until immersed in tub.

He scribbled an automatic postscript to this one before he crumpled the page: "What better picture of man's wide, rich, lusty, flibbertigibbet soul than a pecker with a bow tie in its hair?" But the thought was purely mechanical, venting nothing.

He had never written his novel because – Morse was right. A novel had to squint, to keep its target focused. He couldn't squint. He could never block off his side-vision the way Morse could. Unencompassable devils of wonder came at him from all directions. Beside them Morse's devils of profusion were tractable as kittens.

Used as Morse was to the focalizing of himself to pinpoint in the constant climaxes of intercourse with others, he could now constrict himself to pinpoint at will. Dispersed and somehow incoalagulable as he himself was by his very self-sufficiency, he could never bring himself totally to bear at any one spot. It was like trying to draw with the whitewash brush of consciousness rather than its pencil. And, more than that, amusement at the spectacle of any earnestness, his own no less than others', had always promptly robbed his writing of that snow-blind ardency which writing takes.

But now it was neither earnestness he felt nor amusement, as he crumpled one sheet after another.

Until his glance fell on a sentence that all at once had eyes: "People, shedding their leaves at the moment of leaving, never leaf out the same again; but a re-leafing tree is exactly the friend of last year."

He remembered the moment he'd written those lines. He was back inside its very flesh.

He looked out the window at the leafing trees swaying in the wind. A bluish haze hung over the wood's edge. The colour, he thought, just that shade off being a sad colour, of faithfulness. His eyes touched the trees that didn't judge, that didn't exact, that didn't change toward you for anything else's changing toward you; that, if you loved them, let down on you a rain of cleanness and eternity when you walked beneath them – his eyes touched them like hands.

Whatever else he'd felt about dying, he'd never felt real sadness for himself. But now he suddenly felt a sadness for his eyes . . . for their having too, to die, just because his heart had so chosen. The heart murdering its own family.

As if in recompense for his thought, his eyes brought him at that very moment a definitive picture of the word "grace." The deer bounded from the woods into the field, swivelled, and then, the only thing without clumsiness in flight, bounded again into the deeper forest across the road.

And suddenly Paul's graven thoughts livened, leapt with it.

He could outwit his blackmailing heart. There was a way he could rescue his eyes. Bequeath them to an eye bank. Give them a life in someone else. More than that, bequeath his whole body to the anatomists . . . for whatever research they chose . . .

Paul always heard his thoughts speak themselves in words, as if there was a second tongue inside his brain. He heard them now. Embarrassing. Theatrical. He promptly crimped them with wryness: Scrap this bloody body for parts.

But nonetheless he felt a savage tingling freedom. That stand against invasion he'd engarrisoned all his life, that lifelong trick he'd perpetrated on himself – by what final stroke of freedom from it could he fly more neatly in its face than this? He would –

"Paul!" Letty's voice came urgent from the foot of the stairs. "Can you come here a minute?"

He wondered what had flustered her. When he was at his desk she never thought of breaking in on him.

"In a second!" he called back.

"Well . . . don't take too long."

"All right," he said. "In a second."

He wrote quickly on the bottom of the last sheet: "Life game: Take the 'hurt' out of 'truth' and make it 'ruth'?" And then crumpling this sheet too, he threw it into the wastebasket and went downstairs.

"Look!" Letty said. "Over there. That smoke. Ain't it a fire somewheres? And the wind. It's blowin' right this way."

Paul could see now that it *was* smoke, not haze.

"It's smoke, certainly," he said. "But I think it's on the other side of the brook. They're probably burning edgings at the mill."

Letty relaxed. She always took his word as gospel, even in matters where his judgement was so random he derided it himself. If he said he didn't think it was likely to rain, she'd hang her clothes out without a qualm, no matter what the sky threatened.

But just as they turned back from the doorstep to the kitchen, Paul saw a great grey roiling intestine of smoke shoot upward with such force that not even distance and the wind could break its shape. He knew that this wasn't tame smoke. And though he still couldn't tell which side of the brook it was on, it had that startling personal characteristic of a menace which has crossed the shadowy line between the near and the far.

Letty saw him hesitate. She studied his face, rather than the smoke, for the cue whether or not to take alarm. The wind and smoke began to subjugate the clean domestic morning, give it the lunar, intergalactic quality of an eclipse. Paul felt an odd exhilaration.

"What if it is a fire?" Letty said. "This side of the brook."

"Don't worry," Paul said. "It couldn't jump the field."

But he still watched the smoke. (She had the momentary thought: I'm glad I didn't bring him down for nothing.) And she still studied his face. As if it were within the power of *its* expression to decide the fire's course.

"You're not afraid, are you?" Paul said.

He moved closer to her not to have to shout against the wind, and clasped her shoulder briefly with his hand. Her own hands went quiet.

"No," she said, "I'm not afraid."

CHAPTER

By the time Kate and Morse reached the bridge, both sections of the meadow which the brook bisected and made into a definition of its own gentleness hung thick with smoke.

The deer, fleeing the smoke, broke from the far edge of the woods and ran toward them. Both cars stopped.

Something lifted inside Kate, as if her consciousness were challenged to match the deer's challenging grace. Until it came directly opposite. It passed so close that she could see the texture of its eyes and its hair. She saw that its hair was not silken, but coarse. She had from its eyes that trampling look of animals braving their timidity of people in escape from a greater danger.

It swam the brook, bounded across the far section of the meadow, and disappeared again into the woods toward Paul's. Morse's eye followed every leap it made, keeping the cross of an imaginary gun's telescopic sight focused exactly over its heart.

Kate left her car and ran ahead to where Morse was standing beside his.

"Morse," she said, "I don't think that's mill smoke. It must be a forest fire – to terrify the deer like that."

Up to now she'd been only mildly anxious. Now, something unleashed and nostrillish about the deer had communicated itself to the whole morning. It left her trembling.

"Not necessarily," Morse said. "The least scent of smoke, they take to their heels. And if it *is* a fire, I don't think it's anywhere near the road."

It didn't appear to be, but the road was so crooked there was no telling.

"But what if it is?" she said.

"Well, what if it is?" he said impatiently. "The road's not flammable. Come on. If it is a fire, we're just wasting our time dithering around here."

"Morse," she said, "I can't. I'm afraid. Let's turn back. There might be no place *to* turn farther on."

"Turn back?" he said. "There's a damn sight better chance of being trapped back there than if we make a dash for it."

"Then you do think it may be dangerous?" she said.

For an instant she was solaced to have company in her judgement; and then more dismayed than ever.

"No," he said. "I was just testing your nerve. What the hell kind of a bride are you, that you wouldn't go through fire with your husband?"

He maintained a jokingly derisive note, but he knew that the danger was in fact quite real. He had a nose for danger. He could feel its sharp tingle demarcating all his senses, as if he'd just been passed a telegram. Danger challenged his consciousness the way beauty challenged Kate's; turned his thoughts into rogue animals. And yet some impartial dictum in the threat itself always steered him with the surest tones of all.

It instructed him now.

He had gone to Paul's to rinse the sour taste of writing from his mouth, to escape it altogether. Now, strangely enough, it was the very rebirth of this writing that commanded him. Threatened in this vulnerable car, the fragments of his new novel had suddenly a voice he'd never heard in them before. More than that intermittent life the eye bestowed on them, they all at once had independent life enough to cry out to be saved. He knew there was one way only he could save them. He must take them *through* the danger, and beyond it. Retreat, even with safety, would only suffocate them. Nothing on earth would have made him turn round.

"But Paul," Kate said. "Back there alone."

"All right," Morse said. "What if there is danger? How could we help him if we *were* there?"

"But you said he could be trapped."

"No," he said. "I don't say Paul could be trapped there. I said we could be. Don't ask me to explain why I feel we could be and he couldn't. But don't ever worry about Paul, Kate. Don't kid yourself that he can't make out in any jam whatever. Anywhere. He's indestructible, I mean it, by any agencies yet known to man.

277

If he had to, he could load himself and Letty on that deer and take off like Peer Gynt. What'll you bet it wouldn't come into the old clown's head, anyway?"

"I know," she said. "You can joke. But – "

"But you'd rather be trapped there with Paul than risk it out with me. Is that it?" His voice was only a breath, restraint's, off accusation. He laughed. "So the book comes true after all. One more accident to set things up and I was writing nothing less than prophecy about you two."

They were both in the front seat of Morse's car now, to escape the wind. The situation had steadily increased in tremor, but not yet to that point where the fixed emplacements from which the mind delivers its words were themselves rocked loose.

Now, just as Morse spoke, flame raced up a pine tree so tall and so much closer than they'd judged the smoke to be that they could actually see the top of the tree burning, wild and blasphemous, like a woman with her hair on fire. The firing bases of Kate's words were themselves sent hurtling.

"Morse!" she begged. "Please! Please let's turn back. Please give in to me. Just this once. *Please*."

"No!" he said. "Listen to me, Kate. Are you going to turn back – face back – all your life? Are you? No, darling. Just . . . this . . . once – " he pressed her hand with his own at each word, not as a loan of courage but solely for emphasis – "just this once, you show me you can go ahead with something."

"I can't." She was crying. "Morse, I can't."

He took his hand away. The look he gave her sealed them into separate compartments.

"All right," he said. "There's no need to cry. If you can't, you can't. That's definite enough. I thought you could, that's all. But if you can't . . ." He kept looking at her with that impersonal, dislocating stare. "And now, darling," he said, "forgive me if this seems abrupt, but I really must be off."

He turned on the ignition. Another tree, closer still, burst into flames.

"Morse!" she said. "You can't go through there alone! I can't let you – "

"Good-bye, Kate," he said.

"Good-bye?"

"Of course," he said. He reached over and opened the door on her side. "Let's not be too symbolic about it, but you'll never find a better place to turn than right here. And don't worry. I'll be all right. And you'll be all right. You'll get some kind of seat with Paul on some kind of deer going the other way."

More because she didn't know what look to give him that that look of his wouldn't dismember, she turned her face away and leaned forward to leave the car. Without a word.

In that curious self-externalizing of absolute distractedness, she watched herself stepping out of the car, her movements a triumph of artificiality. And in one of those rags of irrelevance that some cretin of the mind laps before the mind's eye when all its sensible thoughts are so ajostle as to be helplessly blurred, she thought: I look like one of those actresses in this very scene in a bad movie whose spuriousness is so glaringly exposed when the sound track fails.

Tottering in the wind, nearly taken off her feet by it, she ran back to her own car.

Father . . . her mind cried . . . Paul . . . You wouldn't exact a thing like this of me.

The smoke was darkening with malice by the moment. How could this be the morning of two hours ago, that had hung gentle and patient as window curtains?

Oh God, why had she ever left Paul's? Why hadn't she pleaded with him to let her stay? Why had she ever left home at all?

Teeming lost syllables of the peace of home bombarded her without quarter. Home, where there was never a raw, bare-faced moment like this – its jaws open for the strike – when you *had* to make a choice in the face of those very jaws that paralysed all choice. Father . . . Paul . . . You always made your*selves* exactionless when any moment faced me with exaction. But Morse . . .

She got into her car. Nothing told her what to do. The nightmare indecision mounted.

She turned on the ignition. It gave her no advice. She looked automatically into the rear mirror. Everything was clear behind. And then she swung her head around to focus in it, trying to crystallize herself with her own image. A single glance encompassed Morse's moving car and her own still face.

She saw again the selfsame face the mirror had shown her the night she mourned her father. Kate Fennison. She saw in it the face that women had, were left with, who were not proof against the suction of the men who never claimed, exacted. A scarf of smoke hid Morse's car. Kate Halliday. In a sudden wild centaur of decision, she put the car in gear and shot the wheels beautifully grindingly ahead on the harsh gravel. She overtook Morse in a hard weaponish thrust of speed, blowing her horn as if she would over-ride him.

He didn't stop. There was no stopping now. The road was too narrow for any chance to turn, and the smoke made it seem like one of those paths at dusk that only your concentration holds in place. Lift your eyes from it for a second and it disappears. But he sounded his horn back at her in a riotously celebrant rhythm. She had a glimpse of his arm out the window, brandishing the victor's circle of thumb and forefinger.

The smoke thickened almost immediately. One car length at a time was all that vision could win from it. They drove then with an almost vying deadliness of caution. Blowing to each other almost constantly, to signal that each was holding to the road and to warn against collision. Keeping the road clamped down into place beneath the lakes of smoke with their intentness.

Sometimes Morse's car vanished completely and Kate would feel a choke of terror threaten to engulf her. And then her vision would just barely win his car back from the smoke again. Her feet chattered on the gas pedal, but her hands were absolutely steady. She felt that stringent livingness that one completely strange to danger feels when, in the thick of it, some body member on which life or death depends astounds itself with expertise beyond accounting.

She had never been so frightened in her life, but she was no longer afraid. She felt as if the car had broken out her personal standard.

And then the smoke seemed to get thinner. Not as before, when it had slackened only as pain sometimes slackens, to regroup for a greater cloud. But really thinner. She felt a gust of relief. The fire itself must be deep in the woods. The road was veering away from it.

She increased her speed to the top of the hill where the road went down into the long hollow – and there, with no more warning than a fist of sudden heat, she saw, wherever the road paralleled the course of the wind, the wind driving the first demented witches of blood-red flame straight toward them.

As far as she could see on that side of the road, it looked like a valley of hell. Ablaze at every twisting, exploding, crazy, crisscross angle. Roaring-angry, and burning even its own hissing, frying, crackling roar.

The wind tore tips off the geysers of flame and scattered them in the roiling air like brazen leaves. The wilder flames had ridden ahead on the wind deeper into the woods, to pillage. These were the vicious father flames that had stayed to eat. The great gust of wind that had cleared the smoke at the top of the hill revealed the woods like a house stricken to its timbers. Tattered sails of flame tongued out from the tree masts. And that fist of heat that makes the stun of a great burn so different from the smart of a small struck hardest where it was absolutely invisible.

She inhaled one long breath of dismay. Perhaps the fire couldn't cross the road against the wind – but if it *had* crossed the road anywhere, they were encircled. For a moment her mind almost stalled. She almost stalled the car.

And then she heard Morse's horn blow hard and long. She saw his speed increase. She knew he was signalling that now they had to make a blind race for it.

"Morse!" she screamed, pleading for his safety – and forgot her own.

The road was still visible as far as the river of smoke that transversed and submerged it at the bottom of the hollow, and she could see it climbing the opposite grade; and though it had twisted constantly before, here it was mercifully straight.

By some resource of concentration entirely unlike will she crowned her hands masters of her body and, brilliantly masterful for their new honour of taking over from the head, they guided her hurtling down the hill.

She struck the blind of smoke in the hollow and again the sudden fist of heat. She disappeared inside it. She could see absolutely nothing. For the first few seconds that seemed like hundreds she didn't know where she was. If her hands had still been subject rather than ruler she could so easily have taken them off the wheel in an ecstasy of abandonment.

But by a miracle they kept the car on the straight line her mind kept drawn for them between the broken ends of the road and, steadily and steadyingly hearing her car *not* crash into Morse's, she shot up the far bank of the smoke and into the clear. She saw Morse's car ahead of her almost at the top of the grade and she climbed the grade behind him. At the top of the grade the road swung straight away from the fire and they hadn't driven ten car-lengths before she could see, beginning to cry, that these trees here were drowsy with innocence.

Morse stopped. And she stopped. For a moment neither moved. It was like that gaping moment after a crash, when the bystander wonders if the stillness inside the cars is of death and falters at what crawling nest of stun and blood he may open the door onto. Then Morse bounded from his car like someone wakening with the start of oversleep.

He ran back toward Kate and Kate ran ahead to meet him. They gripped each other and he said, "Kate. Kate. Kate . . ."

Her lips were speechless with trembling, but in every limb of her mind she felt a strange new firmness. As if the fire had tempered her.

"My God, Kate," he said, the accents of penitence and exultation battling to a draw, "I never dreamed I was tempting you into anything like that. Do you think if I had, I'd have . . ?" It was the first time she'd ever heard him speak a sentence that was not in some way writing-talking. "My God, I never dreamed it would be such a . . ."

He got no further. The fire ranger's car came shooting at them round the bend from town. With the Kewpie doll lurching back and forth in its rear window and its brakes screaming almost childishly with self-importance, it somehow suggested a Mack Sennett car. It was this slight touch of the ludicrous that struck calm the moment's exclamatory pitch in both Kate and Morse, returned them both to their disparate normalities.

Driver and car made the perfect combination. He yanked his door open and sprinted toward them, bristling with function. He had a way of answering his own questions by the way he asked them. They could scarcely get a word in.

"Ain't this hellish!" he called to Morse before he was quite abreast. He twitched his head toward Endlaw. "You and the missus. You come through there? It ain't crossed the road nowheres? No? Well. The wind . . ." He indicated the direction of the wind. "Who's the other car?" He indicated Morse's car.

"They're both ours," Morse said.

"Oh, yes. Well . . . I sent some men down the log road round the turn there – keep it away from the mill." He had shares in the mill. "Can't cross the brook."

"How did it start?" Morse said.

"Can't tell," he said. "Some goddam – excuse me, missus – some fisherman, I suppose. Dry, y'know. *Dry*. Name's Farquharson," he offered suddenly. "Leander Farquharson."

It took them oddly unawares to hear he had so much name and could pronounce it so smoothly.

"Morse Halliday here," Morse said. "And Kate."

"Pleased to meet ya. And the missus." The man bobbed to Kate. "Well. I'll send a few men ahead, to watch it don't cross the road. Can't cross the brook. Can't get nowheres there. Have to watch the wind don't shift, it come back on the mill. Says rain – radio says."

He looked at the sky. The wind clouds *were* beginning to darken. And then as if he'd been caught star-gazing in a crisis he should command, he turned back to his car more bustling than ever.

"Well. I'll git outa yer way – I kin pull off down the log road there. You won't have no more trouble from here in. There ain't nothin' ahead."

His car shot back the road and disappeared.

"The caretakers of this world!" Morse said. Kate saw that he was already writing-talking again.

"You *knew* the fire couldn't cross the brook, didn't you?" she said. "But you didn't tell me. I never thought about the brook."

"Of course I didn't tell you," he said. "I wanted to make your test a real one."

"You knew we'd have been safe at Paul's."

"Safe, yes. Physically safe. But . . . I can't explain . . . My God!" he said, so suddenly softly it was his sharpest exclamation of the morning. "I've got it."

"Got what?" Kate said.

"The book! The ending for the book. Abso*lute*ly right this time. And for once you'll like it." He was so intent that the fire burning behind them was almost forgotten. "Listen. You *didn't* turn back, did you? You actually didn't. For once the great fouling bully at the helm of things overplayed its hand. There's a kind of last straw that *straightens* the camel's back. That's the whole thing in a nutshell."

He was rattling it off extempore, with none of his usual breaks to rewrite it first in his mind; and it was as strangely disconcerting as an actor's offstage speech . . . without semblance of any kind to the tailored onstage lines which had always seemed to be the truth of him.

"I'm listening," she said dutifully, but only half-attentive.

"Let's say something such happened with the others too. Even with your precious Rex. Above all, with your precious Rex. Let's concede *him* the maverick act of bravery that brings all three of them safe through the fire. Sheila and Bruce and himself. One that – I know this sounds as obscure as hell – but one that somehow makes all three of them . . . *friends.* Or . . . not exactly friends. Not folksy. Chummy. Not that. But the kind of – well, of all being made to see each other's homely, individual . . . lighting . . . by the light of a common overbearing fate. So that this love tangle amongst them becomes a sort of *family* trouble, if you know what I mean."

I should, she thought. It's an echo of my own sermon.

"Mere lovers the bully can trample to its heart's content," he raced on. "Love can be burned or broken. But this business of seeing each other's *lighting* plain, that's the only fibre in the world that's indestructible. The king can own the flesh and blood of every subject in the land, but that's the single thing he can't command – that umbilical cord his very tyranny sets up in them, one with another. The bully can grind them otherwise to dust, but that thing he only strengthens. When it tramples these three into

283

friends, that's the subtlest self-undoing it could manage. Darling, I've got to hand it to you. You were on the right track all the time. Those same alliances in us which nothing *but* the bully's imposition could set up *are* the bully's only possible defeat."

He watched for the shine in her eyes that greets the proselyte, the convert.

"I thought I had the ending right at Paul's," he said. "But that was only thinking. I know I've got it right now. Dead right. There's such a certainty about the twist with Rex I'm sure this must have been the very way it happened. Darling, will you help me get it down absolutely true? Once and for all?"

She nodded, smiling. At last she had her convert. Her victory. And now she had it – what did it amount to? The smile went crooked. Her Pyrrhic victory, that's what it amounted to.

Morse on the side of the angels! It would sound absolutely false. Soft. As if the spine in him had melted. And this whole struggle she had whetted in him – what a farce!

You'll never get it right, she thought. No writer ever gets it right. How can they get it true to life when life's not true or faithful to itself? . . . or people to themselves? When there's no consistency in anything? One day ago, I *was* concerned with Rex. He almost turned the tables in my heart against you. He bores me now. There's your consistency.

"You and the missus," the ranger had said: her face must have a wifely look already. The one impulse in her mind was to consolidate that look. Everyone, everything else was a blinding impatience away. Paul himself was at the farthest possible remove: a fleshly selfishness away. And it couldn't matter less to her if Morse were never to produce another line.

"Well?" Morse said. "What's the big silence? What about it? Does it make sense to you?"

"Lose your sense and gain your senses," she said foolishly.

Morse stared at her. He wouldn't have believed that Kate could ever have a silly look. Stricken, yes. Frustrated, yes. Pitiable, maybe. But never silly. She sure as hell looked silly now, though. As plain and simply silly as the most proverbial spinster tickled by the prospect of a man.

She motioned to the cars. "Come on, come on," she said. "What are we dallying here for?"

They went – married already by that first tender flinching at each other's unconscious absurdities.

The fire scarcely halted at the brook. Outriders of the wind bore down a thunder scorch on the peaceful meadow grass beyond

anything the faint green could possibly combat, and flames
tumbling down to the wood's edge rolled and snarled across the
meadow to the bank. The brook stood helpless while the wind
hurled little parachutes of burning "fog" across it at its narrowest
point. They infested the grass on the other side. The grass there
burned in separate pockets for the time it took to recognize the
sound of fire in themselves, and then they formed an army and
advanced, jealous-fuming, against the far woods.

They made a beachhead in the pine needles on the ground and
then they stormed the pines themselves and then the pines began
to join them with their own gunbursts of flame, and the fire,
recruiting smoke and swelter as it went until it had again set its
own roaring guts ablaze, drove straight on toward Paul's.

CHAPTER

In rain and storm thought leaps instinctively to the peace beyond
this spot the elements punish. Fire makes the whole world seem
on fire. And of all innocences turned rogue, the grass fire, literally
running, is the most incredibly savage.

Paul and Letty were midway down the field. The field was
ablaze. A curling ring of torchlights advanced and constricted
around them like the petals of some terrible flower. The pall of
smoke settling in behind them made the top of the house look like
a Gothic castle emerging from some Arthurian lake.

But it was the accurate little smoke grenades bursting in their
faces that baffled and disturbed them, continually turning them
in each other's view from flesh to shadow, flesh to shadow. Their
thoughts flashed in blades like the flame and then in clouds like
the smoke.

("Kate, Kate" – a cry of thankfulness in Paul's brain kept
threading through the maze and thump of physical sensation and
instant's challenge, like the interstitial threads of flame flashing
then disappearing inside the roiling smoke – "thank God you're
safe. The fire must have missed you altogether." If she'd as much
as seen the smoke she'd have been so worried she'd have turned
around. Thank God she didn't know what they were into. Thank
God she wasn't here.)

The woods fire had followed the tunnel of the wind. But the
grass fire raced in all directions.

Letty had hacked brush brooms off the sentinel spruce beside the house and soaked them with water. She and Paul lunged and stamped and thrashed at what flames they could see with these. But the flames scurried and proliferated like yellow ants. Flying cinders from the woods infested the grass at their backs. And from moment to moment a puffball of smoke and singe would break in their faces and for a flailing retreating instant, fighting for vision and breath, they couldn't tell if the fire line was before them or behind them.

It was plain that their stand here was becoming hopeless.

The boat was tied to the tall thin hackmatack at the edge of the lake.

"Letty!" Paul called fiercely for the second time. "Get in that *boat* and go over to the island. Do you hear me?"

"Are you comin' too?" she shouted back.

"No."

There'd never been an instant's doubt in him that he would stay and battle for the house. Threatened, it had lost its stillness, altogether. He felt a cleaving to it as never before. It was something, some*one* almost that, giving him back his will to live, he'd risk his life to save. He'd never fought like this for anything in his life before. Physically. Angrily. The shrug become second nature, he'd never known what a glorious intoxication it was to fight for something in anger. His blood was pounding, but his heart felt newly indomitable.

"*Letty!* he shouted again. "Get in that *boat*. Do you hear me?"

"If you ain't comin, than I ain't."

Of all obstinacies the one that stems from loyalty itself is the most intensely exasperating. He could almost have struck her.

Suddenly Letty pointed to where the lake coved in close to the house. "Up there."

He saw what she had in mind. There, in the direct aim of the wind, was the narrowest front they could choose to make a final stand on. A stone wall came part-way from the cove to the house. And, joining the stone wall, the ploughed land for the garden. That left only one short stretch of grass between the top of the garden and the house. If the driveway held on one side of the house . . . and the stone wall and the garden on the other . . . and *if* they could stop the flames at this narrow pass . . .

It was just possible they could. The woods fire was still hurling great birds'-nests of flaming twigs toward the house, but they were falling shorter and shorter of their target. And though unnoticeably, so hard was it to tell the wind's draft from the fire's, the wind was dropping. The grass fire was losing its backing and its reinforcements.

At the top of the incline where the house stood, the smoke was thinner. Here they could see what they were doing. They had a few moments to prepare their defence.

"Are you all right?" Paul shouted, as if the wind were still deafening.

"Yes. Are you?"

"Yes."

"Paul!" she screamed, "you're afire!"

He felt the bee sting of burn on the inside of his thigh. A spark had lodged unnoticed there and smouldered through his pants and underwear. A lazy little flame was breaking out. Letty instinctively struck at the flame with her hands.

"Letty!" he shouted, fending her off. "You'll burn your hands. For God's *sake*!"

There was but one thing to do. He stripped off his pants and shorts. His shirt flying loose in the wind, he ground out the flame in his pants and yanked them on again. He didn't bother with his shorts.

"The car!" Letty shouted. "Will I drive it down on the ploughed land?"

"The hell with the car!"

She felt a sudden tide of strength. He'd never spoken to her like that before. Harry used to speak to her like that sometimes—Paul never had.

She had an inspiration.

"The sprayer!" she shouted. "What's wrong with us? Right under our noses."

"Yes – that might do it! If we have time." The fire was coming quickly closer.

The sprayer was a light wheeled tank for watering the garden. It was standing by the faucet in the cellar wall. Rex had put its pumps and valves in first-class order.

"If they ain't dreened the well with their infernal baths every whipstitch," Letty sputtered; tension exploding in her one of those little spites so wildly out of scale with present crisis – and this the first time she'd ever taken them to task in front of *him* like that. "You'd think a speck o' good clean dirt'd kill 'em. If they was as careful about their tongues as they are about – "

"Get the hose," Paul commanded.

She ran to the tool-shed for the hose.

They attached the hose to the faucet. Now they had narrowed their concentration to this one front, the smoke and fire of their excitement itself seemed to narrow and condense. It became the tremor of intentness. And the other fronts, trusted on their own responsibility to hold, seemed stronger somehow than if they'd been manned.

"Wet our clothes," Paul said. "Quick. Douse me with the hose and I'll douse you."

They soaked each other's clothing until it was plastered to their skins, then filled the sprayer tank.

"I'll wheel the tank," Paul said. "You use the pump. It works like nothing now."

"No," Letty said. "I'll wheel the tank and you – "

"I'll *wheel* it!" Paul shouted. "For God's sake, Letty, we haven't got time to argue."

Again she felt the lift. They had never argued before.

They soaked a strip of grass almost as far as the garden's edge – and then the tank went dry. There was no question of refilling: it would take too long. Here too now, the smoke unrolling ahead of the unrolling carpet of fire was so thick they could scarcely breathe. They couldn't see the flame, but they could feel its heat.

Paul knew they would win or lose in a matter of moments.

"Get the broom!" he shouted to Letty, "and keep watch on the upper end there. I'll get the spade and fight it here." All the other fronts seemed to be holding.

The wind had died to that oracular lull between wind and rain that gives the day an other-planetary touch. But the rain was still held tight in the clouds' grip. The grass behind the house had not been cut last year. If the flames outflanked them here and got a foothold into that or – Paul started suddenly – into the brush he'd banked the cold north corner of the kitchen with last winter . . . he'd neglected to take the brush away this spring and it was tinder-dry.

Bruce always left the spade at the head of the garden. The garden wasn't twenty paces off. Paul started for the spade.

And then remembered: it wasn't there. The spade was up behind the house where he and Kate had dug the lilac. There wasn't time to – God*dam* that lilac! He almost cursed Kate as well.

He had no weapon. Again he stripped his pants off. Now he could see the flames – and he began to beat them with his pants. He felt a kind of demonic glee as the smack of wet cloth turned them into snarling smoke.

The smoke was thick as ever. But no longer coming in volcanoes. You could box it, rushing in and out. And though the heat smote hard against his nakedness, it wasn't felling. It had lost its muscle. It was just exactly bearable.

The flames still crawled toward him. But they weren't leap-frogging now, their self-increase was just equal to what he could handle. He knew he was winning. He'd never felt such rampant freedom.

He looked toward the house to see if Letty too was winning. He couldn't see her anywhere. His heart itself missed her, like a skipped a beat. It was totally unlike the way he'd ever missed her any time before. He scrambled back into his pants. He left his post and ran to find her.

"Letty!" he called.

"Here!" she answered.

He saw her then: patrolling inside the curtain of smoke. Her brush broom had itself caught fire and she'd had to put it down. She'd taken off her skirt and was beating at the flames with that. Almost on her knees, *rubbing* them out, so that no sparks would fly behind her.

She too was winning. The grass they'd wet had held. And now, attacking, she had gained some ground beyond it. There were times when she had to *wait* for more flame to appear.

And in an instant's thinning of the smoke he glimpsed the drive-way. It too had held. A grass fire's strength – and weakness – lies in nothing but its speed. It cannot halt. Its feeding must go forward every second, having eaten up its own retreat. The fire had reached the driveway, halted and died.

"I think that's all right, Letty," Paul called. "Come give me a hand down here."

The fire had livened again next the garden. No longer brazenly, but crawling stealthily from tuft to tuft. Letty attacked these pockets with her skirt and Paul stamped his feet on them like someone heading off a string of ants.

He *knew* now that victory was near. For all at once it struck him what a clownish spectacle they both presented. Letty was flailing about her with her skirt, her bloomers plastered tight to her skin – and himself, wet-slinked as a doused pup, bouncing up and down like some crackpot native in a fertility dance . . . He inhaled a chuckle almost.

And then – in a transmutation of it quick enough to be made between breaths, he exhaled the pain.

The first exploratory spit of pain and the first rain struck him together. There was no more rain for the moment. But the pain blossomed as instantly as if an eagle's talons had fastened them-selves inside his flesh.

He felt for the pills inside his shirt pocket, but the water had turned them into paste. It was the kind of belting pain you don't flinch back from: it strikes you down. He sank in his tracks.

"*Paul!*" Letty screamed.

He couldn't speak.

She left her post and ran to him, beseeching him over and over with his own name. He still couldn't speak. "Paul!" she cried. His eyes were closed against the pain, as if daylight too were alive with it. She thought he was dead.

She dragged him back beyond the fire's reach. Brokenly gently, thinking he was dead. Beyond her courage to do it, she knelt down to see if he was breathing. And when she saw that he was still breathing she grasped him and kissed him.

"Paul! Paul! Paul!" she beseeched him back with his own name.

He opened his eyes and she saw him living there in them. Right here again. Her face, in a glorious tumult of the inexpressible, expressed her completely. Its springing phrases of strength and delicacy, eye-moulding the irrelevant flesh, were far more beautiful than beauty's single frozen sentence.

It's not a work face at all, Paul thought. And he knew that she loved him as no one else had ever done.

"Paul!" she said. "You scared the liverpins outa me. What . . . ?"

He calculated the number of words he could pronounce.

"I'm all right. I guess the smoke . . ."

"You look so white," she said. "But the fire's out! It can't go nowheres now. Paul, you're *not* all right!"

She put a hand on his forehead. It wasn't a work hand at all.

"Just let me rest," he said. He closed his eyes again.

He couldn't, for the life of him, have moved a muscle toward the one surviving ant of fire that was right now sneaking around the gap at the garden's edge. Stealing into the long grass.

Oh God, Letty cried silently. I spoke too soon.

For a moment she was so spent she simply couldn't rally to the pitch of crisis a second time. Reviving dangers are more tiresome than challenging. There was a terrible temptation to close her eyes on it. But she knew this tiny flame could be the deadliest of all. It was already spoking out into larger ones.

Oh God . . . She couldn't leave Paul lying there alone, looking again like someone dying. And what if she couldn't head these new flames off? What if she'd only be wasting precious moments trying? Moments that should be used to move him from their path?

She got up and left him. And when she reached the flames her vengeance toward them, her fury at their gluttonousness beyond all decency, beat them out as irresistibly as if she were despising them to death. She gave a sweeping glance around. Yes, the flames were conquered everywhere. And then she shook the cinders off her skirt and put it on again: her proud, bedraggled battle colour.

Paul missed her and opened his eyes. He watched her.

Her clothing didn't strike him funny now, but like a cruel joke on her. A woman's flesh, he thought, when no one any longer thinks it's pretty, has that hurt child's reconciliation with *itself* about it. She damn near broke his heart. But in that curious way that lets its updraft free.

When she had kissed him the touch of her surprising flesh had opened his own as none had ever done before. The deepest questionings that constantly impinge against the consciousness are never recognized – until they frame themselves enormously when their own enormous answer swings open before them. Did he love her? Had he loved her all along? He had. He had.

The eagle of pain had lit, and settled. Then it had crouched there, quiet. But he knew it hadn't flown away. Now, with a final twist of its talons, he felt it fly away.

And then he felt nothing but a sumptuous lassitude and freedom. He watched Letty running back toward him. She seemed completely solid, yet full of shade. The others, except for Bruce, weren't like that at all. They had that harrowing transparency which fever gives, with all their shade talked up and burned away.

"Paul," she said, out of breath and in still another intonation of his name, "are you sure you're all right? You looked so – "

"I'm all right," he said. "As good as ever."

"Don't you want to go to the house then?" she said. "Everything's safe. You can see all over now. Right then I could see clear'n to the woods. The fire's still goin' on in the woods, some, but it can't get nowheres." She shook her head. "Fooo! Wasn't that some session!"

"It was that, all right," Paul said. "They say a grass fire's every bit as good as fertilizer, but I guess we'll hang off for a calmer day to burn that patch behind the house, won't we?"

She caught a deep breath. This was the first time he'd ever joked with her in just that way.

"And if it damn well hadn't been for you, Letty . . ." Paul said.

"Aach!" she said, embarrassed fussy. And then: "Don't you think we really oughta go, Paul, and get you outa them wet things?"

"No," he said. "Not just yet. Let's just rest a little longer."

She sat beside him until the rain came; both quietly watching the field not burning and the house not burning, and she luxuriously letting her thankfulness come to the point of tears and then stopping them just in time. She felt his steady recognition of her. Each absorbed the other's climate as salt gathers moisture. I must stop saying "ain't," she thought – I *know* better'n that. Her hands were as contented as if they were knitting or shelling peas.

And after the rain came in a swift soft-trumpeting sheet they still stayed there. Listening luxuriously to the neighbourly drum of it on the snug house roof. Listening to its gentleness, so much stronger than the fire's spite, conquer the fire in the woods. The fire, fuming with frustration, hissed against it like the devil flinching from the holy wafer, but the rain did not even change countenance.

They were still in that same spot when Farquharson drove up. He couldn't make it out at all. Settin' there in the rain!

"What's wrong, what?" he said. "Are you all right?"

"Sure," Paul said. "We're fine now."

"My God," he said. "You must've had a real . . . We never dreamt it'd cross the brook. Now who would? Anyone'd think the meadow . . . what? You sure everything's all right?"

"Everything's fine," Paul said.

"Look, man," the ranger kept apologizing, "if we'd as much as *thought* it might jump the brook . . . we'd a got here somehow, what? But like I said to Halliday and the missus, it can't jump the *brook*."

"Where did you see the . . . Hallidays?" Paul said.

Letty's eyes alerted, watching for his face to change. It didn't change.

"Oh, back there be the long holler. I guess they had a pretty tough time of it too, drivin' through all that smoke. But they never had no trouble."

"Good," Paul said. "Good." But his face still didn't change.

"My God, man," the ranger said. "You oughta have a telephone here. You coulda bin . . . what? And no one'd ever knew."

"Yes," Paul said. "I guess you're right. We'll have to get a telephone – eh, Letty?"

These tears were too quick for her to head off. He wasn't leaving then! He wasn't sending her away! He'd said "We"! And a telephone – it was some sort of sign. She looked at him and that terrible closed look he'd had when Kate and Morse drove off was altogether gone.

It was only when he was forced to rest a second time on the walk to the house that Letty again felt the stitch of dread. One panic dissolved seems to dissolve the grounds for all other panics of the same moment. It had been like that with Paul's seizure and the fire. This was the sharp dismay when you see that the one's pattern of scare and deliverance may *not* be the pattern of the other.

292

"Paul," she said anxiously, "I know what I oughta do. I oughta take you to the doctor."

"All right," he said. "Tomorrow maybe."

It was curious, he didn't have the slightest feeling now about invasion by the doctor.

"But just let's rest today," he said.

"Well you're goin' right to bed, anyways!"

Indoors, the clean white rain-smoke bouncing off the window-sills and drumming off the roof made the house a stroke of snugness as miraculous as the perfect freehand circle.

Paul went to bed. In Letty's room. She begged him not to climb the stairs to his own. And inside the house inside the rain, with the two of them closer now than two people disclosing themselves to each other inside a drink, he told her the facts about his heart.

She cried; but strengthening, even as she cried, against her dismay. And almost like feeling famous with the drink, he felt her lift her end of this dark knowledge he'd borne so long alone, and he knew something like the incomparable narcosis of drifting off to sleep, young, in the rain. It was the beautiful difference between stillness and calm.

She helped him undress.

"Don't mind me," she said. "Everyone's seen them things before."

It was crying-joking; but with more tenderness in it and with less mythographic nonsense than he'd ever heard before in mention of that particular flesh. And this time, having her see him naked gave him that oddly enhancing, oddly self-startling and self-stroking stun of animality.

She went to the closet and got dry garments of her own. She headed for the kitchen with them.

"Don't mind me," Paul said.

She hesitated to see if he was joking. She saw that he wasn't, except as special circumstance sometimes obliges common sense to take that form. She put the garments on a chair and, half in obedience and half indulgent of a sensual stir which the obedience cloaked and left her innocent of perpetrating, began to change.

He glimpsed that part of her flesh where flesh is absolutely honest – where the mind can't possibly refine it or prim it or fancify it or deny it, as it can the face. And he felt the instantaneously opened, long lengthening homing eye of longing in the part of his own flesh that was most instinctively one-visioned and honest.

This of Letty's was natural flesh, with none of the wisenesses and innuendo about it which, in women like Kate, you couldn't help remembering from their faces and their clothing. In them, the separate maintenances of delicacy in the face and of the indelicate here got in the way of this part's honest statement. You couldn't quite believe it. With this natural, this above all consistent flesh of Letty's there would be absolute freedom. She could reduce the mythographic to the magnificently ordinary.

In a way he loved Kate none the less; but there are loves so intricate, regulated by such a complex maze of tone and volume dials, that in the loss of them you can't help recognizing an element of release. It was as if their differing escapes from the fire had somehow been an escape from each other.

It rained all afternoon and evening. And all that time Letty sat there with him inside the house inside the rain.

"Do you want me to get you a book?" she said once, afraid that he would ask for some title she couldn't make out.

"No," he said. "No."

He didn't want books. He didn't want talk. The talk he'd been used to. That was forever on its toes, twisting and interlocking knowledgeable allusion; that was forever a tiring octave higher than the key speech is written in, as if it were always talk to be overheard, like the talk in books. He had a sudden disrelish – almost to loathing – for books and that kind of talk. As if they were unslept drinking partners of the night before turning up the next morning, dredged and shallow-eyed, and wanting to take it up again right where you'd left off – but you wanting nothing but to rinse out the frowzy memory of them with cold water and fresh air.

He and Letty talked and they didn't talk. And when they talked they didn't break out the words like flags : their words merely showed quietly above the surface as the lap-back in some wave of sentience exposed them, or as the wave broke quietly against thought into a little spray. It was like the talk when one is winding into a ball the skein of yarn another holds stretched across his wrists. And when they didn't talk they had no sense at all of time mounting in the silence.

They had never talked much when they were alone. But their silences before had been quite different. Then, their paths of sentience had seemed so far beyond calling distance apart that this very distance spared constraint. Now, their silent ease with each other was more like that of pairs whose two equations may contain quite different powers and arrangements of the x and y and z, but in whose feeling there's the recognition that in either case the *value* for each basic variable is the same.

When it came past her bedtime Paul said, "You'd better go up to my room and get some sleep."

"No," she said. "I'm not leavin' you alone. I leave you, you'll be paradin' all over the place, likely."

"No," he said. "I promise you. I won't budge."

"I ain't tired," she said.

He knew she wouldn't leave him.

"Well then," he said, "lie down beside me on the bed here. There's no point sitting up all night."

For some reason he felt the first strange mortification at his own correct syntax, as if it were some foppish garment specious to a wonted ground of trust.

She lay down on the very edge of the bed.

Lying on a bed with her clothes on gave her a mussed feeling inside. When she was sure Paul's sleep was sound, she got up and slipped into her nightgown. In just her nightgown it was cold outside the covers and she snuggled in beneath them. There was no harm in that, she told herself explicitly, outstating the implicit wish for once to feel his bed warmth next her: she'd be awake and dressed before the daylight came.

Daylight, brushing shadows from the lilacs across Paul's face, awakened him. He could hear Letty in the kitchen. He wondered how she could have left the bed without disturbing him. He really must have slept soundly.

He went to the window. He saw the ragged ink-spill of burn on the woods and field. But the woods wound was smaller than he'd have believed. It would be pleasant to walk there now, remembering the fire's inordinate boast. And overnight, he could see, the rain had started up the grass's second blading, greener on the scorched field than it would be in any other spot.

The rain had brought out the first *thick* sigh of green on everything; and tree and bush stood as stuporously-dotingly delivered of their leaves as animals of their young. The breeze was teaching movement to the miniature leaves. Teaching them to dip and sway. The sun was high as a bell, but fatherly in every glance. It was the tallest, nearest, openest morning he had ever seen.

His flesh strutted. Struck out instead of in. And his mind, as if it were his flesh's wife, kept up a gentle pensiveness beside it.

That inviolacy he had always prized above all else. How could he have ever thought that . . . ?

But right *there* was the crowning trickery in thought. You never could believe that what you thought at any given moment could be wrong, for that was all that consciousness consisted of: what you presently believed; and thought was nothing but the

295

sound of that belief. You never really doubted that it was within your power to "correct" for any factors that might prejudice your judgement. . . . And then a thing as simple as the one last night could (with that same trickery of the actual) make your certainties of another time as incredible as one generation's to another's.

He was not deceived by what had happened last night. It *was* the simplest of all things. But his mind and his heart felt pruned by it; as physically pruned of their clusterous, strangling ivy of wilted clauses as the one declarative sentence this morning spoke. He felt a like sparkle of unification. And to think of Letty was to turn from the tattered complications – or no, the complicatifying – of the others, and to touch a safety warm as the stinging reallegiance to some tie you'd come within a fool's breath of denying. He felt beautifully simple, and she was the beautiful monosyllable of home.

He had awakened in the night and felt the warm lake of her simple flesh stretched out beside him . . . and the long stretching plumbing eye of longing, beckoned to put its eye out at the lake's utmost depth, was so instantly commanding and free that there was no time for thought.

And inside the dark inside the bed inside the house inside the rain where the pain couldn't find him, he had come to her. And gone to her. And with coming and going become the instantly reversing inside out one of the other and it good and natural with Letty without fuss or fear or finick or fancy, he had felt his spirit charging faster and faster into freedom than any other thing could hope to race against.

And in the moment when his flesh was exquisitely pitted of its stone, he had a glimpse of Death's losing face dissolving far far behind . . .

Letty had left dry clothing for him on the chair. He began to dress. He tried to call up the look Death would have for him now. But its face was as blank as a proper name. His living consciousness, coursing without interstice, gave it no chink to insert itself. And this time he felt no desperation whatsoever not to be able to configure it.

All I ask to see, he thought, are four more seasons. Ensuring them by the very modesty of his claim. Spring. Summer. Autumn. Winter. Maybe it will look like one of them. Nothing can help looking like one or the other of them. He grinned. I don't care what it looks like. I don't care if it looks like a bee hive. Or a piccolo. Or a stump . . .

From habit he tested his freedom against the wryest challenge

296

he could summon. That inviolacy business . . . That false premise right at the start . . . All my life . . . All that waste . . .

He grimaced, but his peace remained intact. Not even rue could chip a single flake off it.

And I thought I was some kind of hero, he pressed the challenge. Oh yes, I did. Not consciously; but underneath somewhere I had that picture of myself. The old inviolate, self-sufficient, nohow seducible hero. Oh, I've really tricked myself ten ways from Sunday!

Again he grimaced, but again his grimace was no more than a chuckling incredulity at himself. His peace, this tricking morning, was invulnerable.

He raised the window. The sun's warmth rested gently on the back of his hand and he inhaled the fresh, sweet, rain-emancipated air.

He felt a strange rejoicing. As if he'd worked harder and steadier at his life's thinking than the others and got it finished sooner and now he could watch them from some cool shady vantage still wrestling with theirs.

I might marry Letty, he thought.

I will marry Letty, he knew.

Letty heard him raise the window. At the sound, requickening memory of the night, there was a stroke of tautness inside her as when the clock in a room stops. Her hands went uncertain.

And then she heard him humming. It was the first time he had ever hummed when they were by themselves. It was the first time she had ever heard him hum at all. The tautness vanished.

But when his steps approached the kitchen threshold, it seized her again. She busied herself aligning the dishes on the breakfast table, glancing half-fearfully at his face.

He was grinning. But in no way wryly now. Discoveringly now, and rediscoveringly – as when you glimpse beneath the masks and shadows of another's speech and flesh that one great equal sign between you that most men search a lifetime for and never find. This they had now was love and more: each the rallying point of the other's bedrock faithfulness; each to the other the walls of an invisible house which sprang up to enclose them at any alien trespass on either.

"Hi, Letty," he said. "Did you sleep well?"

She read his face exactly and the gentle wink behind his words. And touching the breakfast plates with her suddenly liberated hands and looking down at them as if their simple circularity were something splendid, her face itself became quite splendid – and all at once assured as his.

She had a nice surprise for him. She'd show him she could talk as proper as "they" did if she put her mind to it. She'd watch it every minute.

"Yes," she answered him. Then, smiling proudly: "Now remember, after you've had your breakfast and drank your coffee, we'll see about the doctor." She stressed it again. "Just as soon as you've *drank* your coffee . . ."

Paul winced.

And then he grinned.

For a moment the April morning seemed to preen itself in that faultlessness which so mocks the one alone. And in that moment they felt the one inimitable safety. That great, sweet, wonderful safety from the cry of things not understood, of things said and things not said, of things done and things not done, of what is near and what far-off, and the sound of time and the sound of time gone by . . .

THE NEW CANADIAN LIBRARY